GRAYSON SPRINGS

a novel
by

RON GAMBREL

Rough River Publishing

Rough River Publishing LLC
Louisville, KY

Published by
ROUGH RIVER PUBLISHING LLC
PO BOX 58844
LOUISVILLE, KY 40268

GRAYSON SPRINGS is a work of fiction. Names, characters, businesses, places, events and incidents are either products of the author's imagination or used in a fictitious manner. All modern era characters are completely fictional and any resemblance to actual persons, living or dead, is purely coincidental.

Release May 2015

ISBN: 978-0-9908562-0-7

DEDICATION

This novel is dedicated to the memory of my great-aunt,
Mary Ann (Annie) Boone
February 10, 1887 - June 9, 2001

Annie's was the daughter of Mary Elizabeth Pierce Lush.

ACKNOWLEDGMENTS

Larry Myers: the man who taught me the art of literary writing. I will be forever grateful to him for his professional critique, his encouragements, and his insistence on perfection.

Rachel Rice: for encouraging me to write this story, and for editing my early drafts.

Jo McKim: storyline editor. Thanks Jo for believing in my story and for setting the standards high.

Kelsey McKim: grammar editor. It's a hard job. Somebody has to do it, and you did well. Thank you ... thank you ... thank you.

Many thanks also to the following pre-publication readers for their time, and inputs. You thoughts and opinions make me better:

Wendy Robertson
Dr. Daniel Withers
Dinah Haycraft
Mary Doris Simon
Brenda, Joe, and Louise Schmidt
Bob and Lynn Gambrell
Bruce Gambrell Sr.
Bruce Gambrell Jr.
Haley Kelly
Marilyn Guethe
Lauren (Tod) Myers

The following experts graciously assisted in my historical research:
Joe Hylas: Renowned Coin expert.
Tamara Elliot: Reference Librarian US Senate Historical Office
Katherine Scott, PHD: US Senate Historical Office
Don Kennon: United States Capitol Historical Society
Jerry A. McCoy: Martin Luther King, Jr. Memorial Library
Thomas L. Owen: Associate Archivist, University of Louisville
Jody Thompson: (EEC) Ecologist and Forest Health Specialist
Katherine Gibson Fougera: author of **<u>With Custer's Cavalry</u>**

GRAYSON SPRINGS

Chapter 1

"Fuck you!" I screamed over Beethoven's sixth symphony, Melanie's high-society choice in music. "You hate my clothes—you, you—don't like how I walk, how I talk. You fucking tell me what to eat—"

"I do not *tell* you what to eat. I make suggestions."

"Liar! You even tell me how *much* to eat—"

"I do not!"

"And, and now you want to tell me who I can be friends with!"

"Brooke, don't you see what this new school has done to you? You're becoming like one of those—"

"Those what? How can you? *You* do what *you* do and you want to call *me*—"

"What do you mean, what *I* do? What *do* I do?" she shouted while waddling up against me.

"Don't act stupid Melanie—and get the hell out of my face!"

"Don't curse me, and don't call me Melanie! I'm your mother, and I'll get in your face if I want to!"

"You're not my *real* mother. And if you think I won't bust you because you're pregnant—"

"You wouldn't!" she dared, standing so close that I could feel her spit hit my cheeks.

One instinctive right-hook sent my 43-year-old mother-by-adoption backwards over Daddy's leather recliner. Seconds later I knew I'd screwed up. She lay there on the floor on her back, barely conscious, with both hands holding the bulge of her nearly eight-month-

1

pregnancy. Blood trickled from her nose, and the skin around her left eye had already begun to discolor and swell. "Oh shit," I whispered. "I'm ... so sorry ... you were in my face."

Kneeling on the floor, sitting on my heels, I propped her head up on my legs and thought, *God don't let that baby be hurt.* Her blood dripped onto my black leather Rag & Bone skinny jeans.

Eyes still closed, Melanie mumbled, "Help me."

Anxious to the point of nausea, I pulled out my phone and dialed 911.

* * * One month later * * *

"All rise!" demanded the sheriff's deputy. "This session of the New York Family Court is now in session. Presiding will be the Honorable Judge Bernard Stinson."

"Please be seated," spoke the robed, middle-aged man as he stepped to his high backed chair, poured a glass of water, and then took a seat himself. While he settled in, looking down at papers, everyone else in the room seemed to be going about their own business.

I sat there at the defendant's table next to my attorney, Mr. John Sebastian. He's the only man I know who can dress sloppy in a thousand-dollar suit. And to think he told me to "tidy up a bit" in a Ralph Lauren skirt and jacket. Daddy hired him more than once to get me out of trouble.

A young male assistant from the Juvenile Prosecutor's Office winked when he saw me looking. His unsightly, senior counterpart, Mary Anne Glover, Esq., could very well have been the reincarnation of Boston's first known witch. When she stared at me over her reading glasses I felt something scary drift between us.

My parents were directly behind me in the first row of seats. Daddy—Dr. George Green—is a sixty-year-old practicing psychiatrist. His thin, bony face and long silver hair, tied up in a ponytail, reek of the mystique one might associate with a man who has for so long made his living treating mental illness. Melanie, beautifully blonde and only days away from delivery, sat leaning against him. Anyone with

2

common sense could tell they were not my real parents—Daddy at 6'1" and her being 5'8". Hell, I'm 5'3" and not likely to ever grow another inch. And my hair is blood red.

Mrs. Jackson, a well-dressed guidance counselor from my school, Stuyvesant High, stared at her cell phone, texting I suppose. The only other people in the room were a court reporter, two sheriff's deputies, the Court Clerk, and, in the back of the room, a man I'd never seen before. Judge Stinson kept looking toward the guy and whispering to his Court Clerk.

Finally, the clerk turned and said, "Would the defendant please rise?"

Mr. Sebastian and I both stood as Judge Stinson began. "I hope we all had a good weekend. Our docket is full today. I want everyone to pay close attention so we do not waste time. If your cell phone rings in my court, it will be confiscated." He scanned the room one more time and said, "In the case of the State of New York vs. Elizabeth Brooke Green, we are here this morning for the sole purpose of delivering sentence...."

"Excuse me, Your Honor," interrupted my attorney.

"Mr. Sebastian, I say we are in a hurry, yet you interrupt."

"May I approach the bench?"

"I must remind you, Counselor, that we have already heard this case. If you insist, make it snappy. Would the prosecution approach also?"

I stood there unaware of what was going on. Turning, I received a smirk from Melanie and knew right away that something bad was about to happen. The group up front spoke quietly, until the judge raised his voice.

"Postpone! For how long?"

After more whispering, he blurted again, "Six weeks! You honestly believe six weeks can change this girl?"

A few whispers later, the prosecutor grinned, and my stomach began to churn. As the attorneys returned to their places, Mr. Sebastian winked at Daddy. *Not good*, I thought. *Something tells me I'm screwed.*

Judge Stinson again glanced around the room, and then spoke. "Miss Green, this is in fact the third time I've had to consider your fate. This court anticipates that young people will learn from their mistakes. Yet, with you it is as if you can't even remember the first time you were in trouble..."

.....*Hell yes, I remember. I was living in hell, that place where no one cared. Having to bathe and sleep with others, older kids who put their hands on me in the middle of the night. They called me evil because I fought. But why shouldn't I? The first time I got in trouble, I was five years old. They sent me to see a lady doctor in a white coat because I surprised a boy in his sleep and beat his face with my fist, over and over until he bled all over the sheets. I didn't talk to the doctor. Didn't talk to anyone in those days. Why should I? I hated them all.....*

"Twice," continued Judge Stinson, "you've been granted leniency, and now here you are again. I cannot with good conscience disregard the path of destruction that you have chosen. You first came before this court for theft. Shoplifting at a young age is often considered in statistics of normal societal behavior. However, I still find it most unusual that an eleven-year-old would steal a firearm. You somehow convinced the court that you did not know why you stole the weapon. When you returned at fourteen for beating a classmate, you had tested positive for marijuana. Could anyone blame Sacred Heart Academy for expelling you? Do you even realize how much money your parents have spent on your education? How you managed to gain enrollment at Stuyvesant High is beyond me and at least a testament to that institution's dedication to our city's brightest students. Most with your IQ would jump at such an opportunity. And now look at you. Despite the patience of this court ... despite the patience of those who care for you—"

Yeah, right.

"—you return for attacking the very woman who has raised you. Do you have no respect for the unborn baby she carries?"

"I feel sorry for it!"

"Do not speak out in my court, young lady," scorned the judge.

"You asked me a question."

"I did?"

"You did, Your Honor," reminded the clerk.

"Well, I didn't mean for you to speak, and do not until I grant you permission."

Oh my God. What kind of drug is this guy on?

"Miss Green, your excuses for the things you do are as troubling as the acts themselves. One might suspect conditions not revealed in your psychoanalysis. You keep making unwise decisions. May I remind you that the defining difference between me, your father—"

You don't know my father. Not my real father.

"—and anyone else in this room, as opposed to those spending their nights in jail, is discipline. We all consider stupid acts sometimes in our lives. But it is those who lack discipline who carelessly act *stupidly* upon their *stupid* thoughts. One must take time to think before acting. Consequences, Ms. Green ... acts of stupidity carry consequences. Do you understand what I am telling you?"

For some reason, I did. And the judge was right. *But what about all those other stupid people who ruined my life, abandoned me, left me to be abused?* Rather than speak, I nodded slowly.

"And I tell you right now," rambled the judge, "were you eighteen years old today, I would likely be sentencing you to time in an adult facility."

Judge Stinson hesitated, glancing down at the papers given to him by Mr. Sebastian. Looking back up he said, "Now, it is my understanding that your parents are requesting a postponement on your sentencing so that you might participate in some rehab program of their choosing. Miss Green, are you aware of this arrangement?"

I stood silent while the judge stared into my eyes. *You've seen them before, asshole.* It's been the same each time I appear before him. He stares and stares. It's as if I were cursed at birth with eyes so different that everyone I meet looks at me like I'm a freak. Those few seconds seemed forever, like a dream, as I glared back, rapt in what seemed like a standoff. My mind drifted into his, reading some sort of sympathy in his thoughts, and I began to wonder if perhaps he was not as mean as he had let on to be.

"Young lady, do not ignore my question."

"You ... have not granted me permission ... sir."

After a deep breath for patience, Judge Stinson said, "You have my permission. Now answer the question, please."

"No, sir, I *was not* aware of their arrangements, but I guess I am now."

"And do you believe that time away in such a facility can bring you back to reality?"

"Is it like the prison I've been in for the last month?"

"Prison! Miss Green, I can assure you that the juvenile center where you've been held is not a prison. Its conditions are nothing like what you may soon be facing."

Bite me.

Focusing on the row behind me, Judge Stinson said, "I would like the parents of the defendant to stand also."

Glancing back, I saw that the man in back of the room had removed his glasses. He seemed concerned. After Daddy helped Melanie to her feet, the judge continued. "Dr. and Mrs. Green, in six weeks your daughter will no longer be a juvenile. For me to postpone sentencing today, you *and* your daughter must agree that when she returns from the Grayson Springs facility in Kentucky, this Court will have the option of sentencing her as an adult."

"Kentucky?" I blurted. "How could you?"

"Miss Green," the judge scolded. "Hold your comments!" After hesitation, he continued, "As I was saying, if your daughter does not come back with a good report and a better attitude, I warn you now that she may be spending time in jail. Not a juvenile center, but an adult facility."

I turned to Daddy and whispered, "How could you?"

"Do you as legal guardians understand and agree?" reiterated the judge.

In unison, both stated, "Yes, Your Honor, we do."

"And you Ms. Green ... do you fully understand the ramifications of postponing your sentencing as I have described?"

Fuck yes, I understand! They're sending me back to hell. "Yes, Your Honor ... I do."

"Good," announced the judge. "Let the Court make record that the defendant and her parents have indicated they fully understand all that has been said.... Dr. and Mrs. Green, though I have no control over such, I suggest you avoid contact with your daughter during her time away. She has ignored your good advice, as well as that of this Court and her school advisors. Perhaps time away will do her good. She needs to miss you and to see what she is potentially giving up." After scanning his calendar, he continued, "Ms. Green ... today is Maaaaaaaay the sixteenth. Your program is to start on ... the twenty-third. Six weeks will put us in the holiday week of the Fourth of July. I'll not return to court myself until the following week. You be back in my court on Monday, July the eleventh. I suggest you make the best of your time away. Come back here a changed woman, or your Independence Day celebration will be short lived.... Next case."

Outside the courtroom, my parents stopped to speak to Mr. Sebastian. Two of my classmates from Stuyvesant were waiting for me. Jason—dressed in black, decorated with a studded necklace, multiple piercings, and coal black hair—greeted me with a quick kiss on the cheek. "Sorrrrreeee, sweetie. It was already started when we got here, so we were afraid to interrupt. You okay?" he asked.

"No," I answered honestly.

"What's the verdict?" asked Darleen, a female version of Jason.

"I have to go away."

"To prison?" Darleen shrieked. Over her shoulder, I grinned at my girlfriend from Sacred Heart, Shauna, a well-dressed opposite to Jason and Darleen, as she hurriedly joined us.

"No," I answered. "Some place in Kentucky."

Pushing between Darleen and me, Shauna gave me a hug and then a quick kiss on the lips. Releasing her squeeze, she backed off and said, "You told me ten o'clock. What the hell happened?"

"They moved it up."

"And the judge sent you out of state? Can he do that?"

"My parents are sending me there. His *Honor* called it a rehab."

"Well, if it's anything like where my Uncle Charles went, it'll be a resort."

"Don't worry, girlfriend," encouraged Jason. "Your parents aren't going to send their baby girl to a bad place."

"You don't know my parents."

"Brooke's right," Darleen agreed. "Her parents suck."

"By the way," added Shauna as she took a step back, "you look nice in that outfit."

"Fuck you."

Chapter 2

Episodes of disagreement with Melanie often ended with me crying myself to sleep, trying to remember something, anything about my real parents. Who were they? What did they look like? Why did they leave me? My heart longed for what my mind seemed determined to forget. While counselors and psychologists prodded for details, Daddy, the man who took me away from the dark woods and into the city lights, refused to share things he surely had to know.

For a whole week, the thought of returning to those hills of Kentucky brought back flashes of the bad years, and it scared the shit out of me. It didn't help that I'd seen movies like *US Marshals*, and *Fire Down Below*, where rural Kentuckians were portrayed as a bunch of inbred hillbillies. I anticipated thick skinned, toothless people that drove old cars and hung their clothes out on a line in the yard.

For the trip, I wore my hair up under a Yankee's baseball cap, in a ponytail that hung to the center of my back. My low rise, denim jeans and a dark blue full length jacket were from Dolce & Gabbana. The smallest breasts in the senior class at Stuyvesant High were covered with a baby blue t-shirt that displayed "Screw the World," a statement hidden from Daddy by my buttoned-up jacket. My handbag was an oversized Balenciaga, and the black Lanvin sneakers on my feet were a seventeenth birthday present from Grandma Green.

Daddy's dialogue free drive to LaGuardia airport came as no surprise. Since being arrested, I'd gotten little attention from him. There never had been a whole lot of talking in the Green household. We lived in an apartment on Manhattan's Upper East Side, right across from Central Park. Meals were usually on the run, conversations too scholarly, too sophisticated to enjoy. In a way, I even felt sorry for Melanie. She'd wasted her youth with a man old enough to be her father. I suspected an affair. The woman had been spending way too much time primping for someone—not likely the old husband who spends too much time with patients—and there had been a couple occasions when she cut a phone call short upon my untimely arrival.

As we sat waiting in the airport near the ticket counter, Daddy leaned forward, elbows on his knees, chin in his hands, and broke the silence. "How has it come to this, Elizabeth?"

"My friends call me Brooke, thank you. If you were around enough you'd know that. Even your wife calls me Brooke."

"I'm sorry. Brooke is fine. But please. Tell me why this had to happen."

"Why? Your wife hates me and always has."

"I'm sorry you feel that way. She's your mother, and she's a good woman."

"Yea right. Pregnant after alllll these years and going to have 'my own little baby,' in her words. Daddy, do you seriously think that baby is yours?"

"Brooke, don't. Even if ... that would not give you the right to physically attack her. You could have harmed the fetus."

"Oh, my God. You sent me to Sacred Heart Academy, and then call it a fetus. It's a baby, for Christ's sake ... not just some chemical react—" I cut myself short, realizing for the first time that Melanie's pregnancy might have been derived artificially. "You're right, you know, I could have hurt the baby, but I didn't. All I did was give Melanie the reason she wanted—what she needed to get rid of me. If she hadn't been pregnant, I might have really let her have it."

"Melanie and I have spent years trying to pull you out of whatever it is that bothers you so."

"You've spent years trying to fix me. You've never stopped treating me like one of your patients. All I wanted was someone to love me. Every time Melanie tells you I said thiiisss or did thaaat, you start analyzing. I'm not supposed to be your patient. I'm supposed to be your daughter. You really want to know what is wrong with me? Count all the missed opportunities to hug me and hold me quietly, or just listen to what I have to say about *my* day. All you ever get about me is what *she* tells you. And believe me, she's no shrink. The woman has no idea what is on my mind."

"I, I do love you—"

"Daddy, do you even know what love is?"

"Brooke—"

"I would love to read your definition of love. Write it down. Text it to me so I can see if you even have a clue."

"Amazing," observed Dr. Green. "To think I met you because you wouldn't speak. Now listen to you."

.....I remember it well. The boy who spit on me during my first and only day in kindergarten. I beat him so badly that they kicked me out. Two days later, a strange man came to see me. He made the ugly people leave the room. At first, being alone with him was frightening. He said he was a doctor, but he didn't wear a white coat. He was nice. He seemed to understand why I didn't talk. He asked me to draw pictures about how I felt, and so I did, and it made me feel better. That night I did not cry. When the man came back the next day, I knew he liked me. I drew more pictures. On the third day, the doctor asked if he could brush my hair. It was always a mess, tangled. I never let the ugly people touch me. The man gave me a mirror to hold while he brushed. It hurt when he took out the tangles, but I loved the way it felt, someone touching me in a good way. When he finished, he said, "You are so pretty." I looked into the mirror and for the first time saw pretty. I hugged Dr. Green and said, "Could you be my daddy?".....

The PA system broke my trance. "Would Elizabeth Brooke Green, please report to the Gate 17 ticket counter? Elizabeth Brooke Green to Gate 17 ticket counter."

Daddy had been gawking at my sudden silence. We both stood, and I said, "I loved you because you seemed to understand me. You didn't scream at me for not talking. And when I did, you listened."

He wrapped his arms around me, squeezed tight and said, "Brooke, honey, I'm not the one who's changed. I still listen, but when I do, you say I'm analyzing."

I pushed away from the hug and stared at his statement. His grin spoke before he did. "Now who's analyzing whom?" he asked.

I knew he cared about me, but something was missing. *The look of love in his eyes when he rocked me on his knee and called me...* "Daddy, when did you quit calling me Sunshine?"

He looked surprised and said, "Baby, I've never called you Sunshine."

Ughhhhhh. He doesn't even remember. I shouldered my Balenciaga and said, "I've got to go," then added, "Regardless of how it got there, it's a baby. Don't treat it like a fetus. If you treat it like an experiment, it will not feel loved. Believe me, I know." That said, I turned to walk away.

"Brooke, wait," he begged. I looked back and he said, "In all these years, you've never quite adjusted...."

"So you're sending me back, like a faulty product! You think someone there can fix me?"

"I'm sending you back further than you think...."

"And what the hell does that mean?"

"You'll know soon enough. It's kind of like going back in time."

If only I could, I thought. *If only I could go back far enough to meet my real parents.*

"Try to enjoy the ride," he continued. "Just be careful. We want you back in one piece."

"Better talk to Mommy Dearest about that," I said as I began walking away. Glancing over my shoulder I added, "And don't forget, this was your idea."

At the Gate 17 ticket desk, an assistant checked my reservation. "Miss Green, we have alternate instructions for you." As the lady spoke, another woman behind the counter overheard the conversation and interceded.

"Ah, yes. This must be our special guest today. Please follow me, miss."

The employee escorted me ahead of the group of passengers waiting in line to board. For an instant, I felt privileged, like a celebrity. Before entering the tarmac, I glanced back to see Daddy still standing, watching, looking as if he were heartbroken. He mouthed the words, "I love you." I blew him a kiss and then followed the attendant.

Entering the plane, there were greetings from two flight attendants, the plane's captain, and his younger co-pilot.

"Good evening, Ms. Green. My name is Captain Johnson. I hope you will find our flight accommodations suitable. After we land, please remain seated until your escort arrives." I sensed sarcasm. When the pilot turned toward the plane's cabin, his co-pilot smiled, winked, and followed.

As Flight 3056 taxied toward the runway, a flight attendant began announcing instructions over the PA system. I pushed the call button. The second attendant glanced at her partner, shook her head, and then walked toward me. With that, *here we go attitude*, she asked, "Is there something I can do for you?"

Sensing animosity, I replied politely, "Yes ma'am. I was wondering if I might move to the window seat."

There were only a handful of passengers in first class, all adults, dressed in business attire. Both seats between mine and the window had been left empty. Apparently relieved at my politeness, the stewardess said, "Go ahead."

At 10:57 p.m. the engines revved and the scenery outside passed quickly. When the jet airliner tilted upward, I watched my world, my friends, and my Manhattan city lights being left behind. I plugged in headphones, selected music, and then relaxed into the luxurious seat.

Chapter 3

Long dress ... fresh, but old fashioned ... hair longer ... to my waist, wavy ... flowers in a bouquet ... rain is falling...

"Please fasten your seatbelts!" woke me. The headphones were down around my neck, still playing music. I had fallen asleep somewhere on the two hour and 16 minute flight from New York to Kentucky. Through the window, at a distance, I could see an illuminated oasis of what was supposed to be the state's largest municipality.

"Oh, my God, where's the city?" brought a smile to the face of the nearby flight attendant.

She commented, "My exact reaction the first time I came here."

"How could they do this to me?"

"Don't worry. It's not New York, but it's not bad."

"I bet."

"Seriously," continued the attendant, "and everybody knows everybody, so watch what you say about people."

Five minutes later, the plane taxied into the airport terminal. While other passengers made their exit, a light skinned African American woman boarded the plane. She had long, wavy hair, looked to be in her late 30s, and wore blue jeans, western boots, and a white button-up blouse. On her belt, a badge read Kentucky State Police. Until she spoke, I envisioned one of those black lady cops on TV—sharp, authoritatively demanding, maybe even a little on the seductive side. The flight attendant pointed me out.

"Brooke Green?" asked the officer.

Holy shit! She sounds sooo hick! I rose and stretched, displaying my 'Screw the World' message. The flight attendant smiled, then went about her business.

"I'm Officer Porter."

I almost broke out laughing, and I believe she could tell. I hadn't heard such a hideous accent since eighth grade, when some kid from Texas came to Sacred Heart Academy. The woman did wear a pleasantly clean fragrance. "You smell nice for a cop. Am I under arrest?"

"Thank you. And no, you're not under—"

"So why did they send a cop?"

"I'd say because you're a smart ass rich kid with a tendency toward violence and an attitude in need of adjustment. Now, the best thing your bad little ass can do is cover up that shirt and that attitude.... You understand me girl?"

Jesus, this woman loves her job. "My attitude offends you?"

"Attitude shows character, providing the engine pushin' it is trainable. And we're gonna find out about that soon enough. But I'm not the one you have to worry about. Unless you come to order quick, you're gonna really piss off the Colonel."

Colonel? "Who's the Colonel?"

"For the next six weeks, honey, he's your god."

Yeah, right, I thought while pulling on my jacket and shouldering my purse. "First of all, Officer Porter, I'm *not* your honey." I scanned her up and down, and then messed with her. "Unless you really want me to be."

Bitch just stood there, staring at my eyes, like she was contemplating shooting me or something. Finally she said, "Am I gonna be able to trust you to behave?"

"I'm not a criminal."

"So, you think you're just here on vacation?"

"Fuck you."

"Time out, girlfriend—"

"I'm not your girlfriend!"

The flight attendant, who'd been gathering trash from one of the seats, stopped to listen. The cop took a deep breath and said, "Ms. Green, folks in New York might put up with that mouth, but you're in Kentucky now. And while you're here you *will not* speak in that tone. Right now you're real close to me sending your little ass back home with another arrest on your record. And we both know that won't look good when you go back before the judge."

The flight attendant's eyes widened and she shrugged her shoulders as the cop continued.

"They said you were spoiled. Look at you standin' there in a thousand bucks worth of clothes, carryin' a twelve-hundred dollar bag."

"It's not my fault you have to wear Levi's."

"Won't be long, girl, you'll be dreaming of Levi's."

"What does that mean?"

"You'll find out soon enough.... So, can I count on you actin' right?"

Loathing the officer's vernacular, I sassed in a most disgusting southern country accent. "Contrary to what yaw hillbillies think, we Manhattan girls can be civilized."

"Good. Stay with me.... Believe you *do* have a little country in you."

When Officer Porter turned, I felt an urge to kick her in the ass, but instead I said, "Well now, you *do* fill out those jeans nicely."

She stopped, mumbled "Jesus," and then motioned me to go first.

In the terminal area, an old white man operating a carpet cleaner dodged what few travelers there were. I said, "Not very crowded for an International Airport?"

"Should have seen it two weeks ago. Couldn't move in here."

"Why's that?"

"Kentucky Derby. Whole lotta spoiled ass rich folks come through here that week."

"Oh yeah. I've seen it on TV. My parents attended last year."

"They like it?"

"I have no idea. We don't talk that much."

Officer Porter mumbled again, "No wonder the girl gets in trouble."

After a short walk, we stopped in front of a food court. An elderly uniformed member of airport security rose from his seat. He seemed to have been babysitting a girl my age. She sat silent, eyes closed, listening to her iPod. When Officer Porter said, "Sure appreciate your help sir," the girl opened her eyes, but remained seated.

"No problem," he replied. "Glad to be of service." The old guy gave me a look, and then glanced down at the other girl. "You sure you can handle these two by yourself?"

"They give me problems, I'll cuff 'em. That don't work, I'll shoot 'em and bury their bodies in the woods."

"Believe you would," smiled the old man.

Officer Porter reached down, pulled one of the girl's earbuds, and said, "On your feet, LA. We ain't got all night."

When the girl stood, she was a little taller than me. She appeared to be mixed, with long dark, curly hair, fashionably thick lips, and big boobs. Her uncaring glance landed on my handbag. She wore MEK Amsterdam low rise, factory torn, blue jeans; camo hiking boots; and carried a small, matching camo backpack. *Yuk!* Figuring she could not hear me, I lipped, "So last season."

Officer Porter said, "New York, meet LA. You two are gonna be best friends for the next six weeks."

Yeah, right.

Outside the airport, bright lights made it seem like daytime. There were a few cars and taxis pulling up to or away from the loading / unloading zone. As soon as we cleared the doorway, I lit a cigarette, took a long draw, and exhaled with the satisfaction of a junkie getting a fix.

"That'll like, kill you some day," were the first words I heard from LA.

"Don't plan on living forever."

"See that container over there," motioned Officer Porter, "that's where the cigarette goes."

Bite me, I thought while stepping toward the cigarette depository, grabbing two more draws along the way. LA and I were ushered into the back seat of a Kentucky State Police cruiser and ordered to put on our seat belts. She sat, silently checking out our confining surroundings. I figured it was her first police car experience. As Officer Porter pulled away from the curb, LA grinned at me and said, "Feels like I should be receiving my Miranda rights."

Well, maybe she has been in a cop car before.

Officer Porter spoke through the rearview mirror. "You ladies get to know one another. Use your phones, music players, whatever all you want for the next hour. You'll be givin' 'em up after that."

"No fucking way!" complained LA. "I'm not giving up my phone."

I felt the same, but decided to let LA do the talking. Officer Porter merged onto a highway, accelerated into the traffic, and then said, "I feel you, girl, but trust me, you won't need a phone. Besides, where we're goin', most visitor's phones don't work anyway. You'll see."

"Where exactly are we going?" LA asked.

"Back in time, honey. We're all goin' back in time. You two divas are about to experience things you never dreamed of. And keep in mind, your parents have already signed off on all of it."

I tried dialing Daddy's phone. It rang four times and then went to voice mail. Hitting the 'End' button, I closed my eyes and prayed that we could somehow go far enough back in time for me to meet someone who knows who I really am. Maybe I could meet my real parents, tell them how much I've missed them, how I love them, and how I hate them for leaving me alone.

Those thoughts were interrupted by the sound of LA talking on her cell phone. I kept my eyes shut and listened.

"Dad, how could you...? How could you, like, send me somewhere where I can't even have a phone...? But I have to give it up in an hour, for six weeks...! But I thought this was someplace special...? Nooo. We're in the back of a police car, like some kind of criminals.... Yes, a girl from New York.... But, how can I relax when I have to give up my phone? Can you speak to them...? But I can't live without a phone! I'll die!"

I could see tears in her eyes.

"But, Dad ... but, Dad ... bye." LA shoved her phone into her purse and said, "He's so full of shit. Tells me to relax and enjoy the quiet times. I don't want quiet, I want my phone." Then she began staring at me as though she suddenly realized I had been quietly listening to her conversation.

"What's your problem?" I asked.

"No problem," spoke LA, hesitantly. "Just wondered why you weren't talking to anyone."

"They won't answer. It's that fucking judge. He told them they shouldn't have contact with me. He thinks it'll make me miss them. Swear to God, I'll never forgive my parents for this."

LA said, "My mother wouldn't talk to me. Had to call my father, and he's all lecture-y and stuff. Can you believe this shit? We're screwed, you know."

The girl is right. We are both screwed. "My name is Brooke Green."

LA looked over, grinned, and said, "I'm Sherri Reid." She thought for a second. "You got a boyfriend?" When I did not answer, she asked, "Girlfriend?" I said nothing, yet the girl's head tilted, her eyebrows raised, and I read her assumption. "Oh well," she continued, "call yours while I call mine. Might be our last chance." We both began dialing numbers.

Chapter 4

Officer Porter dialed her own cell phone, spoke briefly, and then left the interstate at an exit that read, U.S.31-W Bypass, Elizabethtown. By the end of the ramp, we were entering a mist of fog. After stopping at a traffic light, she turned left and headed down a dark, two-lane state road. Though fog thickened the further we drove out of town, I could tell we were moving parallel to a railroad track.

LA whispered, "You think we're almost there?"

"Don't believe we've gone back in time yet."

"How can you tell? I can't see a damn thing."

As the cruiser slowed, a cone of soft light appeared ahead over a small building. When we left the road, the cruiser's headlights shined on a boarded up one-story building. Old gas pumps stood like sentries guarding the ruins. When Officer Porter killed the engine, I knew we'd reached some sort of destination, and from the look of things, we were definitely moving back in time. She exited the car, stood in front of it looking around for a moment, and then stepped toward the back. Passing my side, she opened the door and said, "Okay ladies, this is where we get out."

LA's eyes were wide open as she whispered, "Is this where she plans to bury our bodies?"

While Officer Porter opened the trunk lid, I answered, "Saw a movie where some creep made girls dig their own graves."

"I think I'm going to be sick."

From behind the vehicle came, "Move it ladies, we're on a schedule."

When I crawled out, LA grabbed her backpack and slid my way. Outside the car, night noises surrounded us.

"Y'all come around here."

Oh shit, she's gonna make us carry the shovels.

Three backpacks lay in the trunk. Each had an ID tag zip-tied to it. "Take the one with your name on it."

After LA and I pulled our bags out, Officer Porter removed her own and then dropped the lid.

I asked, "Are we there?"

"Hell no. Be a couple more hours at least."

LA almost hyperventilated. "We, we have to walk for two hours?"

"No, dear. Unless of course you want to. You wearin' those fancy boots, I figured you might enjoy a thirty mile hike.... Just bring the backpack and follow me."

"But I already have a backpack."

"Guess you'll have to carry two, or leave yours behind."

Things were not making sense. I asked, "You're going to leave the car here?"

As Officer Porter started walking toward the road, she replied, "It won't be there for long." At the blacktop, she looked back and said, "Come on girls. Let's play follow the leader."

LA frowned at me and said, "You know, I'm part Jewish ... and this doesn't feel right ... we're like sheep following some nutcase to our death."

"Listen," I said.

"To what?"

"I love the sounds of all those bugs. I feel too alive to die. Come on."

LA carried a backpack on each shoulder. I put my backpack on and carried my purse. We followed Officer Porter across the road. Looking back, while the building remained in soft light, the cruiser had already begun to blend into the mist. Near the railroad tracks, we stopped at a concrete culvert that allowed water to flow under the tracks. Cop lady sat down on the culvert and said, "Have a seat. Shouldn't be long."

"What are we waiting for?" LA asked.

21

"The train."

LA glanced at me, mouth wide open. "We're catching a train right here in the middle of nowhere?"

"Were you expecting an Amtrak Station?" sassed the officer.

I whispered into LA's ear, "Now *I* feel Jewish."

My whispering disturbed the officer. Her eyes squinted. Lips wrinkled. I needed to go to a good place. Closing my eyes, my mind drifted to the night noises. Their symphony stirred something inside me. Memories dulled by time. When I was 4, 5, maybe 6, living in the bad place with the ugly people, I heard these same intense noises. They eased me then. They were easing me again.

"New York!" blurted the cop. "Wake up. You okay?"

"I ... I'm listening to those beautiful sounds. Can you tell me what they are?"

"Crickets, katydids, tree frogs, bullfrogs, whip-r-wills. Why you ask?"

"They're lovely."

"They're frigging noisy, if you ask me," LA complained.

Instead of commenting, Officer Porter sat staring at us. I'd seen that look a million times at home with Daddy. She was analyzing.

I can't remember which came first, the vibrations in the concrete on which we sat or the rumble of noise down track in the direction from which we drove. Officer Porter stood and said, "Tharrr she blows," as if she were Ahab at sea, spotting a great white whale. LA and I stood also. The train's headlight appeared as a small beacon in the distance, growing by the second. "All right ladies, here's the deal. The train will soon begin to slow. We stay put until the engine passes. Then we move up close to the track. The train will come to a stop, but only momentarily. There's gonna be a boxcar near the end with its door open. We throw in our gear and then climb aboard. Train takes off again. It's that simple. Any questions?"

It felt like déjà vu. Like maybe I'd seen this before.

Sherri said, "Are you sure my father agreed to this?"

Officer Porter ignored the question and said, "There'll be a metal ladder connected to the front side of the opening. LA, you go first.

Toss your bags into the car, and then grab the ladder and pull yourself up. You'll only have to climb three or four rungs and then slip into the car. Turn and see if New York needs help. She'll start up as soon as you get in. I'll come aboard last."

The engine passed quickly, blowing its horn at intervals. Noise became so overwhelming that we had to cover our ears. After a multitude of clanging, rocking train cars flashed by, the engine's roar subsided, and for a moment the sound of brakes screeched. Though slowing, the train continued moving. An opened boxcar appeared near the end.

"Something's wrong!" the officer shouted. "It should have stopped by now!"

It didn't seem to be moving all that fast to me. "I've seen this before, on the movies! Can't we just run and jump on?"

"No way!" shouted the officer. "It's too dangerous!"

"I couldn't run that fast anyway!" screamed LA.

"Oh, I get it, Californian girls can't run."

"Fuck you!" she shouted.

"No. Fuck you!"

"That's enough ladies!" shouted the cop. "I said never mind the train. It's too dangerous!"

LA growled, and then surprised me. As the open car passed, she took off trotting like some sort of human sized penguin with a backpack in each hand.

"I said forget it LA!"

LA kept running. "Californian girls can run!"

I looked back at Officer Porter. She hollered, "Go! If we're gonna do this, we can't wait!"

I began running with the backpack in one hand and my purse in the other. Officer Porter ran on my heels. By the time we caught up to LA, she ran alongside of the open boxcar. My Lavin sneakers were not made for running. Rocks were killing the bottoms of my feet. Officer Porter screamed, "Throw in your bags, ladies!"

LA slung her right hand backpack first as I did mine. Then she switched hands and tossed the second. My Balenciaga slid across the dirty wooden floor, landing against straw bales. Officer Porter's backpack hit the bales in flight. She began shouting, "LA, you're in front. You have to go first! Grab the ladder!"

Without the burden of two backpacks, LA ran with the lope of a deer. She grabbed the ladder's left side, took two more steps and latched on with her right. At first it was her knee that found a rung. Then she pulled up to get a foothold. Within seconds she had climbed into the boxcar screaming, "I did it!"

Growing tired, I had slowed a bit. "Faster, New York!" shouted Officer Porter.

Though the rocks were killing my feet, I somehow accelerated.

"Come on!" screamed LA. "If I can do it, you can!"

Imitating LA's success, I managed to grab the ladder and began pulling myself up. My shoe soles were slick and slipped as I struggled upward, banging my right knee on a rung. Seeing my dilemma, LA offered one hand while holding onto the door facing with her other. We locked grips on one another's wrists, and I somehow made it into the train car. Apparently, Officer Porter was in a lesser condition than she thought. Her pace had slowed and she huffed along midway at the opening. "She's not going to make it," I screamed at LA.

My cohort shuffled to the back of the opening, held on and offered a hand to the officer. "Here!" she shouted. "We can pull you in!"

I joined LA, holding her belt with one hand while gripping an inside rail with the other. Officer Porter grabbed LA's hand and about pulled us both from the train when she lunged from the ground, trying to find a foot hold. As she hung on, the train's engine grew louder and we could feel the increase in speed.

LA shouted back at me, "Don't let go!" then offered her second hand to the cop. Struggling to hold on, I couldn't even see the woman around LA. Some sharp item dug into my right hand, but I knew letting go would cause both LA and the cop to fall. Finally, I could see Officer Porter's head emerging like some crazy version of adult birthing. Her shoulders appeared, then her torso, then victory. The woman scrambled to a safe spot and collapsed on her back on the straw-covered floor. LA and I joined her. We lay silently with Officer Porter breathing heavily between us.

I reached for my purse. Didn't matter what anyone else thought, I had to have a cigarette. When I lit up, Officer Porter mumbled, "Careful. The straw will ignite easily."

After I had a couple draws, LA said, "My friend at home claims she has to have a cigarette after sex. Is that why I feel like I should smoke right now?"

"You didn't have sex," I replied.

"I know, but I might have gotten off."

After a slight chuckle from Cop Lady, I said, "You're fucked up, LA."

"You're smoking. Does that mean you got off?"

"It means I wanted a cigarette."

I finished my smoke while staring at distant stars out the boxcar doorway. At first it shocked me when Officer Porter took my right hand in hers. It felt warm and sent a fuzzy feeling to my brain. She began to speak softly, and I sensed she had LA's hand also. "You guys were great. Guess I'm not in as good a shape as I used to be."

"You had to run longer than either of us," I replied.

LA chimed, "That was the most exciting thing I've ever done in my whole life."

Before I could comment, Officer Porter said, "What the—" as she released my hand. Rising to her knees, she continued, "New York, you're bleeding!"

I held my hand and barely-visible drops of blood dripped onto my chest. "Something was cutting into my hand, but I couldn't let go. I was afraid you and LA would fall."

Without hesitation, cop lady pulled a pocket knife from her jeans. "Who's got hand sanitizer?"

"I do," replied LA as she went for her small backpack.

After slicing through the hem of her blouse, Officer Porter ripped the entire bottom off to create a bandage for my hand. The hand sanitizer stung. Within a minute or two, my hand was cleaned and wrapped, and we were all sitting on our heels staring at one another.

Officer Porter said, "I've been around the world, seen action, and have rarely experienced any better display of valor than what I witnessed here tonight. You ladies reached inside in a pinch and found the strength to do what had to be done to assist someone you barely know. Not because you had to, but because you somehow realized it was the right thing to do. That's the shit heroes are made of."

"You were in the military?" I asked.

"Army MP." Tears ran down her cheek as she finished. "I owe you both."

It didn't take long for Officer Porter to regain composure and default back to her dutiful self. "Okay, ladies. We've accomplished one phase, yet fallen behind on our mission. Let's hustle back on track. Our backpacks contain clothing, shoes, and a jacket. We have to change into what's in the bag. Put what you are wearing now, plus your jewelry, cellphones, *and* your purses, into the bag. It will all be returned after the six weeks."

Without arguing, LA and I began opening our bags to see what fashions were in store. "What the hell?" LA shrieked.

Even in dim light, I could see the most disgusting apparel on Earth. "What the fuck is this?"

"It's clothing from the era we're gonna spend the next six weeks in."

"But I can't wear this crap," whined LA.

"Oh yes you can. And it'll be very much appropriate for where we're goin'."

I asked again, "Just where *are* we going?"

"Already told you. Back in time."

"Middle Ages?" asked LA.

"Not quite. Just get dressed, ladies." Removing her vest, she added, "We're gonna be there soon. Better to dress now in privacy, than after we meet up with the Colonel."

Seeing no option, I began to undress. My backpack was stuffed full with a pale brown, full length skirt, tall white socks, long sleeve plain button blouse, leather shoes, old fashioned bloomers, and a dull, brown overcoat that looked like something a cowboy in a western movie might wear. Noticing how Officer Porter had opened her overcoat onto a straw bale for a place to sit, I followed suit.

Holding up her new bloomers, LA complained, "You expect us to wear these?"

Officer Porter sat removing her shoes. She chuckled and said, "Ain't up to me, honey. Just do it, and do it quick."

I had already taken off my shoes and shirt while LA stood waiting.

Officer Porter asked her, "What's your problem?"

"Can't you at least turn around?"

"Girl, this ain't high school."

I said, "Quit whining. Let's just get this over with." LA turned her back and began removing her attire.

Officer Porter removed her bra, and I found myself staring at what I always wanted. She seemed to notice and quickly covered herself with the blouse from her backpack. When I took off my jeans, she saw my thong and said, "New York, believe you'll be glad they gave you them bloomers."

"Bet this was all they had when you were a kid."

"Excuse me? I'm not that old."

LA huffed, "You two think this is funny?"

"Not about funny," replied Officer Porter. "It's about making the best of a situation."

"There's no bra," LA continued. "Does that mean we get to keep ours?"

"Sorry, sugar. Guess back in the day they didn't have bras."

Slipping into my bloomers, I smiled and said, "You'll get used to it."

"That's easy for you to say," jabbed LA, unsnapping the bra and exposing her 36-Cs.

"Fuck you."

"You two behave," ordered Officer Porter. As she spoke with her back to me, she dropped her Levis. She and LA both had perfectly rounded buttocks. I figured it was a black thing. They probably thought my ass looked like a boy's.

Eventually, we were all dressed and stuffing our belongings into the backpacks. I kept out my cigarettes and lighter. For a moment, we stood staring at one another. Finally, Officer Porter spoke. "Now ain't we a sight for sore eyes?"

Chapter 5

Kentucky isn't all hills. As the train chugged along, my eyes adjusted to the darkness, and I could make out dim images of farmlands, vast fields dotted with an occasional lit oasis of a farmhouse surrounded by a few shade trees, barns, and a silo. When the freight train rumbled across a railroad trestle, I moved close to the doorway to grasp what I expected would be a breathtaking view. Instead, all I saw was a blanket of fog. Officer Porter pulled a straw bale over, and we sat together.

She asked, "What'd you think?"

"Just wondering how far down it is?"

"Sixty meters, I'd say. Been one or two who carelessly found out the hard way."

"No shit?"

I lit a cigarette and exhaled into the vastness. Officer Porter said, "There won't be anywhere to buy cigarettes during your stay."

"Oh, well. Guess I'll have to quit."

"I'm told you were born in Grayson County."

"Suppose you know all about me."

"Not really. Do you remember your childhood?"

"Some ... mostly bad stuff."

"Everybody has bad stuff in their past."

LA had propped herself between two bales and seemed to be napping. I nodded her way and said, "You think she has bad stuff?"

"Wouldn't be here if she didn't."

By the time I finished my cigarette, the locomotive's roar eased, and the train began to slow. Seconds later, the brakes on the boxcars woke LA with another abusive round of noise.

"We there?" she asked.

"We're somewhere." Through the darkness, shadows of a small town appeared. The backs of a mix of one- and two-story framed buildings ran parallel to the track. I turned to LA and said, "We've been removed from civilization."

Officer Porter shook her head and said, "You have no idea, girlfriend."

"I told you, I'm not your girlfriend." As soon as I said it, I realized my deliverance of the message was much less aggressive than the last time I said it. I believe she realized it also.

With a grin, she asked, "How's the hand?"

"Okay."

"Good."

LA stood, balanced herself with the train's movement and asked, "New York, you still sucking ass?"

The train screeched to an abrupt stop, rocking us all. There were no lights on in the whole town. Not even a street light. "Creepy."

Suddenly, a man appeared out of nowhere. Looking up at us, he said, "Best-looking bunch of hobos I've ever seen."

"Mornin', Colonel…. Ladies this is Colonel Ron. Colonel, this is LA, and New York."

Colonel Ron, at 5'9" and around 160 pounds, wore an *Indiana Jones*-looking hat over short hair. In dim light, I guessed his age at mid to late 40's.

He said, "LA and New York ... intriguing. Welcome to Clarkson, Kentucky. Hand me your bags and then climb down. We need to move on. Train's gotta stay on schedule."

Colonel Ron set our bags on the ground and then watched while we descended the ladder. As I reached the ground, he asked, "What happened to your hand?"

"Long story," Officer Porter answered for me. "Fill you in on the ride."

We each gathered our belongings. Colonel Ron offered to carry my backpack, but I held on to it. We followed him to the back car and then across the tracks to the opposite side of the train.

LA moaned, "You've got to be kidding." Our transportation was of the four-legged variety. There was a two-horse, old fashioned buckboard, right out of the TV Westerns I'd watched with Daddy. Two additional horses, saddled for riding, were tied to the back.

"Toss your stuff in the back," ordered Colonel Ron. "Officer Porter will join me while you two ride saddle."

"But I've…never ridden a horse," pleaded LA.

"Makes two of us," I admitted.

"No time better than the present. We're gonna take it easy. These horses are gentle. They're not likely to give you problems unless you make a mistake. Pay attention as I give you a crash course on what to do and what not to do. First of all, you always mount from the left side. Go to the right side of a horse, and it'll know you don't have a clue." He pulled a piece of yarn from his pocket, held it by the ends and said, "Ladies, I'm going to use an unconventional method to quickly teach you how to start, stop, and guide a horse. My method may seem a bit odd or perhaps even offensive, but if you bear with me, you'll soon see my point. He then asked LA to open her mouth.

"Excuse me?"

"I'm not gonna hurt you. I promise. And the string is clean. Just open your mouth please."

Officer Porter said, "Go ahead, LA. Trust me; it's the quickest way to learn."

I was glad he didn't ask me. When LA reluctantly opened up, he slid the middle of the yarn into her mouth. "Now shut your mouth please." LA obeyed. The Colonel stepped behind her, holding the ends of the strings and said, "Pay attention to what I do with the strings." As he spoke, he lightly tugged the string on the left side. "Feel that?"

"Uh huh," nodded LA.

"That would tell the horse to turn left." He tugged the right string and said, "That means right turn. Now check this out." As he spoke, Colonel Ron sort of pulled the left string against LA's neck. "Notice

I'm not pulling back on the string, but more or less leaning it against the left side of your neck to, in theory, push you right. Switching, he pushed the right string against the right side of her neck. "That tells you to go left. It's called neck reining. Make sense?"

LA nodded her head up and down to say yes.

"Either way works to guide the horse; however, neck reining allows you to guide the horse using only one hand. It's the process a cowboy uses to free up the hand he uses for roping." He glanced at me and said, "You paying attention?"

I nodded yes.

"Next lesson." Colonel Ron pulled back lightly on both strings ends at the same time. "That means slow down. If I keep the pressure on, you will slow to a stop. Got it?" She nodded again. "Good. Now how about this?" He yanked on the strings, jerking LA's head backwards.

"Excuse me!" she complained.

"Didn't like that, did you? I promise the horse won't like it either. So don't be jerkin' her head too hard. That's a good way to get the horse to rear up and possibly throw you off.... Okay, we know how to stop a horse, so let's talk about how we get it to move. Right now, if I want you to start walking, I could push you in the back like this." LA stumbled forward. "But since you'll be sittin' on the horses back, that won't work. Instead, we do this." He poked his fingers into LA's sides while saying "Getup."

She jumped and said, "What the—"

"Got your attention didn't it. That's what we do to get the horse to move. We nudge 'em in the ribs with our heels while saying *getup*. The harder you poke, the faster they will take off." He then sort of clicking with his tongue. "Do that when you kick her, and the horse will likely jump to a trot or maybe even a run. Therefore; do not cluck unless you really want to get a move on.... You can take the string out now. So," he asked, "do you get the picture?"

"Makes sense to me," she answered.

He pulled out another string, looked my way, and said, "Do you need a lesson also?"

I backed off and said, "No thanks. I got it."

"Good. Remember ladies, these horses get it too. As long as you give them commands they are used to, they'll serve you well."

Colonel Ron untied the darker horse. He held the reins with his left hand, while gripping the horse's mane just in front of the saddle. "Keeping a grip on the reins gives me control at all times." Standing with his left side to the horse, he turned the stirrup and placed his left foot into it. He then grabbed the saddle horn with his right hand. "Now watch." He pulled himself up until standing in the stirrup on one foot. "Notice," he said, "I still have control with my left hand. Now, I am going to raise my right leg over the saddle." Once he did, he put his other foot into the stirrup on the other side. "See how easy that was. To get off, you pretty much do the same in reverse. While you're up here, it's important that you keep your feet inside the stirrups. The stirrups are adjusted to my height so that I can balance myself or stand up in the saddle if I desire. In time you will learn to post." He demonstrated by sort of gyrating up and down in the saddle. "At a trot, you will do this in time with the horse's stride to keep from beating yourself to death."

LA looked at me and smiled.

Colonel Ron continued, "Make sure the only tension on the reigns is what you apply as a command. Now watch." He said, "Getup," as he nudged the horse's ribs with his heels. Immediately it began to walk forward. Then he said, "Whoa," as he slightly pulled back on the reigns. The horse stopped. "That's pretty much all you need to know for now."

He dismounted and said, "LA, this one's for you."

Colonel Ron held the horse's halter as LA held the reins, grabbed the horse's mane, raised her leg into the stirrup, and tried to copy the Colonel's directions. She did manage to mount the horse despite struggling. Her skirt made it a bit awkward at first, but she soon adjusted. Colonel Ron then adjusted the stirrups for her height.

"She's a mare. Her name is Birdie. Introduce yourself while I get New York going."

Colonel Ron untied the other horse, called it "Becca," and motioned me to its left side. I'd rather have done it on my own, but he insisted on helping. I copied his instructions, without LA's struggles. It felt as if I'd done it many times before.

"Good job," announced Officer Porter.

"You guys are naturals," agreed the Colonel. "I'm gonna get on the wagon now. When I get the team moving, your horses are probably gonna follow. If they do, fine. If not, just nudge 'em and say '*getup*.' Are we good?"

LA and I both nodded. As the Colonel climbed aboard the wagon, I practiced standing in the stirrups. My right hand being sore, I held the reins with my left as shown. When Colonel Ron ordered his horses forward, LA's Birdie followed on its own. Becca stood still.

Oh shit, I thought. *You might know mine would be stubborn.*

"Give 'er a nudge, New York," insisted Officer Porter, looking back.

"Getup," I commanded, while nudging with my heels. Thank God, the horse started moving.

"Good job!" shouted Officer Porter.

Chapter 6

Colonel Ron guided his team away from the train. Moments later, we were all clip-clopping down Main Street in Clarkson. Riding next to LA, following the wagon, I said, "Looks like something from the past." She did not reply.

The freight train could be heard roaring back into motion as we left town and marched toward nothingness. A hundred yards down the road, I heard something and looked back. "LA, check it out."

"What?"

"Back there. I think someone just blocked the road."

"Glancing back, she said, "Hell, I can't see anything."

"Well, I saw it. Someone was putting something in the road. Doesn't any of this seem a little creepy to you?"

"Not really."

Moonlight came and went with the moving clouds, providing occasional opportunities of visibility. I asked, "Hey, Colonel Ron! Do I have to stay behind the wagon?"

"No!" he replied. "You can move up ... won't be any traffic."

Cool, I thought. *Now how do I do this? Since I'm already moving, how do I go faster?* I whispered, "Getup." When the horse failed to respond, I did the click-click sound Colonel Ron had showed us while jabbing my heels into its side. Immediately, the old horse jumped to a trot and continued right past the buckboard with me bouncing roughly in the saddle.

Colonel Ron yelled, "Pull 'er up!"

I hollered "Wooooaaah," while pulling back on the reins.

"Not so hard!" continued the colonel as Becca slowed to a stop and then lowered her rear end. "Remember what I said—she'll—" Before he could say it, the horse reared up nearly vertical. I squeezed so tight with my legs that it hurt, held the saddle horn, and somehow managed to hang on while lessoning my pull on the reins. The horse dropped its front legs to the ground and then stood like a statue.

LA somehow halted her horse, and Colonel Ron stopped his team short of the unruly old mare. "I warned you that might happen if you pulled too tight."

"I—just wanted her to speed up—a little."

"Well, you got that part right. You just did a poor job of putting on the brakes. Once she starts trotting, if you pull straight back gently, she'll slow down to a walk."

"Sorrrrryyy."

"Don't have to be sorry. You'll get the hang of it. You okay now?"

"Yes, I'm fine."

"Notice how rough it was when she trotted. That's when you need to post in the saddle to smooth things out."

"I know that—*thank you*. I'm not stupid! You think I already forgot? I just didn't have time to do it! Okay? Can we continue now?"

Colonel Ron turned to Officer Porter and said, "There's that attitude you talked about."

I wanted to give them both the finger, but I refrained.

"Okay," continued the Colonel, "remember what I said. Do not use the clicking sound unless you wanna go fast, and if you do, don't get carried away when you have to pull the reins to slow down."

Two miles outside of Clarkson, streaks of daylight began bleeding through the partly cloudy horizon. Hints of rolling fields became visible on each side of the blacktop road. I could see the silhouettes of beef cattle grazing in the distance. Roosters crowed from every direction, apparently associated with farm houses and barns that sat at the end of long lanes connected to the main road. Dozens of black crows called loudly as they flew across the morning sky.

Eventually, open fields turned into wooded hills, and the road began a gradual downward slope. Under the forest canopy it became dark again—really dark—and the rapid clip-clopping of horse-shoes on the pavement echoed noticeably louder. The sound of running water to the right indicated a creek close by in the woods.

"Now this *is* creepy," worried LA.

I stared as deep as I could into the woods. "Very creepy."

"Excuse me, Colonel Ron," LA asked, "can you see the road?"

"Don't need to see it. The horses know their way."

Yeah, right.

It became so dark that I could only hear LA clip-clopping along. My horse blindly followed. The air became moist and cool.

"You ladies okay back there?" asked Officer Porter.

I replied, "I'm good."

LA said, "I'm fine, but why is it getting so wet and cold?"

"It's the fog," replied Colonel Ron. "You'll see it in a minute when we leave the woods."

Eventually the road began to level, the canopy opened, and daylight highlighted the misty haze. Colonel Ron guided the team across a small bridge and then pulled left off the road at what looked like the dilapidated remains of a gated entrance. As he did, a large black and tan hound dog bellowed in stride toward the wagon and then followed alongside.

"Meet Bruno," announced the Colonel. "He's our protector here at Grayson Springs."

"Protector from what?" asked LA.

"From anything that might crawl out of them woods," answered Officer Porter. "Fox, coyote, snakes, you name it...the woods are full of critters."

"Great," mumbled LA.

On each side of the drive, a framed wooden post served as the beginning of a dilapidated four-rail fence. To the left, it ran to the bank of the creek. On the right side, four 8-foot sections ended at the edge of a steep wooded area.

"Whoooaaa," commanded Colonel Ron. The team halted some twenty feet inside the fence line. Bruno stood up against the buckboard, allowing his master to rub his head. "Missed me, didn't you boy?" He raised from his seat, turned and said, "Welcome to Grayson Springs! This'll be your home for the next six weeks. Looks a little run down now, but by the time you two leave, it'll look much better."

I sat in the saddle, oddly relaxed, absorbing my rough surroundings and thinking, *we must be the Colonel's first clients*. Small trees and shrubs ran along the creek bank forming the eastern border of a grassy opening, much longer and wider than a football field. At the far end, barely visible through the fog, stood a two story, white-board structure with a silver looking metal roof. The building's backside faced the creek. On the front were tall pillars holding up a porch covering that ran its entire length. A stone fireplace stood against the north end with its chimney rising past the roof's crest. Large cedar and white oak trees lined the west side of the grassy opening.

LA broke my trance. "So we are going to be your cheap labor?"

"Oh no," replied the Colonel. "Cheap would imply that I was gonna pay you for your service. The only pay you're gonna get is three squares meals a day and a roof over your head."

"I feel like a slave," whined LA.

Chapter 7

After a short description of the property—its sulfur and natural springs, steep wooded hills, several dilapidated outbuildings, flat fields, and a new barn that he himself helped build—Colonel Ron drove his horse-drawn buckboard down the same lane used by countless visitors over countless years. LA and I followed. Bending left, the slender pathway became lined with giant cedar trees. Unfortunately, undergrowth had taken over much of a once-scenic entrance to a southern style resort.

Stopping her horse, LA complained, "What's that smell?"

Colonel Ron halted his rig and said, "It's the sulfur springs I spoke of. They're currently hidden in the weeds. Starting tomorrow, we'll be sprucing up this area. Believe it or not, there are pathways between each of the springs."

"But it stinks so badly," continued LA.

"I used to think the same thing," replied the Colonel. "Over the years, I've gotten used to it."

"You've lived here all your life?"

"Grew up just down the road. Visited often as a child. Been around the world, and this is still one of my favorite places."

I let LA ask all the questions while my mind drifted toward sounds; trinkets from my past—birds chirping, the breeze blowing leaves, crickets, katydids, flies buzzing, and the horses plucking grass from the pathway. Sounds I had not heard for years. Some were surely present in Manhattan, only masked by the reverberations of a more civilized society.

"How about you, Officer Porter? You from around here?"

"No. I'm a transplant. Grew up in Mississippi. Moved here after Iraq..."

Colonel Ron interrupted, "Getup," urging the team forward.

Bruno trotted ahead like an escort as Becca and Birdie instinctively followed the buckboard. I'd seen cedar trees before, but none so large. Their trunks were massive ribbed columns with stringy, hanging bark and an aroma all their own.

Proceeding down the lane, the building came into a clearer view to the left between trees. It reminded me of a dilapidated version of Tara from *Gone With The Wind*. After about a hundred yards, the lane forked—left to the building, and right toward the creek. On the other side of the creek rested the barn through remnants of the foggy mist.

"Whooaa," commanded Colonel Ron. Officer Porter climbed off the buckboard and stretched. Bruno begged for attention, and she gave it. Colonel Ron remained in place. "Ladies, y'all follow me to the barn."

Officer Porter stood watching as Colonel Ron urged the team toward the creek. "So," she asked, "What do y'all think so far?"

"After that bumpy ass ride," sassed LA, "I think my tits are already sagging."

Officer Porter cupped her own breast with her hands and said, "To be honest, I don't think the Colonel put much thought into that situation. I'll speak to him about it tonight."

"Tonight? So you are staying here with us?"

"Oh yeah. Be here for the whole six weeks."

"You don't have to do police work?"

"Actually, I'm on leave. Took some vacation time and the rest is without pay. Of course, I'll be getting paid by the Colonel for my services here. If all works out, I'll be doing this full time in the future.... Now you two best get on up to the barn."

LA and I followed Colonel Ron's path. The creek bank had been cut down to allow easier access. In crossing, the horses paused for a drink. The creek bed was at least twenty feet wide, mostly large flat rocks with water running only down a narrow path in its center. There were a few wider, deeper pools scattered about. Schools of minnows darted away from the horses' intrusions. Thirty yards farther sat the barn. Rays of sunshine bled through the hill's jagged treetops, streaking down upon the foggy field and reflecting a blinding light off the barn's wet, metal gambrel roof. It felt as though I were approaching the entrance to another world. Daddy had said I was going back into the past. At that moment, it seemed I had arrived. Colonel Ron waited at the barn's entrance. "You can dismount now."

LA made it to the ground first. "Ouch!" She stood stiff, rubbing her rear.

"A little sore there?" asked Colonel Ron.

While straightening her skirt, she replied, "Not used to that."

"Wait 'till tomorrow. You'll really feel it then."

I slid off easily while LA rattled, "You say you built this barn?"

"With help from my Amish neighbors."

"Amish? As in no modern conveniences?"

"That's right. And for the next six weeks, you girls are gonna be a lot like them."

I flipped up the stirrup on Becca's saddle and began uncinching the girth.

"So you've ridden before," observed the Colonel.

Suddenly, it hit me, *Why am I doing this? I've never done this before. How could I know...?*

The Colonel turned to help LA. I watched as he released Birdie's cinch, breast, and buck straps, and then slid the saddle off. When I attempted to copy his moves, the saddle turned out to be heavier than I thought. It hit the ground, causing Becca to side step. Colonel Ron said, "I'll get that. You lead Becca on into the barn ... third stall on the left."

Becca followed easily. Several light brown hens and a multi-colored rooster clucked loud complaints and scattered as we entered the 30-foot-wide, 40-foot-long barn. A 10-foot-wide runway ran from one end to the other. The opening at the far end was blocked by a wooden gate. There were four stalls on the left, plus one more stall and tack and supply rooms on the right. At the third stall, a sliding door had been left open. On that door, the word *Becca* had been carved into a wooden placard. I led the horse in and turned her so that she faced the door.

"Put 'er in that first stall," I heard the Colonel telling LA. For a moment, I stood looking at Becca's bridle, considering how it might come off.

"I'll take it off," spoke Colonel Ron, standing at the stall door holding a halter.

Suddenly I felt trapped, and without thinking, moved to the other side of the horse. When the Colonel took another step toward Becca, I found myself cowering further into the back of the stall. The horse became restless, as if sensing my demons.

"Easy, girl," Colonel Ron took Becca by the jaw straps of her bridle, pulling her head down. The horse began stomping and kicking. "Knock it off, dammit!" His voice projected harsh and commanding. I felt small, threatened, and paralyzed, crouched in the corner, blinded by flashing visions of the ugly people. My arms were crossed over my breast, palms covering my cheeks and I felt the warmth of urine seeping down my legs. Then I heard his voice.

"I'm, I'm leaving now," he spoke softly while backing out of the stall, leading Becca into the runway.

By then, LA stood at the doorway looking in. "What's wrong with her? Did that horse hurt her? Is she okay?"

Colonel Ron didn't answer. He looked back toward me and said, "LA and I are going to put Becca in another stall. Take your time. Come out when you're ready."

I couldn't move. How could I? My clothes were wet. Tears ran down my face. Like a ghost from the past, the ugly people had crept into that stall with me. Daddy wasn't there to protect me. I was alone. Back in Grayson County. Back in hell.

Eventually, those voices from the past faded to LA's in the next stall, quizzing Colonel Ron. "Is there something wrong with her?"

"Watch me. This is how you take the bridle off."

"Is she ill?"

"Put the halter loosely around her neck first."

"Are you ignoring me?"

"Are you paying attention? Unbuckle and then slip the bridle off her ears. Slide the bit out of her mouth. Place the bridle over your shoulder while you finish putting on the halter."

"You are ignoring me."

"LA! Stop talking. I'm not ignoring you.... Go to the Inn. Tell Loretta that New York needs her."

"Loretta?"

"Officer Porter.... Ask her to bring a blanket."

On her way out of the barn, LA paused to look in at me. She whispered, "I'm going to go get the lady," and then disappeared. I heard her trotting, and then it got quiet. Chickens passed the door making their mild *wock, wock* noises, glancing in but then continuing on as if sensing my uneasiness. There were horse sounds and a bell rang somewhere in the distance. I heard Colonel Ron closing the door to the stall after finishing with Becca. Like LA, he looked in. "You okay?"

Instead of speaking, I nodded.

"I'm gonna unhitch the team. Officer Porter will be here soon."

I nodded again. He left, and I heard the clanging bell again. Chickens. The team. Flies buzzing. Becca snorting her concerns at a crack in the boards dividing the two stalls. The bell. Birds fluttering in the barn rafters. I began to calm down.

When Officer Porter arrived, she stood alone at the door like those before her, a blanket draped over her left arm. Her stare reminded me of Daddy's in his attempts to read my mind. This lady gave up quicker than he. Walking in, she offered the blanket. "Take the wet stuff off and cover yourself with this."

I stood, accepted the blanket, and asked, "How did he know?"

"He's good at what he does … and kind.... Whenever you're ready, we can talk about this?"

"What's to talk about?"

"You tell me."

I tried to think of what it was I should say.

.....Brooke, you obviously have a fear of men, brought on by some traumatic event or events from your early childhood. You've been abused dear, and it will take time to get over your fears.....

Tears began to flow, and Officer Porter knew it was not a good time to talk. Her eyes glistened, and she squeezed her lips together while we stared at one another. She whispered, "We'll talk later," and then turned away.

I said, "Hey." Officer Porter looked back, revealing her own tears. "Can you wait for me?"

She nodded, turned her back, and stood guard. When I left that stall, cloaked in the blanket, I bumped her purposely, tried to smile, and said quietly, "When *you're* ready, we both can talk about this."

Outside the barn, Colonel Ron and LA were unhitching the team from the buckboard. They looked up. I felt ridiculous cloaked in a blanket, trying to hold my soiled clothing out of sight. Colonel Ron seemed to avoid staring or speaking, but LA asked, "You okay?"

"I'm good."

As Officer Porter and I walked toward the creek, I heard the bell again. "What is that?"

"What, the bell?"

It clanged again. "Yeah, that."

"It's a cowbell. Bertha, our milk cow, wears it so we know where she is ... her and her calf."

I strained to see the animals through the mist but could not. "Cool."

"We'll meet Bertha later. Right now you need a clean change of clothes."

After we crossed the creek and turned toward the Inn, I glanced back and could no longer see the Colonel and LA. "Are we the only ones here?"

"Just us. Three women and one man."

"What would happen if I dropped this blanket and ran naked?"

"You have that desire?"

"Always wondered what it would feel like to be naked outside. I mean, haven't you ever wondered why humans wear clothing?"

"Protection from the elements, I'd say, and to cover up our ugly-ass bodies."

"Do you think women's bodies are ugly?"

"I'd say some are."

I quit walking, dropped my dirty clothes, and then held the blanket open like wings, exposing my body to Officer Porter. "You think I'm ugly?"

She stopped, turned and stared. I didn't really think she would, but she did. My nipples hardened as she scanned me slowly from head to toe and then back up as if taking in every detail. I anticipated some sort of comment about my petite body, my fair skin, my small breasts, something, but I got nothing. Instead, she stared emotionless into my eyes, like waiting for me to give up and cover up. I tilted my head, thinking, *"Well?"*

Finally, I did give up, rewrapped myself, grabbed my clothes, and began walking. Officer Porter caught up, bumped me like I had her earlier, and said, "You feel better now?"

I felt stupid.

Chapter 8

Officer Porter pushed opened the inn's front door, motioning me in ahead of her. I stepped in and stood for a moment, marveling at some deserted lobby area from the past. It occupied the first floor's entire northwest quarter. A wall clock's pendulum tossed loud echoing seconds into a room with no furniture. It felt like an Edgar Allen Poe moment. *What have I gotten myself into?*

Two tall windows to my left were evenly spaced between the door and the north end. Another pane of similar size stood between the front corner and a stone fireplace. Inadequate morning light bled in. A wooden mantel served as a base for a large, framed portrait of an older man with long, wavy, white hair. Studying, I asked, "Who is he?"

Officer Porter stepped next to me. "Colonel picked that old thing up at a yard sale. He declares it to be an original portrait of M.P. Clarkson, the man who first established the Grayson Springs resort."

"So they named the town after him?"

"Apparently."

To my right, steep, narrow steps led to the second floor. Plaster walls were dull white with a few blemishes, and all the stained wood trim had lost its luster to a coat of dust. Supports for the second floor ran exposed from the outside walls to another one-foot-square wood-thing that looked as though it might stretch the building's length in the center. The floors were hardwood, scuffed and worn by commercial traffic of the past. The word *ghost* came to mind.

"Is the whole building this empty?" I asked.

"No. We'll get to this room eventually."

"So we really are your first clients."

"Yes. That bother you?"

"Not sure I want to be someone's experiment."

"Life is one big experiment," she claimed while disappearing through an opening. I followed, and I swear we were in a hundred-year-old version of Betty Crocker's kitchen.

Officer Porter tugged open the back door, and a cool morning breeze swept dust bunnies across the floor toward a wood burning cook stove that sat near the north wall. Next to it, under the window, a metal box held kindling. The wall adjacent to the lobby had upper and lower cabinets—some sort of antiquated metal with a thick wooden countertop. On the back wall, windows provided light and a view for any user of a large metal sink. On either side of the basin, additional lower cabinets completed the wall. Millions of dusty, micro-particles danced in the rays of light shining in. An oak kitchen table sat in the middle of the room. Its six matching chairs had rope woven seats.

Officer Porter pointed and said, "Pitch your dirty clothes into that bucket by the door. We'll clean 'em later." As I did, she leaned against the cabinet and said, "I love this room. It reminds me of my great-grandmother's kitchen in Mississippi, when I was a child."

I can't even remember my mother, and this lady speaks of her mother's mother's mother.

"You okay?" brought me out of my trance.

"Yeah."

"You seem to drift off a lot."

"You too," I replied.

She smiled and began staring. I stared back. After a weird moment, she said, "I bet a lot of people comment on your unusual ... beautiful eyes."

It should be flattering, but after a hundred people comment on your eyes, it begins to become annoying.

She continued, "I see 'em as a pathway to what's goin' on in that head of yours."

Good grief. Here comes the shrink shit.

As if reading my mind, she said, "I suspect you have ill feelings for your father's profession. Yet, I believe you are smart enough to

47

understand that without doctors like him, a lot of people would suffer needlessly. He apparently rescued *you* from some..."

"*Rescued* me? Lady, I'm not a dog!"

"I'm sorry. He *removed* you from a bad place in your young life." Her bullshit speech got interrupted by the chatter of Colonel Ron and LA approaching the back door. "Please," she finished, "Don't compare the Colonel or me to your father. Give us a chance."

Colonel Ron and LA sounded chirpy as they stepped onto the back porch. He opened the screen door for her like a true gentleman. "Welcome to our humble abode."

Our?

When Colonel Ron entered, he let go of the screen door and an attached spring slammed it against the wood frame. Startled, LA jumped, and then began her rattling. "Still in that blanket? You look like Pocahontas."

"In case you haven't looked into a mirror, you're not exactly making any fashion statements."

Loretta said, "Easy, ladies. How about I show y'all to your room so New York can get dressed."

"Room?" blurted LA. "We have to share..."

"This is not the Ritz," answered Colonel Ron.

"Oh, my God, I'm sharing a room with Pocahontas."

Oh, my God, I'm sharing a room with a bitch.

"Well," continued LA, "I hope there is a bathroom in *our* room, because I really have to pee."

Colonel Ron grinned, looked at Officer Porter, and said, "Would you please escort LA to the ladies room, which incidentally is also the men's room."

When Officer Porter stepped to the back door, LA's jaw dropped. "Its outside?"

"Oh yeah. Finest outhouse in Grayson County. New York, you might as well join us."

The outhouse, a five-foot-wide, four-foot-deep, seven-foot-tall vertical plank boarded structure, rested at the end of a 25 foot stone walkway behind the Inn. I stood with Officer Porter as LA entered.

"You've got to be kidding," she complained as she closed the door. "There's not much light in here! And it stinks!"

As Officer Porter and I stood waiting, I closed my eyes, absorbing the gentle breeze and the sound of water trickling over rocks in the nearby creek. The smell of methane reeking from the outhouse triggered a memory, and I whispered, "I remember this."

"Remember what?" asked Officer Porter.

"The outside facility. We had one when I lived with the ugly people. Boys stared in through the cracks when I went to pee."

"Eeeeeeiiiiii!" LA screamed from inside the outhouse.

"You okay in there?" asked Officer Porter.

"There's something in here!"

"What is it?"

"It's alive! Help me! Somebody do something! Eeeeeiiii!"

Officer Porter opened the wooden door and poked her head in. LA stood on top of the sitting spot. "It's a lizard for Christ sake."

"Get it out of here—paleeeeze!"

"You calm down, girl. That thing's not gonna hurt you. And you best get used to it. You'll be encountering all sorts of critters around here—insects, snakes, and the like. Most won't bother you if you don't bother them."

"I want to see it," I begged.

Officer Porter backed out to give me a view. I stuck my head through the doorway. To my left, a six-inch, striped lizard curled into the corner. "You're afraid of that little thing?"

"That little thing could bite."

"Bull."

"All right girls, y'all come on out."

I backed out. LA followed, rearranging her clothing.

Officer Porter winked at me and said, "They usually come in twos you know. Better make sure one didn't crawl up your skirt."

"Oh my God, oh my God," panted LA as she jumped around shaking her skirt. "I hate these clothes."

Back in the kitchen, Colonel Ron listened to LA's rants about the outhouse, and then he said, "Okay ladies ... before we go any further, let's do a little orientation here. Have a seat please."

We sat ourselves around the table. Nobody seemed concerned that I remained naked under a blanket.

"First off, I'm already growing tired of calling my associate 'Officer Porter.' She and I have known one another for a long time. I'm used to calling her Loretta, and as far as I'm concerned, if it's okay with her, we all will."

Nodding, Loretta said, "That's fine with me."

"Good." He turned. "So, let's see if I have it right. LA ... is Sherri Reid?" She nodded approval. "And New York is Elizabeth Green?"

"I prefer Brooke."

"Then Brooke it will be."

"So," asked Sherri Reid, "do we call you Ron?"

"Actually, I'd rather you call me Colonel, or Colonel Ron."

Sherri's eyebrows rose and she asked, "Does Officer ... Loretta call you Colonel?"

"Yes I do," replied Loretta. "Always have."

"Now that we have names squared away," continued Colonel Ron, "let me throw in some ground rules. Most importantly, neither of you leaves this property without my permission. At all times, Loretta or I, or both of us will know where you are."

"I'm in prison," mumbled Sherri.

"No, dear," Loretta corrected, "this is not prison. This is an effort to keep you out of prison. Each of your parents has decided that six weeks here will be well worth the time and cost if it breaks the paths of destruction you've been paving."

"She's right, guys," continued the Colonel. "For six weeks, you two are going to live like you are in the 1800s. We have no running water and no electricity. Therefore, TV's, music players, and phones are a thing of your past. That may seem like prison to you, at first, but I believe there's not a person in jail that wouldn't rather be here, close to nature. You have no idea what it's like to live in a cell, no windows, no sunshine, trees, grass, or even the sound of birds. But, believe me, if you screw up here, you may find out."

Sherri asked, "If we have no phones, what if there's an emergency?"

"Loretta has a phone. So do I. We'll only use them when necessary.... Your parents have agreed to the conditions and situations you will experience here at Grayson Springs. Our goal is to take you away from the atmosphere you've been in long enough to teach you a better respect for the law, and for yourself. It has been my experience that when people, young and old, act out of the norm, it is often because they do not like who or what they are...."

Sherri said, "But I like who I am."

"Maybe you do," the Colonel continued, "and I won't argue that point ... for now. But please remain open-minded. As the days go by, accept the idea that maybe you just *think* you like who you are. Sometimes the only way we realize that we don't like who or what we are is by reaching another point in our psychological growth and looking back."

"So," I asked, "You think that I think I like who I am ... because I really don't know who I am?"

Colonel Ron scratched his neck and said, "I think it's complicated. Often people put up a front, pretend they're happy when deep down they're not." He was glancing back and forth at Sherri and me. "It's our nature to make the best of what life hands us. In our youth, the environment we are placed in and the attitudes of those raising us become significant factors in the formation of our personalities. As adults, it can be difficult to recognize why we do the things we do. Typically, our adult behaviors are influenced by the experiences, good or bad, of our youth. If we do not like what we've become, change is possible, though usually difficult. And it often requires a little help in the form of professional guidance." He then looked into my eyes and said, "One thing I have learned in my years of practice is that professional guidance rarely comes from the ones we love."

"You're saying my father cannot be my guidance?"

"I'm not saying it's impossible. I'm saying it would be difficult. His love for you would get in the way both personally and professionally.

It's been my experience that most people have a hard time really opening up to someone they care about. In other words, if one avoids saying what needs to be said for fear of hurting the feelings of a loved one, it will get in the way of an already difficult task."

Why have I never heard this from my father?

Sherri shook her head and said, "Colonel, sir, you are giving me a headache." She at least brought a smile to all our faces.

"Sorry. If I get too preachy, you girls let me know. And if at times I seem to be barking orders, it's because that's what I did for so long ... in the service."

"In other words," I jabbed, "*You* continue to be affected by the environment of *your* past."

Loretta, who had been listening quietly, covered her mouth to keep from laughing. Colonel Ron shook his head and said, "This is going to be an interesting six weeks. And what you just did is acceptable and encouraged. Speak what's on your mind any time ... providing you do so respectfully."

"Respectfully then," asked Sherri, "when do we eat? I'm starved."

"Soon, but let me finish.... From time to time, we will have visitors. Part of our agenda here includes refurbishing this old place to look like it did in the past. Some of our Amish friends may be lending us a hand. When outsiders are here, you must treat them with respect. Do not make light of their beliefs. These people choose to live a simple life. It's their choice, and it works well for them."

"You guys'll like 'em," added Loretta. "They're the friendliest people you'll ever meet."

"For today, we are going to get settled in, eat, and maybe do a few chores. I don't know your sleeping habits, but we must all get on the same program. Since you've been up all night, by sundown you should be ready for bed. There is little to do after dark around here. This time of year, while the nights are short, you will be encouraged to sleep from dusk to dawn. We have oil lamps, but we will not use them to stay up all night. We rise early six days a week. Get used to it. On Sundays we rest a bit. If you don't know how to cook, you'll learn. We share cooking and cleaning."

Sherri raised her hand. "Colonel?"

"Yes, LA."

"If there is no water, where do we shower?"

"Good question. Simply put, we don't—"

"Oh my God," I snapped.

"Hold on, now. We do bathe. Cleanliness is a must. But until we take time to design and build some sort of shower, bathing will be one either with a wash basin, or in a tub."

"Can we start on the shower tomorrow?" asked Sherri. "I can't even remember the last time I took a bath."

Loretta smiled and said, "I'll second that motion."

"We'll put it on our list."

I looked pointedly at Loretta, and gripped the blanket tightly. Finally, she got the message.

"Oh, I'm sorry. Colonel, our guest needs to clean up and get fresh clothes."

"That she does," he replied. "Your clothes are already upstairs. We have several rooms on the second floor. So far, only two have been renovated. One is Loretta's, and you girls will share the other. Most of the furniture in the rooms had been destroyed by varmints or the leaky roof. The furnishings in your room were donated. We asked for old furniture to replicate the 1800s. What we got is really old, but in fairly good shape."

"So where do you sleep?" Sherri asked.

"My room is down here, off the front lobby."

Sherri said, "I can share a room, but please don't tell me I have to share a bed with Pocahontas."

"No you won't," answered Loretta. Looking at me, she added, "House rules: one bed, one person."

Chapter 9

On the second floor, a landing provided access to the bedrooms. There were two doors on each side and one at the south end. Loretta's room appeared to be adjacent the back of the building, directly over the kitchen area. Ours was across from hers, bordering the front. The room had been symmetrically divided. A single bed, nightstand, dresser, and chifferobe sat on each side like mirror images. At the end of each bed, a narrow table held a pitcher and a bowl on top, with towels and washcloths on a shelf underneath. On the floor, below each shelf, there sat a porcelain pot with a lid. Each nightstand held a small oil lamp. Between the two nightstands, one window divided the room in half. Both beds had metal framing and chicken-feather mattresses covered by hand-stitched quilts. The pillows were also stuffed with chicken feathers.

"Brooke, your clothes are in the chifferobe on the right," Loretta directed as she pointed at an old wooden box that looked like it belonged in a barn.

Sherri stepped left and opened the double doors of her chifferobe. "Gross," she mumbled, at the sight of more clothing similar to what we wore. "I'm going to kill my father for putting me here."

"You don't mean that. And you should never make such a statement in front of a cop." Loretta excused herself. "I'm going back downstairs to start breakfast. Bloomers are in the drawer, Brooke. There's already water in the pitcher in case y'all wanna wash off. Settle in and then join us."

Sherri and I began exploring the room. We further inspected the hanging clothes and then searched the drawers. The window had curtains held open by strings tied to nails in the frame. For a moment, I stood staring out across the front lawn. It all seemed so familiar: the woods, the slowly diminishing mist of fog, and the red-breasted robins bouncing around in search of a morning worm. "Wow, would you look at the size of that thing?"

"What?" Sherri asked, moving closer.

"That monster of a bird," I replied while pointing toward a red-tailed hawk that perched on a limb of an oak tree some fifty feet away.

After a glance, Sherri said, "We're stuck here in this godforsaken place and all you can think about is some big bird?"

While she stood venting at the bird, I moved to the end of the bed and dropped my blanket. My back was to her. I had already poured water into the bowl when I noticed Sherri staring. Her eyes remained locked on mine as her head turned. I'd seen the look often. It still made me nervous. "What?" I asked.

"Nothing," she replied, "just checking out the color of your skin."

"You were looking at my eyes."

She walked to the end of her bed, and said, "Honey, you have got to be the whitest white girl I have ever seen."

"Please don't make fun of the way I look."

"I'm not making fun of you."

"You got something against a real white girl?"

I'm intrigued."

"Well, you don't have to stare while I clean up."

As I continued, Sherri pulled out her porcelain pot. "What is this?" she asked.

"I remember using one of these when I was little, on cold winter nights instead of going outside."

"For what?"

"To pee in."

"No frigging way!"

The scent of something frying entered the room. "Food!" I announced. "I'm starved."

Sherri turned and said, "What is it?"

"Smells like ham, I think, and coffee."

A loud noise erupted from outside. Some sort of metal clanging over and over for about twenty seconds. Sherri asked, "What the hell is that?"

"It's a dinner bell. Old fashioned for 'come and get it.'"

"Do what?"

"It means it's time to eat. You go on down. I'll dress and then join you."

After Sherri left the room, I felt petrified, alone, homesick, and I cried.

By the time I entered the kitchen, Sherri had armed herself with a flyswatter. She bounced around the room chasing a number of potential victims.

"Damn these things. If I'm going to eat, they have to go."

"Should have had you when I was overseas," sassed Loretta. "They were everywhere." The table had been decorated with ceramic plates and cups and cloth napkins. A bowl of biscuits sat in the center, covered with a cloth to keep flies off. Loretta glanced my way and then continued shoving wood into the bottom of the stove. "You okay?"

I nodded.

"Well, you at least look more comfortable."

"Blanket wasn't that bad."

Coffee brewed on the stovetop, next to a skillet of scrambled eggs. Colonel Ron stepped in the back door with more wood. He hesitated in the doorway. "Don't know about you ladies, but I'm starving."

Sherri shook her swatter at the Colonel and bitched, "Close that door, you're letting in flies."

I stepped to the stove where Loretta attended the eggs. "You need help?"

"Sure. It's been a long night. Everyone's gonna need coffee. You pour."

As I began filling cups, Colonel Ron took a seat at the end of the table. My stomach growled. When Loretta sat her hot skillet on the table, breakfast was a done deal. She took a seat opposite the Colonel and said, "What do y'all think?"

"Let's eat," chimed Sherri, reaching to remove the covering from the biscuits.

"Hold on, LA," demanded the Colonel. "Let's bless our food first. Thank you, Lord, for this food. Thank you for bringing us together, and thank you for keeping us healthy. Please help us all to be wiser, more understanding and more loving. Amen."

"Aaaamennn," repeated Loretta enthusiastically, while staring at Sherri and me, waiting for us to do the same.

Taking the hint, we did, and then Colonel Ron said, "Let's eat."

....the table was similar, flies in the room, everyone grabbing to fill their plates ... ugly people screaming obscenities and taking back some of what had been grabbed ... leaving the table humiliated, sometimes full, sometimes still hungry....

"Earth to Brooke?"

Loretta's words brought me back. Sherri had begun eating, but Colonel Ron's eyes were fixed on mine. I could feel him analyzing, like Daddy but different. His eyes were kind, and wet, as if he felt my pain.

"Yes, ma'am," I answered Loretta while trying to read Colonel Ron's thoughts. *Is he upset for me, or does he have his own demons?* Loretta and Sherri became aware of our stare.

Sherri said, "You guys are killing me."

Loretta added, "Should we talk about this now, or later?"

Without speaking, I began to fill my plate with a fat slice of country ham, eggs, and hot biscuits. Sherri said, "This reminds me of breakfast with my parents, back home on the terrace."

Thinking back, I couldn't remember a single time when Daddy, Melanie, and I had sat down for breakfast like this in New York. As if by instinct, I ate fast, aware that the Colonel and Loretta were observing.

Sherri said, "This is really salty."

"Real country ham is always salty," replied the Colonel. "Has to be to preserve it. Remember, we don't have a refrigerator here."

"You've got to be kidding! Where do you keep soft drinks?"

Loretta laughed and said, "You won't see any of those around here. Remember, guys, we are living in the 1800s."

Sherri looked at me and said, "Hey there Pocahontas, cat got your tongue? You like this salty food?"

"Sure. Tastes like what we get on the reservation."

Loretta said, "Sherri, maybe you should lighten up on the Pocahontas thing—"

"No," I snapped. "I don't mind. I like the salty ham, and the coffee's better than Starbucks."

"Yeah, right," replied Sherri. "You sure you're from New York?"

Colonel Ron interrupted. "Loretta and I have determined that much of what causes today's teens to get into trouble is the lifestyle they've been raised in. Here at Grayson Springs, we will attempt to take you back to a less complicated time when simply surviving took up the better part of a day. Both of you will experience many different aspects of the daily lifestyle of the 1800s. In the Army, we learned that the larger variety of jobs one experienced, the more appreciative each soldier became of his or her comrades. Therefore, as the days go by, you each will get a chance to experience a variety of chores."

"So what exactly are these chores?" asked Sherri.

"I'll try to make it simple," replied Colonel Ron. "We have to eat, we have clean, and then there is yard work. Our clothes and bed sheets will be washed by hand, the old fashion way. You will hang them on a clothesline to dry. The yard work will introduce you both to labor. It won't be easy, but you'll get used to it. We cook, bring in wood for the stove, milk the cow, feed animals, clean stalls, and gather eggs. We'll go fishing in the creek, and maybe even slaughter a chicken to fry."

"Slaughter, as in kill them?" questioned Sherri.

"Yes, slaughter means kill. It's a dirty job, but someone has to do it. If you wanna eat meat, somebody has to kill something."

"Yuck."

I asked, "How can you store food here without a refrigerator?"

"Good question," Loretta replied. "We have a food cellar built into the hillside. It stays at a reasonably cool temperature. We store potatoes, canned vegetables, and cured meats there. The ham we are eating hung there until we were ready to use it. What we didn't cook today, I cut up and stuffed into Mason jars. Colonel Ron already took those jars to the springhouse. The water there stays at around 48 degrees. Keeps milk and meats fresh for days."

"Where do we get water to drink?" Sherri asked.

"Water is always plentiful here at Grayson Springs."

"Surely you don't expect us to drink that stinky water?" Sherri barked.

"Oh, no. We have both sulfur and natural water springs here. The bottled water you guys pay for at home, we have here in an unlimited supply."

"Bottom line," added Loretta, "we are going to experience life as it was in a more simple time. Most of the conveniences you enjoyed are gone for the next six weeks. Hopefully, at the end of your stay here you will have at least a better respect for those conveniences and a better perspective of what your ancestors went through."

"Are you saying we are spoiled?" Sherri asked.

Loretta looked at the Colonel. He said, "Six weeks from now, I'll let you answer that question."

Chapter 10

After breakfast, we were asked to join Loretta in cleaning up the kitchen. As I washed dishes, Sherri reluctantly dried them with a towel and then placed each item in the cabinets above. It appeared to be a new chore for her. I'm sure she grew up with a housekeeper that took care of such things.

With the sink positioned in front of a window, my mind wandered. The back porch had a single-story covering. Beyond that, approximately thirty feet of grass, then a tree line that ran along the creek. Spring wildflowers decorated the grassy edge. It looked as if one tree had been removed in creating a pathway to the water. While Bruno came plopping back across the creek from God knows where, I asked, "What's the wooden structure out by the creek?"

Sherri leaned my way. Loretta stopped her floor sweeping, came to the window, and squeezed between us. Sherri slid sideways enough to avoid touching. I did not. Instead, my hip held firm against Loretta's almost like a puppy dog snuggling against its mother. It felt comforting. Loretta chose not to react. Instead, she focused out the window and said, "That there's the remains of what used to be a swinging footbridge. Colonel wants to rebuild it."

Still leaning over the sink, I closed my eyes, breathed deeply, and in my mind's eye saw the bridge. "I see it."

"See what?" asked Sherri as Loretta stepped back.

"The footbridge. I see the footbridge, and—"

"And what?"

I tiptoed. "—and someone on it."

"Who?"

The vision faded like a dream in those fleeting moments after being awakened. Opening my eyes, I said, "I don't know. It's gone. Couldn't see the face."

Sherri said, "You are one crazy girl."

"Crazy people hear voices. I do not hear voices. Please don't call me crazy."

She stood cautiously silent.

Loretta intervened. "You don't hear voices, but you do *see* things?"

Ignoring the comment, I asked, "Can I help?"

"Help what?"

"Build the bridge."

"You want to build a bridge?" questioned Sherri with a frown.

Loretta shook her head and smiled. "Why not? Just make Colonel Ron aware of your interest."

After finishing with the kitchen, we joined the Colonel in front of the Inn. He had obviously been picking up woody debris from the yard, creating quite a pile in the center of the grassy opening, and was currently gathering creek rock to form a circle around that pile.

"Looks like we'll have a fire this evening," commented Loretta.

Sherri asked, "Why do I feel like I'm at camp?"

"Because you are," replied Colonel Ron.

I asked him, "You need help?"

"Sure. Need a few more."

Sherri and Loretta followed us to the creek, where Colonel Ron pointed out proper sized rocks. On our way back, Sherri asked, "Are we going to roast marshmallows tonight?"

"Hot dogs would be better," I added.

Colonel Ron said, "Don't forget we're living in the 1800s. Do you really think people roasted marshmallows and hot dogs in those days?"

When we had placed our rocks, finishing the circle, Sherri leaned to Loretta and whispered something.

"Ask him yourself," Loretta spoke out loud. "Don't be shy, girl. We're all adults here."

Colonel Ron sensed a question and hesitated, waiting for Sherri to speak. When she did not, he said, "If you have a problem, share it."

Upset that Loretta didn't ask, Sherri used her hands to lift her boobs and said, "I have two problems ... sir."

"What the—" Colonel Ron started.

"Loretta says they had no bras in the 1800s. Well, I'm sorry sir, but I do not want to be sagging to my belly button when I leave this place."

The Colonel's mouth hung open. When he glanced at me, I asked, "What the hell you looking at?"

"Just considering if you might have the same problem."

"Well, I don't ... at least not to the extent that she does. But I do think you should give her back her bra. How can you expect her to ride a horse like that?"

Sherri nodded and said, "Thank you, Pocahontas."

"Be nice," ordered the Colonel. Then speaking to Sherri, he said, "We'll figure something out." Looking back at Loretta, he admitted, "Didn't think about that."

Loretta glanced down at her own breast, and then attempted to change the subject. "Any more questions?"

"That smell," I asked, "the sulfur, can we go see the spring where it comes from?"

"Sure," replied Colonel Ron. "And it's springs, as in plural. There are several. Follow me."

On the east side of the yard, just past the cedar-lined entrance lane, the sulfur springs were scattered about in an area the size of a baseball infield. Narrow paths had been cut from spring to spring. One bubbled up through the ancient, petrified stump of a cedar tree, two feet in diameter.

"Is this something you did?" I asked.

"No. It came up that way on its own. No tellin' how long ago. Looks the same now as it did when I was a kid."

"The water preserves the stump," speculated Sherri.

"I know the water didn't do this," I added, pointing at a spring that ran over a large stone that had been carved into a basin.

"True," replied the Colonel, "but again, it was done long before my time."

I remained next to the stump-spring, inhaling the strong scent of sulfur, allowing its peculiarity to tickle old dreams I'd had as a young girl. As Sherri and the Colonel progressed from one water hole to the next, Loretta joined me. "Wha'cha thinkin'?" she asked.

"All my life, I've had dreams or ... I don't know what exactly to call them ... visions maybe. Today I realized that some were from things I'd seen or done as a child. In the kitchen, looking out where the swinging bridge used to be, it happened. When you mentioned the walking bridge, I could see it in my mind, as if I'd seen it in person. Makes no sense."

"Everything makes sense in the end. We all have little moments."

"Sure, but have you dreamed about this place ... this stump?" I squatted and touched the water with the fingertips of my right hand and continued. "When I was younger, the dreams scared me because they were so real. They would wake me up, and I couldn't go back to sleep. Couple years ago, a friend turned me on to pot. Said it would make me sleep better, without dreaming."

"Did it?"

"Hell yes. Slept like a rock. But then I got caught buying a bag to split with a classmate. The police accused me of dealing. No one, including my parents, believed I only wanted the pot to help me sleep."

"Brooke..."

I didn't reply, but only continued looking into the crystal clear water that filled the stump.

"Brooke," repeated Loretta. When I finally raised my head, she said, "I'm a cop, and I believe you."

Chapter 11

For much of the first day, we were familiarized with oil lamps, firewood, and the use of natural spring water for drinking. There had been no lunch, and dinner was simple: bean soup, biscuits with homemade jam, and water. As evening approached, we prepared for the fire. Several buckets of fresh spring water were emptied around the outside of the fire pit, and then refilled in case the fire should get out of hand.

Two-foot-long sections of logs were placed about for sitting. On the woodpile, small sticks were covered with larger branches. Underneath all that, dried brush had been stuffed, waiting to be ignited.

"I've seen matches," admitted Sherri, "but I can't say that I have ever actually used one."

Colonel Ron asked, "Would you like to do the honors?"

"Really, you want me to do it ... to light the fire?"

"Why not?"

She failed miserably, breaking the first match.

"Don't press so hard," advised Loretta.

On her second, slower, smoother attempt, Sherri made flame, and squealed, "All right!"

"Hurry, LA!" ordered the Colonel. "Light it at the bottom!"

The brush burned quickly, staying lit long enough to ignite the twigs, and then the larger branches. Within minutes, five-foot flames danced, lighting the night and emitting heat.

"Y'all have a seat," suggested Colonel Ron. "Part of our program here at Grayson Springs will be dialogue. At this point, all I know about you is what I've read and what I've seen today. Loretta and I hope to learn more about each of you as we enjoy this fire. This will be your opportunity to vent about being here and about how you came to be here...."

"Yeah, right," Sherri moaned. "You want me to tell you things I did so you can record it to use against me later on."

Colonel Ron raised his hand and said, "1800s."

"So you are saying that there are no recorders on this property."

"That's right. No cameras, no voice recorders, and no one interested in using anything you say against you. This place is unbelievably simple."

"Who wants to go first?" asked Loretta.

Colonel Ron used a long tree branch to manipulate the fire as Sherri and I sat staring at one another. I had shared my story with so many psychologists in the past; one more wouldn't be such a stretch. *Perhaps*, I thought, *someone here will listen, maybe even give a shit.* But what about LA? *Look at her. Girl doesn't seem like the type that has ever needed to talk out her past, her worries, or her inhibitions.* "What, no volunteers? LA, you seem like a girl with a lot to say."

"And you, sir, seem like a man who says too much."

When she stood, Colonel Ron suggested, "You can keep your seat."

"I prefer to stand when addressing a crowd."

Second thought, the bitch can't wait to dump her shit out to these strangers.

Sherri shifted to avoid the smoke and then began. "If anyone laughs at me, I'll quit." Everyone smiled, of course. "I'm a bitch and I know it. Can't help it. Get it, honestly, from my mother. I don't want to be here. Why should I go one day without calling or texting my friends? Why should I stand here and reveal myself to you people who I don't even know? I want my clothes back ... especially my bra, dammit. I hate bugs and nosey people. So far, this place is full of both."

"Ooooowwww," ribbed the Colonel.

"My father played basketball for the Lakers..."

Sherri Reid, I thought, then blurted, "Your father is Shayquan Reid? No way!"

"Yes, he is. And he has enough money so that I may never have to work, if I don't want to. I wear good clothes and deplore what I am wearing right now. I shop. That is what I do. That and computers. Don't ask me why, but I have a way with technology. And that's what got me here. If you ask me, it is not my fault. My teacher taught me and a couple others how to hack, and after that, I liked the challenge. Give me a laptop and a fast connection, and I can go places you can't imagine. I see advertisements all the time that say 'make money on the internet.' So I tried. I wrote a program to transfer money from other accounts to mine."

"You can do that?" I asked.

"Sure. Once you hack into a server, you read the programs and simply copy their formats."

"So how'd you get caught?"

"Fucking FBI...."

"Hold on, LA," interrupted Colonel Ron. "Please refrain from using the f-word while you are here."

Sherri looked at him like he was afflicted or something and then continued. "The little bank I hacked into was smart enough to write a program that monitors all transactions traffic for inconsistencies. Apparently, several thousand transfers of less than fifty cents per month alerted the system."

"No shit," I mumbled.

"My computer teacher told me he was impressed. The bank was not. They alerted the FBI, and the rest is history. Anyway, since it was my first offense, I didn't get into too much trouble. My father says if I had been over eighteen it would have been on my record forever."

Colonel said, "And he's right about that."

I asked, "If you didn't get into trouble, how come you're here?"

"Good question. My parents are the ones who decided I should come here. I have no idea how they knew about this place or what they think it's going to do for me. All I know for sure is that I had to come here or lose everything ... my car, phone, credit card, everything."

Sherri sat back down on her stump. Loretta said, "All I can say is that I am totally impressed with anyone who understands computer technology. And at least you won't be tempted here for the next six weeks."

"No, but I'll have a gazillion emails and texts when I get back."

"Oh well," mumbled the Colonel. "Imagine how many you'd have after six months in jail."

"Blah, blah, blah, you sound like Mr. Gonzalez, the principal at school, and my father, and that prosecutor guy, and the judge."

"So," interrupted Colonel Ron, "sounds like you have a problem with men."

"Hell no! That's Brooke's issue, not mine."

I stood and said, "Excuse me?"

"I *like* men," she sassed. "You're the one who—"

"Easy now, LA," interrupted the Colonel. "Let's not make unfair assumptions. You told your story. We'll let Brooke tell hers."

"Fine," Sherri blurted, "but I have one more thing to say. You call Loretta, Loretta, and Brooke, Brooke, so why do you continue to call me LA?"

Colonel Ron's face distorted a bit. He chewed his bottom lip a couple times, and then said, "My mother's name was Sherry. She was the sweetest lady in the world. So far, you come in here bitching and ranting like you *hate* the world. I'm sorry, but I just can't bring myself to call you by her name."

Loretta spoke up, "Brooke, I believe it's your turn to speak."

Sherri seemed stunned and sat down without saying a word. Seconds earlier, I had felt like punching her for her comments about me and men. Having watched the Colonel put her in her place, I kind of felt sorry for the bitch. "Let's go ahead and get something straight, the problem I have with men is they think all girls are put here for their pleasure. Guy buys you a burger and fries, and he thinks you owe him a blow job."

Sherri crossed her arms and put her hand over her mouth as if to keep from commenting.

"Seriously," I continued, avoiding eye contact with Colonel Ron, "it seems the only guys a girl can go out with, just for fun, are the gay ones. At least they're not gawking at you constantly with that look...."

When Sherri said, "You're right about that," Colonel Ron gave her the *it's her turn, you be quiet* look.

"Do I mind being here? At the airport in Manhattan, I acted like it didn't bother me. On the plane, I cried. Seeing my world left behind for this godforsaken place was not what I wanted. But truthfully, there are things going on in my life that I cannot explain. Maybe I'll figure some of it out while I'm here. At home, no one listens. No one has the time. Too much hustle and bustle with everyone trying to impress the world. On the plane in Louisville, when I met Loretta, I hated her."

Loretta forced a sad expression, and then grinned.

"Welllll, you seemed like a bitch. When we left the airport, Sherri and I both thought you were an asshole. Shit, you said you might kill us and bury us."

"You said that?" asked Colonel Ron.

Loretta replied, "I was just kidding."

Colonel Ron shook his head and said, "Go ahead, Brooke."

"I didn't really think *you* would kill *us*. But, when you said we had to give up our phones, I began thinking maybe *we* should kill *you*...."

"I was thinking the same thing," chimed in Sherri.

"But you know what? Right now, I don't miss my phone. I doubt anyone at home misses talking to me anyway. They're probably out having a good time ... glad I'm out of their hair." With my eyes closed, I swayed my head back and forth enjoying the fire's heat on my cheeks. "In a way, it's good to be ... someplace else." I could feel my words slowing. "Hanging out by this fire feels good ... like I'm in another ... time. The fire ... the darkness ... your faces ... glowing in the yellow light of the flame. Sparks riiiiising and disappeeeeeearing like, like shooting stars in reverse. I ... I ... love ... this feeeeling."

My words had become whispers. My breathing slow. I was thinking, *what the fuc...*

"Brooke. Brooke!" The voice of Colonel Ron brought me back. "You okay?"

I stood there, knowing I should speak, but not sure what to say. Oddly, the only thing that came to mind was, "Why are you so offended by the f-word?"

Colonel Ron seemed to be contemplating my bizarre question. "I'm not offended. Concerned, maybe, but not offended. Denying your freedom of speech is not my intention. Changing your attitude is."

As I remained standing, the Colonel tried to explain. "When I was in high school, there was a guy in my class who got into tattoos. You have tattoos, Brooke?"

"No. Daddy would not allow it."

"How about you?" he asked, glancing toward Sherri.

Sherri and Loretta both raised their hands.

"Not you, Loretta. Already know about yours—"

"Oooohh," Sherri cooed.

"—anyway," continued Colonel Ron, "one day at school, our Algebra II teacher made a comment about the tattoo George Henderson had on his neck. Of course George got offended and started going off, saying stuff like, 'it ain't none of your business,' and 'I have the right,' and 'it's not my fault you're old fashioned,' and all that."

"And he was right," said Sherri.

"To an extent, he was. But here's the point. To the class's surprise, Mr. Stinson began unbuttoning his shirt. Our mouths hung open as he revealed tattoos on his arms. When he removed his t-shirt, we all about died. The man was tattooed over most of his chest."

"Cool," said Sherri.

"Cool?" questioned the Colonel. "Yeah, that's what several in the class thought. George Henderson said, 'What gives you the right to criticize me?' Mr. Stinson then explained that he wasn't being critical, just concerned. He went on to say that at a time in his life, after college, he had decided to become a politician. Wanted to make a difference. Problem was, when his opponent found out about the tattoos, he made an issue of it, and Mr. Stinson lost in a landslide. Thus ending his political career."

"That's bull," Sherri bitched. "People should not hold it against the man because he has a tattoo. He might have been a great politician."

"Exactly. He could have been a great politician. Problem was, in his youth, he did something that prevented him from ever making that difference. His tattoos were harmless, but detrimental all the same.

What Mr. Stinson was trying to get across to George and the rest of the class was that we never know in our youth what we might want to be or do when we get older. And it breaks a teacher's heart when he or she spends months or years educating an individual with the skills needed to achieve future dreams, and then right before graduation, that person goes out and gets a tattoo, or a bunch of piercings that will in some fashion, right or wrong, lessen those possibilities. One day I was standing with a friend of mine in his sports equipment shop when a young college student approached him for a job. The kid was neat, well spoken, and probably had all the skills needed to work in the shop. My friend spoke nicely to him. Told him to fill out an application and give it to the girl at the counter. When the kid walked away, my friend said, 'I would never hire that guy to greet my customers. Did you see all those earrings?' The guy had several rings in each ear. They weren't hurting a thing, except that they were offensive to his prospective employer, who never said a word about it until the kid walked away."

"What an asshole," complained Sherri. "That man turned down a good employee because he had piercings?"

"And that's my point, ladies," replied Colonel Ron. "Right or wrong, the kid missed out on the job he wanted because of his prospective employer's prejudice against piercings. My point is that if you want a piercing or a tattoo, you need to consider its ramifications on your future. Don't put them where they can be seen by a potential employer. A tattoo on your upper arm might be okay if you can cover it with a shirt. Just don't put one on your neck."

I said, "People shouldn't judge you by your appearance."

"But they do, honey," offered Loretta. "That's what Colonel Ron is trying to explain. Right or wrong, they do. It's a fact of life."

"So what's all this got to do with the f-word?"

"Okay," continued the Colonel, "a tattoo or a piercing is something you wear. People see it and may or may not judge you accordingly. Placed properly, you can cover it up. What you say, however, cannot be covered up. The f-word doesn't offend me nearly as much as it does some, but I know for a fact that it does offend many of the people you and I will need to impress to get where we want to go. What you say follows you more than what you wear. People record it. They write it down and publish it. All I'm saying is that while you are here, I want to teach you to consider the whole you, both now and in the future.... Does any of that make sense?"

Without speaking, I slightly nodded and started to sit down, but then stood back up. "Oh, about why I'm here.... I went off on Melanie ... Daddy's wife. She's legally my mother, she's pregnant, and she's a bitch. I gave her a black eye. She deserved more than that, but I didn't want to hurt the baby. I spent a month in a juvenile center. The judge says if I don't come back with a good report from—from you people here at Grayson Springs, he's going to put me in jail."

"A month in juvie?" questioned Sherri. "And he's going to put you in jail for a black eye?"

"That wasn't my first time in court. When I was eleven, I stole a gun...."

"You were in a gang at eleven?"

"Noooo. It wasn't like that. I went to a gun show on Long Island with my father. There were guns everywhere and for some reason I liked them all. But there was this one old gun that really drew my interest. It reminded me of my dreams. Something came over me and I took it ... stuck it under my coat. Of course, I got caught going out the door. Bad part was they thought my father put me up to it. Hell, he can afford any gun he wants. And he would never take something that doesn't belong to him."

"It was a .45 caliber, single action Colt—1873 model," explained the Colonel.

"How do you know that?" I snapped.

"I spoke with your father."

"So you know everything about me."

"Does your father know everything about you?"

"Noooo."

"Then I guess I don't know everything about you. But I do find it interesting that you say you have—what—historical dreams?"

"What do you mean?"

"That gun you were so interested in was an Army issue—from the 1800s."

"All I know is they said it was worth a lot of money."

Sherri interrupted, "You took a gun, *and* you hit your mother?"

"She's not the first. Over the years, I've hurt others."

"Wow," said Sherri, "You are crazy."

"And if you call me crazy one more time, I might go off and kick *your* ass."

"Whoa, time out, Brooke," warned the Colonel. "We're not here to threaten one another. If you get disrespected here, you have to learn to control your violent tendencies. You go off and hurt someone ... I'll have to send you home with another blemish on your record. Understand?"

When I didn't answer, he repeated, "Understand?"

I couldn't hold back the tears. "Don't expect me to be like every other girl, because I'm not. I'm me and that's it. And it's not my fault I know how to fight."

"No one is complaining about your fighting ability. Look at Loretta. She's been through boot camp and Iraq. You think she doesn't know how to fight? I've seen her in action. But along with her fighting abilities, she was taught discipline. Knowing when to fight and when not to is a big part of it."

"Discipline ... now you sound like that judge." Instead of sitting down, I walked away from the fire. Bruno followed. As I stood next to one of the giant cedar trees, scratching Bruno's head, I heard someone approach. Loretta asked, "You okay?"

Instead of turning to face her or speaking, I nodded.

Remaining behind me, Loretta told a story. "When I was twelve, I spent the night with a friend. She and I were sleeping in her bed. In the middle of the night her father came in. There was just a small amount of light. He sat on my side of the bed. When he slid his hands under the blanket, I froze.... I wanted to scream but nothing came out. What that bastard did that night with his hands scarred me for life. It hurt so bad that I finally screamed out. That's when I realized that Sheila was awake and crying."

I turned to face Loretta.

"For the longest time," she continued, "I hated men. All men."

"What about *your* father?"

"I wouldn't know the man if he walked up right here right now ... never met him. But honey, I'm all grown up now. I've been to college and around the world and believe me, I have met good men."

"Colonel Ron?"

"Colonel Ron is the most trustworthy human being I've ever met. I promise he would never put a bad hand on you or me or any other girl, woman, or child."

"You love him, don't you?"

Chapter 12

Sleep seemed to come easy for Sherri Reid. Her heavy breathing blended with a symphony of night sounds drifting in through the open window. Sleep did not come so easy for me. I lay awake for a long time thinking about the story Officer Porter had told me, wondering about her assessment of the Colonel. *Is the man truly trustworthy?*

A hint of daylight filtered through trees as Sherri and I both woke to the sound of a rooster's persistent crowing somewhere in the yard. "What the hell?" Sherri complained. "Can't someone shut that thing up?"

I pulled the blanket over my face and said, "It's not like it has a snooze button. Believe they just do it when the sun is coming up."

"Oh ... my ... god. Are you telling me that thing is going to wake us up every morning?"

Peeking out, I said, "Unless one of us kills it." For a moment, we remained quiet. Along with the rooster's alarm, the songbirds sang and the crows cawed. I said, "Listen to all those birds. What can they be saying?"

"Saying? You actually think they talk to one another?"

"Well, it would seem they have to communicate ... at least within their species."

"So I guess New York is a frigging animal geek."

"I've got your geek, bitch."

"Don't call me a bitch," Sherri snapped, rising up in the bed.

"Then don't call me a geek." Crawling out of the bed, I rubbed my inner thighs and buns and said, "Oh man am I sore."

"From the horse?" Sherri asked.

"Hell yes," I replied while parting the curtains to see outside.

"What's going on out there?"

"The Colonel's coming down the lane on Becca. Wonder where he's been so early?"

As I watched the Colonel ride toward the barn, Bruno running ahead of the horse, Loretta knocked on the door and ordered, "Rise and shine, ladies. It's a new day. Time to get moving."

"Go away!" Sherri complained.

Loretta opened the door, stepped in, and smiled. "What's wrong, girls? Not used to getting up at the crack of dawn?"

"You are a cop, right?" Sherri asked.

"Yeeessss."

"So, you have a gun?"

"Yeeessss."

"Good. Can you let Brooke borrow it? She's gonna shoot that damned rooster thingy."

"Me? Why can't you do it?"

"Because it was your idea."

When I didn't reply, Loretta said, "So, you wanna kill my rooster?"

"Your rooster?" Sherri and I questioned at the same time.

"That's right. I bought him from the Amish at a flea market."

"Second thought, New York: kill her and the rooster."

Breakfast didn't come as easily as it had the day before. In the kitchen, Colonel Ron said, "Gonna go milk the cow and gather some eggs. Either of you ladies interested?"

"Interested?" I questioned.

"In joining me. Giving me a hand."

"Can we both come?"

"One of you should stay and help Loretta."

Sherri quickly said, "Take Brooke, I'll stay."

When I took a deep breath, Loretta said, "Colonel, maybe you should go alone today."

"It's okay. I'll go." As I stepped past Loretta, I whispered, "You said I could trust him."

Colonel Ron carried towels and a pail of water. I carried a clean empty bucket with a lid and a basket for eggs.

"You milk the cow every morning?"

"Not every morning. Bertha's got a calf, still not weaned ... don't wanna take too much of her milk."

"Is it safe to drink unpasteurized milk?"

"Some say it is, but we don't. We actually pasteurize it ourselves. You'll see how when we get back to the kitchen."

Bruno knew his job well and had already found Bertha and the calf feeding in the middle of the field that stretches some forty acres beyond the barn. Bear Creek bordered the right side of the field. State Road 88 ran along the other. Though the road was not visible from the barn, an occasional automobile could be heard passing in the distance. At the far end, there were more trees as the terrain rose into the hills. To the west side of the barn, just beyond the creek, a narrow stretch of thicket separated the water from the steep woods.

"What's up that hill?"

"Trees, trees, and more trees. Actually, there used to be a Civil War era military camp in those woods. Still signs of it if you know what you're looking for."

As we neared the barn, Colonel Ron said, "You sure you're gonna be alright in the barn, alone with me?"

Still walking, I asked, "You going to shove me into a stall, push me on the ground, put your lips on mine, pull my dress up over my head..."

"That's enough Brooke. You're out of line."

When I stopped, he did too. "Fu ... Screw you! I thought we were supposed to talk. I thought you were going to listen."

At first he seemed shocked. "So, you're saying these things actually happened to you?"

I stood silent.

"Who? When?"

"One of the ugly people."

76

"But you were only—"

"Five. Maybe six."

"Jesus. I'm sorry Brooke. And so you were thinking of that yesterday, in the stall."

"It was the first time I remembered it."

"So, Dr. Green doesn't know about this?"

"No. Told you, I just remembered it yesterday."

"You do realize the person who did this to you could be prosecuted."

"He was a foster child like me. Maybe a teenager."

"You refer to the ugly people. Were they really that ugly?"

"What they did was ugly."

Colonel Ron stood staring into my eyes and I could sense his pain for me. "I'm glad we had this talk. Please, never hesitate."

By the time we entered one end of the barn, Bruno had Bertha and her calf waiting at the other. Colonel Ron opened the gate, and Bertha came right in. Just inside the barn there sat a small stool. Leather straps hung from each side of the runway. Both had a snap on the end that Colonel Ron hooked to Bertha's halter, securing her in the center of the runway. Against the wall, a feed trough had been mounted to an iron rod bent to a 90-degree angle. Pulling on the trough swung it out into the middle of the runway, directly in front of the Jersey cow. Bertha's calf remained a safe distance away just outside the barn, bawling an occasional discontent with her mother being temporarily detained.

Pointing, Colonel Ron said, "Inside that stall is a wooden bucket and three feed bins ... oats for the horses, grain for the cow, and scratch for the chickens. Bring me half a bucket of grain."

"Grain?" I asked.

"Corn, my dear. Corn is grain."

When I returned he said, "Pour it in the trough so Bertha can eat while I show you how to clean her teats and draw milk."

"Teats?"

"Her nipples."

"Oh, tits."

"No, their real name is teats."

I know someone milked the cow when I was a child, but I couldn't remember actually watching. Colonel Ron sat on a little stool, washing the cow's teats and then began squeezing and pulling them to draw milk. I did find the process interesting. After showing me how, he allowed me to do the milking. *Jesus, this seems weird.*

When our bucket was three-fourths full, we capped it and allowed Bertha to rejoin her calf. The cute baby bovine seemed anxious to make sure we hadn't emptied mamma. Colonel Ron said, "Now, take the feed bucket back and bring me about this much scratch." He held his thumb and index finger about 1-1/2 inches apart. "Scratch is the one that looks like a mixture of crushed corn and some seeds."

When I returned with scratch, Colonel Ron directed me to the stall next to the tack room. The side and back walls were lined with hay-filled wooden boxes where chickens laid their eggs. Two hens sitting on eggs complained as Colonel Ron led me into the room. Glancing back, he asked, "You okay?"

I nodded yes. Loretta's rooster and a few chickens followed us into the stall, squawking and carrying on as if we had rang Pavlov's bell. Some pranced in through the door. Others flew up to the stall window and down to the surface inside. When I began scattering scratch on the ground, the sitting hens jumped from their nests to compete for a meal. Most of the boxes contained eggs. Colonel Ron gathered enough for our breakfast, making sure not to disturb the warm ones.

Back in the kitchen, Loretta and Sherri were frying country ham while waiting to scramble the fresh eggs. On the stove, an iron pot of water sat heated with a thermometer sticking out in preparation for the milk. Loretta took the bucket from Colonel Ron, removed the lid and began skimming the heavy cream off the top. She poured the rest into a clean pail covered with cloth for filtering. That pail was then placed into the heated water.

"So," I said, "this is how you pasteurize?"

"Sure is," Loretta answered. "We try to keep the temperature at 145 degrees for forty minutes. Then we'll poor the milk into mason jars and suspend them into cold water down at the spring house. It'll keep longer than what it takes for us to drink it all."

"Would Louis Pasteur approve?"

"Sure he would," answered the Colonel. "He'd be proud of our little process."

"So this is it?" asked Sherri. "All we have to do is act like pioneers for six weeks and we're done?"

Colonel Ron glanced at Loretta for a second and then at Sherri. "You make it sound simple, but let me assure you, there is a lot of work involved in what we will be doing."

After breakfast, the Colonel disappeared outside while we ladies began cleaning up the mess. When things were nearly done, I asked, "Mind if I go to the ladies room?"

"Go ahead," replied Loretta. "We can handle this."

As I exited by the back door, Colonel Ron stood near the creek with Bruno by his side. I walked to the outhouse, did my business, and then joined him. He was smoking a cigarette. Hearing my approach, he turned and joked, "Did you flush?"

I ignored his humor, and asked, "Can I get a cigarette?"

He spoke through an exhaled draw. "You're gonna cause me to quit, you know."

"Why, didn't everybody smoke in the old days?"

"I'd say most of the men did, but not so many women."

"Well, maybe you shouldn't think of me as a woman."

Colonel Ron thought for a few seconds, and then said, "You talking in general, or just about cigarettes?"

"What's that supposed to mean?"

"I think that's what I'm asking you."

"So, is this about my sexual preference?"

"You tell me."

I knew what he was doing. Psych people are all alike. Never really say what is on their mind. Just a bunch of open ended questions.

"Hear all those birds? I've never heard birds like that at home." While the Colonel glanced around as if identifying the sound makers, I added, "Give me one of those cigarettes, and I'll try to explain."

"1800s," he replied.

"Excuse me?"

"In the 1800s, people had to roll their own."

"I can handle that."

When the Colonel produced a pouch of tobacco and the rolling papers, I sat down Indian style and impressed him by how fast I could roll.

"Looks like you've had practice," he commented.

"Not with tobacco."

He offered a light, and then watched me choke on the filter-less cigarette. "Not what you expected, is it?"

Recuperating, I said, "No wonder you're thinking about quitting."

"Maybe we'll quit together.... So, you were going to explain?"

After another, more conservative, draw, and without making eye contact, I said, "You want to know if I am a lesbian."

"Didn't say that. But if that's what you want to talk about."

"Jesus, you're just like Daddy. I'm not saying I am, and I'm not saying I'm not. Really don't know. For as long as I can remember, I thought maybe I should have been a boy. Not that I don't like girly things. I do, you know. But now and then something happens that makes me wonder."

"Like what?"

"Like seeing a girl with a nice butt and finding it attractive."

"Hold on ... is this a conversation you and I should be having?"

"You asked, asshole."

"Just asking if you would be more comfortable having this conversation with Loretta."

"I came a thousand miles to be around people who are supposed to listen ... and you don't want me to talk?"

"Didn't say that."

"Uuugghhh! You people kill me. I've always found it easier to talk to boys than girls. Loretta says I can trust you. So, to be quite honest, I'd rather have this conversation with you!"

"Okay." Then as he had earlier, Colonel Ron stood gazing.

I said, "People always stare at my eyes."

"They're unusual."

"Unusual?"

"Don't mean that badly. Your eyes are beau—" He cut himself short.

"Colonel, sir ... we're alone. I'll say what is on my mind if you'll do the same."

He dropped his cigarette and stepped on it. "God blessed you with beautiful eyes. It's hard not to stare."

"Thank you."

"Tell you what ... you say perhaps I shouldn't think of you as a woman ... how about when we talk like this, just you and me, we talk man to man?"

"Man to man?"

"In other words, I don't want anything you or I say to be taken as sexual innuendo."

"Oh, I get it. You're afraid of a lawsuit."

"No. I'm afraid of you taking me wrong. I do not wanna disrespect you in any way, and I don't want you to think that you can't trust me. It's that simple."

"Oh."

"Deal?"

I reached out for a *manly* handshake. When the Colonel accepted, I said, "Deal," and then turned and began walking back toward the kitchen.

"Thought we were gonna talk?"

"We did. You're a smart guy, Colonel. Believe you can infer the rest of *that* conversation."

"Put the cigarette out."

Without looking back I asked, "When are we going to rebuild the swinging bridge?"

"Walking kind of funny, aren't you?"

"Quit looking at my ass."

Chapter 13

Some adjustments come naturally when people are isolated, like the excitement that occurs when visitors arrive. Bruno began barking one of those barks that indicates a stranger, and we all left the kitchen at once. A one-horse carriage passed through the still dilapidated gated entrance. As it neared, the driver and passenger were easily identified as a man and women by their attire. He wore a wide-brim straw hat, long-sleeve white shirt, suspenders, and an untrimmed beard. His partner wore a simple full-length dress and a bonnet.

"Mormons?" I asked."

"Amish," replied Loretta.

"O-M-G," complained Sherri. "Is everyone around here backward?"

"Easy, girl. One could accuse you of profiling. And I believe you will find them anything but backwards."

Their little one-horse buggy flashed past the giant cedars. After rounding the curve, the man commanded, "Whoa." Snorts and whinnies came from near the barn as the horses recognized the presence of another. "Howdy Ben, Charlotte," greeted the Colonel.

The man, in his late twenties, tipped his hat and said, "Colonel, Loretta. See the Inn finally has ... guests." The man's eyes met mine as he spoke, and he seemed disturbed.

"Yes we do, and special guests at that."

Charlotte wore a friendly smile. Her skin was milky white, and her eyes were dark and caring. Only the tips of coal dark hair stuck out from beneath her bonnet.

Loretta said, "Come on down here, girl. Let me see that belly."

Colonel Ron quickly met Charlotte to assist her dismount. As she stood, her advanced pregnancy became obvious. On the ground, she hugged the Colonel and accepted a mafia-style kiss on each cheek. Loretta received the same from Ben.

Colonel Ron began introductions. "Charlotte and Ben, this is Brooke, and LA. They are indeed our first guests at Grayson Springs."

"Nice to meet you ladies." As he spoke, Ben reached to shake Sherri's hand. When he turned to me he seemed startled. With his back to Loretta and his wife, he scanned me up and down. "Have we met?"

Colonel Ron answered for me. "She lives in New York. Perhaps in your travels?"

"No. I was thinking here." He broke his stare, turned to the Colonel, and said, "You always wanted to move your practice to the woods. Didn't anticipate your first clients would be so—" Glancing back at Sherri and me, he finished, "—so pleasant."

I wanted to say, *What the fuck did you expect,* but held my tongue.

"Colonel's been dreaming of this project for a long time. Hope you ladies realize how much this means to him. He and Loretta are good people."

"Why thank you," curtseyed Loretta in appreciation. Then to the lady, she said, "As you can see, our friend Charlotte is with child. She's due about the time y'all go home."

Sherri said, "Better watch Brooke. She beats up on pregnant women!"

"Bitch!" Without thinking, I shoved her so hard she landed on her ass.

"Whoa, whoa, whoa!" In an instant, both the Colonel and Loretta were between us as Sherri rose to her feet like she might want a piece of me.

"She had no right to say that."

"Well, it's the truth, isn't it?"

"I didn't punch Melanie because she's pregnant. She's an asshole. Just like you."

"You're not," Loretta snapped, "gonna punch anyone here. You hear me, girl?"

I answered with a snarl. The pregnant lady seemed to be in shock, leaning against the buggy as if ready to leave. I curtsied and said, "Ma'am, I do apologize if this Californian bitch has given you an unsightly opinion of me. I'm not nearly as dangerous as she would have you think." Without speaking, the lady nodded her acceptance.

Sherri kept looking me over, and I couldn't tell if she was planning an attack or fearing that I might be. Colonel Ron, with one eye on me and the other on Sherri, said, "If you ladies are done feuding, we can carry on."

I would have expected more of a reaction, but the Colonel seemed intent on ignoring my bad behavior.

"As I was about to say," he continued, "Ben and Charlotte live close by. Normally they'd walk, but with the pregnancy and all, well, you know."

"And," added Ben, "if it happens to rain, we can't cross the creek."

"Yeah, but we intend to fix that problem," replied the Colonel. "Charlotte, if you wanna join the ladies inside, Ben and I can do a little figuring on fixing the footbridge."

I wanted to be a part of the bridge restructuring. While Loretta removed Charlotte's bag from the buggy, I sensed Sherri watching me watching the men.

Loretta said, "Come on in, girls. We have a surprise."

As Sherri and I lagged behind, she squinted at me and then whispered, "Sorry for what I said." When I glanced back toward the men, she asked, "Are you attracted to that guy?"

"No."

"You sure?"

"It's not what you think. There's something about him that bothers me."

"Like what? He seems nice."

"Not sure. It's in the way he looked at me."

Entering the kitchen, Sherri asked, "So what's the surprise?"

Though my thoughts were elsewhere, I was at least attracted to the word 'surprise.' Charlotte removed her bonnet, allowing dark curls to fall to mid-length on her back. Loretta explained, "Our friend here is gifted with a needle and thread."

"Can she make me a pair of jeans?" Sherri begged.

"Noooo," replied Loretta, "but she can make you a bra."

Immediately, Sherri became interested. While Charlotte emptied the contents of her bag—cloth, ribbon, and sewing supplies—I watched Colonel Ron and Ben through the window. They were standing near the spot where the Colonel and I had spoken earlier. Sherri could think of nothing except lifting her boobs. Noticing my focus, Loretta placed her hand on my shoulder and whispered, "Join us out of respect for Charlotte, and I'll make sure you get to be a part of the construction."

"Promise?"

"Promise."

The process of building a bra wasn't as boring as I had expected. Charlotte took some sort of cotton cloth, used scissors to cut it into two large squares and then folded each into triangles. She then slipped a long ribbon through both triangles at the fold.

"I see," announced Sherri. "It's going to be like a bikini top."

"That's right," Charlotte answered as she threaded her needle. "I'll sew the tips of the triangles together where they meet and then add a ribbon to each for neck straps."

It only took ten minutes or so for Charlotte to sew the two neck straps into place. "Okay now. We'll have to try it on for adjustment before I sew the bottom ribbon into place."

Sherri suddenly realized she was expected to disrobe for fitting. "Here?" she asked.

"Sure," Loretta answered. "We're all adults. Brooke can watch out the window to make sure the men aren't returning."

"Oh well," Sherri mumbled, anxious to try on her new bra. As she unbuttoned her blouse, exposing her hugeness, I glanced back and forth between men and boobs.

Charlotte said, "Oh my. Hope I made it big enough."

Loretta tied the lower ribbon around Sherri's back, and then pulled the straps over her shoulders. "How's it feel?"

"Better," replied Sherri as she lifted her breasts to a comfortable height.

Loretta tied a bow and walked around to see the results. "Charlotte, you are a genius."

Charlotte stood and adjusted the cotton cups to get the proper separation. "Okay. Let's take it off and I'll sew the bottom ribbon into place."

When Loretta began untying the straps, my attention was on Sherri instead of the guard duty I'd been assigned. I heard footsteps and turned. Ben stepped slowly to the open door just as Sherri's monsters were exposed. He stood staring until he noticed me watching him. "I'm sorry," he apologized. "Had no idea."

"Brooke! You bitch!" shouted Sherri as she turned away. "You did that on purpose!"

While Sherri covered herself, Charlotte gave me a look to kill before asking, "What can we do for you, Ben?"

"Colonel wants Brooke to join us if she can."

Loretta replied, "We'll send her out as soon as we finish here."

Ben turned and said, "Thank you, and pardon my interruption." He grinned at me and tipped his hat before leaving the porch.

I said, "Colonel Ron knows I want to help with the bridge."

"Yeah, well, it can wait. We still have to make your bra."

"Shouldn't take long," jabbed Sherri.

"Fu..." I caught myself again.

"Don't you dare, young lady," snapped Loretta. "And don't go gettin' pissy. We trusted you to do something for us and you blew it."

Charlotte finished sewing Sherri's bra, and then started mine. As I unbuttoned for fitting, Loretta said, "I'll keep watch this time."

"Why worry," Sherri chirped. "There's not much for them to see anyway."

I wanted to turn loose with a tongue lashing, but held back. When my small breasts were exposed, Charlotte said, "Now those nipples were made for breast feeding."

The words passed blankly through my mind as I admired Charlotte's high cheekbones and her dark flowing hair. The way it fell

86

softly across her shoulders and down the front of her blouse. Our eyes met for the first time and she stared the same way Colonel Ron had. It felt weird. If no one else had been around, I might have kissed her. Finally, she said, "Let's get you covered up," as if she knew it was her attention having a reaction on my nipples.

Noticing, Sherri said, "Gross," and then assisted in the fitting.

As Loretta continued her post, I spoke frankly to Charlotte. "Do you wear a bra?"

"Yes, I do."

"I thought Amish women were not allowed to wear bras."

Loretta answered for Charlotte. "I told you, Ben and Charlotte are not your average Amish."

No shit. He likes Sherri's boobs, and she likes my nipples.

"Ben and I cherish the simple way of the Amish, but that doesn't mean we have to adhere to all its practices. I, for one, refuse to be blindly obedient to Ben or any other man. And I refuse to live without a phone."

I nodded my approval. *Maybe I do like her.*

The room was filled with wordless thoughts and questionable glances as my bra was completed. Before buttoning my blouse, I leaned down to the seated Charlotte, hugged her neck and whispered, "You are a beautiful lady, and I thank you for your kindness." Then, turning to Loretta, I asked, "May I leave now?"

"As soon as you apologize to Sherri."

Looking at Sherri, and excited about going out to be with the men, I said, "I bet it made Ben's day..."

"Brooke!" interrupted Loretta. "You're being rude."

Charlotte said, "It's okay. She's probably right."

Finishing my apology, I said, "Sherri, if I offended you, I truly am sorry."

While I stood buttoning my blouse, Sherri replied, "You're so full of shit."

I stepped close and gave her a quick kiss to the lips, before darting out the door.

Again Loretta blurted, "Brooke!"

As I scooted across the porch, I heard Sherri say, "She's okay."

The men had moved to the opposite side of the creek for further inspection. Without hesitation, I pulled up my skirt and started running toward the shallow crossing point of the creek near the barn.

In about a minute I reached the men, out of breath and with the bottom of my skirt dampened from a quick crossing of the creak.

"Whoa there, girl," said the Colonel. "No need to hurry."

Noticing their stares, I said, "What? You two never seen a girl run before?"

Ben replied, "Need to introduce you to my baby brother. Boy loves to run."

Without replying to his comment, I asked, "So, what did I miss? When do we start on the bridge?"

"Slow down honey," advised the Colonel. "It'll take time to mill the wood and acquire the cables."

"Man to man, I'd rather you didn't call me honey."

Ben let out a, "Ooooweee," and it felt as though I'd missed something. Looking at Ben, I asked, "Do you wear that hat all the time?"

"Don't be rude, Brooke," snapped the Colonel.

Ben said, "It's okay. The hat protects me from the sun. I don't carry sunscreen in my pocket, and I certainly don't want melanoma on my ears when I get older.... Does that answer your question?"

When I replied, "Yes, sir," Ben got his first good stare. I tried to read his mind. *Sometimes I think I see more than I should.*

Chapter 14

When the bridge planning had been completed, we returned to the kitchen. Colonel Ron took a seat, and said, "Okay girls, in the back of Ben's carriage, you'll find a lawn mower. Remove it, making sure you don't damage it or the buggy, and then take it to the sulfur springs area. I want all the pathways cut at twice the width of the mower. It'll be hard work, so take turns with the mower. I'll be along later to see how it's going."

Ben said, "It's a simple machine. Just try not to dull it on rocks."

"So," Sherri sighed, "how long is this going to take?"

Colonel Ron grinned. "Doesn't really matter. You girls got nothing but time."

Before we could leave, Loretta said, "Best be watchin' out for snakes."

"And ticks," Charlotte added.

"What kind of snakes," Sherri asked. "Are they poisonous?"

"Mostly copperheads," replied Loretta, "and maybe a water moccasin when you're near the creek. If you see one, don't panic. They're more afraid of you than you are of them."

"Yeah, right," I mumbled as I turned and left the room.

Outside, Sherri caught up with me and said, "Don't ever leave me alone with those two again. They're like two old women, telling stories about *the old days*."

I knew we were about to do manual labor, yet it felt good to be away from adults. We easily lifted the mower out of the buggy and then stood there figuring it out. "What's the deal?" I wondered aloud.

Sherri complained, "Can you believe this shit? This thing doesn't even have an engine...."

"1800s, stupid."

"So how does it work?"

I held the handle and said, "I believe like this," The mower was nothing more than a long shaft with a tee handle on top, connected to an axel at the bottom with wheels on each end. The wheels were all that drove the rotary blades which ran parallel to the axel. Pushing the contraption forward caused the horizontal blades to turn, thus cutting grass.

"Oh my god," Sherri laughed. "It'll take for-ev-er."

"Colonel says we should take turns. I'll go first." I began dragging the machine toward the sulfur springs area. "Come on. Let's get started. It might be fun."

"Work? Fun? Have you lost your mind?"

Crossing the lane, just past the cedars, I stopped dragging and said, "I believe this is where we should start. I began the process of pushing forward and pulling back at short intervals. Grass and weeds flew.

"Damn, you're good, Brooke," Sherri praised. "Let me know when you're tired and I'll hide."

"Colonel Ron said not to dull it on rocks. Maybe you should go ahead to clean debris from the pathway."

"Ahead to where?

"The path to each spring, stupid."

"Quit calling me stupid!"

After she had cleared rocks and sticks from the first pathway, Sherri leaned against one of the cedars. Her interests seemed to fall on white flowers that were growing in abundance near and around the springs. As I created a clean, double-wide path to the first spring, she waded into the flowers, picked one, and asked, "You ever seen one of these before?"

"They were all along the road on our way in. Probably shouldn't be handling any plants until you know what they are. You might get poison ivy."

"Poison!"

"And don't forget what they said about snakes and ticks."

Sherri asked, "What exactly are ticks?"

"Ticks are little blood sucking parasites that cling to your skin. Haven't you ever seen one on a dog? The more blood they suck, the bigger they get."

"Don't tell me that!" screamed Sherri as she darted out of the weed-patch and began scanning her dress for signs of insects.

"Your turn. My hands are hurting."

When Sherri took over the push mower, I began clearing things from the next barely visible path. After about an hour of alternating on the mower and breathing sulfuric fumes, we had clean pathways and blisters on our hands. For a moment, we stood admiring the fruits of our labor.

Sherri held her hands up and said, "If my friends at home saw me like this, they would never speak to me again."

I heard her words, but my mind was drawn to the woods on the hill in front of me. When I didn't reply, Sherri asked, "What the hell are you looking at?"

"Not sure. Does it look to you like the path should continue?"

"Maybe at one time," she considered while inspecting the briary foliage that had grown across the pathway. "But it's almost like someone planted this crap here to keep people from continuing."

"Yeah," I replied, while admiring the small white blooms that covered the thorny barriers. "That's what I'm thinking. I'd like to go up there and see what we can find."

"Already told you what's up there," said Colonel Ron from behind us.

Startled, Sherri and I turned to see him and Ben standing fifteen feet away on our freshly cut path. When my eyes met the Colonel's, he asked, "What's wrong?"

"Not sure. I feel attracted to that hill, almost like I've been up there before."

Ben said, "There's a curse on that hill."

"A curse?" asked Sherri.

I turned to the Colonel. "You didn't mention a curse."

Ben asked, "You say you feel like you've been up there?"

"Brooke has a gift. She has historical dreams, or visions, or something," Colonel Ron replied for me.

I said, "This one's more like déjà vu."

"Really?" replied Ben, staring as if he'd seen a ghost. "You been on that hill before, ain't you girl?"

"Not in this life," I joked. "But sir, I would like to hear more about the curse." Ben turned away as if I'd made him uncomfortable.

Colonel Ron scratched his head. "It's nothing really ... the curse is more like a rumor...."

"Rumor?" Ben obviously disagreed.

Colonel Ron tried to play it off. "Just because you and a few old timers around here talk that stuff, that don't make it a fact. I've been on that hill—"

"And I bet it was raining, wasn't it?" Ben asked.

"What about the rain?" Sherri questioned.

Ben replied, "It rains up there every day. The story says that's why Grayson Springs has an unlimited flow of spring water."

"Like a rain forest," Sherri speculated.

"Like a curse," Ben repeated.

"So, can I go up there?" I asked.

Colonel Ron replied, "We have no reason to go up there. Right now I think we should déjà vu our way back to the inn."

On our return walk, I could tell that Sherri, like me, sensed it was not the first time the Colonel and Ben had debated over the curse on the hill. Colonel Ron changed the subject. "You girls did one heck of a job on these pathways." At the edge of the front lawn, he stopped, put his hands on his hips and said, "By the end of the week, we'll have all this looking great."

I asked, "How do you cut all that grass from the road to the Inn?"

"I don't. You girls do. And you just got a taste of how."

"No way!" Sherri huffed.

"You've got to be kidding," I added, staring at nearly an acre of grass.

Sherri and I, tired and thirsty, limped into the kitchen ahead of the men. Besides being saddle sore, we now had blisters. And the ones on my hands were not nearly as bad as the ones on my heels from the stiff new shoes. Running had irritated my heels, and then the continued walking just made it worse. Loretta ordered, "Back outside, ladies. We need to check you for ticks. I see one on Sherri's dress already."

"Tick!" Sherri screamed. "Where?"

On the porch, Loretta asked the men to go inside so she and Charlotte could look us over for ticks. We sat in chairs while they checked our hair. Charlotte said, "Now you girls can see why I wear a bonnet. If I get time, I'll make y'all one.... Or you could just cut your hair."

"Not me!" blurted Sherri. "Make me a bonnet."

I thought about the idea of cutting my hair, but instead said, "I'd prefer a hat like Ben's."

It felt good the way Charlotte ran her fingers through my hair. Reminded me of the way it felt when the black girls at school did me up in braids. Though my hair was clear of parasites, Charlotte did find one little tick on the hem of my dress. Kneeling down, she began raising my dress to search my legs.

.....He was tying my shoes when he began rubbing his hands up my dress. It scared me and I gasped. He put his finger to his lips as if to say, be quiet.....

Loretta noticed my tears, and said, "Charlotte ... perhaps she should check herself," nodding toward my face.

Seeing my condition, Charlotte struggled to her feet and said, "I'm sorry. Did I do something out of...?"

"No," Loretta interrupted. "It's not you."

I stood and limped quickly off the porch and around the building to the outhouse. Inside, I closed the door and latched it. Just enough light bled in through the cracks between boards for me to search my legs for bloodsucking parasites. I did find one behind my left knee and from there checked every sweaty inch of my body. After several minutes, I heard someone approaching. Through the cracks, I identified the Colonel walking my way.

"You okay in there?"

"Yes."

"Need anything?"

"A cigarette."

Pouch, papers, and a book of matches slid under the door. "Don't be long. Charlotte and Ben are about to leave and she needs to know you're okay before she leaves." At that, he walked away. I quickly rolled three cigarettes. Smoked one, saved one in my dress pocket, and left one in the pouch for Colonel Ron.

When I returned to the kitchen, Charlotte looked up in despair. I walked to her, reached for her hand, and said, "May I walk you to the buggy?" She seemed shocked, but adhered. On our way out the door, I looked at Ben and said, "Give us a few minutes, please?"

At the buggy, Ben's horse looked happy to see us. I assisted Charlotte up to the bench seat. She said, "Thank you."

"Thank *you*," I replied.

"For what?"

"A while ago, I recalled something that has apparently been bothering me for years. When your hands went up my leg, it reminded me of something that occurred when I was very young. Something terribly inappropriate."

Charlotte said, "I am so sorry," as she started to brush back my hair, but then pulled back.

"Please don't pull away. I'm okay now. It won't bother me. I enjoyed your touch as you checked my head. It was heavenly. It's just that ... you know."

"I do understand. And apparently everyone else does too. Remember, Colonel Ron is a professional, and Loretta has a psychology degree also."

"But what about Ben?"

"Ben ... well, Ben is Ben. He understands everything."

"Are you mad at me for the boob thing?"

"No. You didn't do it on purpose."

"I can't say that for sure. Might have heard someone coming."

"You did it to get at her?"

"Maybe."

"Well, I'm sure you made Ben's day. Just keep in mind: it's not the kind of thing a pregnant woman wants her husband looking at. Not feeling too attractive at the moment."

I stared deep into her eyes and saw the same insecurity I'd seen in Melanie. "Charlotte, you're pregnant, not fat. And you are beautiful. Don't ever think otherwise. Two or three months from now you'll be the same knockout you were before you got pregnant."

She smiled.

Turning toward the hill behind the springs, I asked, "By the way, you ever been up on that hill?"

She looked and said, "Can't say I have."

"You know anything about a curse on that hill?"

She seemed surprised. "Ben tell you that?"

"He mentioned it."

"Well, I'll tell you right now, I don't believe in ghosts."

Ghosts? My enquiry got cut short by the approach of Ben and the others. Sherri thanked Charlotte for her homemade bra and reminded her of the need for a bonnet. Colonel Ron begged them to stay for supper, but Ben said they were expecting company.

That evening, as Sherri and I did dishes, Loretta joined Colonel Ron for his after-dinner cigarette. I said, "He probably wants to talk to her about my *strange* behavior."

Sherri shook her head. "Everything's not about you, you know. I believe she likes him."

"You think? Hell, I believe she's in love. And by the way, I asked Charlotte about the curse on the hill thing. She said something about a ghost."

"No shit. I guess that settles it then. Snakes and ghosts. I'm not going up on that hill."

As we spoke, Sherri scratched at her groin area through her dress.

"You okay?"

"Still itching. Can't stop thinking about the blood sucking ticks."

"You don't have one, do you?"

"No, I checked."

That evening, as we prepared for bed, I said, "I need to pee, but I swear I'm too sore to go back down those steps."

"Why don't you use the potty thingy?"

Looking at the porcelain pot, I said, "You know, I believe I've used one of these when I was little."

"No shit?"

"Did I tell you that I was born near here?"

"Noooo. So you are like a real-live hillbilly?"

"Ha ha. I left here when I was five or six ... didn't I see toilet paper in one of these drawers?"

Sherri leaned down and slid open the bottom drawer of her nightstand. "I've got a roll here. Check yours."

My drawer slid out, but not nearly as far as the one on Sherri's nightstand. I removed the small roll and thought out loud, "Did they even have toilet paper in the 1800s?"

"Hope so. I read somewhere that the early Egyptians used dogs."

"Dogs?"

"Yeah. They let the dog lick their butts clean."

"Gross," I replied while raising my gown, lowering my bloomers, and then squatting over the pot.

Sherri laughed at the sight and the sound. "Guess it beats going down those steps again."

After finishing my business, I gazed out the open window at how the sunset illuminated the treetops on the cursed hill. "At least we have a screen to keep the bugs out."

"Our only modern convenience is a screen."

"There's a lot of grass out there, you know."

"Don't remind me. Is it even legal for them to make slaves out of us?"

Looking at my blistered hands, I said, "Not sure about legal, but it certainly is cruel."

"My father would never make me cut grass."

"Oh, well."

"You think it's funny. I can tell. You want me to get all dirty and break my nails and—"

"Quit whining. You think I do labor in Manhattan? Before today, I'd never cut grass in my life." Turning from the window, I noticed Sherri was scratching again. "You've got something, you know. Probably some creepy disease from those weeds you were in."

"It's not fair," she whined. "All this because I learned how to hack."

"All this because you broke the law, and because your parents don't want you to go to prison."

"It was my first offense. Why couldn't they just give me a break?"

"Believe that's what they consider this ... a break." While speaking, I opened the top drawer of my nightstand and removed a matchbox. "It's going to be dark soon. Want me to light this lantern thing?"

"Not for me. I'm exhausted. Since you didn't shoot the rooster, I need to start my sleep early."

I pulled out the cigarette I'd rolled earlier.

Sherri smiled. "Is that what I think it is?"

"I wish. It's a cigarette. Down here, they roll their own."

"The Colonel gave you that?"

I said, "Not exactly," while striking the match and lighting the cigarette.

"So you *are* a thief."

"Fuck you."

"I'm going to tellllll."

"I might be worn out, but I can still kick your ass."

"Fuck you too then."

We both smiled. Replacing the matchbox, I realized the top drawer was opened further than the bottom one had. "Makes no sense."

"What?"

I looked over and Sherri was flat on her back, staring at the ceiling. Her hand was under the cover, moving. "You know that looks gross, what you are doing."

"I can't help it. It itches. Sorry if it excites you to watch."

"Go to sleep, pervert."

Chapter 15

That next morning, the rooster had only just begun to crow when Loretta knocked on our door. "Rise and shine, ladies. Big day ahead of us." Ten minutes later, Sherri and I were sharing our complaints over strong coffee when Colonel Ron popped in off the back porch, carrying a shovel.

"Why can't *you* get milk, eggs, and meat?" Sherri complained to him. "I'm so sleepy I can hardly see."

"Because, Miss LA," he answered, "I'm about to shovel out the sewage under the outhouse. If you would prefer to join me...?"

"Hell no! Take Brooke."

"Not me," I said while grabbing the egg basket. I dreaded being in the barn with Loretta and morning bitch girl, but had no desire to shovel shit.

The Colonel grinned as Sherri and I hustled away. The rooster crowed as if mocking us while Loretta, carrying a bucket, caught up. "Slow down, girls. We're in no hurry."

Sherri said, "I'm not in a hurry. Just mad."

"Why are you mad?"

When Sherri stopped, I continued to the creek bed, stopped and looked back at her rant. "Why am I mad? Are you f-f-frigging kidding me...?"

"Easy now," Loretta advised.

"Ughhhhh. I'm stuck out here in this godforsaken place, I need a shower, I've already got some kind of eff'n disease, and you ask why I'm mad! Give me a break."

"Disease?" asked Loretta. "What on earth are you talkin' about?"

"Those blood sucking bugs gave me something and it's driving me crazy."

"You mean the ticks? You still have one?"

"I'm itching like hell."

"She has a rash," I added.

"Where?" Loretta asked.

After a deep breath, Sherri started walking and said, "I'll show you when we get to the barn."

Loretta shook her head, and we all continued across the creek. By the time we reached the barn, the dog had Bertha and her calf rounded up near the east entrance. "Good job Bruno, but we're not milking today."

Sherri bitched, "Thought you said we were going to get milk?"

"We are. But we're gonna get the milk we pasteurized yesterday. It's cooling in the spring house. We'll grab it on our way back."

"I don't get to milk the cow?"

"You wanted to?"

I said, "I told her how much fun it was."

Noticing Sherri scratching, Loretta asked, "So, what about your disease?"

After looking out to make sure no one was coming, Sherri lifted her skirt, held it up with one hand, and then pulled her bloomers down enough to reveal red spots on her groin area. She said, "Looks like measles to me."

Loretta grinned and said, "Honey, all you have is a bad case of chiggers."

"Chiggers? What the hell is that?"

"Well, you were right about one thing. It is a bug, but not a tick. Chiggers are so small you can't see 'em. Look out yonder. See those weeds with the white flowers. Those are chigger weeds."

"Oh-my-god!"

I couldn't help but giggle. "Told you so."

"You get against them and the chiggers get on you," Loretta continued. "They crawl right through your clothes and go for your groin. They like the moist, warm area."

"So how do I get rid of them?"

"Time. They'll die on their own, but it'll take a few days. Meanwhile, you'd best quit scratching or they'll get infected."

Dropping her skirt hem, Sherri said, "I can't help it."

As I tossed chicken scratch about, all the hens and the rooster ran, flew, and clucked toward their morning meal. Loretta and Sherri took the opportunity to rob nests of several eggs. "Never dreamed I'd be doing this shit," Sherri mumbled.

Loretta waited until we had left the stall to reply. "Y'all come with me."

"Where?" Sherri asked.

"Set your eggs down and follow me."

At the end of the runway, Loretta opened the gate and motioned for us to step out. Behind the barn, two old metal chairs, hand-painted green, sat side by side under a sugar-maple, facing towards the pasture. She used her hand to brush away dew and debris, and said, "You two have a seat." I shrugged my shoulders and we both plopped down. Loretta continued. "The Colonel and I sit here sometimes and just take in the world. Look out there and tell me you don't see heaven."

Streaks of radiance from the morning sun peaked through leaves of trees at the top of the hill, giving the whole pasture a heavenly look. Fog drifted from Bear Creek, through a narrow line of sycamore, hickory, and oak trees, and out onto the field's edge. Around fifty yards away, Bertha stood chewing her cud while the calf sucked a meal from one of her teats. Further out, all three horses nibbled non-stop in the grass, tails swishing flies from their rumps. Standing behind us, Loretta said, "Now close your eyes. Relax. Listen to the sounds. Smell the smells."

Leaning back, I began to notice a variety of songbirds performing their unique melodies. Leaves rustled in the breeze, chickens clucked behind us in the barn, and the aroma of Bertha's fresh cow dung gave the air its own unique country appeal. Loretta asked, "You ever in your life felt anything so peaceful?"

Sherri admitted, "Nothing like this. It is peaceful, but I'm not sure it's worth all the work that goes along with it."

"Honey, you call what we do here work. We call it heaven. Think about it. Both Ben and Charlotte have been out in the world. They've seen the U.S. from New York to LA, even parts of Europe, and still they choose to live a simple life in Grayson County. Both of you kids have—"

"We're not kids," I complained.

"Sorry. You ladies have parents so tied up in their own way of survival that they don't have time to enjoy you or the precious little things in life. In these old hills of Kentucky, you're gonna see, feel, smell, and hear things most city folks never experience."

Sherri said, "Bet my father would like this."

"He probably ain't seen anything this peaceful since Georgia Te—" Loretta cut herself short. "After six weeks, you ladies will never forget this place. Someday when you are young mothers, about to pull your hair out from the hustle and bustle of the daily hum drum, you can take a moment, close your eyes, and come here in your own private way. It will take the edge off an otherwise bad day. Colonel says there were times when thinking about these hills was the only thing that kept his sanity in Iraq."

When we opened our eyes, Sherri saw the look on my face. She asked, "Loretta, how did you know my father went to Georgia Tech?"

"That's where I did my undergraduate work."

"So you knew my father?"

"Yes."

"How well?"

"We were friends."

"Oohhh, I see," she stated while turning to look at Loretta. "Before he met my mother?"

"Yes. We took walks in the park."

"Did you have sex?"

"We enjoyed our walks."

"But did you have—"

Loretta's glare said, *don't go there.*

I kept my mouth shut, thinking *Colonel Ron wasn't her first confidant.*

"So," continued Sherri's interrogation, "how come my dad didn't marry you?"

I glanced back in time to see pain in Loretta's hesitation. She mumbled, "I was in the reserves. Got shipped out. We went our separate ways."

"How did you wind up here?"

"Served under Colonel Ron in Iraq. We became friends."

"Friends? Like with my father?"

"Just friends. Officers are not allowed to conduct personal relationships with those under their command. There's a very strict code on fraternization."

"But that was then," I finally interjected. "You're not in the Army now."

Sherri said, "You must have feelings, or you wouldn't have followed him here."

"When we first got back from Iraq, Colonel Ron and I were stationed at Fort Knox. He asked me to join him here for some R&R. I'd heard so much about this place, figured I'd have to see it with my own eyes to find out if he was exaggerating. Only took a couple days for me to fall in love."

"With Grayson Springs, or the Colonel?"

Instead of answering, Loretta said, "Believe we need to get moving."

The spring house—an eight-foot by ten-foot framed building—had been constructed overtop a natural water pool, four-feet in diameter. A contraption over the water reminded me of a wishing well. Loretta rotated the crank until it pulled up a basket full of Mason jars. Some held milk, some meat. "You have to be careful not to break 'em." She removed a jar of milk and handed it to Sherri.

"Wow, it *is* cool."

"Technically, the milk should last a couple weeks. To be on the safe side, we only pasteurize what we can consume in a week."

I asked, "Does this freeze in the winter?"

"No. Running water doesn't freeze. Just a little around the edges, but never completely."

Looking at the shelves on the walls, Sherri asked, "So, you guys use this for a refrigerator?"

"You could say that ... You want bacon today or ham?"

"Bacon, please. The ham is too salty."

"Get used to that. We can soak it, but it will always be more salty than what you're accustomed to."

On our walk back to the Inn, Sherri said, "People sure had it rough in the old days."

"Yes, they did. But it was a much simpler life. No traffic, no bad news on the radio and TV every day..."

"No beach. No car. No phone. No music."

"I hear you. But I still bet later when you're at home, you'll miss this."

A few steps later, Loretta and I noticed that Sherri had stopped walking. We looked back. She turned in place, taking in her surroundings. "This is what my father meant when he said, 'Relax and enjoy the quiet times.' I still don't want to be here, but I will say this: when we came through here before, I didn't hear water running from the springs or those little frogs jumping in as we walked by. I paid no attention to the sounds of the birds, the bugs, or the leaves in the breeze. Now, thanks to you, I do."

When Sherri turned and rejoined us, Loretta had tears running down her cheeks. Sherri asked, "What's wrong?"

After wiping her face, Loretta wrapped her arms around Sherri and whispered, "About twenty years ago, as your father and I walked in the park, he said almost those same words to me."

Chapter 16

By the time we got back to the Inn, Colonel Ron had finished his nasty chore and was holding a jar full of worms. I asked, "Did you get them out of the poop?"

"No, I got them out of the dirt where I buried the—the waste. Gonna use them for bait."

"And what are you baiting?" Sherri asked.

"Thought you ladies might like fresh fish for dinner this evening. Wanna join me?"

"Are there chigger weeds out there?"

Colonel Ron grinned and said, "I can't guarantee there's not."

"Well, then you can count me out."

"I'll go," I interrupted.

"How about it, Loretta? Can you two handle breakfast while Brooke and I catch a few?"

Loretta looked at Sherri as if to say, *Do you mind?*

Sherri said, "Hell, let her go. I hope she gets a chigger so she can see how I feel."

Colonel Ron and I walked down a misty footpath next to the creek. We each carried a cane pole complete with six feet of line, a bobber, and a hook temporarily snagged into the handle end of the pole. He let me lead the way, and I soon found out why. "What the—" I nearly ran into a huge, intricate spider web stretched across the path. I stepped back.

Smiling, Colonel Ron said, "Oh yeah, I forgot to warn you." The web had drops of moisture clinging to it like tiny crystals. In the middle, a colorful spider the size of a silver dollar lay in waiting for prey.

"Should I kill it?"

"Why? It's not bothering us. We're bothering it."

I stared closely at the spider. "It really is beautiful. I seem to recall these from my youth." He used his pole to break the web and swing out of our way.

Thirty feet farther, a gap in the foliage revealed a wide pool of water. Our approach startled a dark brown, flat-tailed something that jumped into the water and began swimming downstream.

"Was that a—?"

"Beaver."

"Don't see that in Central Park."

Pointing out remains of several small trees that had been cut off six inches or so from the ground, Colonel Ron said, "You can be sure there's beaver around when you see teeth marks on stumps. Their damming up the creek is part of what provides us with this fishing pool."

By stepping closer to the bank, I could see the beaver dam stretching across the creek some thirty yards further downstream, under the blanket of fog. *There was a pond in the woods. I fell in and came out with a leach on my foot.* Nearby, a water snake wiggled across the creek's surface, its head sticking up. "Oh, my god. There's a snake!"

"They're around here," advised the Colonel, "so be careful where you step, sit, or put your hands."

"It feels like we're in a movie, all these animals and reptiles and such."

"But these are real. Nice, isn't it?"

"Uh, yeah—long as we don't get bit." I watched as Colonel Ron ran a fishhook most the way down through a worm and then back out.

> *.....They laughed while they did it to worms,*
> *caterpillars, crickets, hell, anything small that*
> *moved after they hooked it. It was a boy thing.*

As the only girl, I was only supposed to watch.
Now I get a chance to do it, but it.....

"It seems cruel, doesn't it? How would you like some giant to do this to you?"

"Animals kill one another daily for consumption. Mankind's been doin' this for thousands of years. It's called survival."

"Yeah, but we don't have to do this to survive."

"Well, let's put it this way, if you and I don't catch fish this morning, we don't eat tonight, unless of course, you have a better idea."

"McDonald's," I said, while holding my pole out, watching my bobber, waiting for a bite. "I'll take a Big Mac and fries."

"No comment," was the Colonel's only reply.

"Oh my god! Oh my god!" I squealed, as my bobber disappeared.

"You've got a bite! Pull it in!"

As the end of my fishing line zigzagged in the water, I gasped.

"Come on Brooke ... raise the end of the pole before it gets away."

I did as advised, and a beautiful, seven-inch fish glittered in the sunlight, dangling from the end of my line, flip-flopping for its life.

"That's a big bluegill. Bring it around this way before it gets off the hook." When I turned the pole over the bank, Colonel Ron grabbed the line. "You slide your hand down from the head so you don't stab yourself with its fins. They're sharp as needles."

"Can't believe I did it! Can't believe I caught a frigging fish!"

"You sure did," replied my pleased teacher, "and a nice one at that. At least now we know *you'll* eat tonight."

After little more than an hour, Colonel Ron and I returned from our fishing expedition. Besides my cane pole, I proudly carried the stringer with eight good-size bluegills. Bruno had searched us out and was leading the way home. Colonel Ron said, "I smell bacon."

"But I want to eat the fish."

"They're for dinner, I told you. Give me the stringer. You go inside and tell Loretta that you and I are going to clean fish. Then join me at the creek, down by the barn. We can have these things done in a jiffy."

I skipped up the back porch and into the kitchen.

"About time," ribbed Sherri.

"It was fun. I caught three fish all by myself. Colonel caught five."

"Good," said Loretta. "That'll be supper tonight."

"He and I are going to butcher them down by the creek."

Loretta began gathering items. "*Clean* them," she corrected. "Livestock gets butchered. You clean a fish."

"What ev-er," I sassed as she handed me a pan, a spoon, and a knife.

On my way out, Sherri said, "Next time I want to go fishing."

Loretta shouted, "Don't you run with that knife! It's really sharp."

Colonel Ron filled the pan with creek water. Then, after placing a flat board on top of a rock for a table, he used his knife to cut into the brain portion of a fish's head. At first, I cringed. "Gross ... that's so inhumane." The other seven fish were gasping for air.

"Inhumane," repeated the Colonel. "Inhumane would be if I cleaned these puppies alive. Some people do, you know."

"They say serial killers start out on animals."

"Are you insinuating I might be a serial killer?"

"Are you?"

"Not hardly," replied Colonel Ron as he used the spoon to scrape off the fish's scales. Then, after using the knife to remove its head, he pulled out and discarded entrails and tossed what remained into the pan.

"That's it?" I asked. "We eat the fins?"

"Sure do. Fry 'em up real crisp and they're good."

"Yuck."

"You'll see."

As he completed the second fish and tossed it into the pan, I asked, "Can I do one?"

"You want to?"

"Yes, I do."

"Might as well, then," replied the Colonel as he grabbed a third fish to further demonstrate. "You have to be careful. See how I hold it so it can't fin me?"

"Yeah, I've been watching."

Accepting the knife, I grabbed the fish and forced the blade into its brain without hesitation. Colonel Ron smiled and said, "Just like a true serial killer."

"And don't you forget it," I joked, while holding the bluegill's tail and scraping off scales with the spoon. "Melanie should see me now."

Colonel Ron pulled out his tobacco pouch and said, "Thanks for rolling me one."

"*De nad,*" I replied.

After he lit the cigarette and took a draw, he asked, "You ever killed an animal before?"

"No. But I do enjoy swatting flies."

"That's different."

"How so?" I asked, "Taking a life is taking a life. How can you consider the life of one species more important than another?"

"Some say God put certain animals here for food, others for companionship or working."

"You don't believe that, do you?"

"I was asking you," Colonel Ron replied with a psychologist tone.

Grabbing another fish, I said, "If there is a God, he didn't decide that horses were for riding. Man did. We could all be vegetarians, but most of us choose to eat fish and chickens and cows because we're frigging carnivores. Our ancestors were, and we'll probably continue going about the business of killing innocent animals for the luxury of eating as long as man exists."

"And how do you feel about that?"

"Do you think God would hold it against a cat for eating a mouse?"

"No," he answered with a grin.

"Then why would he hold it against me or you for eating a mouse, or a cat for that matter?"

"Interesting."

"God, you're sooo much like Daddy."

"Well, you're right about one thing. Our ancestors were carnivores, or at least omnivores, which is what most of us are now. But for the moment, I'm more like Pavlov's dog because the smell of that bacon frying is making me salivate." He dropped his cigarette and stepped it out. "Let's finish here and go eat."

Glancing down at the snubbed cigarette, I said, "Thanks for the draw, asshole."

That morning's breakfast turned into a grand session of unspoken dialogue. Colonel Ron noticed right away a change in Sherri, and with eye contact, gave credit to Loretta. She smiled back her appreciation. I could sense him trying to read my mind. *Good luck with that.* When he saw that I had finished eating, he asked, "Loretta, you mind if Miss Green and I take a little walk before cleanup starts?" She tilted her head as if puzzled. "We'll only be a few minutes."

On our way out the door, I heard Sherri ask, "What did *she* do wrong?"

Near the entrance to the pathways of the sulfur springs, Colonel Ron said, "Much nicer since you guys cut the grass." He pulled out his tobacco pouch. "Here," he said, "You're better at it than me. Roll us a couple."

I sat on a rock performing my task. As I handed him his and started on mine, I said, "Wish this were a joint."

"But it's not."

As the Colonel lit up, he said, "Let's walk." We started a stroll through the freshly cut paths. I lit my cigarette and said, "I know you know these are bad for me. Why do you let me smoke them?"

"You were already a smoker. Let's just say I'm giving you a chance to wean from them slowly. Are you not smoking less than before?"

"Yes, but I figured you were smoking with me as some sort of bonding situation."

"Are we?"

I blew smoke at him and said, "Yeah."

"Good."

"So, man to man, why did you ask me out here?"

"Truth is I'm interested in the things you said earlier about killing animals."

"Oh my god, you really do think I'm a serial killer."

"No ... at least I hope not. Just wondering though, have you always been so philosophical?"

Grinning, I said, "Grandma Green says I have an old spirit."

"Meaning?"

"She thinks my spirit's been around longer than my body."

"Interesting. So what do *you* think?"

"Not sure. All I can say is that for as long as I can remember, I've had dreams about things I have never seen. I wake up and it's like, déjà vu."

"You've mentioned that before. Define déjà vu."

"You know. Going somewhere new and feeling like you've been there before."

"As in?"

"As in coming down here on the train. Looking out across those fields in the moonlight ... it, it felt like something I'd seen before. Not like on TV or in a movie, and not as a child, but like I'd actually seen those places in person, as an adult."

The Colonel took a draw from his cigarette, exhaled and said, "I'm sure that happens to people all the time."

"Sure it does. That's why they have the term déjà vu. But I just wonder if it happens to others as much as it does me. And sometimes mine is different from what I've read about."

"In that?"

"Sometimes I do things I've never done before as if I had been doing it all my life."

"Is that right?"

"I'd never ridden a horse before, yet, when we got here and I got off Becca, I started removing the saddle as if I'd done it before. Not like I'd seen it done and figured it out. It came too easy. Like I'd performed the task a hundred times."

"Must admit, I wondered about that when you did it."

"I've tried to talk to Daddy and Melanie about these things. They pretend to listen, but rarely comment. They don't really listen. Not like you."

"So, you don't think I am just listening because it's my job?"

"Maybe, to some extent. But I do find myself listening to you, and I'm not getting paid. I think you are at least interested in me ... or my mind ... or whatever. You know what I mean."

"Yes I do. And may I say that while I am doing a service, it makes my job much easier when the person I am speaking with is as personable as you are."

"Personable. No one ever called me that before."

"Now, back to déjà vu."

"When I was eleven, I stole a gun. I did it because I felt like it was mine. It was an old gun. Something a soldier might have used back in the ... the 1800s."

"I read your file."

"The girl I beat up. She said she was going to scalp me. We were already pushing each other. But when the words came out of her mouth, it was like someone turned a switch inside of me. I couldn't help myself. If someone hadn't stopped me, I might have killed her. I feel bad about it now, but at the time, it seemed like something I had to do."

"Did you tell this to the doctors?"

"Yes I did, but they just looked at me like I was crazy. Said it sounded like I was making excuses. Loretta says you're a fair man, a good listener. Do you think I'm crazy?"

Colonel Ron smiled and said, "No, I don't think you're crazy. But do me a favor. Anytime you feel one of these, these mysterious moments, let me know. You don't have to necessarily say anything, just give me a look. I'll get the message."

We continued our talk and soon reached the end of the mowed pathway. I stood for a moment, staring up toward the hill, the place that had attracted me the day before.

"What?" the Colonel asked.

I turned and gave him a look.

"What?" he repeated.

Tilting my head, I crossed my eyes and pressed my lips together. Then it hit him. "You're having one now?"

"Thank you. Yes. Same as yesterday when we cut the grass. There's something about that hill that draws me, like I *have* been up there before."

"You are nuts—"

"Fuck you!" I spurted, turning to walk away.

"Watch that mouth."

"Then screw you," I shouted while fast-walking back the way we had come. "You don't really care. You're just like everybody else."

"Hold on, Brooke. That's not fair," he begged while catching up. "Wait a second."

When he put his hand on my shoulder, I turned as if to hit him. Colonel Ron backed off, held his hands up, and said, "Brooke, I was just joking. Honest. I didn't mean it."

"Then don't say it. I'm not crazy, and don't you act like I am."

"It'll never happen again. I promise."

I stood there doubting his word. Then he said, "When I was a kid, the pathway continued up that hill. People used to walk in under the shade of the trees. On top is where the old military post used to be. Over the years, the path grew up with foliage and no one ever bothered to clean that part again."

"Do you believe me when I say I feel like I've been up there before?"

He hesitated as if thinking about the absurdity of my claim. "Seriously, I don't think you've ever physically been up there before, but, I am open to the possibility that there's something to your feelings. Don't quote me on that, but again, please let me know when this stuff happens so we can try and figure it out. Fair enough?"

In my mind, I still questioned his sincerity, yet realized that his offer was the best I'd had so far. At least someone was listening. I nodded.

Chapter 17

Each morning after breakfast cleanup, we had an hour to make beds, take care of personal hygiene, and relax before working. Officially time was kept by the old wind-up clock in the lobby. Colonel Ron had his pocket watch synchronized to it and made sure Sherri and I remained on schedule.

Grass cutting became a daily ritual at Grayson Springs. We were expected to do yard work for two hours at a spirited pace. Initially, Colonel Ron and Loretta kept watch to make sure we took turns at pushing the mower. They didn't need to. Sherri and I rotated duties without guidance. Getting off the mower didn't necessarily mean a break. Between turns, there were plenty other things to tend to. Shrubbery in front of the Inn had to be pruned, as did the ornamental trees around the patio adjacent to the building's north end. Hand snips were all we had to trim the edging. The longer we worked, the more satisfaction I found in changes we were making, and I am quite certain Sherri felt the same. I had often watched yard keepers in New York, and could now further appreciate their efforts.

By Friday of the first week, the grounds had become presentable. After breakfast, Sherri and I could hear the Colonel and Loretta talking outside as we finished dishes. The morning sun had become hidden by dark clouds. Colonel Ron said, "Hope the storm holds off until chores are done. Believe I'll have the girls clean up around the entrance."

"Today's not a good day," Loretta replied.

"Excuse me?"

"Believe we should give Brooke a little time to herself."

"Time for what?"

"To adjust."

"Adjust to what?" probed the Colonel.

"Her period."

"Her period? She's never had a period?"

"Not in the 1800s."

"Ooooooohhh," he cringed. "So what *are* they gonna do?"

"Don't worry, I took care of it."

Sherri giggled.

I whispered, "It ain't funny, bitch."

Loretta had given me what she called a sanitary belt and a bag full of bath towels cut into pieces. The belt held the rags, folded and positioned to absorb menstrual bleeding. I felt sorry for myself, but more so for the millions of women who had to do this shit monthly in the past. The cramping was bad enough. The whole belt issue only added insult to injury.

Loretta continued. "I believe it's a good day for you to spend some time with Sherri. She wants to milk the cow and go fishing. And, you need to know, she feels disrespected because you refuse to call her by her name."

"My *mother's* name."

Loretta shook her head and said, "You're being childish. People have the same name. Besides, Sherri didn't choose hers. And she *is* a good girl. I can tell."

"Wow," I whispered to Sherri, "sounds like you've been sucking ass."

"Up yours," Sherri whispered back.

"You really want to milk the cow?"

"Why not? You did."

An hour later, I found myself alone in the bedroom. Colonel Ron and Sherri were off together. Loretta hung out downstairs doing God knows what. Probably cherishing a bit of free time. I lay on the bed missing Manhattan so much that I cried. *Wonder if Melanie has had her baby yet? Do they miss me? Doubt it.*

Reaching over, I slid open the bottom drawer of my nightstand to remove the roll of toilet tissue. Again, it bothered me that the darn thing wouldn't come all the way out. At home, I'd had similar problems. Overstuffing would force something to fall out the back, lodge underneath the drawer, and cause it to stick.

Curious, I removed the top drawer, which came out rather easily. Then, reaching behind the bottom drawer, I slid my hand underneath and felt something. *Voila!* Pushing the drawer in a little released tension and allowed me to slide the object out. Thousands of hairline cracks adorned the leather cover of some sort of book. It had no title. Goosebumps rose on my arms as I blew away dust. Opening the cover revealed cursive writing on musty pages, browned around the edges:

Elizabeth Pierce

Wednesday, April 19, 1876

I got this here diary for Christmas, but have never had anything worth writing in it. Today, I reckon I do. This morning, when I first laid eyes on John Crittenden, I knew he was different. I had just walked down the hill on Grayson Springs road on my way to work. Was hurrying across the Bear Creek footbridge and there he was, midpoint over the water, leaning on the rail, looking at something down the way. He wore blue military pants, suspenders, and a white shirt. When I said, Pardon me, he rose upright, but remained in the center of the walkway. Avoiding eye contact, I said, Could I pass please Sir? Instead of speaking down on me as I had commonly experienced from resort guests, he smiled, glanced past my ragged dress and worn shoes covered in road dust, and said, Anyone ever told you how pretty you are?

I melted inside as the words left his mouth. Struggling to speak, I said, Well thank you Sir. You are too kind. But my work bell has already rang, and I can ill afford to be late. Mr. Van Meter's done warned me once.

You work here at Grayson Springs? he asked, as if he didn't already know from my appearance. When I nodded, he said, Then I must accompany you to ensure Captain Van Meter that it was I who held you up.

For the first time I looked directly at his face and noticed something strange about his stare. It was as if only one eye looked at me. I told him, Hotel employees are not allowed to associate with guests. I will get into more trouble. Please Sir, just let me by.

Scurrying off the bridge, I could feel his stare. My insides fluttered strangely. After each room I cleaned today, I glanced about trying to catch sight of the man who made my heart race. By quitting time, I had given up. When I started back this way, there he was waiting at the bridge, this time wearing his blue army jacket and hat. He took his hat off, and acted all proper. He said, If I cannot walk you to work, surely I may walk you home.

No one appeared to be watching from the hotel, so I said, It is nearly two miles, mostly uphill.

Half way home, I couldn't be sure if Lieutenant John Jordan Crittenden III was pulling my leg or was actually a member of a very prominent family. He claimed that his grandfather had been the Governor of Kentucky, a U.S. Senator, the U.S. Attorney General, and Kentucky's State Treasurer.

I said, Sure, and my Daddy is the grandson of President Franklin Pierce.

Mr. Crittenden stopped dead in his tracks and asked, Do you believe I have lied to you?

I felt guilty and stood staring at his hurt expression.

After a moment of silence, he said, You can tell, can you not?

I was not sure what he meant, but then he told me that his right eye was not real. I found myself backing off a bit.

He told the story of how he lost his eye in a hunting accident out at Fort Abercrombie. Said a shotgun cartridge blew up in his face as he unloaded his gun. He said some doctor in Cincinnati took out his dead eye and replaced it with one made of glass.

I said, Oh my, while wondering if he had grown his full beard to cover scars.

The man said he came to Grayson Springs to relax for a few days.

I felt sorry for him and said so.

He told me I ought not feel sorry for him since he had already become accustomed to having only one eye. But he said he was a bit concerned about how it looks.

I told him, I will make you a deal. Will not feel sorry for you if you promise to not feel sorry for yourself. He grinned.

I could see relief on his face and a new lightness in his step as John continued to tell me about his father, Thomas, and his uncle, George. How both served as generals in the War, one for the north and one for the south. Man sure does love the military.

John told me he had been commissioned as a Second Lieutenant by President Grant himself, and would soon be heading west to fight Indians with the 7th Calvary.

By the end of our walk, I decided Mr. Crittenden is either the biggest liar on earth, or the most important man I have ever met. His flattery overwhelmed any feelings of distrust I might have had.

When we reached the gate in front of my house, he picked a wildflower. I could see Mamma staring out the window as John removed his hat, bowed and said, For you, my lady.

No one ever called me a lady before. Always been called little girl, or just girl, or perhaps young lady when Momma or Daddy gets mad.

When he asked if he could accompany me to the door, I warned, Not in that there blue uniform. Believe your uncle George would have been more to my daddy's liking.

After I told him I had to work again tomorrow, he assured me he would be present at the bridge. By then I could see three sets of eyes staring from the house windows. Leaving him at the gate, I made a point not to glance back before reaching the door. He was still looking and I waved before coming in. Then I watched him walk away and out of sight while trying to answer Momma's questions.

As I finished reading the first entry of what appeared to be a diary, I wondered how long it had been under the drawer. *1876. So long ago. Like history. Did the Pierce family donate the furniture?* Voices interrupted my daydreaming. Looking out the window, I could see Colonel Ron and Sherri returning from the barn. I placed the diary in my top drawer, under items, where it could be kept my secret.

When Sherri opened the door, she seemed to sense that I had just jumped into bed. For a few seconds, she stood silent.

"What?" I asked.

Shaking her head, she said, "Nothing ... how you feeling?"

"You have no idea. Now I truly know what it means to be *on the rag*."

"Gross. I think I smell you."

"It's in the potty thingy."

"What?"

"The rags ... the dirty ones."

"No way. What are you going to do with them?"

"Loretta says I have to wash them to reuse."

"No way."

Chapter 18

For lunch, Loretta had concocted a soup using leftover baked potatoes, cream, and spices. "Not bad," Sherri complimented.

"Glad you like it."

"Hard work makes anything taste good," chimed Colonel Ron.

"What's that supposed to mean," Loretta snapped with a frown.

"No. No. I didn't mean it that way. It *is* good, but I'm just saying that hard work creates a healthy appetite."

"Sounded like a Freudian slip to me," Loretta sassed, "especially considering no one did any work this morning." Noticing that I still hadn't taken a bite, she asked, "You okay, Brooke?"

"I'm good."

"I see ... no appetite?"

"Not real hungry." I leaned back in my chair and asked, "Colonel Ron, where is the Grayson Springs Road?"

A bit surprised, he answered, "It's a portion of State Road 1214 ... the road that runs in front of our entrance here. Starts just the other side of the creek."

"Does it run up a big hill?"

"Yes it does, but why would you ask?"

"Just curious."

Colonel Ron glanced at Loretta as if to say, *Where the hell did that come from?* Loretta shrugged her shoulders.

"Is it a dirt road?"

"Dirt road? Maybe a hundred years ago. It's blacktop now. Who's been talking to you about Grayson Springs Road?"

"No one," I answered honestly.

Thunder clapped in the distance. Colonel Ron said, "Sounds like a storm. Suddenly, raindrops began tapping on the metal roof of the back porch. Jumping up, he said, "Y'all give me a hand. Need to close windows. I'll get these down here."

Loretta started up the stairs with Sherri following. I said, "I'll get the front rooms."

"Just the end ones," suggested the Colonel as he headed toward his room. "The porches will protect the front and back windows."

I struggled with the window next to the fireplace as Colonel Ron reentered the lobby. "Here, let me help," he said. When he reached over my shoulder it felt creepy. I jumped, sucking wind and backing away several feet. Colonel Ron forced the window closed and then turned to face me. Instead of reacting to my behavior, he stepped to the door, opened it, and said calmly, "Wanna watch the rain?"

Following him onto the porch, I didn't know what to expect. Was he offended? Would he go into some sort of psycho-philosophical speech? The world outside was in a furry. Thunder roared. Sheets of water slid horizontally off the porch roof. Skies were dark, and for as far as I could see, trees rocked violently back and forth in the high winds.

Noticing my awe, Colonel Ron said, "Beautiful isn't it?"

"Oh my god! Is there going to be a tornado or something?"

"Hope not. Never can tell, though."

"Should we go in?"

"Are you afraid?"

I scanned the area again, looked back at the Colonel, and said, "Hell no. I think it's cool."

He pulled out an already rolled cigarette and lit it.

I said, "Guess in the old days, this was a form of entertainment."

"Still is, if you appreciate rain. In Manhattan, you can go without for six months. Here, no rain means nothing grows. No corn, beans, cucumbers, tobacco. No grass for the livestock. Farmers have to appreciate the rain." After a draw from his cigarette, he offered it my way.

"No thanks."

"Can I ask you a question, Brooke?"

Here it comes, I thought. "Sure, why not?"

"Why'd you ask about the Grayson Springs Road?"

Oh, that. Not wanting to reveal my source, I said, "Just curious."

"But how'd you know it was called the Grayson Springs Road?"

"That's two questions, Colonel. Let me ask you one?"

"Okay."

"Will you take me up the Grayson Springs Road?"

His forehead wrinkled and he said, "Only old timers refer to it as *the* Grayson Springs Road.... We might ride up that way."

"But I don't want to ride. I want to walk."

"Are you kidding? You wanna walk up that hill?"

"Just two miles."

Colonel Ron shook his head in disbelief. The whole conversation had him befuddled. "We'll see."

The screen door creaked open, and Sherri joined us. "What's up out here?"

"Just watching the rain," I replied.

Loretta stepped out and said, "It's a mess, isn't it?"

"Not if you truly appreciate the rain."

The Colonel's eyebrows rose. Winds shifted and rain began blowing in on the porch. "Believe we best go in." He went through the door first, followed by Sherri.

Before entering, Loretta tapped my shoulder and said, "By the way, Sherri says your room stinks. There's a nail on the right side of the outhouse. Hang your bucket on it until we get a chance to clean those rags.

Being sarcastic, I used my best hick voice and said, "Round here, we *cleans* fish, and we *wash* our rags."

Loretta shook her head. "Guess I deserved that. Just go get the bucket."

"Alright already."

As I started in, Loretta stopped me again. "Colonel Ron still giving you cigarettes?"

"No ma'am. He says I have to quit."

In Kentucky, weather systems blow up quick, but rarely last long. Twenty minutes after the storm started, the wind calmed and the sun began to shine. Colonel Ron told us to re-open our windows and then meet him at the creek near the barn.

"What for?" asked Sherri.

"Just hurry and do as I say, please."

Loretta seemed to know what was coming as we all gathered at the creek. Colonel Ron said, "I want you to stand quietly and listen."

"Listen to what?" asked the ever-inquisitive Sherri.

"LA, you talk too much."

Loretta shook her head.

Colonel Ron continued, "Obviously, if you listen quietly, you'll be able to answer your own question."

Sherri and I stood puzzled, staring back and forth, waiting for whatever it was the Colonel wanted us to hear. To that point it was nothing more than the breeze circulating through trees, tiny raindrops dripping from their leaves, birds whistling unique calls to one another, insects buzzing, and the gentle trickle of water running down the creek. Then suddenly Sherri's expression changed. She heard it first. Then I noticed the odd rustling, almost percussive sound coming from up-creek.

"What is it?" I asked.

"Is it alive?" sounded Sherri.

"Just keep an eye up the creek," urged Colonel Ron, "and remember—few people get to see this."

As the sound grew closer, it became louder. We stood dazed, as if expecting some prehistoric dinosaur to come crashing through the woods at any second. Then, there it was. Coming around the curve in the creek some fifty yards away was a wall of water as wide as the creek bed and two feet tall, splashing violently, covering everything in its path. In a matter of seconds, the creek that had been little more than a trickle became thirty feet wide and two feet deep.

"Wow!" exclaimed Sherri.

"Oh my god!" I added. "It's a tidal wave!"

Colonel Ron said, "Not quite," as the water flooded past carrying woody debris, "but it is dangerous. If you happen to be in its path, it'll wash you away. People drown every year when they get caught in the backwater." Sherri seemed infatuated with what was going on.

"So," I asked, "why is this happening?"

"What do you think, LA?" the Colonel asked. "I see your mind working over there. Got it figured out yet?"

Looking upstream, she said, "This is the water coming off those hills. It flows down from different contributories and hits the creek pretty much all at once, building along the way. Probably won't last too long."

"Not since the rain quit suddenly," explained the Colonel. "But when it rains for a while, the creek keeps rising, sometimes over the banks, and stays that way for days. Years ago, before the roads and bridges were built, people got cut off from the outside world. That's why they needed footbridges."

I looked back at the Inn and said, "Why did they build the Inn where it is? Didn't they realize the water would be an issue?"

Loretta answered, "Honey, they built Grayson Springs where it is because of the springs. It was the springs that people came for. They thought they had healing powers. Therefore, it only made sense to build the resort close to the springs. Notice it has a stone foundation. Water would have to cover the whole yard and that field out yonder before it could get up into the floor."

Sherri asked, "Why do you call it a resort?"

"In its heyday, Grayson Springs was considered a resort. It had several structures large enough to house hundreds. The grounds provided visitors with all sorts of entertainment along with the endless supply of healing waters. Most of it burned down. All that's left now are the few spring houses and this old Inn."

I listened to what Loretta said, while staring up the hill toward the area that once held Camp Grayson Springs, the military outpost. Then I turned back to the water and said quietly, "I've seen this before."

Colonel Ron said, "Excuse me. Say again."

Instead of speaking, I simply gave him the look.

Chapter 19

That night at supper, I asked, "Are there any books here that I can read?"

Loretta looked at the Colonel and said, "We shoulda thought of that."

"What sort of reading would you like?" asked Colonel Ron.

"J.K. Rowling would be nice."

"1800s," reminded the Colonel.

"Are you kidding? We can only read stuff from the 1800s?"

"Or before."

"Did they even write back then?"

Sherri's jaw dropped. "You're not serious? You've never read *Heidi*, or *Little Women*?"

"Not really."

Colonel Ron leaned back in his chair and said, "There's plenty titles from those days that you should recognize. How about *Moby Dick* or *Tom Sawyer*?"

"Or Edgar Allen Poe?" added Sherri.

"Poe is from that era," agreed the Colonel. "I'd have to research to see if he'd been published in book form.... Brooke, have you read *Uncle Tom's Cabin*?"

"A—no—but the title does sound familiar."

"I have," Sherri bragged.

On the second floor, at the south end of the hall, Colonel Ron used a skeleton key to open a door. He carried an oil lantern as Sherri and I followed. The room appeared to be like an attic—dark, hot and musty.

Gusts of air and dim planes of light bled in through the broken sideboards and the vents at the gable end. Shadows rotated as Colonel Ron turned with the lantern. Sherri said, "This place is creepy," while observing her dust-covered surroundings—a freestanding mirror, a dilapidated wooden rocker, an open box of blue-colored Mason jars, a wooden storage chest secured by a large bronzed padlock, and two dozen or more wooden crates filled with who knows what.

Colonel Ron moved next to a sheet-covered group of crates. "Hold this," he ordered, handing me the lantern. I immediately turned, looking around. "Stay still please. I need to see."

"Excuuuusssse me."

Sherri moved next to the Colonel. "What're you looking for?"

While pulling away the sheet, Colonel Ron said, "A book. Something for Brooke to read. One I'm sure *you'll* find interesting. I saw it some time back while scavenging through this stuff."

From the crate, Colonel Ron removed an old cigar box. "Check this out," he said, opening its lid. Inside were two fat pencils, a six-inch ruler, an eraser, and a few copper paper clips. You girls ever use one of these in school?"

"One of what?" I asked.

"A cigar box."

"For what?"

The Colonel smiled and said, "Actually, it's a little before my time. My parents said they used these things to hold their school supplies."

"They didn't have backpacks?"

"Not hardly."

"May I see it?" asked Sherri.

Colonel Ron handed over the box and continued removing items from the crate. I stood quietly holding the lantern steady.

"Ahhh, here it is," announced the Colonel as he pulled out a weathered book. Rubbing dust from its cover, he said, "Check it out."

Sherri set down the cigar box and centered her attention on the small hardback book. Its edges were partially frayed, the cover illustration barely decipherable—water lilies in a pond and some sort of plant. At the top of the spine it had the image of a plant—some sort of flower—and the words UNCLE TOM'S CABIN and H.B. STOWE.

"Are you shitting me?" squealed Sherri. "Tell me this is not like an original copy? It's got to be worth a fortune."

"Welll111, not exactly. I checked. It's like a reprint from 1898. The original copies were printed in 1852 and were a two volume set. They're worth thousands. This one is probably worth less than a hundred dollars. It is valuable to me however, just to have something that old. As you'll notice inside, it was given as a Christmas gift to someone named Ralph B. Lyon, by his teacher. Brooke, I believe you will find this interesting to read."

"Uncle ... Tom's ... Cabin?" In my mind, I thought, *have I read this before*? "You're not afraid I'll mess it up by reading it?"

"I've already paged through it. Don't believe it'll fall apart. I trust you'll take good care."

"I will.... Colonel, what's in the chest?" As I spoke, both Colonel Ron and Sherri turned their attention toward the chest. I stepped closer and suddenly the lantern's light fell on the bulky wooden box. It had metal edges and some fancy designs in the wood. Obviously, someone had cleaned much of the dust off of it lately.

"Mostly clothes. I found that old chest buried among all these crates. It was shoved so far back you couldn't even see it until I began going through things. The crates covered with sheets are the ones I've been through. Mostly junk, but who knows what might be hidden in them. I mean, *Uncle Tom's Cabin* is no small find."

Nor is the diary of Elizabeth Pierce. "Can you open the chest?"

"Not right now. I don't have the key on me. Had to pick the old lock to get in it. The lock that's on it is one I found downstairs in a drawer. And it's only got one key."

Sunset at Grayson Springs meant bedtime since there was really nothing else to do. Tired from another day's activity, Sherri welcomed the comfort of her feather mattress. I came into the dimly lit room carrying my porcelain potty.

"I swear when I get home, I'll never complain about my period again. If the girls at school knew what I just did they'd die."

"Where'd you clean them?" Sherri asked.

"In the creek. Just squatted on a big rock and washed them in the water."

"Gross, you bloodied up the creek."

"The water was going by so fast, you couldn't even tell it."

"Still nasty."

"Truthfully, once you get past the idea of what you are doing, it's not that bad."

"Should be a while before I have to deal with it."

"What do you mean? Don't you have periods?"

"I've got the patch."

"No way," I spoke in disbelief. "How'd you manage that?"

"Had it on already. Figured if they'd make me give up my bra, they'd take my patch as well, so I made sure not to turn it towards Loretta in the caboose."

"Hell, I didn't see it either."

"Don't see how you missed it. I saw you checking me out."

"Where's it at?"

"On my hip." Sherri raised her gown enough to expose the patch that stuck to her left hip.

"Guess I was too busy looking at your boobs. You were making such a big deal."

"Oh, by the way. Sorry about the comment I made."

"You mean about me being small."

"Yeah."

"Don't worry about it. I'm used to it."

"You could have implants."

I placed my hands on my chest, sized myself up and said, "Maybe someday. My Aunt Ruth says I'm better off without them. Hers hurt her back and shoulders."

"Guys love 'em."

"Hmmph."

Sherri rolled over and said, "Maybe you *don't* need implants."

I thought, *Bitch*, and then used a match to light the oil lamp on my nightstand. "You mind if I read?"

"Not at all. Late in the afternoon of a chilly day in February..."

"Excuse me?"

"Uncle Tom's Cabin," yawned the sleepy Sherri, still facing away.

I picked up the old book, opened it and thought out loud, "Wonder who Ralph B. Lyon is?"

"Was, you mean," mumbled Sherri. "He's long dead by now."

The pages were browned by time, darkest around the edges. In my mind, I created an image of some young kid named Ralph, reading this same copy by lamplight more than a century ago. On its title page were the words

UNCLE TOM'S CABIN

-OR-

LIFE AMONG THE LOWLY

-BY-

HARRIET BEECHER STOWE

SIEGEL, COOPER CO.,

NEW YORK.   CHICAGO.

On the next page I began reading the PREFACE:

The scenes of this story, as the title indicates, lie among a race hitherto ignored by the associations of polite and refined society;....

After skimming through the Preface and the biography of Harriet Beecher Stowe, I came to the first chapter and read, **Late in the afternoon of a chilly day in February...** "Are you kidding me? You are such a geek. You were quoting the first line."

Sherri, already asleep, didn't answer. I continued reading and nearly became nauseous at my introduction to the real world of slavery. In one short chapter of *Uncle Tom's Cabin*, I realized why blacks in America have such a hard time overcoming their past—their horrid past. The sheer thought of an otherwise distinguished man named Shelby, considering Tom, or Harry the little boy, or Eliza, his mother, as property fit to be bought or sold. And for the first time in my life, I saw the word *nigger* used in its original context, as a derogatory title for a black person, who was considered to be a lesser human being, someone's property. I wondered why they don't make all kids read this.

For a moment, I stared at Sherri's sleeping bulk, wondering how reading such a book had affected her. Sickened by the reading, I slid open the top drawer of my nightstand and quietly exchanged one 19th century writer for another. Harriet Beecher Stowe for Elizabeth Pierce. Relaxing back into my pillow, I opened the worn diary to its second entry and read:

Saturday, April 20, 1876

Got up earlier this morning. Daddy was out feeding stock while Momma made coffee and fried bacon. I stepped in just as she poured a cup. She asked me why I was up so early.

Told her I was having trouble sleeping so I figured I might as well get up.

She asked if my not sleeping had something to do with that young man come walking me home yesterday.

I said, Oh Momma.

She said, Do not oh Momma me. She went on and on about beau stuff and it went in one ear and out the other cause I done heard it all before. She never made mention of it to Daddy at breakfast and I was glad. The youngins were dying to tell on me, but it seemed Mamma musta warned them they best not.

When I left the house a bit early for work Momma glanced me a look and said I best behave.

For some reason my trip down the Grayson Springs road seemed much different this morning. I swear they was more birds singing than usual. The sky clear as a bell and the only bad part of the walk was me a worrying whether or not I would actually get to see John. On my way past the Haycraft place Hershel stopped his plow mule. His boys followed behind him picking up rocks and arrowheads. He hollered Good morning and asked were I not a bit early this morning.

When I said Yes sir, he wanted to know if it had anything to do with that Yankee he seen walking me home yesterday?

I do swear there are no secrets in Grayson County. I hollered, Tell Anna Hi and then walked on ignoring his comment.

When I reached the bottom of the hill old man Clemons was sitting out front of the store smoking a cigar. I greeted him and I swear if he didn't ask me if I wasn't a bit early? Sometimes I think Daddy has the whole world spying on me. I went on up to the porch and gave him a big hug like I usually do on Sunday mornings on the way home from church.

I told him I had me a big day at the hotel and figured maybe I ought to start a bit early. After brushing off his suspicions I headed toward the creek and there he was bigger than life, John, standing right smack in the middle of that bridge just like he was yesterday. Bet a dollar he heard me talking to Mr. Clemons.

It felt like I was floating in the air when I walked out to where he stood. John rose up from the rail and looked my way. He took off his hat and bowed in a gentlemanly way while he said Good morning to you Miss Pierce. You have just made a beautiful day better.

And so have you I thought while seeing how handsome he looked in his brown trousers and white shirt. Even looked as though he might have trimmed the frill off his beard.

He pulled out his pocket watch and looked at it and said I hoped you would arrive early so we might spend some time together before you have to work. Seems my prayer has just been answered.

Looking toward the hotel I told him to follow me. I passed him and moved quickly to the other end of the bridge. He joined me and then I led him past the hotel and on out to the springs. Figured no one would be out there that early and I had always dreamed of walking them paths with a man like I often seen distinguished women folk from the cities do. We went from spring to spring and I told him how much prettier it would be in a month or so when the flowers all bloom. When we reached the last spring John looked up that path that goes into the woods up toward the old military outpost and then he asked me if I ever been up there?

I said nope. Hear tell they ain't much to see.

He said he walked up there yesterday and that I was correct cause he did not see much of interest. He said he did however find a natural bench in the woods, and thought perhaps we could sit there a while and talk.

Thinking them woods out of site would be best anyway I submitted to his desire. When we started into them trees and up the hill John reached for my hand as if I could not make it on my own but I feel sure it was just an excuse. My hand in his felt like new butter on a hot potato and I coulda fainted except it would have ended our walk. He led me off the path to the big rock that he found to be of interest. He said it had broken off the ledge further uphill. When it rolled downhill it landed against a beech tree. The edge that broke off was sticking up and looked like a bench. He believed that at one time, Indians had used it to grind acorns since it had a hole drilled nearly through it.

We sat there long as I could. John did most the talking telling stories about growing up in Frankfort being a Grandson of a Governor and all the things he got to see and do. I was in heaven. Down that hill behind me sat that old hotel and all that work I had no desire to do. In front of me were all them trees and birds and that warm breeze hitting me in the face. After about thirty minutes my work bell rang and I had to go. John looked at his watch and asked might we meet again later when I get off?

I said People already talking. They see you walking me up that hill again someone will likely go straight to my daddy.

He asked me why that would be such a problem.

I told him I do not know for sure that it would be but could see no real reason to take that chance. Not just yet. Daddy thinks every boy looks at me is trying to give him a grandchild. He says I am not to court nobody until I reach 16.

John said And you are not? I about died. Knew right then he thought I was older. Said he was soon gonna be 22. All I could see in my mind was him taking back calling me a lady and starting to consider me a little girl, like everybody else.

So when he asked me when I was gonna be 16, I told him August 31st, and he said that was close enough.

My heart about exploded.

Chapter 20

Saturday morning at home usually meant sleeping in until nearly noon. At Grayson Springs the rooster had no calendar, and that particular morning its crow was echoed by Bruno's barking. Someone was coming.

"Give me a break," complained the sleepy-eyed Sherri.

I rolled up from the bed enough to raise the blind, and then I peeked out at soft light bleeding through an almost eerie, misty fog. Bruno stood near the flagpole, facing toward the entrance, bellowing some sort of distress. Then, flashing through the cedars, came the horse drawn carriage that could only be Ben and Charlotte. But they weren't alone. Behind them a single rider, wearing a white shirt, dark suspenders, and a wide-brimmed hat, rode a huge black horse. Clip-clopping of hooves and the carriage's rattling drew Sherri's attention. "Who is it?" she asked.

"Looks like Ben and Charlotte, and some new guy on a horse."

"Really?" chimed Sherri. "Young or old?"

"Hold on a second ... it's foggy out, like the first day ... remember?"

Sherri twisted herself out of bed, and joined me at the window just in time to catch a glimpse of the newcomer at the end of the building. The carriage had already pulled under the porch as indicated by the sound of hooves on the brick surface. "Damn, I missed him."

"Let's go down," I suggested.

"Like this?" Sherri complained, looking into the old mirror on her dresser.

After getting dressed, I went downstairs and into the kitchen, where pleasant conversation filled the room. "Good morning," said Loretta. "Didn't have to push you out of bed *this* morning."

After a week of Grayson Springs' solitude, why wouldn't I look forward to seeing someone new? Sherri arrived moments later, spruced up nicely for the unexpected guest. The new guy had removed his hat, revealing shoulder-length, sandy brown hair. Unlike Ben, he had no facial hair. Though he looked strong, his blue eyes sparkled with kindness as he scanned the room. *Are there gay guys in the Amish community?*

Colonel Ron said, "Y'all know Ben and Charlotte. This is Ben's brother, Eli. After Sherri smiled and I nodded a sleepy hello, the Colonel motioned around the room, introducing everyone. "Eli, this is Brooke Green from New York, and ... and Sherri Lynn Reid from Los Angeles."

I could see the joy on Sherri's face at being referred to by her name instead of LA. She sort of curtsied toward the Colonel and then said, "It's nice to meet you Eli."

Eli nodded his reply without speaking. Less interested in the newcomer than the smell of bacon already sizzling in Loretta's iron skillet, I went to Charlotte, who sat drinking a cup of coffee. "How's the baby machine coming along?"

"Growing."

"You look swollen."

"Just got that way of late."

I said, "Might not be getting enough fluids."

"Believe fluids are what's causin' me to swell. Besides, I'm gettin' plenty of fluids." As she spoke, Charlotte held up her coffee cup."

"But that's the wrong kind of fluids," I advised. "Caffeine's a diuretic. Dehydrates you."

Charlotte asked, "If I have too much fluid, why wouldn't I want to dehydrate?"

By now, Ben and Eli had approached, interested in the conversation, and everyone in the room listened. I continued, "I know it seems that way, but if you're not getting enough fluids, your body will automatically start retaining fluid, thus the swelling. I say get off the coffee, start drinking a lot of water, and hopefully you'll see a difference."

"And you know this because?" questioned Ben.

Offended by his tone, I said, "Bi-o-lo-gy and Chem-is-try." Ben seemed equally offended by my sarcasm and it made me feel bad. "Sorry, I didn't mean it that way."

During breakfast, Eli and Ben walked outside. Sherri asked, "They leaving already?"

"They're on their way to the barn," replied the Colonel. "Eli's gonna shoe Becca."

"Shoe Becca?"

"He's a farrier … takes care of horse's feet. Trims their hooves and then shoes 'em."

"He gives horse pedicures?"

"Do what?" I questioned.

Loretta glared. "Yes Sherri, you could say that."

After Eli shoed the old mare, Ben saddled her and rode her back to the Inn. Eli followed on his gelding. Everyone gathered near the flagpole. Colonel Ron announced, "Okay ladies—I know you both had a chance to ride already, but there's still a few things you should know about horses and their equipment. Since Eli's here, I'm gonna let him be the teacher."

I whispered, "You mean he's going to talk."

Sherri leaned into my ear and said, "He can teach me anything he wants."

Instead of answering, I stood silent, staring at Eli's hands as he raised the stirrup and loosened the cinch strap exactly as I had on day one. When the saddle was free, he pulled it from Becca's back and tossed it onto the ground. Then, turning, he said, "I'll say this quick. Anyone has a question, stop me…. Horses, like anything else, come in male and female. When it's born, it's a foal. After it's weaned, we call the male a colt and the female a filly, up until they're three years old. Then we call the colt a stallion or a stud, unless we geld it at which time it becomes a gelding. After three years old, the filly becomes a mare."

When Sherri raised her hand, Eli pointed her way.

"What's geld mean?"

"To geld a horse is to castrate it."

"Why would you do that?"

"Mostly to settle it down. Same as with cattle. If you don't make steers out of the male bovine, they'll fight. Castrate 'em and they become docile. All they do is eat and grow. Bigger they get, the more money they bring at market. Like the steer, a gelding becomes calm, not so aggressive toward the mares, and much easier to train."

"So a steer and a gelding are the same thing?" Sherri continued.

"Same procedure, different species. Bulls become steers. Horses become geldings. "

"How do you do it?"

"For a horse, I use anesthesia to put the animal to sleep. Then it's a simple surgical procedure that takes maybe five minutes at most."

"Sounds soooo cruel."

"Not really," Ben replied. "It's no different than neutering a dog or cat. The animal doesn't realize what's going on and there's very little or no pain involved."

"Did the bull tell you that?"

While everyone giggled, I said, "Your horse is much bigger than Becca. Is it because you cut his nuts off?"

Colonel Ron and Ben shook their heads. I'm sure Eli heard me speak, but he seemed distracted. I waited for an answer as he stood, staring at my eyes, of course. Finally, he blinked, realized his state, and said, "I'm sorry. What was your question?"

"I, I asked is your horse so big because you cut his—"

"Oh yea," Eli interrupted, still staring. "Not really. He's just a larger breed. Horses don't necessarily get bigger when cut."

"Okay now," complained Colonel Ron. "Let's get on with the lesson."

Over the next twenty minutes, Eli pointed out and described all the tack associated with horses—saddle, bridle, blankets, harness, etc.

Becca stood patiently as Sherri and I each saddled, bridled, mounted, dismounted, and then stripped her again. Finally, it came time for us to ride. Eli mounted Becca and began walking her in a circle around us.

"See how I am sitting up straight, holding the reins loosely," instructed Eli. "You have to get used to squeezing with your knees … heels down, toes up."

Sherri said, "Looks easy."

"Actually, it is after you get used to it.... Now then, I'm gonna speed her up a bit so I can explain what we call *sitting the trot*. Until you learn this, trotting will beat you to death."

Colonel Ron said, "It's what I referred to as *posting*."

Eli *click-clicked* with his tongue and Becca jumped to a trot. Simultaneously, our instructor went into some sort of gyrations on the saddle.

Sherri sighed, "Oh my god ... oh, my god."

I whispered, "You are such a weirdo."

"You telling me that doesn't excite you?"

"Shut up, I'm trying to pay attention."

Eli continued, "What you have to do is consciously feel the horse's up and down motion. Feel it in the saddle. Keep your shoulders over your hips and lean forward and back with the rhythm. If you try to wait on gravity to pull you into the saddle, it'll be too late. You'll have to contract and relax the muscles in your hips along with the rhythm."

Sherri whispered, "How about it Brooke? Ever had a contraction between your hips?"

"Sure. About a hundred times while I was riding Becca."

"Liar."

"Pervert."

Eventually it was our turn to ride. Sherri went first. Eli held the end of a twenty-foot lunge line as Becca walked the same circle as before. After two rounds, he said, "Now, I'm going to speed 'er up. Try to sit the trot."

Seconds later, Sherri was bumping up and down terribly in the saddle. I watched to see Eli's reaction as her bra failed miserably. He seemed immune. *Is this guy gay?*

"Thi-i-is i-i-is a-a li-i-ittle ha-a-ard-er..." Sherri tried to speak while bouncing around the circle. I couldn't watch her. My eyes were on Eli. For the moment, he was locked onto Sherri. Eventually she got the hang of posting.

When it was my turn, I leaned close to Loretta and whispered, "I can't do this."

"And why not?" she replied.

"Do you have any idea what this shit between my legs felt like when I was on that saddle?"

"Oh," she replied. "Forgot about that.... Eli, I believe we'll have to wait on Brooke's lesson. She has female issues today."

"Gross," I whispered. "You didn't have to say that."

Eli bowed his head slightly and said, "It's no problem. I understand. We can do it another time."

I felt he truly did understand.

Chapter 21

.....It was dark when I woke to someone's touch. The hand was rough, moving up my leg. When it slid past my knee, I began growling and went off on one of the ugly people.....

Uuuggghhh! I woke in a sweat, heart beating wildly. I'd been shaken awake. It was dark, and without thinking, I grabbed the shaker, rolled over quickly, and struck blindly.

"Stop it, Brooke! Stop it!" Sherri's muffled pleas broke my trance. "What the hell is wrong with you?"

Suddenly realizing who, what and where I was, I released my grip, slid off, and curled into a fetal position next to my frightened roommate. Details of my dream faded into the same old questions and frustrations I'd dealt with all my life. Sherri remained still, listening as I cried. My body rocked back and forth while I wept. After a minute, Sherri rolled over, embracing me. I did not resist. Eventually, my breathing subsided and I slept.

With the rooster crowing, I woke again, still in Sherri's grasp. Loretta stood in the doorway, arms crossed, staring. "Can't believe this," she spoke, disappointedly. "You broke the rules."

"It's not what you think," I pleaded, rising in the bed.

"Sherri! Wake your sorry ass up!"

My roommate stretched, and then rolled over, revealing her bruised face.

"What the hell?" Loretta asked.

Oh my god, I thought. *I did that.*

Sherri and I prepared breakfast alone as Loretta and Colonel Ron powwowed on the back porch. When I tried to speak, Sherri said, "Shhhhh," while rising and moving closer to the screen door. I joined her and we listened.

"She says Brooke was having a terrible nightmare. When she tried to wake her in the dark, Brooke attacked. We're lucky it's not worse."

"We'll have to separate them."

"No. You can't do that. If Sherri's not complaining, why should we? Can't you see ... they've connected?"

Colonel Ron said, "I'll have to talk to them both, individually."

Breakfast involved little or no dialogue. The Colonel appeared to be contemplating my demise. Loretta seemed satisfied to remain silent. When he had finished eating, Colonel Ron said, "Brooke, while I do not want to overreact on this situation, you must understand my concern for Sherri's safety."

"It's okay," Sherri interrupted.

"For you, maybe it is, but for the rest of us, it's not." Then looking at me, he said, "Loretta and I have a responsibility here. How can I be sure you will not seriously hurt someone?"

"I don't know what to say."

"The only way I am going to feel comfortable with this is if we begin a more in-depth conversation about your problems."

Rising from my chair, I leaned against the counter, looking out the window. Suddenly, everything before me seemed orchestrated. Leaves on the trees, swaying in the morning breeze, were in perfect harmony, each one a unique part of something large. A redbird perched on top of the dinner bell, head cocked back, singing its own beautiful version of "where are you lover" to a nearby duller version of itself. Cumulus clouds were slowly drifting by in flawless formation like a marching band in a parade, playing a song called "Fair-Weather Day." My heart beat rapidly and I felt a sense of belonging as though I were a part of it all, one perfect little piece in a beautiful gigantic jigsaw puzzle. I wiped my eyes dry, turned, and said, "Do you all know how much I care about you? In these few days, you've become more my family than anyone at home. I really *do* feel bad about hurting you, Sherri. And then what did you do? You held me. You wrapped your arms around me and held me as I slept. No one has ever done that.... I feel bad that I disappointed you, Colonel. You do seem to want to help me and Sherri. You treat Loretta like a lady, and she treats me like ... like I imagine a good mother treats her daughter. These are things that have been missing in my life. Things I need.... I know this is all temporary, but in a few weeks, when it ends, at least I'll know there are people out there who can treat one another caringly." Looking at Colonel Ron and Loretta, I said, "I know you are getting paid to do all this, but for now, I'd like to know ... I have to know ... do you people really care about me?"

By the time I finished speaking, we were all in tears. When I turned back to the window, they got up and came to me. I had been in group hugs at school, but never one like the one in that kitchen. Colonel Ron squeezed so tight it hurt, but I said nothing. In Manhattan, my friend Darleen had once described her baptism. How she went under the water one person and came out another, saved, reborn into a world of faith. At Grayson Springs, I felt saved.

Loretta volunteered to help Sherri with cleanup in the kitchen. Colonel Ron said he and I needed to take a walk. I dreaded what I knew would be the start of question after question.

"Where are we going?" I asked, following Colonel Ron across the creek and then away from the barn.

"You said you wanted to walk up the Grayson Springs Road."

My heart jumped. I skipped closer to the Colonel, hugged him, and said, "I love you."

He didn't answer, but I knew he loved me too.

When we reached the spot where I had joined Colonel Ron and Ben days earlier in planning the footbridge, I stopped and began surveying.

"What's wrong?"

"Nothing," I answered. "Just trying to see in my mind how this looked years ago."

"Hasn't changed that much."

"But there was a footbridge here."

"Yes, we already talked about that."

For a moment, I imagined being Elizabeth Pierce, and that the Colonel was John Jordan Crittenden III. "Okay Lieutenant, lets walk."

"Lieutenant?" asked the confused Colonel.

I began walking a pathway that in my mind was the right direction. Several steps later, the Colonel had not moved. He stood staring at me. "Now what?" I asked.

"How you know that's the right way?"

"Is it?"

"Yes," he answered while stepping toward me.

"Then don't ask how I knew."

When we passed an old boarded up building, I professed, "This used to be a store."

Grinning, he said, "Yes, it did."

After crossing State Road 88, we began our ascent up the asphalt version of the old Grayson Springs Road. Rolling hills of hardwoods and pastures dotted with cattle stretched as far as my excited eyes could see. I knew our walk involved more than just satisfying my curiosity. Therefore, I wasn't surprised when the Colonel began his inquiry. "If you were in my shoes, how many broken rules would it take before you eliminated someone from the program?"

"If *I* were in *your* shoes, Colonel, I would first analyze the results of the behavior ... before passing judgment."

"Had I judged, you would be on a plane home already. And as for analyzing, I've been trying to be your friend, not just your psychologist. I expect you get plenty of that at home."

"I do."

"And?"

"Believe it or not, Colonel, I *am* smart enough to realize that I need help in understanding my problems. I want to know why I feel the way I do and what I can do about it. When you said we need to have a more in-depth conversation, I was glad.... I came here hoping to talk abo—"

An approaching car distracted my line of thought. The driver waved.

"You know them?" I asked.

"Yes."

Another car passed and the driver waved.

"You know everyone here?"

"Wouldn't matter if I knew them or not. People in the country just wave out of friendly respect."

"Oh."

"Brooke, you're avoiding my question. How many broken rules before you would eliminate someone from the program?"

"Rules? Plural? I see. Loretta must have told you that we were sleeping together."

"Yesssss."

"Do you really think we were doing something wrong?"

"I've already heard LA's version of what was going on."

"So, what exactly do you want from me?"

"Can we speak—uh—man to man here?"

I turned, began walking backwards, facing Colonel Ron, and said, "Sure. What's on your mind, buddy?"

"Can you describe the ugly people?"

I stopped walking. "Look around Colonel. I was five, maybe six years old when I left Kentucky. Yet I feel more at home here than in New York after twelve years. I believe ... I know I was born somewhere in these hills. Sometimes I go to sleep trying to remember my parents ... or anything about my youth. The only things that come to mind are the people who did ugly things to me. I see some things here that I remember as though I've seen them before. But it's not possible. When I was little I was never allowed to leave the place where I lived. At least not that I can recall. They never took me to church, or anywhere. I think I went to school one day. And I'm sure you already know how that turned out. I barely remember leaving that awful place when Daddy, Dr. Green, finally took me away. And it was dark that night. I don't remember much except that it was pitch black. His headlights shined through the darkness and we went up ... up a long hill in the woods. I was so glad to get away from that place and the people who laughed at me ... touched me in ways no child should ever be touched. If you wonder why I attacked Sherri last night, I was dreaming of the ugly people. She woke me up in the dark, and I thought it was part of my dream. I did what I did when I was a little girl."

"Your fighting?"

"You know what, Colonel ... I think I do want to talk to you as my psychologist, for a moment, in that I do not want what I say to you to be repeated."

"You speak with confidentiality."

"Not even Loretta?"

"If that is your wish."

I stared directly into Colonel Ron's eyes, as if reassuring my trust in him. Then, turning away, I asked, "Would it surprise you to know that I am still a virgin?"

"All things considered, no, it would not surprise me."

Turning back to him, I snapped, "Why? Because you think I'm gay?"

"I do not know that."

"But you think it. Colonel, if I were not a fighter I might have lost my virginity at age five. God did not give me a father or a mother to protect me. Not even a brother or a sister. I had to do it all on my own. The very people entrusted to protect me were ugly to me, and they left me alone with kids older than me who held me down and took my clothes off and touched me all over. When I got a chance to hurt one of them, I did, and it felt good. Better than anything I'd ever done before. After that, I talked to no one and no one touched me. They wouldn't even brush my hair. I figured they were afraid of me. Afraid I would come to them in their sleep and hurt them. Somehow, their fear made me feel safe."

"No one has ever held you kindly and made you feel safe?"

Fighting tears, I said, "Last night someone held me. Last night, someone held me ... kindly. Last night I felt safe."

"Your parents. They never held you?"

"My parents ... they don't even hold each other."

The Colonel's eyes watered. That moment reassured me that Loretta's assessment of him was accurate. He was a good man, a man to trust. Another car coming down the road broke the trance between us. Colonel Ron pulled out two cigarettes. The car passed. We both waved and then smoked while walking. At the top of the hill I asked, "How far have we come?"

"Almost two miles, I'd say."

In the distance there were structures. I pointed and asked, "Is there a house up there?"

"Yes."

"May we go that far before turning back?"

A metal mailbox rested on top of a wooden post near the gate of a dilapidated picket-fence. On it were the barely readable letters M. E. White. Wildflowers grew along the front of the fence. I picked one, bowed to Colonel Ron, and said, "For you, my lady."

"Excuse me?"

The house sat in bad repair, its metal roof rusty and bent in places; wood siding peeled as if it hadn't been painted in decades. Weeds grew wild in places likely once groomed. Gutters hung awkwardly under the weight of a broken oak branch. Further back, a barn leaned as if it might fall at any moment. Closing my eyes, I could feel the same spring breeze that brushed the face of Elizabeth Pierce 132 years earlier. Colonel Ron's aftershave sparked my imagination. In my mind, I allowed him to be my Lieutenant John Jordan Crittenden III. I could almost feel the presence of Elizabeth Pierce's mother staring from the window.

"Since we came this far, I should at least say hello," opened my eyes. Colonel Ron was waving at someone who stared from the window.

"Who is that?"

The door opened and a pitiful looking old woman stood gazing out. Colonel Ron waved again and said, "Howdy Mrs. White."

The old woman stepped outside and toward the gate with a stronger stride than her elderly, un-groomed appearance would suggest. "Long time no see, Ronnie Lee. And who is your young friend here?"

"Mrs. White, this is Brooke."

As she reached the gate, I said, "It's good to meet you, ma'am."

"Nice to meet you.... Lord have mercy," spat the old woman, backing off as if she'd seen a ghost.

My head tilted. "Mrs. White, do you know me?"

Squinting suspiciously, the old woman asked, "Ronnie Lee, where on earth did you find this girl?"

"Excuse me?" he asked.

"I could never forget them eyes, and that red hair? Been what, ten, twelve years ago? It's gotta be her. You know she come outa them flats."

The Colonel stood silent.

Mrs. White continued. "Ronnie Lee, don't you act like you don't know who this girl is. Hear tell she ain't nothin' but trouble. Why'd you bring her here?"

Apparently confused by the old woman's knowledge of me, Colonel Ron said, "Mrs. White, it sure is good to see you again. Believe we best continue our walk now."

"But she knows who I am," I pleaded.

"Come on Brooke.... Brooke!"

The Colonel and I had only walked a short distance when Mrs. White, still at the gate, shouted, "You be careful, Ronnie Lee."

"Careful of what?" I asked, walking backwards, staring at the woman.

Colonel Ron did not answer, but kept walking.

I shouted back, "Do you know about someone named Elizabeth Pierce?"

The old woman looked shocked. Then, strangely, she raised her hand and waved as if saying goodbye. Confused, I waved back and then continued with the Colonel. We walked silently for the next hundred yards. He stopped at the entrance to a barely visible dirt road. Running downhill from the blacktop, it had grown up with weeds, and showed very few signs of being traveled. Sunshine highlighted everything around us except that path sloping deep into the woods, darkened by a canopy of trees. Crows called from the treetops. An eastern breeze rose coolly out of the bottom. "What's down there?" I asked.

Colonel Ron lit a cigarette and said, "The Flats."

My knees weakened. I felt a need to sit and did just that, right there on the edge of the asphalt. Colonel Ron joined me. While staring forward as if gazing into the past, he said, "Waaayy down there, the road ends at the farm of Old Man Sherman Henry—"

I know that name, Sherman Henry.

"—When I was a boy, two of my friends took a dare and went down in those flats just to see what it was like. The rest of us waited right here. After about twenty minutes, we heard shotgun blasts. Darrel came back. Billy Ray didn't. We waited and waited for him but he never came out. Eventually, someone went to the house we just came from. Mr. Lush called my father, and together they went looking—"

Mr. Lush?

"—they took a hound with 'em and found Billy Ray in the pine thicket. He'd tripped and fell on a sharp sapling stump. Went right through 'im. My father said the ground was all bloody and tore up around his feet and hands where he clawed and squirmed trying to get off that stump."

"You never went down there?"

"Years later. Took a doctor down there to see what they were calling the wild child."

"You're talking about me! Are you talking about me? Was the doctor—?"

"Didn't really wanna go down there."

"You're talking about my father, Doctor Green. Aren't you?"

Colonel Ron drew off his cigarette and remained silent.

"Did you see me then?"

"No. I didn't go in. Only drove down there to show him where it was. Didn't stick around."

"But how did you know my father?"

"When your father practiced in Kentucky, he also taught psychology at the University of Kentucky. He was my professor. In class one day, I told him of the stories I'd heard about you and your behavior, and how I feared you were being mistreated. He became interested. That's how I wound up showing him where you lived."

"So you already knew where I came from. You, you knew Mrs. White was right when she said I was the girl from the flats."

Colonel Ron didn't have to speak.

"How could you?" I felt hot, angry, betrayed. I turned and started beating his shoulder with my fist. "How could you keep this from me?"

"Stop it Brooke!"

He put his arms up to protect himself, but I kept pounding them over and over. He grabbed me, pulled me to him and wrapped his arms around me, and then held me so tight that I couldn't move. I felt myself hyperventilating. I struggled. I wanted to hurt him, but I didn't want to hurt him. I wanted to hate him, but I—wanted to—

"Brooke ... Brooke ... Brooke, wake up." I heard crows cawing. Opened my eyes to brightness. The ground felt rough on my back. Colonel Ron stood over me. My rage had diminished. I felt—better. "You okay?" Colonel Ron asked.

Without speaking, I nodded. He extended his hand. I took it and he pulled me to a sitting position. I stared past him, down the dark, wooded lane. "My past is down there."

"Your past is a part of your problems. Your father and I discussed it. And I had every intention of discussing it with you—"

"You said '*part* of my problems.'"

"When you started talking about other things, things you had no way of knowing, I knew there was more."

"Can you remember how it looked?"

"How what looked?"

"Down there, in the flats."

"Not much there ... an old two-story house, a barn—"

"And a chicken coop," I added.

"And a chicken coop."

"Let's go down there."

"No. We can't. It may not be safe."

"The ugly people. They still live there?"

Colonel Ron nodded.

"But I want to see them again. I'm not afraid. I want them to see that I survived ... that no one has hurt me since they did. I want them to look at me and know that I remember things...."

Colonel Ron extended his hand again and said, "Gettin' late. Believe we best go back before Loretta starts to worry."

Chapter 22

Friday April 21 1876

Cannot write much now. Daddy is downstairs hollering at Momma about something. Afraid it might be about me and John. By all means I do not want him coming up here and catching me writing about John in this here book.

Saturday April 22 1876

For three days now I been talking to John. During work, I watch from a distance as he associates with other guests, mostly men. He sees me too but acts otherwise. When I take my lunch, we slip off up into the woods and sit on that same old rock. If Daddy knew I was spending time with a bluecoat, nearly six years my elder, he would shoot John and beat me silly. At supper tonight, Mamma went and told Daddy I was talking to a nice young man. He gave me that look that says, there is no such thing as a nice young man.

154

Sunday April 23 1876

Went to church this morning like every Sunday. Sat in Momma's pew waiting for Mass to start when I heard whispers everywhere. Turned around and there he was, Mr. John Jordan Crittenden III, standing in the doorway. I about died right then and there. He looked handsome as ever in his Sunday suit. At least he was smart enough not to wear his Yankee uniform. He saw me staring and stepped our way. Mamma's pew being full like it was he took a seat right behind me. Could hardly breathe knowing he was so close. When I turned, he said, Good morning Miss. Pierce.

Momma pinched my arm so I would turn back around. Her and Daddy started whispering and I got a stare from Daddy. Pretty soon, the singing began and Father Joseph Carmans and his two altar boys came in to start the Mass. I swear I could feel John's breath on the back of my neck.

It was the longest Mass I ever did attend. After it was over, everybody stood outside the church like always, talking and carrying on. Mamma was over looking at Grandpa's grave when John walked right up and introduced himself to Daddy. Daddy shook his hand. Mamma saw what was occurring and came quickly. Daddy said this here's my wife Catherine. When Mamma reached to shake his hand, John took it real gentleman like and kissed it. Thought Daddy might strike him but he didn't. I felt like a little girl again as John and Daddy talked about everything from war to Washington D.C. They acted like I wasn't even there.

Finally John spoke about me by saying how much he enjoyed my company on our walks. Daddy squinted and I knew right then I would be hearing about it later. While they kept talking I walked past Momma and said Know Daddy's going to kill me when we get home. Might as well go to confession now.

She said I best hurry.

When I told Father Carmans that I might be in love with a Yankee, I believe I heard him laugh a little bit. He told me it was not necessarily a sin, but warned about lying to Daddy. He never even gave me penance.

By the time I got back outside Daddy, Momma, and the youngins were all in the wagon waiting on me. John was riding off on his horse. Figured he and Daddy must have had words or he would at least waited and said bye to me. On the way home, Daddy told Mamma how he had trouble believing a man of that status would be seriously talking to his daughter.

He did not kill me tonight like I thought he would. Instead, he told me I best not concern myself with a man that was only passing through.

I said I thought you would not like John because of him being a bluecoat.

Daddy said, That man is no more Yankee than I am.

I can't wait to talk to John to see what him and Daddy really talked about.

I tried to picture Elizabeth Pierce lying in her bed thinking passionately of her John Crittenden. Though I'd never actually been in love, I did feel a twang of warmth, as if I were somehow feeling Elizabeth Pierce's attraction to John. Or was it John's attraction to her?

Monday April 24 1876

This afternoon, John wore civilian clothes and walked me all the way home. He came in to see Daddy, but he was not here. Him and Hershel Haycraft were gone to see a moonshine maker. Momma invited John to eat dinner and he did. Mamma liked him so much it embarrassed me.

Before he left John broke my heart by saying he has to head west day after tomorrow. It made me awfully ill. I am afraid to go to sleep. Might die and not see him before he leaves.

Tuesday April 26 1876

Last night I was afraid of dying. Tonight I want to. And would except I am gonna be waiting for John to return here after he gets done fighting all them Indians out west. We have our own Indians down by the Nolin River. Asked John why he could not just fight them instead. He laughed and said Kentucky Indians were not savages like those out west.

Wednesday April 27 1876

Before he left John and I went back up to our sitting rock. He showed me how he carved our initials into the beech tree it leaned against. It made me so happy I reached up and kissed his cheek.

He said I could rest assured that the whole time he is away he will be thinking of me. Said one of these days we will meet again at the bridge and he is gonna pick me up and carry me off to one of those rooms up on the third floor where we can look out over the springs and, well

John stopped talking. He touched my face real gentle like and then kissed me right on the lips.

Now I have kissed me a boy at school before but never like that. John's kiss lasted forever. I lost my breath and swear I still have not got it all back. When it was over he took a little brown leather box out of his pocket and handed it to me. Said his grandfather's third wife gave it to him after the old man died. John asked if I would keep it while he was away out west.

I said How can I take something your Granddaddy left for you?

John put his arms around me and said I can give it back to him when he returns.

When I started to say what if you don't come back, John stopped me from saying it. Then he whispered to me that if he should not return, the box and its contents would be mine to keep.

Thursday April 28 1876

I miss John. Today I walked alone to our sitting place. Sat there and looked at his and my initials on the tree remembering the kiss. I tried to think of where he might be. How far away could he be in one day?

Friday April 29 1876

I can hardly bear to write about John. He is so far away by now that I fear I will never see him again. I hope to sleep better tonight. Last night I lay awake thinking of him wondering if there are young ladies in towns around where he will be.

Saturday April 30 1876

I miss John.

Sunday May 1 1876

I prayed at Mass for John to return.

Monday May 2 1876

From the sitting rock, I stared down at the sights and sounds of Grayson Springs and wondered if John could close his eyes and hear them and see them.

Yesterday I told Mamma about John's box. Reckon she told Daddy. This morning he asked me if I had opened it. I said no. It would not be proper. It still belongs to him. Daddy said he would *open it and not tell me what was in it if I wanted him to. I hid the box in my room so he would not.*

Tuesday May 3 1876
I miss John.

Wednesday May 4 1876
I miss John.

Page after page, entry after entry, she wrote simply, "I miss John." I could feel her pain. The anguish of wondering if he would ever return. How hard it would have been back then, not being able to text one another or call or email. After another month of writing, "I miss John," it appeared as if she had given up. The rest of the page remained blank. It made me feel empty. Flipping another page, I found a small yellowed envelope wedged between pages, addressed to:

Miss Elizabeth Pierce
Grayson Springs, Kentucky

The THREE CENT postage, green, in the shape of a police badge, had been printed directly onto the envelope. On it, there was an image of a horse rider and a locomotive with two train cars. At the top it read, 1776 US POSTAGE. At the bottom, below the train, THREE CENTS 1876.

The envelope's sealed flap must have been opened by hand as the edges were jagged. I removed a letter on stiff paper, browned by age, and read:

Dearest Elizabeth Pierce,
As the days and months have passed since the massacre of General Custer and his loyal men at

Little Big Horn, I am reminded by the faces of those whose loved ones passed just how privileged I am. My husband, Lieutenant Frank Gibson, was one of the few officers of the 7th Cavalry who survived the massacre. Those same compelling forces that preserved his existence have demanded that I provide solace to those who were less fortunate. It is in that spirit that I write you. Please accept my apology for taking so long to address this issue to you. There have been so many letters to write.

I believe it was in the month of May when I first met Lieutenant John Crittenden. He was considered by some to be an outsider, having never graduated from the Point. Yet I saw through the politics and realized what a dedicated soldier he really was. Observing my understanding, he spoke freely on several occasions. His Kentucky charm outweighed the heaviness of his recent tragedy at Ft. Abercrombie. He viewed with one eye what many of us miss with two. And I must tell you that while the stories of his family's dedication to the military were told with pride, it was his thoughts of you that made him smile.

Like many of my widowed friends, you have been deprived of a future with a man I know to have been good hearted. I understand that your time with

Lieutenant Crittenden was short. Regardless, you should hold precious that in his final days, you were on his mind continuously. He spoke well of your beauty, both of body and spirit, and the walks at the springs and your sitting spot in the woods. In my mind, I can see yours and his initials engraved into that beech tree, a task he claimed to have earned him your kiss.

Perhaps, at a future date, Frank and I might bring our Baby Kate for a visit to the Grayson Springs Resort that Lieutenant Crittenden spoke so highly of.

May life bring you abundant happiness, and may you never forget that Lieutenant John Crittenden had deep and passionate feelings for his little Elizabeth Pierce.

With sympathy,

Katherine Gibson

I wished I had not read the letter. Those words of solace hurt me. There was this strange feeling that I somehow had a connection with the young soldier she spoke of. Horseback riding. Removing a saddle. The firearm I had stolen as a child. No wonder it attracted me. I'd dreamed of all this. The day when I beat the girl at school, she had said she wanted to scalp me. After reading Katherine Gibson's letter, I knew in my heart that Lieutenant John Crittenden had been scalped by Indians. I felt his pain, heard his screams. When I had explained my dreams to Daddy, he told me children often dream of trauma witnessed on TV. He and the court-appointed psychologist discounted my explanations, accusing me of making up excuses for bad behavior.

My anticipated joy in reading the diary had been spoiled because I knew the ending. Yet those old pages contained more entries by Elizabeth Pierce.

Friday December 22 1876

It is now three days away from Christmas. The tree is up in the front room. Mamma handed me a letter this afternoon. I thought it was going to be from John. It was not. It came from a lady out west, Katherine Gibson. She wrote to tell me John died at the hands of Indians. He is never coming back. I feel as if I will die myself. All I have left of him is this little leather box he gave me. Tonight I shall open it.

After all in the house were sleeping, I put fire to my lamp. I took John's leather case from its hiding place and sat it on my bed. I cried. For the first time, I turned the two small latches and open the lid. To my surprise, inside there was another box. This one is of glass. It is painted up so pretty with men on horses and dogs and a little fox running from them. I opened the glass box and inside there are 5 one cent pieces all shiny and new.

Saturday December 23 1876

Tomorrow is Christmas Eve. Mamma says we will likely attend Midnight Mass at St. Augustine's. This morning after breakfast I revealed the contents of John's leather box to Mamma and Daddy. Daddy called the glass case porcelain. He says it is a snuff box and he says it is too fancy for a soldier. Those shiny cent pieces are 20 years old. Daddy says they still look new because of them having never been spent.

Sunday December 24 1876

Mamma says since we are going to Midnight Mass tonight we don't have to attend Sunday Mass this morning. For this I am grateful. Daddy went to see his moonshine friends today and he told them about my fancy snuff box and the coins in it. Someone there convinced him that the box and coins were of considerable value. He says I should let him sell them for their worth. I cannot bear to do so. They are all I have of John. Tomorrow, I will hide them where no one will ever find them.

Chapter 23

Shortly after the rooster called his morning call, Colonel Ron came into the kitchen, surprised at my presence. Having managed to start a fire in the cook stove, I already had coffee brewing and was standing in the open doorway staring out at the creek. "Couldn't sleep?" he asked.

Without turning, I replied, "Had a bad dream. Decided to get up."

"Something you'd like to talk about?"

"Not really. Been there, done that. Doesn't do much good."

"Try me."

I turned, walked to the stove, and said, "You ready for coffee?"

"Sure."

While pouring a cup, I asked, "Is today Sunday?"

"All day."

"I need to go to church."

Colonel Ron smiled, reached for his coffee, and said, "Dream that bad?"

"Can we walk to church from here?"

"Be a long walk."

"Bet it's not much more than a mile."

"How you know it's not ten miles?"

Instead of answering, I gave him the look.

"Bullshit. You had a vision of the church?"

Not wanting to lie, I said, "Not really. But I bet it's old."

"Dah."

"And up on a hill."

The Colonel stared but said nothing.

"Graves close by?"

167

"You feel a need to go to Mass, or do you just wanna see the church?"

"I want to see the church."

"That's what I thought—but why?"

I hesitated, made eye contact, and asked, "Do you think I came here by accident?"

Colonel Ron stared for a few seconds before replying, "No. You came here because of your behavior."

"But why here? Of all the places in the world, how did I wind up coming to Kentucky? To this place. A place I've seen in my dreams."

I suspected Colonel Ron, like all the others, doubted my dreams.

"You came here because I know Dr. Green and because he felt maybe you could open up better with me, someone from the area of your roots, than you had with the psychologists in New York."

"I opened up for them. They didn't believe me. Do you?"

"I—"

"Don't lie please. If you do not believe me, say so."

"I ... I believe there is something special about you. I haven't quite placed my mind on it, but with luck, I will. Unlike those before me, I recognize too many details in what you say ... facts that you cannot possibly make up. I find myself pondering more on why you speak of these things than on their authenticity. So, that said, yes I believe you."

"Then I'd say someone made the right decision—sending me here."

"So, what is it you need to see at the church?"

"Don't know. It's like I have to go there to find out."

The Colonel stood silent, staring. I wondered if he could see my relief. Much of the distress from my dreams and from reading Elizabeth Pierce's diary had subsided with his trust in me. Whether he knew it or not, he had become my confidant. Loretta entered the room witnessing what appeared to be an awkward moment—me staring at Colonel Ron, him staring back, both of us silent. After a few seconds, she asked with contempt, "Am I interrupting something?"

Without breaking his stare, Colonel Ron said, "Brooke wants to go to church this morning."

Sunday was to be a day off from labor on the grounds. During breakfast, Colonel Ron asked if Sherri and Loretta would like to join our trip to St. Augustine Church.

Sherri said, "With this face?"

Colonel looked at his pocket watch and said, "If we leave in the next thirty minutes, Mass will be ending about the time we get there. You won't have to go in."

Loretta said, "I can stay here with Sherri. You two go ahead. We might even walk over to check on Charlotte. I could use a shower anyway."

The word shower excited Sherri. "I'm definitely going with Loretta."

I asked, "We going to walk or ride the horses?"

Colonel replied, "Legs sore from our walk?"

"Yes," I admitted.

"Buckboard or saddle?"

"Saddle."

I put on a fresh set of yuck clothing and then stood in front of the mirror, finger brushing my dirty hair until it was at least presentable.

Watching, Sherri joked, "A little makeup wouldn't hurt."

When I turned to give her a dirty look, she said, "Second thought, you're beautiful without it."

Loretta and Sherri watched us saddle up. I took Becca; Colonel took Birdie. When we were about to leave, Sherri sassed, "You guys say a prayer for me. I'll think about you while I'm over at Charlotte's taking a shower."

Colonel Ron grinned. "Did Loretta tell you Charlotte's shower consists of a bucket with holes in it, hanging from a tree?"

Though the nearby blacktop road ran directly to St. Augustine Church, Colonel Ron led me on a trail that ran parallel to Bear Creek. We passed the spot where we had caught fish and continued south. Sycamore and scaly-bark hickory trees lined the creek bank. On the other side of the water, a forest of trees ran uphill.

"It's not that far to the church. We'll walk the horses the whole way. Don't get too close to the trees. Horse might rub you into one."

I looked back and could no longer see the barn. "I feel like a pioneer."

"Believe it or not," replied the Colonel, "where we are right now hasn't changed much since those days."

"So, why didn't we ride the road?"

Glancing back over his shoulder, he said, "You got something against the woods?"

"The cursed woods?"

"It's not all cursed."

"So, you do believe!"

"No, I do not."

Surveying the field toward the blacktop road, I said, "I'm not afraid of the woods, just wanted to take the route someone might have taken in the 1800s."

After considering my question, he replied, "I'd say this *is* the route they would have taken back then. That road didn't come along until the nineteen hundreds."

"Were there savage Indians in this area?"

"Define savage?"

"You know. The kind that kill white settlers and then take their scalps."

"There were Native Americans in this region. A lot of artifacts have been found in these hills. And I'm sure at some point they were less than civilized. But by the mid-1800s, I'd say most around here were fairly docile."

"Most?"

Without looking back, he said, "Well, I'm just saying there could be one or two still hiding out in these woods, waiting for an unsuspecting pioneer to come riding by on his or her trusty horse."

"You're so full of shit."

He looked back and smiled.

As we continued forward, Becca seemed to be on autopilot. I cherished the quietness. There were sweet sounds, music to my ears— bird noises, the sound of horse hooves, an occasional snort, and the rustling of windblown leaves. When a vehicle passed in the distance, I chose to ignore it. Three quarters of a mile out, Colonel Ron dismounted to open a gate. We left the field, entered the woods, and then started across Bear Creek.

"Won't be long now," announced Colonel Ron as he stopped to let Birdie drink from the crystal-clear running water. I followed suit. A whitetail deer and her two spotted fawns flagged their tails high and trotted off into the woods. The doe began blowing or snorting or something, an obvious warning to other deer.

Colonel Ron lit a pre-rolled cigarette, took a draw, and then offered it to me.

"No, thanks."

"Top of this hill, you'll see one of the oldest Catholic churches in Grayson County ... built in the early 1800s."

As he spoke, I sat there taking in my surroundings. "That church can't be any closer to God than we are right here."

"You like the woods?"

"This is heavenly."

The final stretch to the church property was steep indeed. Emerging from the woods, we were at the back of the building, a brick structure with arched stained glass windows and a steeple. I'd expected something larger. Blessed sounds emerged as a small congregation sang its final hymn. Several cars and pickup trucks filled a parking lot that had been carved into the side of the hill. Mass was ending. A priest and two altar boys came out of the church, soon followed by men, women, and children. Most greeted the priest on way to their vehicles. Some stood around chatting. Colonel Ron waited until the crowd had departed before riding up to Father Ryan.

"Well, well…if it isn't the good Colonel Ronnie Lee."

"Long time no see, Padre."

The priest stood tall, fit, and sun darkened like a farmer in clergy attire. His meticulously groomed, graying hair, looked as if it had been jelled back to cover a balding spot.

"You could have come inside," replied the priest to Colonel Ron. "Afraid the roof might fall in?"

As the two men chat, I sat in the saddle, taking in the hillside spotted with gravestones, large and small, some new, many old and deteriorating. Colonel Ron retrieved my attention when he said, "Father Ryan, I'd like you to meet Elizabeth Brooke Green from New York."

Father Ryan stepped next to Becca, looked up, and said, "Look at me, child." When we made eye contact, he made the sign of the cross and said, "I'd heard, but needed to see with my own eyes ... please, come down."

Without moving, I snapped back, "What exactly *did* you hear, Father?"

"Well ... I heard that the wild child of the Flats was back in Grayson County. Don't be alarmed, dear. I'll not judge you by your past. My ministry is about forgiveness."

Dismounting, I looked up to the priest and said, "Excuse the hell out of me Father, but I don't recall anything from my Grayson County past that should require forgiveness."

"Is that a fact? Then perhaps I should refer to you as the Blessed Mary."

I nearly hit his sarcasm with the F-bomb, but feared I might go to hell for cursing a priest. Seeing my expression, Colonel Ron said, "Easy, Brooke, I can assure you Father Ryan makes his comments respectfully."

Rather than argue morals with a man of the clergy, I curtseyed politely, and then strolled off into the graveyard. I had spotted an old woman on her knees tending a grave some thirty yards away. It was the elderly Mrs. White from the Grayson Springs Road. When I neared, she remained on her knees and spoke without turning. "What do you want from me?"

I stopped and replied, "Yesterday, ma'am, you seemed to recognize me. Please, you must realize, I've never met my parents.... I have no idea who I really am. I'm just trying to find out something. Anything about my past."

"You spoke of Elizabeth Pierce. Who told you that name?"

"I've spoken to no one..."

"Liar."

"I—I read about her—and I have dreamed of her. I feel like I know her."

The old woman looked up and snarled, "You know nothing," and then turned back to her chore.

"In eighteeeeeen seventy six, I believe, Elizabeth lived in the house where you live—her and her mother and father and two younger siblings. She worked at the Grayson Springs Resort, cleaning rooms. And—and she fell in love with a Yankee soldier."

My words stopped Mrs. White's work. Utilizing the grave marker for support, she rose and huffed, "Who told you such a thing?"

Hearing her raised voice, Colonel Ron and Father Ryan walked to us. Seeing the old woman's condition, Father Ryan asked, "Is there a problem?"

She looked at Colonel Ron and asked, "Who's been talking to this girl?"

He said, "Brooke, you cannot bother Mrs. White."

"She is *not* bothering me, but she speaks of things that only I should know."

"Brooke claims to have dreams. She's spoken of several things from the past. At this point, I cannot explain."

Father Ryan said, "Mrs. White, like me, you are familiar with this girl's past from a tainted perspective. Ronnie here has been assigned to work with her as a professional, a psychologist, in order to help her cope with a past that may be more horrid than I had realized. We must try and understand her quest for knowledge of the past. She knows nothing of her blood relatives."

I closed my eyes. Father Ryan's words were suddenly kind and true, and it felt as if I were standing on holy ground, closer to my past than ever before. I wanted to be strong, yet tears came anyway. My heart raced and I felt paralyzed, drifting into another time and place. *A beautiful young lady, dressed like me, walked gracefully from among the graves. She reached for my hand and I took hers, soft and warm, and I knew it was...*

I opened my eyes. It was Mrs. White holding my hand. She said, "If you gentlemen don't mind, I'd like to speak with her in private." Colonel Ron and Father Ryan assumed sincerity in the old woman's voice. They turned and left us. Still grasping my hand, Mrs. White said, "Shall we walk?" and then sort of tugged me into motion.

As we strolled into the resting place of the dead, I asked, "You really want to hold my hand, or do you just need help getting along?"

"Yep."

I smiled and then gently squeezed her hand as we continued our slow walk. The old woman said, "You spoke of my grandmother."

"Elizabeth Pierce was your grandmother?"

"She was."

"And you live in her house?"

"I live in the house her father built. Properties get passed down in these parts."

"You have children?"

Instead of answering, she said, "I saw you only once when you were a child. Came to the Flats to attend to the boy you beat. His face was bruised and bloody. You could have blinded that poor child."

"That *poor child* held me down while he and another put their hands under my clothes in places where no man has touched me since."

Mrs. White stopped walking. "No one knows who you are."

"Did I grow up in the Flats?"

"You and about a dozen others over the years. Wasn't none of 'em belonged to Sherman and Eloise Henry. They just kept youngins for the government checks. Not long after that doctor took you away, the law come and took every one of those kids.... I tried to believe you were the lucky one."

"Why?"

"Why what?"

"Why did you try to believe I was the lucky one?"

"Because ... you were the one who seemed the most disturbed. And I don't mean that in a bad way."

"Why was I there? Why can't I remember my parents or anything before I was there?"

"Honey, you were born down there in the Flats. Your momma was like you. Just another foster child livin' with Sherman and Eloise Henry. Girl died bringin' you into this world."

I felt sick, unable to breathe, standing there imagining my mother being raped by one of the ugly people. *Is that where my violence comes from? Am I one of the ugly people?* "My father? Did you know my father?"

"Look here, child." Mrs. White pointed toward a grave marker that read:

Mary Elizabeth Pierce Lush
Wife of Leo Lush
Born 1860   Died 1945

As I stepped toward the marker, a strange feeling flushed through me. "It says *Mary* Elizabeth."

"Mary is her saint's name. We don't usually address a woman by her saint's name."

"I see." I ran my fingers down the stone's weathered surface to the name *Mary Elizabeth*. My hand quickly jerked away, and I backed off. It felt like the static shock I get from sliding across the seat in Melanie's Lexus.

"What's wrong?" asked the old woman.

"Not sure." I began scanning the nearby graves.

"What is it?"

"I feel something. Is my mother buried here?"

"No, dear."

"Then where is she buried?"

"I'd say somewhere in the Flats. Old man Henry wouldn't pay to bury his own mother. Know damn well he didn't pay to bury little Cin—"

"Little who? You know my mother's name, don't you?"

The old woman turned away and began walking toward the church.

I followed, shouting, "Tell me! Tell me what you know!"

Colonel Ron and Father Ryan heard my elevated voice and recognized Mrs. White's plight. Again, they came to us. "Brooke," demanded Colonel Ron, "that's enough. Can't you see you have upset her?"

I stopped walking. As the Colonel accompanied Mrs. White to her vehicle, I turned back toward the grave. While I stood there gazing at Mary Elizabeth Pierce's marker, Father Ryan spoke from behind me. "What is it child? What troubles you so?"

"I'm—I'm not sure Father. I felt something here. A connection. A comfort. I thought it was this grave."

"You no longer feel this *connection*?"

"I do, I think. But it's not as strong."

"Why did you upset Mrs. White?"

"You have it backwards, Father. She upset me."

Chapter 24

"What the hell happened to you today?" Sherri inquired as we undressed for bed.

"I'm not sure, but for some reason, I felt I was close to my mother."

"In a graveyard?"

"My mother *is* dead."

"Oh, yeah. I'm sorry."

"Don't be. Just help me figure this thing out. Why would I feel such a connection to Mary Elizabeth Pierce, a woman who died 45 years before I was born?"

"I'd say the answer is in that old woman."

"No shit, but Colonel Ron says I have to stay away from her because she is old and she got upset both times she saw me."

"Maybe he's afraid she'll have a heart attack or something."

"Bull. That old woman's too mean to die. She knows my mother's name and won't tell me. I'd like to kick her old ass."

"Brooke. You shouldn't talk like that."

Stepping out of my skirt, I said, "So, how was your shower?"

"It was good."

"Was it outside?"

"Yes. It had a curtain. And the water was warmed by the sun. At least I got to wash my hair."

"Damn."

"You should ask them to take you over there. It felt amazing."

After Sherri dozed off, I reread Elizabeth Pierce's diary entries, longing to learn more about my past. My mother's name. My father's name. The old woman knew more than she was willing to admit. Deep down, I knew she had her own demons.

On Monday of week three, during grass cutting chores, Ben, Charlotte, and Eli came by. Ben's buggy had been replaced by a buckboard full of lumber and ropes for rebuilding the swinging footbridge. In my eagerness to participate, I hustled through chores at an accelerated pace. Sherri couldn't care less.

By noon, the men and I worked adamantly in the open, freshly cut lawn while Sherri, Loretta, and the ever-growing Charlotte watched from seats they'd dragged under a nearby shade tree. Sherri proudly wore her new bonnet created by Charlotte's talented hands.

In the yard, four lengths of rope had been stretched out the distance of the creek span, plus enough extra to tie off to trees on each bank. These long lengths became the horizontal suspension ropes which also served as handrails. They were twisted together, two ropes for each handrail, in case one should break. Colonel Ron and Ben began attaching three-foot lengths of rope at intervals of four feet. These would serve as hanging vertical supports for cross-boards.

Sherri stared while Eli and I took the wagon to the creek. We had been sent to prepare the landings and supports on each side of the creek. Eli utilized a work horse to drag the original rock landings to new positions. Each needed to be placed between two trees. The trees would be tied off with rope to a steel stake, driven into the ground. This would keep the trees from bending under the weight and tension of the bridge. While Eli drove in the first stake with what he called a sledgehammer, he asked me to bring him a length of rope from the wagon. On my return, he said, "Your friend seems to be spying on us from the kitchen."

Turning quickly, I caught a glimpse of Sherri sliding out of sight.

"Is she worried about you?"

"No," I replied. "Knowing Sherri, she's jealous that I'm spending time with you."

"Thought you were..." Eli cut himself short.

"What? You can say it. I'm a big girl."

"So, are you?"

"Are *you*?"

"Me? What makes you think such a thing?"

"In New York, most nice guys are gay."

"What if I told you I only pretend to be nice?"

Unrolling the rope, I said, "You'd be lying."

"You sure about that?"

"Eli, if you're not gay, you're the nicest straight guy I've ever met."

Tying a knot, he said, "I guess I'll take that as a compliment."

"You should," I sassed, while grabbing his hat off his head.

Eli stood up straight and ran his hands through the most beautiful hair I've ever seen on a man. "Give it back, Brooke."

"But I want to wear it," I said, while pulling it onto my head. I expected he would grab it back, but instead he stood there, staring down at my feet. Wasn't sure if I'd hurt his feelings or what. Then he returned to his work and said, "If you wear my hat, people will think we are engaged."

"Won't they ask why you are engaged to a lesbian?"

Walking to the wagon for another length of rope, he said, "So, are you?"

"My friends say I am."

"Not up to your friends."

I looked to make sure Sherri wasn't within hearing distance and then asked, "You ever heard of Sherman and Eloise Henry?"

"They live down in the Flats."

"Do they still have kids there?"

"Not to my knowledge."

"You been down there?"

"Sure. I shoe the old man's horses."

"How old are you?"

"Twenty-one. Why?"

"Don't remember ever seeing you."

"You were one of those kids?"

I nodded.

On his knees tying rope, Eli stopped his work and stared up at me. "You're the fighter, aren't you?"

I tilted my head.

"Where you been all these years?"

"New York.... Right after I was adopted, we moved to Manhattan."

Finishing his knot, Eli stood up and asked, "So, what's that like?"

"Big, fast, and noisy."

"That good or bad?"

"I miss my friends and my clothes, my phone, my music."

"So you don't like it here."

"Can't say that. I'm more comfortable here than I expected. I can tell this is where I was born."

"Where were you born?"

"Are you acquainted with Mrs. White on the Grayson Springs Road?"

"Yes."

"She says I was born in the Flats. My mother was a foster child herself."

"So, who was your father?"

"That I don't know. Was thinking maybe you could take me down there so I could find out."

Eli placed the second spike and said, "You want to drive this one in? I'll hold it."

"You trust me not to hit your hand?"

"Just keep your eye on the spike. I'll have my eye on you." His words felt good. I picked up the heavy hammer, raised it over my shoulder, and then slammed it onto the spike as if I'd done it before. "Not bad for a lady."

Lady sounded good coming from Eli. I raised the hammer again and said, "You didn't answer my question," while striking the spike a second time.

"Can't do it. You're a minor. Colonel Ron's responsible for you. He would have to agree."

"Tomorrow's my birthday. I'll be eighteen. Then I can legally do what I want. I'm going to go to the flats if I have to go by myself. Pleeeaaase?" I begged.

"Not without Colonel Ron's permission. I would never break his trust."

By the time both landings were prepared, Colonel Ron and Ben came dragging the bridge's rope system to the creek. Cross-boards were removed from the wagon and laid next to the inn-side landing. They were rough cut, 2"x6" oak boards, three feet long. Each had a pre-drilled hole in both ends. Eli and I volunteered to enter the water to pull the bridge across as the Colonel and Ben slipped the boards onto the vertical ropes and tied knots under each. The water was cool, but I didn't mind. As we waded backwards, I asked, "Hey Ben, what does it mean if a girl wears a man's hat?"

Ben glanced at the Colonel, shrugged his shoulders, and said, "Guess it means you both have the same size head."

I looked at Eli, and he was smiling. "Bullshitter," I sassed while removing the hat and spinning it to him like a Frisbee. Eli looked inside the hat. "What? You think I have head lice?"

"No. But you could stand to wash that mop."

"What!"

"You heard me. Cleanliness is next to godliness."

"You're an asshole."

"And you need to wash that mouth and hair."

"Screw you!"

"That does it," Eli grumped as he released his grip on the bridge and splashed my way.

Before I could react, he grabbed me and said, "Cleansing time."

"Don't you dare!" I screamed.

I barely heard Colonel Ron scream, "Eli, don't!" as the water caved in around my face. Once submerged, he pulled me back up. Before I could recover, he dunked me again. I heard bubbles and muffled screaming from the bank. When he pulled me up again, Eli released me and just stood there staring. I shook my head and spit water.

Eli smiled and said, "Now you are cleansed and beautiful."

I busted him right in the mouth. Immediate remorse swept over me as I stood dumbfounded, staring at the blood dripping off his chin. By then, Sherri, Loretta, and Charlotte had joined the men. They all stood watching.

Eli cleansed his face with creek water, and then began wadding toward the bridge. "Grab your side. We need to get this done," was all he had to say.

After all the cross-boards were attached to the horizontal ropes, Colonel Ron and Ben secured the Inn-side to the trees. They then came around to the other side. While Eli used the horse to stretch the ropes, they finished tying it to the landing trees. To complete the bridge, ten-foot 2"x10" planks were laid three-wide on top of the cross-boards to serve as a walking surface. At 4:00 pm, I stood in the middle of the bridge, facing downstream, eyes closed, gripping the rail.

"What's she doin'?" Charlotte asked loud enough for me to hear.

"Visualizing," replied Colonel Ron. "Girl claims to have seen the original bridge in her dreams."

Eli stood on the other end of the bridge watching me. I heard Sherri ask, "What's *he* doing?"

Ben said, "Visualizing."

Charlotte asked, "What are we going to do with those two?"

Colonel Ron said, "Not a thing."

Chapter 25

On Tuesday morning, June 3, as Sherri and I worked together cleaning up breakfast dishes, Colonel Ron and Loretta were sitting on the front porch drinking coffee. When Bruno started barking, we ceased working and scooted to the front room to peek out. Not expecting company, we were surprised to see Eli on his gelding entering the property.

Sherri spoke quietly, "Here comes your boyfriend."

"Yeah, right."

"I can tell he likes you."

"Oh well."

"Don't stand there acting like you don't like him."

"I've never had a *boy*friend."

"Oh my god," she whispered. "Have you ever actually had sex with a girl?"

"Shut up."

"Seriously?"

"My friend Shauna and I—well—you know—we've sort of fooled around."

We both stood for a few seconds watching Eli ride down the lane. He led a solid white mare with some sort of wide red ribbon around its neck, tied into a bow. I mumbled, "What the hell?"

Sherri took me by the shoulders and said, "Listen, girlfriend. I don't know anyone who hasn't like, sort of fooled around. You're no more lesbian than I am. Look at me and tell me you don't feel something when he's around."

I guess my silence answered her question and mine. By the time Eli reached the porch, both Colonel Ron and Loretta were standing. Loretta asked, "To what do we owe this pleasure?"

"Sorry about coming by unexpectedly."

By then, Colonel Ron had begun checking out the mare. "Fine-looking animal. What's with the ribbon?"

"It's a birthday present."

"For who?"

"Isn't today Brooke's birthday?"

Sherri whispered, "Today's your birthday?"

"Eli," huffed Loretta, "you can't do that."

"And why not?"

"Hold on, Loretta," spoke the Colonel. "Explain yourself, Eli."

"I think she likes horses, and I think she has difficulty trusting guys. I can't see the problem with showing her that a man can care."

"Really," smiled Loretta.

"She lives in New York City," reiterated Colonel Ron.

"I know that. I'll keep the mare. Anytime she wants to visit, it'll be here. Come on, Colonel, it's her birthday. Didn't you get something special for your eighteenth?"

Loretta's eyebrows rose as she smiled at the Colonel, turned, opened the door, and yelled, "Brooke! Come on out here!"

We were standing right behind the door. "Listen girl," Sherri whispered, "I'd take this guy in a heartbeat, but for some reason, he likes you. Give it a chance. Swear to God, if that hunk kisses you, you'll know for sure."

I almost tripped stepping out the door. Eli smiled and said, "Happy Birthday. Her name is Casper."

While everyone sang Happy Birthday, I went to the horse and stroked its mane, letting the long strands run through my fingers. "She's so beautiful. Thank you, Eli. I—I don't know what to say."

"Give him a kiss," Sherri urged.

I kissed the side of Casper's head.

"Not the horse, dumbass. Kiss Eli."

Tears ran as I contemplated the thought. Eli, realizing my dilemma, held his fist out for a bump. I drew a fist, touched mine to his, and mouthed, "Thank you."

Eli supervised as I saddled the mare, and then he watched me ride around the grounds. When he saw I had adequate command of the horse, he asked Colonel Ron's permission for him and me to take a ride.

"You can take her out around the field or up in the woods. Just don't leave the Grayson Springs property. I trust you'll both behave."

Sherri stood behind the Colonel shaking her head and mouthing, "Kiss him."

Eli led the way along the same path the Colonel and I had taken to Saint Augustine Church. Halfway down the field, he stopped. "Straight takes us around the field. Right goes across the creek and up into the woods. There's a nice view from the top."

Looking to my left, I asked, "Where does that path go?"

"Up to the road. If we go around the field, that's the way we would come back. From the top, you can see it all."

"Then let's go up."

Nearing the creek, Eli dismounted to unlatch a single strand of barbed wire. He led his horse through and then reattached the wire after I passed. Crossing the creek, we stopped to let the horses drink. I asked, "Do you like your lifestyle?"

"If I didn't, I wouldn't be here."

"So you can leave anytime you want?"

"This *is* America. We *are free,* you know."

"Guess I'm not used to being free. Someone's always telling me what to do."

"Well, you're eighteen now. You'll have to get used to making adult decisions."

"Thank God."

"Yeah, well, along with the decision-making comes a lot of responsibility." Eli nudged his gelding forward, and I followed on a path uphill. The gradual slope made for easy riding. At the top, he turned his horse and stopped. "Check it out."

The view was awesome. Hills and trees for as far as the eye could see. "Nice."

"See that road straight over there? That's the one you and Colonel Ron walked up."

"Grayson Springs Road?"

"Yep."

"So the path you said goes toward the road takes you that way."

"Sure does. You can go that way if you don't have a buggy."

Pointing left, I said, "Do you believe those woods are cursed?"

"Ben does. And so do a lot of others. I went in there, and yes it was raining, but that day it was raining everywhere."

As Eli spoke, I caught wind of a familiar scent. "Can you smell that?"

Eli's nostrils flared as he identified the smell. "You know what that is?"

"People do smoke weed in New York."

Two male voices could be heard from just over the ridge. When their heads appeared, Eli said, "Might wanna let me do the talking."

One guy, short and stocky with a Red Man cap, carried some kind of a long-handled shovel. The other, about 5'9" and skinny, had an unshaven face and long, stringy hair. He carried a rifle. Both looked to be in their early twenties. "Eli Clemons, what you doin' up here?" asked the short fellow.

"Jimmy ... William. 'Bout to ask y'all the same."

Jimmy grinned and said, "We's just squirrel huntin'."

"Is that right? Out of season?"

"Ain't never stopped us before."

"You plan on knockin' a squirrel in the head with that spade?"

While Eli spoke with Jimmy, William stepped toward me. "Well, I'll be damned. Looky here, Jimmy. Remember that girl you said I made up. Here she is bigger than life, right in front of me." Staring at my eyes, he said, "Didn't think I'd ever see you again."

"Excuse me," I replied.

"Eli, how you know this wild eyed bitch?"

"She's a guest of Colonel Ron at Grayson Springs."

"Guest!" Jimmy blurted. "Heard he had himself a couple outlaws livin' there."

Gripping Casper's bridle, William said, "You sure I didn't see you in that wet woods over yonder? About a year ago?"

Eli answered for me. "She lives in New York."

"No shit. Ain't never had me no New York girl."

"Sir, I don't know what your intentions are, but I can assure you today is not your day to *have* a New York girl, and furthermore, I'd appreciate it if you would unhand my horse."

"Your horse. Believe this mare belongs to Ol' Man Henry."

Eli said, "It belongs to her now. I bought it from Sherman Henry."

"And you gave it to *her*? Damn, Eli. Bitch must be good."

I slid off the saddle, stood in front of the scraggly, foul-mouthed scoundrel, and said, "Sir, the last guy who called me a bitch got whooped."

As Eli dismounted, William squealed, "Ooooweeee. Eli, you gonna whoop me for calling this girl a bitch?"

"I don't need his help, and I already asked you nicely to let go of my horse."

Still gripping Casper's bridle, William held up his rifle and said, "And what if I don't?"

The words had barely left his mouth when I kicked him between his legs. Shocked and caught off guard, the skinny redneck bent forward, moaning in pain. I began wailing his head with both fists like a cage fighter. He dropped his rifle. Jimmy started to move at me, but Eli grabbed his shirt collar. When William went to his knees, I kicked him once under the chin, sending his thin frame backwards. He landed hard in weeds, unconscious, face bleeding.

"Brooke! No!" screamed Eli as I grabbed the man's rifle. "That's enough!"

I slung the gun out into the weeds.

Jimmy pulled away from Eli's hold and started toward his friend. "Heard tell that bitch was crazy. Look at 'er all foaming at the mouth."

Eli asked, "You sure you wanna call her that?"

"She killed 'im."

Short on breath, and feeling my demons, I wiped my face, looked down at William and said, "He's breathing."

On our way back down the hill, Eli said, "Kind of lost it back there, didn't you?"

"Excuse me?"

"Why would you attack William like that?"

"He wouldn't let go of Casper."

"For that you attack a man?"

"He had bad intentions."

"Did you not think I could take care of the situation?"

"He threatened me, not you."

"You really think he was threatening you?"

"Felt that way to me."

"So am I supposed to forget what I saw?"

"What did you see?"

"I saw a pretty girl turn ugly, out of control, distorted. Girl, you sure as hell were foaming at the mouth."

"It happens when I get mad."

"Damn. So what am I supposed to tell the Colonel?"

"Tell him anything you want."

After crossing the creek, I asked, "Can this horse run?"

"When you're ready, she'll be ready."

I said, "I'm ready," and then kicked Casper into a trot and immediately began bouncing in the saddle.

Eli shouted, "Remember what I said about sitting the trot." He kicked his horse into gear. Catching up he said, "If you wanna run, let's run! Keep your head down."

Eli urged his gelding to a run, and Casper followed. As the horse sped up things got a whole lot smoother. My hair began blowing back in the wind and it felt like heaven. As we rounded the turn at the end of the field, the path widened. Eli slowed until I was next to him. "You okay?"

"Yes!"

"You look good!"

Thirty seconds later we rounded the second turn and were running parallel to the road. A pickup truck honked as it passed and its driver yelled out the window, "Go, Eli, go!"

Casper and the gelding were side by side when we reached the third turn and started back toward the barn. "Pull 'er up!" shouted Eli.

I slowed the mare the way Colonel Ron had instructed on day one. My excitement had me breathing hard. "I've never had that much fun in my life."

"Better than kickin' William's ass?"

"Better."

Eli smiled and said, "You ride well. Just gotta learn how to post." Then he held out his fist for a bump. I reached out and we touched knuckles. "Consider that a kiss." His words made me feel funny, and I wondered if that was what Sherri meant.

Colonel Ron stood waiting at the barn. "Horses are wet. Been running 'em, haven't you?"

"Yes, Sir," replied Eli.

I sat smiling in the saddle. "Colonel Ron, I've never had so much fun!"

"Lucky you didn't kill yourself."

"Girl rides like she's been doing it all her life."

"What happened to your hand?" Colonel Ron asked, noticing blood on one of my bruised fists.

I clammed up.

"Eli," questioned the Colonel, "what happened?"

My riding partner stared at me a few seconds and then spilled his guts. "Up on the hill, we ran into Jimmy Jackson and William Rice. Both of 'em high as hell. William got fresh with Brooke. Wouldn't let go of her horse, so she wore 'im out."

"Did he put his hands on you?"

"No sir," I answered.

"Then you had no right to attack him."

"But..."

"No buts about it. That rage of yours is why you are here. You gotta learn when and when not to use force.... And Eli, why didn't you do something to stop it?"

"It was over in a flash. Girl lives up to her reputation."

"Jesus! Is William hurt?"

"I'd say."

"Dammit, girl, this ain't gonna go away. Boy's liable to press charges." There was an odd silence, as if he were waiting for my comment. I had nothing to say. Colonel Ron closed his eyes momentarily, as if gathering composure. Finally, he looked back up at me and said, "Man to man, I'm gonna need you to write down exactly what happened, and I want it before supper, and dammit, I guess now I *will* have to think twice about letting you out of my sight." Stroking Casper's sweaty neck, he said, "Take 'em to the creek so they can drink and cool off."

Chapter 26

We'd barely gotten into our room that night when Sherri started. "Well?"

"Well what?"

"Don't act stupid. I want to know everything."

"Not much to tell. There were a couple of idiots up on the hill. We were like, sitting on our horses checking out the scene when I smelled them..."

"They were dirty?"

"Well, that too, but they were smoking pot."

"Damn. Wish I was there."

"Don't believe you would want to smoke with these guys. They were a couple of real inbred-looking hillbillies with dirty hair and dirty mouths, and one of them acted like he wanted me."

"No shit? Just like that?"

"Said I was perrrrty and that he'd never had him no New York bitch before."

"So you hit him?"

"I hit him because he wouldn't let go of my horse."

"Good grief. So what did Eli do?"

"Nothing. Wasn't anything for him *to* do. I took care of it."

"Then what? Did they leave?"

"We left. The one guy was still on the ground."

"You are one crazy bitch..."

"Hey. Already told you about that."

"Sorry ... Soooo, no kiss?"

"You heard the Colonel. We behaved ... but we did do something."

Sherri's eyes were big.

"We touched fists again."

"You touched fists. That's it?"

"But I ... I think I felt some of what you were talking about."

"Ohhhh," Sherri smiled, "so there is something going on in that perrrtty little head of yours."

"There's something I want to ask you?"

"Anything. Just call me your one stop source for relationship information."

"Jesus, girl. Get over yourself.... I need you to cover for me while I leave Grayson Springs."

Casper became my best friend. I kept her up in the barn until she got really used to me. Eli shared his system that reminded me of Pavlov's bell. We let Casper out into the lot, on a long lead. As she walked around, I whistled. When I whistled, I drew her to me with the rope and then immediately treated her with a handful of oats and a hug. After a few repetitions, she knew my whistling meant oats and love, and she came without my tug.

Each morning before breakfast, I let Casper into the lot, whistled her back, gave her the treat, and then saddled her for a ride around the field. Once away from the barn, I took the trail toward the road and then ran her down the backstretch. Returning along the creek, I let her have a drink and cool off, hoping Colonel Ron wouldn't suspect we'd been running.

After morning chores, working in the yard became a daily ritual. If there was heavy dew or it had rained overnight, we'd have to wait until the grass dried before cutting it. Colonel Ron had this opinion that idle moments were wasted opportunities. To fill such, he expected, at the very least, *thinking*.

One morning, as we sat on the porch waiting for fog to lift, Loretta drank coffee while Colonel Ron rolled his day's number of cigarettes. I noticed him glancing my way to see if it was teasing me. My desire to smoke had actually been depleted by the unpleasantness of non-filtered cigarettes. They were so strong it took away from the experience. I assumed it was Colonel Ron's frigging psychological approach to getting me to quit on my own.

"We all think, you know," philosophized Colonel Ron, "the whole time we are awake."

"Duh," replied Sherri. "It just happens. Like a dream."

"Exactly," continued the Colonel. "But while we have no control over our dreams, we can control what we think about in our daily routines. If I am relaxing here on this porch, I might choose to think about my day ahead, or I can think toward solving a problem ... my future ... my past. It's all up to me."

"Why," Sherri asked, "would you waste time worrying about the past?"

"Didn't say I would worry about the past. But I might think back to how my life has gotten to this point. The mistakes I've made. The things I enjoyed. Those are the thoughts that shape my future, or at least how I perceive my future. If I avoid looking back, I take the chance of repeating the same mistakes. Don't wanna do that."

I commented, "You think way too much, Colonel."

"No more than you. Of all us on this porch, I'd say you are the thinker."

"So you're saying Loretta doesn't think? Is she like a dense bimbo who sits around staring blankly into nothingness?"

"Damn," spurted Loretta. "Guess I need to *think* about that."

Colonel Ron said, "You've just made my point, Brooke. You took my simple statement and blew it into a short story. Could we not write a book on what you just said about Loretta? True or not, you put a *thought* into your statement and covered a lot of ground in the process."

Sherri stood up and said, "Colonel, you're giving me a headache."

"He has a point," I admitted. "I mean, I think about all sorts of things while pushing the mower. It makes the work go by."

"Me too," Sherri complained, "I think about how much I hate cutting grass!"

Thinking came easy for me. Every stroke with the mower brought me one step closer to my plan to visit Sherman and Eloise Henry. They were the ugly people, but they were also the key to my past, my mother's name, the location of her grave, and my real father's name. Just daydreaming of those tidbits of information made my work go by.

Sunday morning would be my best opportunity to leave Grayson Springs unnoticed. It was sleep-in day for the Colonel and Loretta. Awakening to my absence might not be alarming, since they had already become accustomed to my morning ride on Casper. I lay awake for most of that Saturday night in anticipation of my quest for information. Before leaving the room, I placed my hand on Sherri's shoulder.

"Wake up a minute," I whispered.

She reluctantly rolled over. With the curtains pulled open, just enough moonlight bled in for me to make out her face. "What?" she said out loud.

"Shhhh. Don't be loud. You'll wake someone. I'm getting ready to leave."

Sherri rose up in the bed. "What time is it?" she whispered.

"Not sure. I'd say somewhere around four-thirty."

"You're really gonna do it?"

"Yes. I have to."

"So, what do I tell them if they ask where you are?"

"Just say you thought I was going to take a dump. Chances are, I'll be back before they come looking. If it's after daylight, they'll think I'm out riding Casper."

"Oh yeah, that'll work," she mumbled while rolling back over. "But if you don't come back, I'll have to tell the truth because I'll be worried about you."

"I'll be back."

The stairs seemed to creak louder than usual. With each step down my heart beat faster. By the time I got out the back door, anxiety had me hyperventilating. I had never snuck out of the apartment in New York.

The tree canopy blocked most of the moon's light as I slowly rounded the end of the inn. It sounded as though someone had turned up the volume on all the night creatures. A hoot owl hooted, tree frogs screamed, and bull frogs bellowed from all along the creek. Mosquitoes buzzed around my head like little fairy vampires desiring my blood.

A noise startled me; something splashed through creek water to my left. I stopped in my tracks, waiting, and could hear what sounded like some four-legged animal plowing its way through brush behind me. Then I could no longer hear it at all.

Is it close? Did it go the other way?

Something nudged the back of my leg, and I nearly wet myself. It was Bruno. "Damn, dog," I whispered with as much enthusiasm as I could allow. "You scared the shit out of me."

Nearing the creek, things became more visible, and yet I still stumbled once on a loose rock while crossing. "Shit!"

Apparently the horses heard me. They began snorting at my approach. Inside the barn, chickens cackled quietly at mine and Bruno's untimely arrival. It was too early even for the rooster to crow. When I opened her stall door, Casper became rowdy. I slipped off her halter, slipped on her bridle, and she knew it was time for an early morning ride. After a hug around the neck, I took her into the runway to be saddled. Ten minutes later, I opened the gate so that Casper and I could leave Grayson Springs for an early morning, slightly moonlit adventure. Hairs stood up on my arms as I began my trek. Bruno knew my morning routine and did not follow. I rode Casper at a walk to the pathway that led toward the road. She knew her way well and I urged a trot. By then, I had perfected the posting procedure and could easily ride the pace. I couldn't tell if it was getting lighter or perhaps my eyes were adjusting; nonetheless, I could make out most of my surroundings.

Nearing the road, I hesitated at the sound of an automobile approaching in the distance. Lights appeared and I kept far enough away from the road to prevent being seen. When the car had passed, I dismounted, opened the steel gate and led Casper out of the field. It felt like an escape. After closing the gate I walked her up onto the blacktop before mounting. The loudness of horseshoes on the asphalt worried me. It made sense to ride on the roadside grass for fifty yards or so to the intersection, and then another fifty yards up the road Colonel Ron and I had walked days earlier. At that point, I stepped Casper up onto the road and bumped her to a noisy trot. The clip-clopping sounded even louder than the first night when we rode from Clarkson to Grayson Springs. I wanted to run, but was afraid the steep grade would be too much.

Halfway up, I noticed headlights in the distance, flashing through trees. A patch of cedars provided a large enough hiding place for Casper and me until the pickup truck passed by. I had not anticipated traffic on an early Sunday morning. Continuing, I soon crested the hill and paused in front of the old woman's house. Dawn had reached the horizon. Roosters had already begun to crow. Though the house sat dark, light funneled down from a single unit mounted high on the front of the nearby barn. While I knew in my heart that the old woman possessed more knowledge about my past than she was willing to reveal, my mission lay half a mile away, down a hill, through the woods, in the flats.

"Come on, Casper. Let's go."

At the spot where Colonel Ron and I had sat on the road's edge talking, I recalled the story of his friend dying in the flats. Should I fear the place where I once ran as a child? I could still remember the old house, the barn, the chicken coop, and the outhouse.

As I stepped Casper off the blacktop and into the dark woods, most of dawn's light disappeared, and I again struggled to see. It reminded me of the night I left the flats in Dr. Green's car. Only this time I descended. At least the grassy dirt road eliminated clip-clopping. The downhill grade lasted for about a hundred yards before I saw what looked like the proverbial light at the end of the tunnel. As I left the woods, things leveled into the misty flats. Next to the pathway, a leaning, dilapidated sign read, *No Trespassing*. For a moment, I sat in the saddle, staring out across the property, trying to remember it as it was twelve years earlier. It seemed smaller and more confined by woods. I could see a satellite TV dish on top of the house ahead. Around the house and barn, weeds had taken over much of what had once been kept groomed.

.....We were playing hide-n-go-seek. I came to this spot, hiding behind brush. It was the first time I saw the No Trespassing sign. At some point, I became more interested in the sign than the game and stood in front of it, rubbing my hand across the letters. The ugly boy, James, tagged me and questioned, "What are you doing?" I asked him what the letters on the sign said? He told me it said, "You cannot leave." Looking back, I realize neither of us could read.....

Casper must have gotten scent of another horse. She began snorting, and then I heard a neigh-whinny up near the barn. Seconds later, a dog began barking and I could tell it was approaching. Casper became restless. "Easy, girl. It's okay." The scraggly looking hound came to within thirty feet and then stood at bay, barking his displeasure at my presence. From the house, I heard a squeaky door hinge and then a brusque voice: "Who goes there?"

I was afraid to speak and remained silent.

"Speak up or I'll shoot!"

Jesus, he's going to shoot me. "I come to visit ... sir!"

"Didn't hear no car! You walk in?"

"No sir! I'm riding my horse!"

"You by yourself?"

"Yes, sir!"

"Come closer!"

"Come on, Casper." As I left the protection of shadows, I feared the old man would shoot me. A light was on inside the house, and I could make out the man standing in the doorway with a shotgun and the woman staring out from behind him. I stopped about forty feet away, close enough to hear the woman's mumbling voice, but not enough to understand her words.

"Come closer!" barked the old man.

I stepped Casper another twenty feet.

"That's close enough."

I sat staring, waiting. The woman whispered into his ear. He shouted, "Ain't nobody visits here. Not this time of a mornin'. State your business."

"I want to talk with you."

As I spoke, the woman whispered again, and the old man said, "I know who you are. You got no business coming here. What the hell do you want?"

"I do not want trouble, sir. I only want to learn about my past. I've spent twelve years trying to figure out who I am ... who my parents are."

After more whispering, he asked, "Where'd you get that horse?"

"It was a gift, sir. My friend Eli gave it to me for my birthday."

"Eli Clemons gave you that horse? How the hell you know Eli?"

For the first time, I heard relief in the man's voice. "I'm staying at Grayson Springs. Eli helped us rebuild the footbridge."

"And for that he gave you that horse?"

"We've become friends."

"So, you the one whooped up on William Rice?"

"News travels fast in Grayson County."

"You ain't changed a bit."

"May I speak with you about my past?"

As the woman whispered again, I realized that the old man could not see me. He said, "Git down off that mare. Come on in," and then both of them disappeared into the house.

I tied Casper to a nearby sapling and then stepped up to the door. The sound of a TV and a stench of uncleanliness came from within. I pulled open the same ragged, wooden screen door that I had let slam often as a little girl, shut it quietly, and entered the world of my nightmares. The front room seemed much smaller than I remembered it. A wood stove still stood in the corner. Off to the left was the doorway to the one bedroom shared by me and the boys. In the kitchen, I found the old couple sitting at a table cluttered with mail, a carton of cigarettes, an open pack and lighter, an ashtray full of butts, two coffee cups, a bottle of whiskey, and a small flat screen TV. In the light, I could see that the old man's eyes were cloudy. He felt for a remote, and used it to turn off the TV. The woman's stare was unreadable. She asked, "You drink coffee?"

"Yes, ma'am."

"Take a seat." As I did, she rose and began pouring a cup. "Sorry about the way the place looks. Reckon by now you can tell Sherman's lost most of his eyesight. Hard to keep things up."

"I'm sorry."

"Why you sorry?" grumbled the old man. "Ain't your fault." He stared blindly for a moment, and then said, "Ain't nobody calls me sir. Call me Sherman. Her name is still Eloise, and ifin' I remember correctly, yours is Mary Elizabeth."

Mary Elizabeth? "Excuse me?"

"What? Don't know your own name?"

Mary Elizabeth? I didn't know what to say. I sat suddenly confused. "No one ever called me Mary Elizabeth."

Eloise sat the coffee cup in front of me and said, "We never used your saint's name. Wasn't no one else here had one."

"So why did I?"

"Reckon you got some Catholic in you," opined the old man.

My adopted parents raised me Catholic, but I had never considered that my real parents were Catholic as well. "So I..."

Sherman interrupted, "She says you're dressed like an Amish. Eli done converted you?"

"No, sir. I have to dress this way for six weeks as part of the program I'm going through at Grayson Springs."

"I hear tell that Lee fella's a bit weird."

"Colonel Ron is nice. He's a psychologist."

"And why would you need a psychologist? Didn't you get adopted by a shrink?"

"The court will not allow testimony from my legal guardian."

"What kind of trouble you in?"

"Guess you could say I have a problem with my temper."

"Always did," added Eloise.

"So," asked Sherman, "what is it you want from us?"

"I need to know who I am. Who my parents are, or were. I grew up thinking my mother and father deserted me and that's why I was living here. Now I've been told that I was born here."

"Who told you that?"

"Mrs. White ... lady up on the hill."

Eloise seemed to want to speak, but did not. Sherman slid his hand across the table until he found his pack of cigarettes and a lighter. Suddenly, the sight of filtered cigarettes had me craving. "May I have one?" I asked.

He tapped the pack until one stuck out and offered it my way. "Thank you." Sherman lit his and then held the lighter in my direction.

As I exhaled my first glorious draw, he said, "What else did that old hoot on the hill tell you?"

"Not much. She said my mother died the night I was born. I got the feeling she knew more but kept it to herself."

"How'd you come about talking to her?"

"Colonel Ron introduced us."

The old man took another draw and then said, "Before we go any further here, I want you to know that I've had a bad taste in my mouth ever since your little ass left here."

"Why?" I asked.

"Before you went to causin' problems, we had us a good thing goin'. State paid us a pretty penny for keeping kids. After you left, they come and took 'em all. Now, as you can see, we got nothin'. Livin' on what little social security Uncle Sam gives us. And that ain't much."

"I'm sorry."

"Sorry. Hell, I'd like to know what your problem was. We provided you with clothes, food to eat, and a dry place to sleep. What the hell else did you want from us?"

"I'm sorry, sir, but my memories are not all that pleasant. A lot went on here that should never have happened."

"Like what?"

I could feel myself angering. "Like me having to bathe with boys and them putting their hands on me. They rocked the outhouse and stared at me through the cracks. They took my clothes off and laughed at me when I ran back to the house naked. And that one boy came in the middle of the night and touched me in places where he shouldn't have. Need I continue?"

The old folks sat there silent, like they were stunned. Eloise became teary-eyed.

I said, "I know you knew what was going on."

The old man sucked hard on his cigarette, and I did the same. He reached for the bottle of whiskey, opened it, and took a big swig. Then he spoke. "Girl, I don't know how things are up there in New York, but down here in these hills ... well, we're simple people. You city folks got your high society schools and fancy computers. We never had none of that. Eloise made it to the eighth grade. My old man made me quit after four years. Needed me to work on the farm. And let me tell you right now, we all grew up takin' baths together. By the time water got heated, wasn't no sense in wastin' it. And as for that other stuff, hell, the first hairy pussy I ever seen was my older sister's ... reckon I ran right off in the woods and abused myself."

His lack of couth sickened me. Eloise hung her head as he continued.

"Back in my day, we growed up watchin' farm animals mate. Hell, I reckon we's just as curious as boys in the big cities. We couldn't run out and hire us a whore or watch a dirty movie or look at a book. But ain't none of us didn't peek through the cracks in a outhouse a time or two. Or at least until our mammas wore us out for it."

"And so you think it was okay for that boy to hold me down and touch me and all that?"

"No, I don't. And I didn't back then, neither. Don't reckon you know'd about me whoopin' that boy's ass for what he done. Think I shoulda' hauled you out there in the barn and let you watch? You was a little girl and I didn't feel you needed to see what I done to him."

"But he didn't stop."

"Didn't know that." He turned to Eloise. "She say anything to you?" Eloise shook her head.

I exhaled a draw and said, "That's because I didn't think you did anything about it!"

Sherman downed another drink from the whiskey bottle. When he set it down, Eloise grabbed the bottle and took herself a desperate drink. She exhaled like it burned and then said, "Honey, you was just a little girl when them boys took your clothes off. And I switched 'em all for it. You was the only girl on the place, and that's why they picked on you. If you think you were abused, you shoulda heard some of the stories them young fellas brought with 'em. They were angry, just like you. Had they been good boys, we wouldn't of got 'em in the first place. We done our best. In a way, what we did for kids was like what Mr. Lee is doin' for you. We was givin' 'em a second chance."

I sat there stunned as the people I hated for twelve years were making reasonable arguments for the bad behavior of those I felt abused me. Never had I considered that the boys I grew up with had themselves been abused.

"How old are you now?" Sherman asked.

"Just turned eighteen," I replied while smashing out my cigarette in the ashtray.

"Older you get, more you'll understand the drive behind how young folks acts ... boys *and* girls. Don't know if you're a God fearin' woman or not, but I'd say it's our instincts what makes us sinners. We ain't that much different than any other animal on this earth. A man's gonna have food and water, even if he has to kill for it. Gotta have air to breathe, and sex to multiply, otherwise we'd cease to exist. You been to college?"

"Not yet."

"Well then I reckon I've learned me about as much listenin' to that television set as you have in school. And before I lost my sight, I read me the whole damn Bible, front to back. Lot of things a man does he don't understand 'til he gets old. Then he looks back and sees how his sexual desires controlled his youth. How he woke up thinkin' about it. Thought about it all day, went back to sleep thinkin' about it, and then dreamed about it. Preacher man's gonna tell you it's the devil makin' you feel that way. Well I'm a dumb old country man, and I can tell you it ain't the devil. Believe it's our instincts. I'd say they's the same stuff inside a man's brain that's inside a dog. Makes it jump a fence and mount a bitch it ain't never even seen before. Most of us got enough good raisin' to control ourselves. Act like human beings and not like animals. That boy what messed with you, he had no upbringin' before he got here. Comes a point where they ain't no amount of ass whoopins gonna fix him. Boy like that will likely end up in the penitentiary."

The old man flinched. His cigarette had shortened enough to burn his fingers. He pulled out another, lit it with the last one, and then put out the butt. "Your mamma was one of our girls."

"Your daughter?"

"No," added Eloise, "God never blessed us with one of our own. That's part of why we started raisin' foster children."

"Poor child come here when she was just nine or ten. Only girl we ever took in. Folks round here said her mamma was a witch. She was a squatter down by the lake, 'til she disappeared ... left the child all alone. Wasn't nobody ever knowed for sure who Cynthia's father was."

"Cynthia? My mother's name was Cynthia?"

"That's right. Girl grew up a bit too quick and—"

"Your mamma was beautiful, honey," interrupted Eloise.

"Sure was," continued Sherman, "and she knowed it. Had to take a stick to her and a couple them boys. Difference between you and her was she was old enough to enjoy the attention they was givin'."

Nausea struck me. "My father ... he ... he was one of the boys here?"

"No. I made sure of that."

"Then who was he?"

The old man started to speak, but Eloise interrupted. "Sherman. You can't."

"Can't what?" I asked anxiously.

Sherman sucked hard on his cigarette, and then said, "You leave outa here, you stop back up on the hill and tell that old woman you been talkin' to us. See ifin' she's got anything more to say."

"But ... I think you know."

"I'm sorry girl, but that's all we got to say about that."

I looked up at the clock on the kitchen wall. It read 6:30. "Shit," I screeched, while rising. "I need to go."

"Snuck out, didn't you?" mumbled the old man.

"Yes I did."

"Just like your mama," smiled Eloise.

After starting toward the door, I hesitated. Eloise stood staring. She said, "Sherman let me bring in Cynthia because I wanted a girl so bad. When she passed, it about killed me. Only thing kept me goin' was having you. You were my only baby. Then you went all wild on us. Shut down. When you had to leave, that old hoot on the hill blamed it all on me, said I failed to raise you right."

"Hoot on the hill?"

"Beth ... Old Mrs. White," complained Sherman.

I moved to Eloise and gave her a hug, and we both wept. When I released her, she nodded toward Sherman. As awkward as it seemed, I forced myself to hug him. He jumped at my touch. "Thank you for talking to me," I whispered into his hairy ear, "and I am so sorry for the burdens I might have placed upon you and Eloise." He remained silent, but raised his old hand and gently slid it across my face as if reading brail.

"I *can* see, a little," he spoke with a quiet, choked voice. "Enough to tell you still have that red hair. Your mamma had dark brown hair and not a freckle on 'er. Wasn't nobody down in these flats had red hair. You keep that in mind, Sunshine."

Sunshine! My knees nearly buckled. "You called me Sunshine when I was little?"

"Yes I did. Your hair was wild and tangled and stuck out. Reminded me of the sun."

"Did I ever ride your knee?"

"You did, up until you went wild on us. Then you wouldn't come near me. Never understood. Broke my heart."

"Could I possibly bum another cigarette?"

The old man grinned for the first time and said, "Help yourself."

While I lit one, he felt for the carton, removed a pack and reached out to me. "Take it."

When I accepted the pack, he said, "Now git on out of here before you git in more trouble."

I hugged him again and said, "Thank you."

The old couple stood just outside the door as I mounted Casper. Sherman said, "Eli gave me a pretty penny for that white mare. Boy must think a lot of you."

I patted Casper on the neck and admitted for the first time, "Eli's different. He's the first guy that's ever made me feel good about being a girl."

As I rode away, Eloise asked, "You told him that?"

"No, and you'd best not." Before rounding the curve, I hesitated and hollered back, "What about my mother's grave? I'd like to see it!"

Eloise shouted, "I'll have to mow out a pathway before you come back."

"And what about pictures of my mother?"

"I'll look and see!"

Chapter 27

Let karma be karma. If all the trouble I'd experienced in New York was what it took to get me back in Grayson County, then so be it. I loved Manhattan, with all its hustle and bustle, my friends, Daddy, and, even to some small extent, Melanie. Yet, there I was riding a horse on ground that for the first time in my life felt like home. The Flats wasn't some place I'd been sent to. It was my birthplace. The first ground I ever stepped foot on. Where I learned to walk and talk. It's hard to explain how I felt riding back up the hill. The information I'd received from Sherman and Eloise had shed new light on my nightmares. I could never have imagined that the ugly boys had been abused as much or maybe even more than I had.

In front of Mrs. White's house, I said, "Whoa," and then sat staring. Curtains moved, and I knew she watched. I expected she would come to the door as she had for the Colonel and me. When she did not, I shouted, "I just left Sherman and Eloise. I believe you, and I need to talk!" Apparently she did not want to speak to me. Having no time to waste, I left at a trot.

At the bottom of the hill, several cars passed as I waited to cross the road to reenter Grayson Springs. It had to be near 7:30, normal time for me to be returning from my morning ride. Once through the gate, I kicked Casper into a run. I neared the barn just as Colonel Ron opened the gate to let Bertha back into the field. "Milking on a Sunday?" I asked.

"Well, for you to ask means you weren't here when I started. Or when I got up and made coffee. Looks of that mare, I'd say you took a pretty long ride. You been out all night?"

"No, sir."

"With Eli?"

"No, sir."

"Off the property?"

"Well. Yes, sir."

"First you get in a fight. Now you leave the property. I'm gonna take this milk in to Loretta while you unsaddle. Turn 'er out so she can water herself. When I get back, you and me are gonna have a seat in those green chairs out back of the barn."

I didn't say a word as he walked away. After finishing my chores, I found the green chairs and took a seat. Morning rays were peeking through trees as Casper passed up Bertha and the calf and then disappeared through the creek bank fog. Birds were whistling. *Nature ... why can't my life be so simple*? I sat dreading the Colonel's lecture.

It took forever before I heard him open and shut the gate. Though I knew he paused at the corner of the barn, observing me, I refused to look back. Bruno lay at my feet looking up at his master. Finally, the Colonel came and sat down, but said nothing. After a minute or so, I could take it no longer. "I thought you wanted to talk?"

"Did I say that?"

"You said..."

"I said we were going to take a seat in the green chairs."

"Well, here we are."

"Yes we are."

"Listen, dammit. I've had one hell of a morning, and I could use your advice. So, we gonna talk or not?"

"We can, if that's what you wanna do. You go first."

Now what do I say? "Over the past twelve years in New York, I have never snuck out or even felt the need to. The other day, Eli told me that along with the freedom of being eighteen I get the responsibility of making adult decisions. This morning, I made my first real adult decision. I had to know more about who I am. And the only way to do so was to visit Sherman and Eloise Henry in the Flats."

Colonel Ron raised his eyebrows as if to say, *so that's where you were* and then leaned back into his chair to listen.

"I've been angry for most of my life. Always felt like my real parents abandoned me. And without knowing them, I despised them for that. For making me grow up in the Flats with what I always called the ugly people. Today, I found out that the people I hated actually cared about me. They were unable to have their own children so they started raising foster children. I had no idea that the others there had been abused as much or more as me. And not by the Henrys."

I hesitated, expecting his comments. He said, "Go on."

"My real mother's name was Cynthia. She was a foster child. Mrs. White had told me my mother died the night I was born. The Henrys assured me of that, but what they wouldn't tell me is who my father is. Sherman said I should speak to Mrs. White about it."

"And how does that make you feel?"

God, he sounds like Daddy. "It makes me feel like she knows something she's not telling me. Do you think I could be related to her?" Colonel Ron sat with his chin cupped in his hand. "Well?" I insisted.

"So, you feel she knows something about your father?"

"Yes, I do. Remember the day at the church, in the graveyard? I felt something weird when I touched the gravestone of Mary Elizabeth Pierce, the grandmother of Mrs. White."

Colonel Ron nodded.

"Today, Sherman and Eloise told me that my real name is *Mary* Elizabeth."

"Where did Brooke come from?"

"I made Brooke up because I didn't like being Elizabeth."

After another moment of silence he said, "You made Brooke up. Are you happier as Brooke?"

"What does that mean? I'm still the same person."

"So then, you are saying that Brooke and Elizabeth have the same personality?"

"Sure they do."

"Are you always Brooke now, or do you switch back and forth between Brooke and Elizabeth?"

"Hold on now. You think because I've been abused that I created a split personality? Hell no!"

"I'm not thinking, Brooke. I'm just listening to what you say. If you say Brooke and Elizabeth are the same person *and* personality, then I believe you. But, you do seem to be having a difficult time with your identity ... who you are ... who your real parents were. These are not unusual feelings for someone of your background. Perhaps we do need to talk to Mrs. White."

"I tried, this morning. She wouldn't come out."

"You knocked on her door?"

"No. She knew I was there. I saw the curtains moving."

"She's probably afraid of you. She *is* old, Brooke."

"Do me a favor. Call me Elizabeth, please."

"Does this mean you want to abandon your New York self for the old Kentucky girl you once were?"

"I think it means I'm finally accepting who I really am and where I came from. Daddy would say a child's first five years plays a big part in his or her adolescent behavior."

"Sounds about right, but what is your point?"

"I'm just thinking that the problems I encountered in New York are byproducts of my early years."

"And?"

"And, the things I've gotten in trouble for are probably not that big a deal here in Kentucky."

"So you think stealing a gun is normal in Kentucky?"

"No, but I bet no one here thinks oddly of a girl who shows an interest in one."

"Fighting?"

"I kicked that hillbilly's ass and no one has come to arrest me."

"So, you think he's forgotten about that? You think there is no chance of retaliation?"

"Not unless he wants more of the same."

"Elizabeth has a lot to learn."

"I bet everybody here smokes pot."

"'Everybody' is a big word. You assume old Mrs. White, the Henrys, Ben and Charlotte, and Loretta and I all smoke marijuana?"

"I bet you have sometime in your life."

"Do you consider drugs to be an answer to your problems?"

"Jesus! Can you knock it off with some of the psychoanalytical shit? I smoked pot to avoid the dreams."

"And you didn't like the buzz?"

"Sure I did. And there you go. You wouldn't call it a buzz unless you did it yourself."

"When was the last time you smoked pot?"

"I don't know. A year ago, maybe."

"And what about the dreams? You still have them?"

"I have dreams about things that make no sense."

"We all do. No one's dreams make perfect sense. However, I do find your dreams interesting in that they seem to include some historical aspect."

"Colonel," I asked, "do you know anything about a grave in the woods of Grayson Springs?"

His eyebrows rose again. "Old man Henry talk to you about that?"

"No."

"Then who did?"

"No one spoke to me about it. It's a dream I've had. Not once, but several times. And it's always the same, me taking flowers to a spot in the woods. I'm only assuming it's a grave because of the flowers."

"So what makes you think it's in the woods of Grayson Springs?"

"Because of what Ben said about it always raining in the woods. It always rains in my dream."

Colonel Ron seemed surprised. Then he squinted and stared. I could tell he was trying to decide if I was lying. Finally, he said, "Don't mess with me on this."

"I swear to you on my mother's grave, which I still haven't seen, I am *not lying*. I have no reason to. And, by the look on your face, I suspect there is such a grave."

"I'd be careful who you speak to about this subject. Been hearing that story since I was a kid. Some call it a grave. Some say it's a buried treasure. Probably just a rumor, but some around here take it seriously. Those two boys on the hill the other day, you and Eli assumed they were cultivating marijuana. People don't grow pot up on the hill. Too far to carry water...."

"So what were they doing?"

"Obviously they were smoking pot, but I'd say they were treasure hunting on my property. Seems every year or so someone new decides to dig up the hill, looking for buried treasure."

"What kind of buried treasure?"

"If you asked them, they'd say Civil War-era stuff. Twenty-seventh Regiment used to have a recruitment camp up on the hill back in the eighteen-sixties. Ask me, those young boys don't give a hoot about civil war memorabilia. My guess is they've been talking to some old-timer about the grave or treasure or whatever in the hell it is."

"Who do they think is buried in the grave?"

"Nobody. That's just it. That's what's so confusing about it. Some say grave. Some say treasure."

"Like maybe five shiny Flying Eagle Cent pieces?"

Colonel Ron looked like he'd seen a ghost. "Who told you that?"

"No one."

"There's no way you could know that unless ... did Mrs. White tell you that?"

"No. I swear I haven't spoken to her or anyone else about this."

"You telling me you dreamed..."

Before he could finish, the gate squeaked open and we were joined by Loretta and Sherri, both carrying a cup of coffee. Loretta asked, "You two still goin' at it?"

"We're good," replied the Colonel. "We can continue our conversation later."

Sherri offered her cup to the Colonel. "Loretta said you might need this."

Chapter 28

On Monday morning—week four—Loretta's rooster woke me from a delusional visit with Daddy, Melanie, and their newborn baby boy. Details quickly diminished as I lay there considering why my dream would portray a boy when Melanie had told me she was carrying a baby girl. Then, to my further confusion, I realized that Sherri wasn't in her bed. When the door opened and she popped in, I asked, "Where have *you* been?"

"Outside. Why are you still sleeping? Colonel tell you not to take anymore of your morning rides?"

Did he? I thought. "No. Guess I just didn't wake up. What time is it anyway?"

"A little past seven-thirty."

"Why didn't you wake me when you got up?"

"Girl, you were snoring away. Figured you needed to make up some sleep."

"And you've been..."

"I've been sitting on the porch with Loretta and Colonel Ron. Swear to God I believe they're in love."

"Wouldn't surprise me."

"Loretta just now sent me to wake you up so you and Colonel Ron can cook breakfast while she and I go for a walk."

"A walk?

"Yeah...."

"What's up her sleeve?"

"If I had to guess, I'd say she's gonna ask me not to mention my father and her in front of the Colonel."

"Jesus."

"Get up, girlfriend! I want a biiiiiig breakfast when I get back."

Sherri popped back out as quickly as she entered. I used the pitcher of water to wash off, got dressed, and then went to the kitchen.

Colonel Ron crouched over stoking the woodstove. Sensing my presence, he said, "Good mornin', sleepyhead."

"Good morning," I replied in a beeline for the door. "Gotta pee ... and by the way, did you tell me I couldn't ride in the mornings?"

"No." He squinted and said, "Should I have?"

"Nooo." I left the room, and then stuck my head back in. "Hey, big boy. Would you be interested in a real cigarette?"

He stared for a second, and then said, "You're bad."

"Can I take that as a yes?"

"Hurry back. I've got something to show you."

On my scurry to the outhouse, I wondered what he might want to show me. Sitting there on that wooden seat, with my skirt pulled up under my arms, it dawned on me how good I felt. *Is this what happy is? Are these kind of people my kind of people? Is this where I belong?*

Returning, I said, "Be right back," while rushing through the kitchen and up the stairs. I removed a couple cigarettes from their hiding place and then dashed back down. Colonel Ron had his hands in a bowl, kneading up a mixture of flour, milk, and lard. He had an envelope in his shirt pocket, and I wondered if it might contain what he wanted to show me. "Here," he said, "you finish this while I check the fire. We can go outside while they bake."

He supervised as I managed to create my first flat pan of eleven homemade biscuits. By the time I placed them into the oven, I feared Loretta and Sherri would come back and catch us smoking. "We'd better hurry before they get back."

"Don't worry," he assured. "Sherri wanted to see the top of the hill, the place where you and Eli went. They're walking, so it'll take a while." As he poured a cup of coffee, he asked, "You?"

I suddenly got that feel good feeling again. At home it's never like this. "Sure, coffee and a cigarette. Isn't that like an old people's American tradition?"

"Blah, blah, blah."

Outside, we sat our coffee cups on the small table between the rockers. When I pulled the two filtered cigarettes out of my blouse pocket, the Colonel looked like a child on Christmas. "Let me guess," he said. "Old man Henry?"

"You'd be right," I responded as he lit his and then mine.

For a few seconds, we both sat cherishing the taste. "Damn," he said, "almost forgot how good these are."

"You were going to show me something?"

"Oh yeah," he replied, while removing the envelope from his shirt pocket. "Look me in the eye, Brooke..."

"Elizabeth."

"Elizabeth. What I am about to show you is in confidence. I bought this at a sale in Massachusetts. It caught my interest because of the way it appears to reinforce the old stories of buried treasure here at Grayson Springs, and of a young man who befriended old Mrs. White's great-grandmother..."

"Mary Elizabeth Pierce?"

"That's right." He opened the envelope and pulled out an aged piece of paper. Unfolding it, he said, "The man who sold me this claimed it was a page from the Congressional notes of Senator John Jordan Crittenden. Read it and tell me what you think."

I laid my cigarette on the edge of the table before accepting the fragile sheet that appeared to be a single page from someone's journal.

Saturday, February 21st, 1857

It will be another cold day in the Senate chambers. With floor business about to begin, some members entertain a morning dose of political gossip. In addressing SB90, I asked the good Senator Jones of Tennessee if he still possesses his Flying Eagle proof. He answered affirmatively. I offered him a dollar for it. Mr. Jones wants two. Man drives a hard bargain. Now, I suspect, he sits there next to me, writing about how he is going to outsmart me for that second dollar.

Mr. Henry Rice continues to lobby. Poor man worries himself sick over his HR642. We all know it is a matter of time until Minnesota becomes a state. He also has a proof, which I graciously offered to purchase for one dollar. Senator Jones told him he is holding out for two. Mr. Rice now seems skeptical of my intentions and has shied from my offer. I told him I only want to save the coins for my namesake grandson. The boy is not yet three years old, and perhaps shall live long enough to profit from their future value. Mr. Rice still declined. Knowing him to be a gambling man, I offered a betting proposition. He seems confident that today's vote on HR642 will be unanimous in favor of. I wagered $10 to his one cent piece that someone will vote against it. He then suggested that it would be I or Senator Jones who would change our mind. We both assured that we would not vote nay. He begrudgingly agreed to my wager.

Elizabeth and I will join the Bells for dinner tonight at their 14th Street residence. Elizabeth will precede my arrival as she and Mrs. Bell intend to display their cooking talents. On my way, I shall detour by way of the Carusi's Saloon to join Senator Jones for a shot or two of Old Crow. He insists I invite Mr. Rice to join us. If the man intends to be our future colleague, the least he can do is buy us a drink. I must remind him to bring his proof.

Need to leave Dexter's at six o'clock sharp.

"Who's Dexter?"

"Dexter's is the Hotel where Crittenden and Jones were staying during the 34th Congress, 1856-57."

"Wow. This is sooo cool."

"I researched online and read the congressional minutes for that particular day. SB90 is Senate Bill 90. Its passage gave the Treasury Department permission to make a smaller one cent coin. Before that, the one cent piece was about the size of a quarter. Regardless, the treasury made a number of 1856 Flying Eagle One Cent proofs to distribute among Congress so they might see what they were voting on. Problem was they were not meant to be circulated. Yet nearly all of the coins disappeared."

"People collected them?"

"I'd say."

"And HR642?"

"It was a House Resolution presented to Congress by Henry Rice, delegate from the then-territory of Minnesota. Its passage gave the citizens of that territory the right to create a Constitution in preparation for statehood."

"So how did the vote go?"

"Only one person voted against HR642 that day. It was Senator Thompson, the other Senator from Kentucky."

"That's convenient."

"Thought the same thing myself. Did you notice, nowhere on the page does it actually mention Senator Crittenden by name?"

"That's because he wrote it. Writers don't use their own name in first person."

"True..."

"But you should be able to tell it's him."

"Really," he asked, "how?"

"He talks about Elizabeth. One should be able to verify if that was his wife."

"It was. His third as a matter of fact."

"And he refers to John."

"John?"

I handed the paper back and said, "John Jordan Crittenden the Third ... the writer's namesake grandson, who is also the young man you spoke of that befriended Mary Elizabeth Pierce."

Colonel Ron sat silent.

"What?" I asked while puffing on my cigarette.

"I asked you before, how can you have knowledge of these things if you haven't spoken to anyone?"

"I promise you, no one *told* me any of this!"

"But how could you..."

Colonel Ron's questioning got interrupted by the sound of a scream the likes of which one only hears in a horror movie. "What the hell?" he mumbled, rising from his chair.

"Was that Sherri?" I asked, rising also.

"Wasn't Loretta."

The sound of a gunshot echoed through the woods, followed by muffled shouting.

"*That* was Loretta," insisted Colonel Ron as he stepped off the porch. When someone whistled loudly from atop the hill, he dropped his cigarette butt, stepped on it and took off running.

"What's going on?" I shouted while putting out my own cigarette and picking up the Colonel's.

"She needs help! You stay here!"

"Bullshit!"

He hesitated, but knew darn well that I wasn't about to stay behind. "Okay then! We don't have time to saddle horses! We'll have to run!"

"I'm good!"

I pitched the extinguished butts into the weeds and followed. Instead of crossing the creek, Colonel Ron led the way upstream across rocks and then splashing through a portion of the water until we had bypassed the barn and fence. With one hand, I gathered my wet skirt up to my knees and tried to keep up. He climbed the bank and started running parallel to the creek on a deer trail. By the time I got up the bank, he'd already rounded the curve. As I struggled to catch up, Bruno passed me from out of nowhere in pursuit of his master. Seconds later, I rounded the curve and ran right into Colonel Ron as he scanned the trail ahead, the one Eli and I had used to climb the hill on horseback. Bruno sat breathing hard with his tongue hanging out.

"What are you looking for?" I whispered.

He leaned close. "Can't just jump out in the open. Let's go up through the woods."

As quickly as I nodded my approval, he took off, busting his way through saplings and spider webs. He and I both slipped several times in our efforts. Halfway up, Bruno left us, and I could tell the Colonel was tiring. *Too many cigarettes.* At a level spot, near the top, he paused. Voices could be heard from a short distance away. Loretta said, "Bruno? Where's your buddy?"

Colonel Ron smiled and said, "Let's go."

We waded through the brush and into an opening. Loretta stood ten feet from William Rice and Jimmy Jackson, both on their knees. She held a handgun with both hands, pointed toward the ground.

Sherri stood close by, holding William's rifle. She saw us first and hollered, "Colonel Ron! They grabbed me."

"Is that right? How about you give me the rifle?" He took the gun and then looked at Loretta. "You can relax now. They're not going anywhere."

Raising her blouse, Loretta tucked the pistol into a holster attached to her belt, against her back. "Assholes grabbed Sherri. They didn't let go until I fired a warning shot."

Turning to the hillbillies, Colonel Ron said, "Y'all can stand up now. Either of you tries to run, I'll shoot you in the back." After they rose, he said, "William, what the hell would your old man say if I told him you were up here tryin' to kidnap one of my guests?"

"Her back was turned to me. I thought she was the redhead."

Bullshit.

Colonel Ron said, "And that made it right?"

"I owe her."

"You owe her?" Looking at me, Colonel Ron said, "Walk over next to William."

Yeah, right! "Why?"

"Just do it. He's not gonna hurt you. I promise."

218

I moved next to the lowlife and waited for Colonel Ron to continue.

"William, do you even know who this girl is?"

"Hear tell she's the wild child from down in the flats."

Jimmy added, "My daddy says she ain't right in the head."

"Tell your daddy he can kiss my—"

"Brooke!" barked Colonel Ron. "There'll be none of that, thank you."

"My *name* is Mary Elizabeth."

Ignoring me, he turned back to the boys. "If you guys overheard me talking about someone born just up the road from here ... someone with an attitude, mean and lean, ready to fight in a heartbeat ... couldn't I be talking about one of you?"

Neither answered.

"Couldn't I?"

"Yes, sir," answered Jimmy. "Guess that describes both of us."

"But I wasn't talking about you two. I was describing her. She was born in the flats. She's meaner than a snake. And she truly has a reputation for kicking ass and taking names."

William shook his head.

No one ever described me that way before.

"William, you already know how she can be. How you think those folks in New York felt when she started goin' off?"

Jimmy grinned. William almost cracked a smile.

"If you heard some of the things that got her in trouble, you two boys would be saying, *you go, girl.* Basically, they're about to throw her ass in jail for being just like you. So, how can y'all not like her?"

Loretta and Sherri stood quietly, as if analyzing the Colonel's tactics. William scratched his head and said, "Didn't say I didn't like 'er. Said I owed 'er. Day she kicked me in the nuts I was just tryin' to be nice."

"Well, William, I'm afraid she didn't see it that way. But for now, I think you two should apologize to one another." Glancing my way, he said, "How about we just shake hands and let bygones be bygones."

"Bullshit!" I blurted. "I don't owe him an apology, and I have no intentions of shaking his hand."

Colonel said, "What, you too good for him? Think you're better than him, or Jimmy, or *me* because you've been hangin' out in New York for twelve years?"

"No I don't, but he's rude *and* filthy."

"Try not to judge by appearance. Make no mistake, I do not in any way, shape or form endorse or excuse their behavior. However, I don't believe either one of these boys meant you any real harm."

"Yeah, right."

"He is right," admitted William. "I wasn't gonna hurt you. Just havin' a little fun."

Jimmy added, "Most girls around here wouldn't even a took it the way you did. And hell, William just thought you was the girl he seen last year down in them rainy woods."

Loretta looked at me and said, "I agree that they are repulsively dirty, and they damn near got shot for being stupid." Then she turned to William and Jimmy. "And if you boys want a decent girl, you need to clean up your act." Back to me, she continued, "Truth be known, I bet you have friends in New York who would look like freaks in the eyes of these boys."

William and Jimmy stood there looking pitiful. With a conscious effort to ignore his filth, I reached for William's hand. It felt like shaking hands with one of those kids at school that come from poor neighborhoods. The ones no one liked. The ones I always felt sorry for. As I gripped his hand, he no longer seemed a threat. I released and then offered my hand to Jimmy. After we shook, I turned my right shoulder to William and said, "Go ahead."

"What?"

"You owe me."

"You want me to hit you?"

"Sure. I was wrong to hurt you. You owe me."

He stepped back and said, "That's okay. I never did wanna hurt you. I just thought you were, were..."

"Perrrrty," sassed Sherri.

I moved next to Sherri and said, "Okay now, I have to ask, how in the hell do you mistake this busty, beautifully tanned Californian babe for me?"

Jimmy laughed and said, "Told 'im it wasn't you."

William said, "She had her back turned, and her hair was up under the bonnet." As Sherri and I continued talking with the boys, Loretta spoke with the Colonel privately. Quietly, Sherri asked, "So, you guys have weed?"

Before either of them could answer, Colonel Ron interrupted. "Jimmy, William, exactly what were you guys doing up here?" They looked at one another, but neither spoke. "Seriously," asked the Colonel, "Loretta thinks you boys are growing pot."

William said, "Not up here."

"Then what *are* you doin' up here?"

"We been diggin'."

"Diggin' for what?"

Jimmy answered. "Old man ... a little bird told us there's treasure buried somewhere up here."

"So you guys figure you have a right to dig up my property on some wild goose chase?"

Jimmy blurted, "How you know it's a wild goose chase?"

"How you know it's not?"

"Ain't your hill, Mr. Lee," reasoned William.

"To hell it ain't. I have a deed that says it *is* my hill ... got over a hundred acres here. Boys, when I was a kid, I dug up half this hill myself. Never found anything. And right after I bought the place, I came up here with a metal detector. Found a few military items, but nothing you would call a treasure. It's just not here. So believe me when I say you're wasting your time."

Colonel Ron unloaded the rifle and handed it back to William. "Want you boys to go home and think about what happened here today. Loretta coulda' justifiably shot you...."

"What's that mean?" William asked.

"It means she had the right to shoot your ass because you grabbed this girl with intent to do God knows what. If that'd been the girl's father instead of Loretta, you'd both be dead. World ain't like it used to be. The way y'all talk to girls is considered harassment in the real world."

"What's that mean?" William asked.

"It means you could lose a good job for not treating ladies with respect. And if you grab one against her will, dammit, you're gonna go to jail. Now y'all get on outa here and don't be diggin up my hill. Understand?"

Jimmy and William both shrugged their shoulders. They each lit a cigarette. Jimmy moved toward Sherri and said, "Good to meet you. Sorry about scarin' ya." As he spoke, he reached with both hands to shake hers.

William apologized to Sherri as well and then turned to me. "Still think you're nice, and I still think we've met before."

Before walking away, Jimmy said, "Mr. Lee, we might look stupid, but we ain't. When you was a kid up here diggin', this hill didn't belong to you any more than it does me and William. Believe you bought this place just so you could get to the treasure. You never woulda been up here goin' over every inch of it ifin' you didn't think there was somethin' here."

As they disappeared down the hill, Colonel Ron said, "They'll be back."

Chapter 29

Before we made our way back down the hill, Colonel Ron pointed out where the camp of the 27th Regiment had been located nearly one and a half centuries ago. Expecting a fort like the ones seen on TV shows, I found it disappointing that they had simply pitched tents and had not constructed an actual fortress.

When I worried aloud about my biscuits in the oven back at the Inn, Colonel Ron assured me that the fire would burn out before creating a problem. Nonetheless, on our return, my biscuits were more like briquettes. Staring into the warm oven, Loretta joked, "We could save them for the grill."

Though Sherri's big breakfast lacked bread, there were no complaints. As usual, she and I cleaned dishes while Loretta and the Colonel had coffee out front. After a glance to make sure we were alone, Sherri said, "Check this out." From her dress pocket, she withdrew a skinny joint.

"Where did you get that?"

"That guy Jimmy palmed it to me when he shook my hand."

"You trust it?"

"Well, since he already had it rolled, I say yes."

"When do you plan to smoke it? And how can we do it without them smelling it?"

"We can smoke it while we cut grass ... way down by the entrance. They'll never smell it from there."

"Depends on the wind," I reasoned.

Twenty minutes later, we were heading to the yard. Sherri walked in front of me, dragging the mower rather enthusiastically; a dead giveaway, I thought. As I passed the porch, Colonel Ron asked, "What's *her* hurry?"

"Who knows," I answered, shaking my head and walking quickly to catch up. Sherri didn't slow down until she reached the gated entrance, some hundred yards away. "Are you stupid?" I complained, stomping my way up to her.

"What's your problem?" she asked.

"Hell, Colonel Ron's already asking questions. I mean, how obvious are you? You've never shown any passion for cutting grass, and then all of a sudden you trot out here like you can't wait to get started."

"Calm down," she replied, glancing back towards the Inn. "You might be right. Looks like he *is* watching."

"No shit, dumbass."

"Hey, you calm down, bitch." Pulling the joint out, she said, "I believe this is exactly what you need."

"What I need is for you to stop calling me bitch before I go off."

Ignoring my comment, Sherri said, "Let's act like we're picking up debris. See if they go in."

After a minute or so of dragging sticks to the yard's edge, I grabbed the mower and said, "Obviously, they're not going in until one of us starts pushing this thing. I'll go first."

Almost as soon as I started pushing and pulling my way across the yard, Colonel Ron and Loretta rose from their chairs and disappeared into the Inn. Sherri wasted no time lighting up. "Hold on, stupid!" I whispered loudly while making my way back to her. "They might be looking out the window."

"Bullshit," she replied, holding in smoke. "If they look out the window, it'll be to make sure we don't catch 'em in the act."

"Of what?"

"Don't be so naïve."

"You really think they're in there doing the big nasty?"

"Well, hell yes," she answered before taking another hit, and then offering the joint to me.

"Don't pass it to me. Just set it down on that rock."

"Are you that paranoid?"

"Yessss." After she placed the joint on the rock, I glanced back toward the Inn, ignored the angel on my left shoulder and gave into the devil on my right. A long, hard draw left me coughing.

"Take it easy," Sherri advised.

It had been over a year. Thirty seconds after my second hit, I felt the buzz, noticed the grin on Sherri's face, and knew she felt the same. "Oh my god." I took one more hit and lay it down. Sherri took another hit and then pinched it out, placing the remainder into her pocket.

For a moment, I stood silently, holding the mower handle, admiring the girl in front of me. Her 1800s attire. Her dark, naturally wavy hair. High cheekbones. The way her large breasts protruded behind the material of her white blouse. Her confidence and comfort with who and what she was. When Sherri's head tilted like a puppy, my focus wondered beyond her to the yard, the Inn, the giant cedars. Daddy's words returned. *I'm sending you back in time.* I missed him ... longed to call him and tell him about how much I liked Kentucky. How relaxed I felt with my surroundings. I wanted to ask about Melanie and her baby. A tear tickled my cheek, slowly gravitating to the corner of my mouth.

"You okay?" Sherri asked. "Brooke. New York. Mary Elizabeth!"

"I'm, I'm soooo okay it hurts."

"You are one crazy girl. Give me the mower. I'll cut grass while you get your act together. At least pretend to be doing something."

Standing there watching Sherri take off, rocking that old mower back and forth, rapping lyrics to herself, grass flying, it felt like one of my dreams. Like some sort of revelation waiting to be understood. The sulfur springs area sat in a natural arena surrounded by hills on three sides, to the south, west and north. The old original hotel buildings would have run between where I stood and the Inn. Mary Elizabeth Pierce and John Jordan Crittenden III met for their daily talks on one of the hills that stood before me. The rock mentioned in the diary could still be there. Would their initials in the tree still be visible? The coins—could it be she actually hid them on the hill? Colonel Ron, William, Jimmy, and who knows how many others had been digging up the top of that hill for decades. What none of them knew was that Mary Elizabeth and John never made it to the top of the hill.

Closing my eyes, I held my arms out wide and listened. Sherri, the mower, and her lyrics hip hopped along several yards away. She labored closer, and at some point shouted, "I've known she is crazy all along!"

Ignoring her comment, I began turning like a child in play. Faster and faster I spun until becoming dizzy. It felt awesome, but wasn't a game. Over the years, I'd used the same process whenever I'd lost something in the apartment. I could spin blindly, stop, and more often than not be pointing in the right direction to find what I sought. Standing there, eyes still closed, arms stretched, the sound of Sherri and the mower had ceased and I could no longer tell which direction I faced. *Perfect*, I thought. *So which hill am I facing?*

After a deep breath, I opened my eyes and about died. Straight in front of me, ten feet away, stood Eli Clemons, staring. Next to him stood Sherri doing the same. I felt myself blush. "Having fun?" Eli asked.

I was buzzed and feared speaking would reveal that fact. Sherri said, "Let me guess, you're the scarecrow from the Wizard of Oz."

Still frozen, I glanced left and right at my arms, and said, "There *is* a method to my madness, but nothing either of you would understand."

"I understand the madness," stabbed Sherri.

Without saying a word, Eli closed his eyes and spread his arms like mine. "Jesus Christ," continued Sherri, "you two are a perfect match." That said, she turned and resumed her grass cutting chore.

"Okay," I asked, "are you making fun of me?"

Eli opened one eye just enough to see me and said, "No, just joining the madness. You looked like you were having so much fun, figured I'd try it."

As if reading one another's minds, we both lowered our arms. I was about to explain my childhood positioning exercise when he said, "Heard you had another encounter with Jimmy and William."

How could he know that already? "Who told you?"

"Had breakfast with Ben and Charlotte. He mentioned it."

And who told him? I wondered. "News sure travels fast in Grayson County."

"You got that right. So, you wanna take a walk?"

"Where to?"

"Doesn't matter to me," he replied.

"Well, I don't think the Colonel would want us going back up the hill today. And I'm going to have to do my part of the grass cutting."

"You okay? You look tired."

"Didn't sleep well last night," I lied.

"Tell you what, since you're tired, instead of walking, let's ride."

"But where is your horse?"

"It's at Ben's place. I'll borrow Birdie. You finish your chores while I go say hi to the Colonel and Loretta."

"Ooookay," I answered. "You do that. I'm sure they'll be glad to see you. I'll be along shortly."

Sherri returned with the mower as Eli walked off toward the Inn. "Your turn," she stated. Then, looking at the smirk on my face, she added, "I hope they're done."

"I hope they're not."

"You are one evil woman."

I mumbled, "Something's just not right."

"Excuse me?"

"Nothing. Just thinking out loud."

While finishing my portion of the grass cutting, I noticed Sherri standing behind one of the cedars, striking a match and taking another hit off the joint. *Girl's going to get us caught.*

Chapter 30

The marijuana buzz, though somewhat diminished, still lingered as Eli closed the gate behind us. The comfort I'd had with him before had lost some of its luster. In front of the Colonel and Loretta, I chose not to mention Eli's curious knowledge of the morning's events on the hill.

"So," I asked as we led our horses away from the barn, "how is Charlotte's pregnancy coming along?"

"She looks miserable to me. About to pop." Then he changed the subject. "You knew, didn't you?"

"Knew what?"

"You knew what Colonel Ron and Loretta were doing when I went to the house."

"What *were* they doing?"

"Never mind," he said. "By the way, what's with Sherri this morning? She seems ... different."

"She thinks you and I should do what Colonel Ron and Loretta were doing."

"Whoa!" Eli stopped walking.

I continued a few feet further, looked back and said, "What?"

Instead of answering, he stood there silent. When it became apparent I would not speak, he mounted Birdie, urged her forward and said, "Interesting."

Interesting? I thought, while mounting and pushing Becca to a trot.

As I caught up to Eli, he asked, "Did you tell her you thought I might be gay?"

"Noooo. Are you?"

"Nooooo."

"So, have you entertained the idea of you and me getting together?"

He grinned. "Such bold dialogue today. Does this mean *you* have entertained that idea?"

"I've never had sex with a boy." *Oh shit. Talk about a Freudian slip.*

We were at the intersection in the trails. Eli stopped his horse as if contemplating a direction, but I knew his mind reeled over my comment. Finally, he asked, "Does that mean you've had sex with a girl?"

Oh shit. Now what do I say? "There's a girl from my school. She's lesbian. She tells me I am too."

"So are you?"

"I'm trying to tell you, if you'll just listen."

"I'm sorry. I'm all ears."

"I've always wondered. At Sacred Heart Academy, there were only girls. At some point, I realized that I had an attraction toward them. I mean, I found them attractive. Then I move to Stuyvesant High, and there are lots of boys, but they're ... well, they're different. Some are nasty and disrespectful. I find myself more comfortable around the gay boys. At least they don't paw at you or talk trash. So you could say my little mind had it all figured out, or at least it seemed that way, untilllll I came to Kentucky and met you. I assumed you were gay because you're nice to me and you don't ask for anything in return. But then you say you're *not* gay. Can I just say I'm confused?"

As if inspired by my words, Eli smiled, said, "Follow me," and then kicked his horse into high gear.

Instinctively, I followed. "Where *are* we going?" I yelled.

"Trust me!"

At the end of the field, he veered into the woods, dismounted and opened the fence. I thought, *Surely we're not going to the church?* After splashing across the creek and plowing uphill, it became clear. Casper, not being accustomed to such abuse, snorted and blew snot in our fast ascent. At the top, Eli finally slowed as we rode into the clearing behind St. Augustine Church. I caught up and felt winded as I said, "Eli Clemons, I do trust you, I think, but if you think I'm getting married today, you're full of shit!"

He laughed out loud and said, "God, I love you. No we're not getting married. Just follow me."

While I rode at a walk, around the Church, it dawned on me that he was the first guy to ever say he loved me. *Was that a loose comment, or does he intend it literally?* Instead of going to the Church's entrance, Eli led me to a small frame house nearby. Father Ryan sat on the porch with a cup of coffee, a writing pad, and a Bible. "Well, good afternoon," he spoke first.

"Good day, Father. I believe you've already met Brooke."

"Mary Elizabeth," I corrected.

Eli seemed confused. "Do what?"

"The Henrys told me my real name is Mary Elizabeth. I prefer that."

Father Ryan placed his book and pad on a small table and said, "So you've made progress in your quest for genealogical information. To what do I owe this visit?"

Eli answered. "Father, remember the conversation you and I had about sexual identity?"

The priest's squint told me he had considered the conversation private. Instead of speaking, he answered with a nod.

"I think Brooke ... I'm sorry, Mary Elizabeth could use the same enlightenment."

Father Ryan sat as if pondering our situation. After a sip of his coffee, he looked at me and said, "Is Eli indicating that you have some doubts about your sexuality?"

When I looked at Eli, he said, "Just be honest. If you need, I can leave and come back."

But where will you go? I thought.

He dismounted and then answered my question as if reading my mind. "I'll take a walk in the graveyard. Something I want to see anyway."

God, I wish I hadn't smoked that shit. "Our conversation, Father, will it be in confidence?"

"You can rest assured."

As Eli strolled out into the graveyard, Father Ryan invited me to sit next to him on the porch. "Your rockers are the same as Colonel Ron's."

"The Amish make them locally." He spent an awkward moment staring. "Young lady, I do not mind having this conversation with you provided it is because you want to have it. Not because Eli wants you to have it."

"Father, I've been counseled all my life by psychologists, psychiatrists, school counselors, and friends. If you have anything of value to add to their bullshit, I'm all ears. Eli is part of the reason I am here, but only because his friendship has added to my confusion."

"I see. Can I assume that you and Eli have had some conversation about what we are to discuss?"

"Yes, sir. He knows of my confusion."

"Perhaps we should start with a description of your confusion."

After repeating to Father Ryan what I had admitted to Eli some twenty minutes earlier, I said, "Father, in New York it has been my experience that boys who respect me the way Eli does are all gay. That's why I thought *he* was. And I'm still not sure."

"I will not discuss Eli's situation. Like you, he spoke to me in confidence. Therefore, let's address your situation as if neither of us knows Eli."

"Ooookay. That makes sense. I guess."

"And rest assured; the only thing Eli will know about this conversation is what you tell him."

Father Ryan seemed different from any of my former counselors. His interest appeared driven by spirituality and concern, rather than profit. "Father, I appreciate your discretion."

"That's good. Let me begin by saying that unless you've been living under a rock, so to speak, you should be aware that the priesthood is full of men who have sexuality issues. By nature of our biology, we all have to deal with sexuality. In choosing the priesthood, I created my own sexual depravation. Fortunately, unlike some of my colleagues, I have been able to control my demons. Does that mean they do not still exist? No. What it means is that by virtue of prayer, meditation, and an unusual interpretation of scripture, I have come to understand my sexual dilemma."

"Priests have sexual desires?"

"Choosing the priesthood does not eliminate the needs of the flesh."

"Sex is a flesh need?"

"Like other species on Earth, humans are designed with biological drives to prevent extinction. We must have food, water, air to breathe, and sex to proliferate."

"Are you saying we have instincts of survival?"

"That is exactly what I am saying."

"Does this mean the Church lies when it says the devil causes us to lust?"

"Yes and no. Church doctrine involving the devil was written at a time when mankind used religion to explain things they did not understand, which by the way is very unfair to religion. As man's knowledge increases and we realize the mistakes of our forefathers, it tends to delegitimize God and religion."

"Mistakes?"

"As an example, early Christians believed that it was the presence of a demon which caused a man to have a seizure. Today we know better. We know it is a disease called epilepsy. I referred to my sexual dilemma as a demon. I use this term figuratively because in reality, I know my sexuality is driven by hormones, chemicals created by our flesh bodies to ensure proliferation. Not demonic creatures. Our biological makeup is pretty much the same as all other animals."

"You say we are animals, but are we not different?"

"Sure we are. We have a level of intelligence unparalleled by other earthly species. I personally choose to believe the difference is due to the presence of a celestial body within our flesh bodies. Human beings are the combination of a celestial body and a terrestrial body ... a heavenly spirit and the animal man. And much of what the Church describes as a battle between good and evil is actually a battle between our flesh and spirit."

"That is pretty deep, but I like it. So do you believe in evolution?"

"Of course I do, as does the Catholic Church. We cannot deny truth. Signs of some sort of evolution exist all around us. Does my definition of evolution match that of Darwinism? No, not exactly. Darwin was the Father of Evolution in much the same way that Freud was the Father of Psychology. His ideas were revolutionary. Darwin's theory of evolution began an educated debate concerning how man came about on Earth. For now, let's call it Devine Implemented Evolution. In other words, if God is real, and if scripture is real, then God must have created evolution. Understanding this will make it much easier to comprehend the subject of our conversation."

Father Ryan stopped talking, waiting for my response, as if he'd asked a direct question. But he had not. *What does he want me to say?* "Die," I said.

"Excuse me?" he replied.

"D. I. E. Devine Implemented Evolution. I like it."

"Good," smiled Father Ryan. "Now, before we go any further, may I request that the confidentiality concept goes both ways?"

"I understand, Father. What you are saying is that your views are not all traditional Catholicism and you don't want to get into trouble with the Church."

"Brilliant observation."

I reached out my hand to shake his. We did. He smiled and continued. "Okay, if I open up this Bible and read it as if I had no prior knowledge of its meaning, on the first page I see a description of how God created human beings. He made them in his image. And since his image is a spirit, I can only assume that means he added a spirit to the animal man, thus creating the first human beings. If Devine Implemented Evolution is real, then perhaps man had already evolved to the point of being upright, walking, talking, and even living in pairs before God added the spirit. Let's assume man had already evolved to the stage of Homo sapiens before God added a spirit."

"I get it, Father, and I agree with your analogy thus far, but what does that have to do with my issue?"

"Patience, my dear. I'll get there soon. There's a story in the Bible that describes how God cast Lucifer and his angelic spiritual followers out of Heaven and onto the earth as punishment for their disobediences. We also read Jesus' parables of the prodigal son, the lost lamb, and the lost coins. Each story was told to describe God's attachment to that which he has created. My thought is that his love for those spirits cast from Heaven is just as strong as his love for the prodigal son. We could call them his prodigal spirits."

"So what you are insinuating is that the spirits within us are in fact the spirits God cast out of Heaven."

"Very good."

"Our life then, is it a test or a punishment?"

"Perhaps a bit of both. Biblically speaking, if the spirit within each of us lives a life according to the will of God, then at the death of our flesh body, our spiritual body will be accepted back into Heaven."

"Sounds simple enough."

"Yes, but it gets more complicated. If one reads the Bible carefully, he or she may see a distinct relationship between Adam of the Old Testament and Jesus of the New Testament. It appears that the spirit within Jesus was the same spirit which had formally lived in Adam...."

"Reincarnation?"

"So to speak. Paul writes of the two Adams. The first being Adam from the Old Testament. The second being the Lord, Jesus Christ. Therefore, one could say that the same spirit was in both. The Old Testament is simply a portion of the Hebrew history that runs from Adam to Jesus. Biblically speaking, because Adam gave in to the needs of the flesh, and therefore failed the test in the Garden of Eden, he was not permitted to administer the word of God until his spirit was reborn into the body of Jesus. Of course, the second time around, the spirit of the son of God passed the test in the desert."

"Ooookaaay."

"One must assume that Jesus had a recollection of his past life as Adam, and thus understood the inborn biological needs of the flesh."

"Again Father, I must ask, what this has to do with my issue?"

"For argument's sake, let's assume God offers each of us the same second chance that he offered the spirit of his son. When Jesus said he will come again to judge the living and the dead, could it be that the living are you and I, and the dead are those who have died but were not worthy of heaven ... those waiting for a chance to be reborn into another human flesh body to get a second chance..."

"Or a third?"

"Who knows? My point is this, if a woman lives a long life, yet at the death of her flesh body, her spirit is not worthy of Heaven, what if said spirit gets a second chance? What if that spirit is reborn into the body of a male? Could that man then have a spiritual recollection of his past life and therefore have feminine tendencies?"

"Are you saying that you may have been a woman in your past life?"

"I am simply suggesting there may be a possibility that your confusion is caused by a spiritual recollection of your past life where you lived as a man."

"Oh, my god. If that were true, it would explain why I fight like a man, and why I find women's bodies attractive."

"Perhaps."

"So what should I do?"

"Well, if I were you, I'd keep in mind that for any of this to be the case, your presence on Earth today would indicate that something about your former life was unpleasing to God."

"Are you saying my screwed up life is a punishment for something I did in my past life?"

"Let's remember that my whole theory is speculation. But I'd say if there is a God and he indeed grants our spirits more than one chance, then I can't see him making it any easier. For me, I just plan on living my life according to the will of God in hopes that this will be my last time around."

"Does that mean I should be a nun?"

"No. Of course not. There's a lot involved in a calling to service in the Church. To reach Heaven, I think we simply need to live decent lives, obeying God's commandment to love one another as he loves us."

"So we need to give one another second chances."

"Very good, my dear."

"Father, may I speak freely?"

He grinned and said, "I can't envision you speaking otherwise."

"First of all, you said, 'If there is a God.' Does that mean you have doubts?"

"Not so much doubts as a willingness to admit that no one's interpretation of the word is provable. We take it all by faith. None of us will know for sure until after we are gone from this world."

"Also, Father, you do realize that your hypothesis on sexuality is exactly what you accused our forefathers of doing. Namely, using religion to explain something we do not understand."

"You are correct. It is hypothetical. Nonetheless, until we otherwise explain the sexual identity issues among mankind, is it not better to consider an individual's sexual identity problem as a spiritual issue, rather than considering them to be freaks of nature?"

"To most people, the story you just told would sound like the biggest line of bullshit they'd ever heard. To me, however, while it may be just that, bullshit, it does explain a lot of the issues I've struggled with for most of my life."

"Good. I hope my thoughts will provide you relief on your dilemma. Now, I suggest you join Eli in his stroll among the dead."

Rising from the rocker, I said, "Thank you, Father. And I hope you too will receive some solace from our conversation. I'm sure God will reward your service." I left that porch a different ... woman. The feelings of the past had not disappeared, but they were less discomforting after learning at least a feasible explanation for their existence.

Chapter 31

Father Ryan's thoughts on sexual identity issues rolled in my head as I approached Eli in the graveyard. Standing at the marker of Mary Elizabeth Pierce Lush, he heard me and turned. "How'd it go?"

"Good," I replied.

"And?"

"His ideas are interesting. May I ask why you are looking at this particular grave?"

"Over the years, I've visited many of the graveyards in this area. One thing I've noticed is that back in the day, it wasn't uncommon for a mother to pass her own name to a daughter. Like a man naming his son after himself."

"And?"

"Notice this marker says Mary Elizabeth Pierce Lush. Meaning Mary Elizabeth Pierce married a Lush."

"Okay."

Eli took a few steps to another nearby stone and said, "Look at this one." The grave read *Mary Elizabeth Lush Higdon*. "If you consider the dates," he continued, "you'll see that this grave is that of the daughter of Mary Elizabeth Pierce Lush."

"No shit? Like, Mary Elizabeth Jr.?"

"One more," Eli said as he reached for my hand. I accepted, and he led me to yet another grave: a much newer, larger, fancy six-foot wide stone. "Now check this one out."

The left half of the stone read *George E. White, 1935—2000*. The right side had been pre-marked *Mary Elizabeth Higdon White, 1933—*.

"So this woman is still alive?"

"Exactly. And with all this in mind, do you not find it interesting that the Henrys would name you Mary Elizabeth, as if somehow you belong in that linage?"

On our ride back to the Inn, I kept thinking about the letters *M.E. White* on Mrs. White's mailbox. Eli remained quiet until we got to the bottom of the trail that led up the hill. He stopped and said, "Shame we can't go up there."

"Why's that?" I asked.

"I enjoyed the way we sat looking out over the hills from the top."

In my mind I could hear Sherri chanting, *Do it. Do it. Do it.* Regardless of what Father Ryan had said, it still felt awkward. "Eli," I asked, "what do you know about the treasure Jimmy and William have been looking for up there?"

"Treasure? I thought they were growing pot?"

"Not up there, they said."

"That makes no sense. I mean..." Eli cut himself short.

"What?" I asked.

"How do you know they're looking for the treasure?"

"They said that's what they were doing ... digging for treasure. So, you know about the treasure?"

"Sure I do," he replied. "Everybody in these parts has heard the treasure stories. But I didn't know Jimmy and William were interested. Those boys wouldn't know a treasure if they saw one."

"Would you? I mean, do you know what it is they're looking for?"

"Coins, I've heard ... old cent pieces. Rumor is they're worth a fortune. No one knows for sure that they even exist."

"What if I told you they do?"

"Do what? Exist?"

"Yessss."

"And how would you know that?"

"I'd rather not say, but trust me, they do exist, or at least they did at one time." I kicked Casper into gear and yelled back, "And I believe I know the one person who may know where they are."

When I reached the barn, Eli trailing me, I dismounted at the gate. Colonel Ron and Loretta sat in the green chairs behind the barn. Sherri stood, pacing as if she had been pleading a case in court. The Colonel rose and met us at the gate. "I believe I'm gonna have to create a time limit on these rides."

"Sorry Colonel," I replied as Eli joined us. "We stopped by the church and spoke to Father Ryan."

"Father Ryan?" he asked Eli, suspiciously. "Why would you two be needin' a priest?"

Seeing Eli's blush, I spoke. "Advice, Colonel. Confidential advice."

Sherri and Loretta joined us. Sherri said, "I sure am glad you two got back. These old people have been worrying themselves sick. Of course I told them they needn't. No one's gonna hurt Eli as long as he's with you."

Her words, though meant as innocent play, brought grief to Eli's face. His silence forced me to speak. "Sherri, my dear friend, might I inform you that Eli has strengths beyond your wildest imagination? He certainly doesn't need *me* to protect him. Thank you."

"Ooooooh. I see," she squealed.

"No, dear. That's the problem. You don't see."

"Eli," the Colonel asked, "may I have a word with you?" Eli dismounted, tied Birdie, and then followed Colonel Ron into the barn.

That evening, as Sherri dressed for bed, she complained, "Paleasssse, do not leave me here alone with those two again. They drive me crazy."

"Really? How?"

"They want to counsel me on my ways. They seem to think that when I leave this backward place, I should take the backwards ways with me. I'm a techy and I will always be a techy. When I leave here, I'm gonna steal that push mower and put a motor on it."

I shook my head and asked, "Would you mind covering for me again?"

"No way. Are you crazy?"

"Maybe, but I have to go. It's important, and this time I'm not waiting until morning. Plan on leaving as soon as they go to sleep."

Sherri stood and pulled her gown back off. I found myself staring as her bare boobs hung freely. "Stop that," she complained.

If Father Ryan is right, I must have really liked women in my past life. "What are you doing?" I asked.

"I'm getting dressed. You leave again, I'm going with you."

"But what if we get caught?"

"You got caught last time, and you didn't get into trouble."

"But I'm eighteen."

Bent over tying her left shoe, Sherri looked up and said, "I'll take my chances. Hell, I'm ready for some adventure." After tying the other shoe, she popped up. "So, where are we going?"

"I have to talk to Mrs. White."

"What's with you and that old woman?"

"That's exactly what I need to find out."

We waited another 30 minutes before tiptoeing out of the room and down the stairs. When I opened the wooden door, Bruno sat on the back porch as if he expected our arrival. The old dog escorted us to the creek, but then turned back when we started across the footbridge. Sherri asked, "Why can't we just ride Casper?"

"It makes it harder to hide and a whole lot more difficult to sneak back in."

We crouched in the weeds near the road until a car and a pickup passed, then dashed across Highway 88. From there we began a fast walk uphill on the Grayson Springs Road. About halfway up, Sherri stopped and struck a match. "What are you thinking?" I asked as she lit the rest of the joint we'd started earlier in the day.

"I'm thinking it's a perfect time to finish this." Holding in smoke, she said, "Here, take a hit."

"No thanks. Don't wanna be high when I talk to Mrs. White."

"Suit yourself," she sassed while taking another draw. When she choked on a hit, a dog began barking somewhere nearby.

"Great, dumbass," I whispered. "That's all we need."

I turned and continued my walk. Sherri trotted up next to me and said, "Don't leave me. I'll be lost."

"If I'd known you were gonna get stoned, I'da' left you at the Inn."

The dog continued barking. Sherri grabbed my arm, stopping me. "Hey, don't be mean to me. I'm bored to the bone back there, and I just wanna share your adventure."

"More like *stoned* to the bone." I took her by the hand and said, "Just stay with me and try to be quiet."

As we neared the top of the hill, the dog, long behind us, finally quit barking. Sherri whispered, "You sure we're on the right road?"

Ahead in the distance, I could see the silhouette of a tree line against the sky. "We're almost there."

"What if she's asleep?"

"I'll just have to wake her up."

"How?"

"I don't know. Figure that out when the time comes." I released her hand and we continued. Stopping around 20 feet from Mrs. White's mailbox, I whispered, "No lights are on." When Sherri did not respond, I turned to see her standing with her back to me, arms spread like wings, staring into the sky. I backtracked, tapped her on the shoulder, and asked, "What the hell are you doing?"

"Oh my god," she said quietly, still staring upward. "Please just give me a minute. I love the stars."

I wanted to knock her out so I could do what I came to do, but instead found myself standing next to her, raising my own arms, and sharing her lust for the heavens. Obviously pleased, Sherri reached for my hand. As we stood starring skyward, her warmth spread through me. I turned so we were face to face. She didn't flinch as I wrapped my free arm around her, drawing her closer. Her breasts pushed against mine, and I could smell the marijuana on her breath as my hand lowered on her back. My breathing had already grown heavy when she turned her head, laid it on my shoulder and wrapped her arms around me. It wasn't the slap in the face I'd expected. Nor was it what the man in me wanted. When I tried to separate, she held me tight as if apologizing for not being like me.

Our embrace got interrupted by the sound of a vehicle chugging up the hill from the direction we'd climbed. With headlights appearing through the trees, we crouched together behind roadside growth. She giggled and said, "We'll get chiggers."

The auto, a pickup, slowed as it approached Mrs. White's mailbox. I about died when it pulled into her drive and parked next to the house. "Stay here," I whispered. "I need to see who it is." Keeping low, I moved close enough to get a view. Two men exited the truck, one wearing a cap, the other a wide-brimmed, Amish-style hat. They stepped around to the front and the cap guy began banging on the door. When the porch light came on I immediately recognized the passenger as Ben Clemons. The door opened and I could see Mrs. White. Before she could speak, the two men appeared to force themselves in.

"Oh my god," spoke Sherri from behind me, scaring me shitless. "Did you see that?"

I caught my breath and replied, "Yes. Didn't look right, did it?"

"Should we go get the Colonel?"

"That would take too long." The uncomfortable feeling I'd always gotten from Ben began to make sense. "If you wanna go back, fine, but I have to get a closer look."

"I can't go back alone."

"Then stay with me ... and please be quiet."

When we got to the gate, there were no lights on in the front of the house, so we crept around to the back. Passing the pickup, I noticed that the driver's window was open. "We might need this," she whispered.

Even before reaching the back of the house, I could hear yelling. The windows were too high, so we moved back far enough in the yard to gain a visual. We could see Mrs. White sitting in a chair with the two men standing. The older man did the yelling. I couldn't make out his words. Sherri said, "That's Ben in there." As she spoke, Ben grabbed the old woman by her shoulders and shook her. "Oh my god!" Sherri whispered loudly. "We have to do something!"

With no other option, I picked up the largest rock I could find. It was half the size of a brick. I asked Sherri, "Can you hit that window with this?"

"Honey, I play short stop on the softball team. I can hit that window."

"Good. I'm going back to the truck. I'm gonna honk the horn. As soon as they look like they hear it, you throw the rock, and then dive into those weeds back there beyond that ridge. I'll sneak around the barn and join you."

Glancing back, she asked, "Why can't we just hide behind the barn?"

"Because that's the first place they'll look. Pleeeasssse just do as I say." Sherri reluctantly agreed. "Now, before I go, I want you to join me in a chant."

"Do what?"

"Stare at Mrs. White and quietly repeat what I say. Mrs. White, do not be afraid. I will take care of you. Mrs. White, do not be afraid. I will take care of you. Mrs. White, do not be afraid. I will take care of you." Before we finished the fifth chant, the old woman sat up straight in her chair and stared at the window as if she could see us. I said, "Keep chanting until I hit the horn," and then took off toward the truck.

Reaching in through the open window, I laid my hand on the horn and prayed, "Please God, let me protect that woman." Enraged, I spat on the inside of the windshield, and then pressed hard. The horn's blare pierced the night like a fog horn off Manhattan, so loud that I didn't even hear Sherri's rock crash through the window. Assuming she had tossed it, I dashed for the shadows. As I scooted down the dark side of the barn, men's voices rattled behind me. They were heading for the truck.

Something blocked my way. I tripped, tumbled to the ground, and felt warm blood seeping through my blouse. Thinking, *Can't stop now,* I held my arm while struggling to my feet and stumbling toward the back of the barn. The truck's engine started and lights beamed past the back corner of the barn while I crossed to the opposite side and to the ridge. Sherri giggled at my clumsy arrival in the weeds. Seconds later, Ben appeared at the back of the barn, scanning as if he'd heard us. I lay as quietly as possible, breathing heavily. Sherri, stoned as shit, nearly gave us away when she whispered, "This is not happening."

In his wide-brimmed hat, Ben's dark silhouette reminded me of a creature I had seen in a horror movie. Rotating like a lighthouse, he surveyed the darkness in search of prey. Finally, his partner honked the horn and Ben walked out of sight. We waited patiently until the truck had backed out and noisily chugged away downhill in the direction from which it came. Sherri whispered, "Could be a trick. Ben might have stayed."

I agreed and we waited another minute before peeking. By raising my head, I could see Mrs. White staring out her broken window. "Come on, I believe they're both gone."

Slowly, we slithered up the side of the barn, making sure Ben hadn't waited for us. "Mrs. White," I shouted, "it's me, Mary Elizabeth!"

The old woman appeared to faint, falling below the window. "Come on," I said. "Let's go in!"

We found Mrs. White flat on her back in the kitchen floor. Sitting on my heels, among the broken glass, I propped her head up in my lap.

Sherri squealed, "You're bleeding!"

"No shit. I'll be okay ... more worried about her."

Mrs. White's head began to move, and she opened her gentle eyes. Seeing me brought tears. She whispered, "Mary Elizabeth."

"I'm here, and they're gone. Don't be afraid. I'm gonna protect you."

"Are you okay, Ma'am?" Sherri asked.

Looking at me, Mrs. White enquired, "Who is she?"

"This is my friend Sherri. You needn't worry about her. She's a good person. Now, let's see if we can get you up off the floor."

After helping me lift Mrs. White into a chair, Sherri began sweeping up glass. I drew a cup of water from the kitchen faucet. As the old woman sipped, I asked, "Why was Ben shaking you?"

She squinted and asked, "You know that man?"

"Yes, I've met Ben, but I don't know the other one."

"That was old man Simpson. Known him all my life. Back in the day, when he was a young man, Bartholomew was one of the sweetest fellows I knew. Wound up marryin' my best friend. Now, for some reason, in his old age he just ain't no good."

"Guess we can say the same for Ben. What did they want from you?"

"They kept asking me about the treasure. Where it was buried."

"Did you tell 'em?"

Suddenly, she had a look of distrust. "What do you know about all this?"

"Yeah," asked Sherri, hesitating from her work, "What *do* you know about all this?"

"I could sit here all night trying to explain, but it wouldn't change a thing. Point is, in my heart, I'm certain the treasure that Ben and that old man are after does exist. Or at least it did at one time."

The old woman sat silent. Sherri, stood by the refrigerator, staring at an 8x10 photo held on with magnets. "He has your eyes!"

"Excuse me?" I asked.

Sherri ignored me and asked, "This your son, ma'am?"

The photo was of a boy standing in his high school football uniform, helmet in hand.

"Yes, it is. He was my only child. George and I tried for years. Thought I was barren. Never forget, on my forty-first birthday, thought I had a stomach virus. Turned out I was pregnant."

"You said he *was* your only child ... is he...?"

"Yes. He's gone."

Sherri said, "I'm so sorry ma'am." Then glancing back at me, she asked, "How far from here did you say you were born?"

"Not too far. Just down over the hill."

"Jesus!" continued Sherri, "This is your father." Turning to the woman, she asked, "Are you her grandmother?"

Tears ran freely as Mrs. White admitted, "Yesssss. Yes, I am."

I didn't know what to say. It wasn't like I hadn't sensed it all along. For a moment, my newfound grandmother hung her head, weeping. Finally, she said, "No one knew. George went to his grave not knowing he had a grandchild. Mr. Henry had done been complaining about Jamie coming down there. Said he felt like my Jamie and his wild ass girl, your mamma, had been fooling around out in the woods. George forbade Jamie to go back down there. Poor boy left here without even knowing he was gonna be a daddy. Minute I laid eyes on that child, you, I knew you were Jamie's. Couldn't tell George ... at least not until after I had a chance to tell Jamie ... but he..."

I stepped to the picture and rubbed my hand across it. "Who named me Mary Elizabeth?"

"Sherman Henry done that to spite me."

"So you are ashamed to be my grandmother?"

Shaking her head, Grandmother White cried, "I was not ashamed of you. I wasn't even ashamed of Jamie for makin' a baby out of wedlock. But I was afraid of George and what he might say or do if he knew. He was more backward about those things than most people these days. No dear, don't you think for one second that I was ever ashamed. Things just didn't work out right back then. Eloise loved you like you were her own and she never would have given you up except you went to hurtin' them other youngins. Honey, I figured in the end, you'd be just as wild as your mamma.... And then that doctor took you away before I even knew what was goin' on. State took all the kids from the Henrys. I wondered all the time what had become of you. After George died, I asked Sheriff Simon to look you up. He said you had gotten yourself into some trouble up there in New York. Made it sound like you was no good. Then, when you showed up out of nowhere at my gate with Ronnie Lee, well, I was afraid of what you might be up to. Can you understand why I was afraid of you?"

Before I had a chance, Sherri stepped to my grandmother and began comforting her. "Ma'am, now you know differently. I can assure you that you have one of the nicest granddaughters in the whole world. And I believe you two need one another."

When she looked my way, I asked, "What should I call you? Grandmother? Grandma? Granny?"

"You can call me anything you want. Grandma would be wonderful. Many times over the years, people asked if I had any grandchildren, and I lied. Always broke my heart. If I'm ashamed of anything, it would be me denying your existence."

"Get over it," I said. "If I was going to be mad at you, it would be because you knew I was in New York and you never came to see me. But that's the past. For now, I want you to tell me about my birth father."

While Sherri and I tacked an old shower curtain up as a temporary repair on the window, Grandma White told stories about Jamie White, her only child, my real father. Her loving words painted a portrait of a well-built country boy, an honor roll student, who lost control of his frigging hormones long enough to knock up my mother. To hear Grandma tell it, Cynthia, my mother, was a wild-ass little vixen who seduced her precious little boy. *Yeah, right. It takes two to tango, Grandma.* Unfortunately, I can't ask him about it because he died in some freak helicopter accident on Paris Island while participating in boot camp for the Marines. I found it hard to believe that he left Grayson County and did not know his girlfriend was pregnant.

"Cynthia," Grandmother explained, "was about the third or fourth generation of the wildest bunch of women ever to set foot in Grayson County. Wasn't none of them ever got married to my knowledge. Can't even tell you what the girl's last name was. Do know that Eloise fell in love with the child after her mother run off ... with a man I'd suspect. Eloise and Henry treated your mamma like she was their own. They just never could get the wild out of that girl. She was downright uncontrollable."

"Must have been something good about her. Your son liked her."

"Jamie and her growed up together. When they was younger, George and me didn't pay it much attention. Jamie told me girls and boys at the school had little to do with her, her bein' such a tomboy and all, and because of where she lived I guess, and partly I'd say because she could whip all their asses in a fist fight."

"So, Miss Mary Elizabeth, you like, came about it honest," Sherri interrupted.

Grandma White smiled and continued. "Ask me, Jamie loved that girl long before she became a woman. Him and her went to the woods just like two boys, huntin' rabbits and birds. They had 'em a grapevine over on the bluff where they could swing. If I could walk them woods, I'd show you a big ol' tree with marks carved into it for each squirrel them two shot out of it."

"My mother was a fighter and a hunter?"

"Oh yeah. And a looker."

"A looker?" Sherri asked.

"Honey, somewhere along the line, Eloise Henry's skinny little tomboy blossomed. God meant that girl to be a woman, and she sure was. And I reckon my boy was no match for the temptation. Sherman claimed he caught 'em together."

I had to ask, "Grandma, what exactly do you mean by tomboy?"

She smiled again and said, "Look over yonder in that mirror. Believe you'll see what's left of one."

"So I look like her ... but what does it mean?"

"Used to be if a girl didn't act girly, people called her a tomboy. I'm talkin' about the kind of girl that would rather have a BB gun than a doll. One that wanted to spend most of her time with the boys, out doin' boy things, like fishin' and huntin' and climbin' trees. Most growed out of it and became wives and mothers. Now and then one stayed that way, you know, didn't go for no man in her bed, and then they called her a butch or a queer, or somthin' like that."

"A lesbian," Sherri reiterated.

Grandma just grinned and nodded. "I knowed one girl to be like that. Her parents told her she had a callin' and sent her off to be a nun."

"So," I asked, "you think I'm a tomboy?"

"I think you probably were, but look at you now. You seem beyond that stage. By now I'd say you're either a man lovin' kind of a woman, or..."

"Or a queer? A lesbian?"

"All I know is that you are my granddaughter, and that's all that counts. Rest of that means nothing to me at this point."

Sherri asked, "So what are we going to do about those men. Ben and the other guy?"

I said, "It would be nice if we could tell Loretta, but we can't. Isn't there some kind of sheriff around here?"

Grandma said, "Don't believe that new Sheriff Godfrey would do anything against Bartholomew Simpson, them being brother-in-laws and all."

"Just like the stewardess told me on the plane. Everybody in Kentucky is related."

"Bunch of inbreeds..." Sherri caught herself. "Sorry."

Looking at the phone on the wall, I had an idea. "Grandma, you call that man Simpson and tell him that the two *fellows* who come in here after them said they were going to be paying him and his buddy a visit. Say they don't care much for anyone who would pick on an old woman. That'll likely scare the shit out of him and Ben."

"What am I gonna say if he asks who you are?"

"Tell him you don't know. Say they didn't come here to see you. Say they were following them."

Sherri added, "And tell them we told you next time either one of them steps foot on your property, you should shoot first and ask questions later."

When Grandma White hung up the phone, her expression told it all. She felt like she had put the fear of God in Simpson. She couldn't tell if Ben was with him or not. Regardless, he would pass on the word.

"Now," I asked, "What exactly can you tell me about this treasure everybody is looking for and how it relates to your, *our* ancestors?"

Chapter 32

Grandma White reached into her cabinet and retrieved a bottle of bourbon. After mixing some with diet cola, she relaxed into a kitchen chair and said, "Them stories about buried treasure been rollin' around in these hills for long as I remember. Seems every generation has one or two boys that gets all wrapped up in tryin' to dig up Grayson Springs. And they don't even know what the hell their lookin' for. All they know is some old-timer told 'em there's treasure in them hills. You girl, I can tell you're my boy's child because, like him, you have some kind of extra sense about all this. Like you, he knew stuff no one would expect him to know."

My father knew what I know? How? Did he read the diary? Evidently you didn't. "Mrs. White, Grandma, I need to ask you a crazy question. Colonel Ron told us that the old furniture we are using at the Inn was donated. Did any of it come from you?"

She looked surprised. "It did ... and how would you know that?"

"I'll explain later."

"When I gave that stuff to Ronnie Lee, I knew it was a mistake, but everybody kept tellin' me to move on. In our later years, George and I slept in separate rooms. Not because we didn't love one another, but because he had sleepin' problems. If I moved in bed, it woke him up and then he couldn't go back to sleep. Him and Jamie used the upstairs rooms. I donated both bedroom sets to Ronnie Lee's cause. Stuff was old anyway. He said he could make good use of it."

Sherri asked, "Why do you say it was a mistake?"

"Honey child, people can say what they want, but when an old woman loses her only child and then her husband, it's almost too much to bear. Used to go up there and spend hours dustin' and cleaning like I did when they was alive. It was all I had of 'em." Grandma began to weep.

Together, Sherri and I wrapped her in our arms until the weeping subsided. "Is this too much right now?" I asked. "We can talk later."

"No. Please don't leave yet. You have to understand, you two's the first to put a lovin' hand on me in so long. Let's just talk a while. You askin' all these questions is almost like having Jamie back again."

"Grandma, I know you miss that old furniture, but you can't imagine how much it means to me to discover I've been sleeping on my real father's bed."

"Thank you, dear. That makes it much easier."

In my mind, I could see my father reading that old diary just like I had. That's why he knew the things I know. That antiquated furniture had likely been around since Mary Elizabeth Pierce slept on it in 1876. "Grandma, you say my father knew about things he shouldn't have. Did he ever mention a man, a soldier named John?"

"Yes, he did, and that's what led me to believe he knew things he shouldn't have known."

"How's that?" Sherri asked.

"Jamie was less than a teenager when he began asking questions about things even I didn't know, stuff from the 1800s. There wasn't but one person to ask. I went right down the hill here to see my mother's sister, Aunt Annie. She had to be the oldest person livin' in Kentucky at that time."

"Was it Mary Annie Boone?"

"See there. How do you know such?"

"Nothing special about that, Grandma. I saw her grave at the church. Born in 1887. Died in 2001."

"That's right. Nearly a hundred and fifteen when she passed."

"So let me see if I have this right. You're saying a daughter of Mary Elizabeth Pierce lived until two-thousand and one?"

"That's right."

"So hard to believe. And you asked her about the grave?"

"Yes, as I was sayin', when I mentioned a grave in the hills of Grayson Springs, Aunt Annie about swallowed her dentures. She had memories of goin' down there with her mamma, them pickin' flowers along the way, and then puttin' 'em by a rock in the woods."

I could see Sherri's analytical mind turning. She asked, "So if she knew people were looking for treasure, why didn't she ever talk about where her mamma took her?"

"I asked her that same question. She said when her mother was alive, people called her crazy for takin' flowers to a make-believe grave every year, same day, June 25th. After Grandma died, Annie didn't feel like a bunch of strangers oughta be trompin' on or perhaps diggin' up her momma's memories. She said it wasn't nothin' but a memorial anyway. Wasn't really anybody buried there. It was a place her mamma and some fella she once loved used to sit."

Under my breath, I finished the date, "June 25th, 1876."

"Little Big Horn," echoed Sherri. "That's the day of Custard's Last Stand."

"God, you're such a geek." I took a deep breath and said, "That's the day Lieutenant John Crittenden died at Little Big Horn."

Grandma White sat up straight, took a large swallow of her drink, looked me up and down, and said, "That's the same fellow Jamie asked me about."

"Grandma, John Crittenden was the soldier who befriended your grandmother, Mary Elizabeth Pierce, before he went west to fight the Indians. He gave her some coins to keep until he got back. He told her if he didn't come back, they were hers to keep. My understanding is that those coins are the treasure everyone is looking for. They were uncirculated proofs of the 1856 Flying Eagle Cent pieces. I'm guessing that today they would be worth quite a sum. And they belonged to your grandmother. That means since you are her only next of kin, they belong to you ... at least that's the way I see it."

"But Aunt Annie said men had been diggin' up that hill since she was a child. Had nothing to do with her mamma. Said it was about some outlaw burying stolen money up there in the early 1800s. Someone by the name of Doc Brown."

Sherri said, "I'm so confused. If your Aunt Annie never talked to anyone about this, how did anyone know about the coins in the first place?"

"Her father," I remembered. "Mary Elizabeth's father knew about the coins. He wanted to sell them, and that's why she hid them in the first place."

"So," Sherri asked, "What made people think she hid the coins at Grayson Springs?"

"Sounds like people got two stories mixed up. All I know is she put them somewhere. And if my dreams mean anything, I'd say she buried them at the rock where she and John Crittenden sat."

Sherri speculated, "So why didn't someone just follow her to the grave?"

"I thought about that. The coins were only twenty years old when he gave them to her. Doubt they were considered all that valuable until later, in the nineteen hundreds. By the time people associated the grave with the coins, I'd say Mary Elizabeth was either dead or too old to be walking up there."

Grandma White asked, "Why don't we just leave well enough alone?"

"Because," I said, "People are not going to stop digging up there until somebody finds something. And besides Grandma, that man loved your grandmother. He didn't give her those coins to bury. He gave them to her to hold on to until he returned from the Indian Wars. Those coins and her memories were all she had of him. She buried them because he never came back. Believe it was only five one-cent pieces. To her that was nothing special. She had no idea what they would be worth today. How about we find them and put their value to good use? We can fix this old place up ... make sure you have enough to live on. Maybe help Colonel Ron out with his project. I'd kind of like to see others like Sherri and me get a chance to experience Grayson Springs."

"You would do all that?"

"Yes, I would."

"So, that mean you ain't plannin' on goin' back to New York?"

"I have to go back for a while. I've got a court date. Might even have to do a little time. But after that's over, you can bet your ass I'm coming home. I'd love to live right here with you."

Grandma White put her hands over her face and wept.

Chapter 33

Our walk back down the hill proved uneventful until we neared the bottom. We both turned to the sound of a vehicle approaching from behind us. Just as its headlights began flashing through treetops, we heard a loud noise, almost like a gun-blast. The lights drew nearer but flashed erratically, back and forth from one side of the road to the other. A continuous grinding noise accompanied the chaos. As it drew closer, sparks flew from under the veering mass of metal. Sherri let out a scream as the rear end of a huge old model Ford nearly hit us in an out of control, 360-degree spin.

The car came to a smoking rest, halfway between us and the intersection, so close that we could smell a mixed aroma of burnt rubber and steel. The passenger door flew open and out popped William Rice. He began stumbling around on the blacktop, ranting, "Hot damn, ga-a-awd almighty!"

Jimmy Jackson opened the other door and rolled out into the ditch some 20 feet from us. William whirled around in the middle of the road and slurred, "Damn Jimmy Boy! Son of a bitch. You oughta be a NASCAR driver. That was one hell of a piece of drivin'."

"Shhhh! Shhhhh!" Jimmy tried to silence William. Scrambling next to his friend, he spoke just loud enough for us to hear. "You see what I saw?"

"What?"

"A girl."

"What girl?"

"You didn't hear her scream? Swear I did."

"Damn, Jimmy, you hit somebody?"

"Don't think so...."

An engine roared nearby, and a new set of headlights swung into sight, turning off Highway 88. The truck stopped near Jimmy's car. Lights went out, but the engine continued running. It was the same truck that we encountered at Grandma White's house. Jimmy and William seemed frozen in the middle of the road. Both doors of the truck opened, and out popped Ben and the old man Simpson. "You boys sure are makin' a lot of noise," growled the old man.

"Had me a blooowout," Jimmy slurred.

"Damn near killed us," laughed William as the two men stepped closer.

Ben Clemons said, "You boys think you're pretty smart, throwin' that rock through the window?"

"Do what?" mumbled Jimmy.

"And blowin' the horn," scorned the older man, "and which one of you sorry bastards spit on my windshield?"

"Don't know what the hell you're talkin' about," William pleaded. "We just come from Gracie May's. Got us some whiskey."

"What?" snarled the old man as he sucker-punched Jimmy in the stomach. William tried to attack as Jimmy went to his knees and began throwing up on the road. Ben cut poor William off and struck him in the face several times. Too drunk to protect himself, the confused hillbilly crouched on the ground. Ben shouted, "We been cuttin' you boys in on this deal. Now you want to go behind our back! Y'all think you can scare us off and take everything for yourselves?"

As William looked up, blood running from his mouth, the old man kicked Jimmy and screamed, "What'd she tell you?"

Sherri whispered, "We've got to do something."

Shaking my head, I whispered back, "Not yet."

Jimmy cried out, "Damn you, old man. Don't know what the hell you're talkin' about."

"I'll kill you right here you little bastard," screamed Simpson as yet another set of lights appeared from the intersection. Blue and red streaks began flashing through the darkness, across nearby trees.

Sherri whispered, "Cops."

256

A spotlight caught four men in the middle of the road—two standing and two on their knees in agony. "Don't anybody move!" bellowed a deep voice from a loud speaker. Again, two doors opened. From the driver's side, a tall, overweight man wearing a uniform emerged wielding a flashlight in one hand and a firearm in the other. On the passenger side, it was Loretta with her own light and gun.

"Ben, what the hell's goin ' on here?" asked Loretta as she and the officer cautiously approached.

"We just got here."

Simpson said, "Hey, Pete. Good thing you came along. Appears these boys had an accident."

While lighting a cigarette, the fat officer asked, "Porter, you know these boys?"

"Sure do," Loretta answered. "What say you, Jimmy?"

"Had me a blowout ma'am. Lost control."

Observing Jimmy's half-digested dinner on the road, the sheriff asked, "Boy, how much you had to drink?"

Frightened, Jimmy lied. "None at all, Sir."

Simpson said, "We heard the commotion. Thought we'd help 'em get back on the road, but quite frankly, Pete, don't believe either one of 'em's in shape to be drivin'."

Loretta moved closer and asked, "Don't lie to me, William ... you boys been drinkin'?"

"Yes ma'am. We had us a little whiskey."

"What happened to your face?" she asked. "You look beat up."

"Reckon I hit the dashboard," William lied. I knew right then that he was afraid of Ben and the old man.

The officer shook his head and said, "Bet money wasn't neither one wearin' a seat belt." Turning to the old man, he asked, "Bart, you been a drinkin'?"

"Hell no. You know me better than that."

Loretta said, "I can vouch for Ben."

While the officer spoke on his two way radio, Ben asked, "Loretta, what are you doin' out with the sheriff?"

Sheriff? I thought.

257

"Out looking for our girls. They went AWOL." Raising her voice, she asked, "Ain't any of y'all seen 'em, have you, Brooke and Sherri?"

Waves of worry and surprise were so thick I could feel it from the ditch we likely shared with bugs, lizards, snakes and who knows what else. Ben and the old man stared at one another. William glared at Jimmy. And I sensed Loretta noticing Jimmy glancing around.

"Oh shit," Sherri whispered.

That lying-ass Simpson, said, "Didn't you boys say somethin' about girls a while ago?"

"Hell no!" spoke William. "We ain't been with no girls tonight."

Loretta seemed suspicious now, as if doubting William. The sheriff turned and said, "Bart, you and Mr. Ben here best go on home. Looks like I'm gonna be bookin' these boys for DUI and public intoxication, and anything they might know about those missin' girls."

Sherri's warm lips touched my ear and she whispered, "The old man knows the sheriff. I bet that's his brother-in-law."

"No shit, Sherlock," I whispered back.

As the two men turned to leave, Ben said, "Y'all want us to help look for the girls?"

Loretta answered, "No, Ben. You go on home. Stay close to Charlotte in case she goes into labor. I'll call you if we need help."

Ben tilted his head and then his hat as he and the old man climbed into the pickup—engine still running. Loretta stood watching the truck leave, stop at the intersection, and then turn left and out of sight. On her way back to the sheriff, Jimmy, and William, she scanned in our direction. At one point she seemed to stare at me right through the darkness.

Another police car arrived. We watched poor Jimmy and William, already handcuffed, being loaded into the back seat. I could feel Sherri shaking. She whispered, "We've got to do something. We can't let them lock those boys up."

"We can, and we will. They're both drunk. And I'm not about to say anything to Loretta in front of Sheriff fat-ass frigging brother-in-law, Godfrey."

When the second cruiser left with Jimmy and William, Loretta began walking around with her flashlight, checking out the damage to the old Ford. "You 'bout ready?" asked the sheriff.

"You go ahead, Pete. I'm gonna snoop around here for a while. Make sure there's no sign of the girls in this car. With the new footbridge, I can walk back to the Inn in a matter of minutes."

"You sure? Hate to leave you here alone."

"I'm a big girl. How about you drive up to the church and make sure they're not hangin' out up there. Call me if they are."

"Have it your way," replied Fat Ass as he squeezed back into his squad car. He backed up to the intersection before turning off his flashing lights. Funny thing, as he drove away, Loretta jumped the ditch, climbed over a barbed wire fence, and then trotted up the hill. Her silhouette stood against the moonlit sky for more than a minute while Sherri and I became increasingly nervous.

"What the hell is she doing?" Sherri whispered.

"She's watching the sheriff. Don't believe she trusts him any more than we do."

"Should we stay here or try to sneak back to the Inn?"

"Hold on. She's coming."

Loretta retraced her steps nearly to the vehicle and then turned in our direction. "Seems we're pretty much alone now. Do I need to call in a dog, or are you ladies ready to go home?"

Sherri whispered, "What now?"

I stood and asked, "At what point did you figure it out?"

As Sherri rose from her cramped squat, Loretta shined her light on us and replied, "When Jimmy whispered to me that he heard a girl scream. Didn't see any blood on the car or the road, so I figured you were still alive. Now get your sorry asses down here."

We gladly crossed the ditch before pleading our case. Standing in the middle of the road, Sherri said, "Loretta, you're like not going to believe what happened."

"You best hope I believe. And I can tell you right now, Colonel Ron's gonna have both your asses on a plane home tomorrow."

"Not me," I snarled.

"Excuse me?"

"I'm not going anywhere. I'm eighteen, and this is my home. I'll go back for my court date, but I *will* be back. This is where I belong, and I have a grandmother living just up the road who needs me."

"Jesus Christ. We do have a lot to talk about."

"Not here," I replied. "I don't want to be here when that crooked sheriff comes back. You do know that old man was his brother-in-law?"

"Who in the world told you that?"

"Her grandmother," smiled Sherri. "Right after we rescued her from that old man Simpson and Ben."

"Rescued?"

I said, "They were roughing her up, trying to get information concerning the buried treasure on Colonel Ron's hill."

"Ben wouldn't do that!"

"I've been trying to tell you about that man."

Sherri added, "Loretta, we saw Ben violently shaking old Mrs. White. They were screaming at her."

"She alright?"

"Yes, my grandma is okay. We scared them off without showing our faces. Problem is, they thought it was Jimmy and William. We were walking home when the boys crashed right here. Then along comes Ben and the old man. They accused the boys of double-crossing them. When they denied it, the men began beating them up. They've all been in on the boys digging up the hill."

"Trust me," added Sherri, "neither of those boys were injured before Ben and that old man came along."

"And the old man was threatening to kill Jimmy when you guys came along."

"Hold on a minute." Loretta dialed her cell. "Colonel, I've got the girls. They're fine, but they've got something really important to tell you.... We're right here at the intersection....Yes, it was Jimmy and William. Looks like they had a blowout coming down the hill.... We'll be right there. Now do me a favor. Call Sheriff Godfrey on his cell and tell him the girls are back at the Inn. Tell him you already called me and that I'm walking back. Discourage him from coming by. I'll explain later. Looks like I'm going back on duty tonight.... Because I may have to get a warrant for Ben Clemons' arrest."

Loretta pulled the phone from her ear, and the Colonel's voice scattered across the darkness. When he stopped screaming, she finished, "Ron, just calm down please. We'll be there in ten minutes, and I'll explain. And whatever you do, don't call Ben."

Chapter 34

By the time we reached the swinging bridge, smoke rolled from the Inn's chimney, drifting in our direction. Colonel Ron and Bruno were barely visible on the opposite bank, waiting as if we were their prey. I would have preferred that Loretta lead the way, but she insisted we go first. Sherri followed me onto the wooden planks. The Colonel didn't wait. He turned and marched toward the Inn. Light bleeding out of the open backdoor highlighted his stout frame. Already, I sensed a change in our host. Less psychologist. More rage. It was in his stride and his silence, and I suspected we were about to meet the military side of Colonel Ron.

We joined him in the kitchen as he poured a cup of coffee. I couldn't tell if the steam rose from the stove or him. Before Loretta could even speak, he started. "I hope you ladies know you've just about killed my project here. How the hell can I attract clients when I can't even keep you two on the property?"

"Ron..." tried Loretta.

"What part of 'you may not leave the property' don't you get? I hope you both go to jail!"

"Colonel..." I tried.

"Don't you even start! I trusted you! Treated you like an adult, and to what end? You shit all over me, and ... and ... and what the hell happened to your arm?"

"Oh, shit!" screeched Loretta. "I hadn't noticed. You said the car didn't hit you!"

"It didn't. I fell at my grandmother's house, running from Ben and that old man."

"Dammit!" screamed the Colonel. "Would somebody explain to me—"

Sherri cringed as if she'd never seen an angry man.

"I would," shouted Loretta, "if you'd shut the hell up for a minute. This is not like you. You're losin' your cool when we need you the most!"

Colonel Ron fell silent. His face changed, and I could see his embarrassment. Seconds passed and then he said, quietly, "Okay, let's doctor that arm, and then we can all take a seat and start over."

As she cleaned my wound, Loretta said, "Colonel, I would like to introduce you to Mary Elizabeth Green, granddaughter of Mary Elizabeth White."

Without speaking, he seemed to be waiting for my two cents. "I felt the connection all along. At her gate with you and at the graveyard. Believe Eli figured it out first. Turns out Jamie White is, or was my father. Only ones who knew it were the Henrys and my grandmother. My grandfather and my father died without knowing."

The Colonel squirmed in his chair and asked, "So how does this involve Ben?"

"Ben is bad," butted in Sherri. "He and that old man Simpson are after the treasure."

Colonel Ron looked at me. I said, "I told Eli I thought I knew someone who might know where the treasure is buried. He must have mentioned that to Ben. Colonel, we saw Ben and that old man trying to scare information out of my grandmother. If he wants that treasure bad enough to frighten an old woman, God knows what he might do."

Loretta said, "Colonel, she's had Ben's number for some time. She mentioned her distrust for him early on, but I played it off and even discouraged her from thinking that way."

"Exactly what did you girls see?"

Sherri blurted, "We saw them through the window. Ben and that Simpson guy, like, screaming at her. Ben acted as if he was going to hit her in the face."

"But he didn't?"

"No. But he grabbed her by the shoulders and shook her violently."

"And you did what?"

"When Elizabeth pushed on the horn of their truck, I threw a rock through the kitchen window. It scared them and..."

"And I ran back to where Sherri was hiding in the weeds. I fell on the way, and that's when I hurt my arm. We stayed down until they quit looking and left, and then we went in to make sure Grandma was alright."

"And was she?"

"She's okay. But, we had her call Simpson and tell him that it was two men who ran them off. You know, just to scare him and Ben so they wouldn't come back. Then, when we were on our way home, Jimmy and William had their wreck right in front of us. Ben and Simpson came and they evidently thought it was Jimmy and William who scared them off, so they started beating on them and threatening to kill them, and that's when Loretta and that crooked sheriff came along."

"Crooked sheriff?"

"Sheriff Godfrey," assured Loretta. "Turns out he's Simpson's brother-in-law. Believe he knew that Simpson had been drinking, yet he locked up those boys and let his brother-in-law drive home."

Apparently the Colonel was more convinced by Loretta's instincts than by my or Sherri's testimony. While he called my grandmother, Loretta contacted the State Police. Sometime later, as Sherri and I sat fighting sleep, a cruiser arrived. The trooper suggested waiting until morning to take a statement from Grandma White. Colonel Ron assured him that she was waiting up for them. The three of us stood on the porch watching the trooper and Loretta drive away. Colonel Ron settled into a rocker. He looked distraught. Sherri excused herself to the outhouse, providing my first alone moment with the Colonel, all night.

"I'm sorry I left the property, and I'm sorry for all that I am putting you and Loretta through, and I'm sorry if I messed up your project. But..." I wasn't sure if I should ask him right then, but I wanted to know, so I threw it out there. "But ... did you know my father?"

He stopped rocking, stared at me for a while, and then said, "I'm sorry for losing my cool and for raising my voice..."

"Don't be. I deserved it."

"I didn't really hang out with Jamie White, him being at least ten years younger than me. But I did see him at church every Sunday. There were always stories about him and that girl he hung out with, down in the flats..."

"Cynthia. My mother."

"Apparently."

"So, asshole, you already knew who my mother was!"

"No, not really. No one I know of even knew the girl was pregnant. Knew she died, but that was about it. People around here thought the Wild Child was just another foster kid."

"They really called me the Wild Child?"

"Can't say as I blame 'em. Shoe fits."

"Blah, blah, blah. Tell me, Colonel, do you believe there really is a treasure buried on your property?"

"Anything's possible. Most of the hilltop's been dug up at one time or another by those who believe it. Guess I gave up worrying about it long ago."

"If there is, who do you think it belongs to?"

"Wellll, technically, if it is on my property, it's mine. But since no one knows for sure of its whereabouts, I'd say it will belong to whoever finds it. Only a fool would admit where they found it."

Sherri returned, we talked a while, and Colonel Ron suggested we turn in for what was left of the night. We were about to do just that when Loretta and Trooper Johnson returned from Grandmother's. There was talk about the possible whereabouts of the so-called Treasure of Grayson Springs. It seemed my grandmother, while admitting to the possible existence of a treasure, had not revealed the details she had spoken about with Sherri and me.

Officer Johnson said that Sherri and I may have to make sworn statements after he speaks with Jimmy and William. He admitted that even though Mrs. White refused to press charges on Ben Clemons and Bartholomew Simpson, he had hopes that Jimmy and William would.

"And regardless," he stated, "there will likely be an internal ethics investigation into the actions of Sheriff Godfrey."

Before his departure, I addressed the officer about his vehicle. "Sir, would it be possible on future visits for you to park your vehicle outside of the Grayson Springs grounds? With all due respect, it somewhat destroys the sanctity of what Colonel Ron and Loretta have created here for us."

"I agree," chimed in Sherri. "Seeing your cruiser roll down the lane hurt me as well. Though we resisted at first, there is a certain serenity here that we may never match once we leave."

Colonel Ron and Loretta grinned at one another. When the officer was seated behind the wheel of his cruiser, I asked, "Colonel, would it be all right if I followed Officer Johnson to the gate? I would like to borrow his cell phone long enough to call my grandmother and make sure she is okay."

Officer Johnson held up his phone and said, "You can use it here," before realizing my intention to keep technology off the premises. He drove ahead of me as I walked to the gate. On my arrival, he tapped in the number and then handed me the phone through the window. As the phone rang, I stepped away and spoke to Grandma White in privacy.

Upon my quick return, I said, "Thank you so much. She seems much more comfortable having spoken with you and Loretta."

The trooper said, "I'd feel much more at ease if she'd agree to press charges. I've dealt with rascals like them before. If they truly believe there is profit to be found in those hills, they'll stop at nothing to find it. Since we apparently can't trust Sheriff Godfrey, I'll make sure someone from the department checks on your grandmother daily by phone or visit for the next few weeks. If need be, we can get a restraining order to keep 'em away from her."

"Thanks," I said.

For a moment, he looked into my eyes. His gaze reminded me of the Colonel's: kind and respectful. "Gotta ask," he started, "that speech you gave back there about keeping this place serene, was that just a show to make the Colonel feel better, or what?"

I took a deep breath, and said, "Sir, when I left New York, my opinion of Kentucky was based on an unfortunate collection of childhood memories. As you may well know, my time in Manhattan has been checkered with events that disappointed my parents, my schools, and the court system. I've always known there was a reason for my behavior beyond the obvious. In the past few weeks, I've found not only my true identity, but also a better understanding of my behavior."

"Really, and what might that be?"

"Sir, I have roots that are as wild as those two boys Sheriff Godfrey arrested. I myself kicked William's ass right up there on that hill when he dissed me and refused to unhand my horse. Having spoken to him since, I realize that though he is a bit backwards, that doesn't make him a bad person. And I believe he recognizes the hill girl in me. I was born not too far from here. Who knows; maybe this is where I belong. These clothes I'm wearing feel as natural as any I've ever worn. My adopted parents spent the better part of twelve years trying to refine me, to mold me into their high society culture. Though my vernacular has evolved, I am not at all offended by that of these hill people. Any psychologist will tell you that a person's first five years have a major effect on their adult personality. When I return to Manhattan, I will not forget my time at Grayson Springs. The labor I have experienced is hard, yet rewarding in an odd sort of way. The serenity of this place gives me peace of mind. Were it not for what I have experienced here at the guidance of Colonel Ron and Loretta, none of my present state of understanding would exist. I'd likely be locked up in some jail in New York, still contemplating the cause of my unusual behavior. I want Grayson Springs to stay exactly as it is so others like Sherri and me might come here, get away from whatever is killing them inside, and perhaps find a peace that they can take home with them. Are you a native Kentuckian, sir?"

"Well, yes I am. I was born maybe twenty miles from here, just the other side of Caneyville."

"Then might I suggest that if you were to migrate to Manhattan, you too would feel out of place and be looked upon differently. There is a great variety of cultures in New York, but I've never seen anyone there quite like what I've met here. And sir, I've got me a grandma living up on the Grayson Springs Road. To my knowledge, she is my only living true blood relative. In my heart, I feel some responsibility to take care of her."

He replied, "Haven't heard anybody call it *the* Grayson Springs Road for some time." After starting his engine, he said, "Young lady, you sure are a talker ... but I like what you say." As he pulled away, Officer Johnson talked out the window. "Hope to see you around, neighbor." His words were planted in my heart as I began my light-footed stroll back to the Inn.

Chapter 35

The atmosphere at Grayson Springs had certainly changed. It seemed I'd aged several years in a matter of days. Though he never said so, I sensed that my conversation with Officer Johnson had somehow found its way back to the Colonel. Nearing the end of our six-week stay, while Loretta took care of personal needs at the Inn, the Colonel invited both Sherri and me on a post-breakfast visit to the barn. After tending to the chickens, he led us up a wooden ladder to the loft of the barn. I had not previously noticed the loft's existence. Like me, Sherri seemed intrigued by the elevated position, dark and dusty, with an open view of the barn's runway. Bales of hay were stacked several-high along the outside walls, with a few scattered near the opening over the barn's runway. Dim vertical planes of morning light intruded through gaps in boards on either end. The stale smell of fescue became diluted with fresh air when Colonel Ron opened a set of double-doors, providing a four-foot-square source of ventilation. He sat in the middle of the opening and asked us to join him. Sherri chuckled and said, "You really expect both our fat asses to fit in there?"

I joked, "Speak for yourself, asshole."

"Humor me, ladies. Squeeze in. We'll not be here for long."

Sherri glanced at me. I shrugged my shoulders as if to say, "Why not?" She lowered herself first, and then I squeezed in. It was indeed a snug fit. Yet, unlike in my recent past, sitting against the Colonel's physique did not necessarily discomfort me. Actually, being at least ten feet off the ground with our feet dangling made the tight fit more inviting. Just below us sat the green chairs.

"My God," uttered Sherri, "what a beautiful sight."

A blanket of fog covered the field. Bertha, her calf, and the horses drifted through the mist at a distance as they grazed. Dew dripped a steady beat, almost like rain, as it fell from the leafy tops of trees. At a distance, the red-tailed hawk I'd seen often perched on a high hickory tree limb, waiting for any small varmint that might expose itself long enough for a swoop and snag.

Colonel Ron said, "The memories of views like this carried me through some pretty tough times overseas. I hope in the future, on bad days, you two can find a quiet spot, meditate, and put yourself here the way I have. Now, as we enjoy this wonderful view, I'd like each of you to share your opinions on Grayson Springs. Sherri, tell me what you think about this place, your pros and cons, and don't hold back. Be honest. It'll be *my* way of growing from *your* experience."

"This is not fair, Colonel. How can I say anything bad about a place that looks so heavenly?"

"That's a plus, but I had anticipated a bit more input."

Sherri sat silently for a moment and then said, "I hate not having electronics. I miss texting, checking out my social sites, shopping online and all that, but there are some things about this place that I will miss. I haven't had to use make-up for weeks. My skin is better than ever. I've slept more. And I haven't had to worry about kissing ass or sucking up to anyone, or trying to be someone I'm..." She strangely cut herself off, hesitated, and then added, "I won't miss the outhouse, that's for sure."

Like me, Colonel Ron seemed to be analyzing Sherri's stumble. "All that said," he asked, "how do you see this experience affecting your legal dilemma at home?"

"My legal dilemma? Truthfully, Colonel, I don't see myself as having a legal dilemma. It's not like I'm going to go home, grab a computer, and start hacking. Learned my lesson on that. Hell, I still blame it on my teacher. He gave me the skills to hack and then didn't even take up for me when I got caught."

Colonel Ron waited for Sherri to finish. "You make a good point in that your instructor should have emphasized responsibility in the process of teaching you to hack. However, I'm sure he recognized your skills and anticipated your using what he taught you for legitimate actions."

"As in?"

"Perhaps the man foresaw a future for you within the FBI, CIA, or Homeland Security. Those agencies use hacking for the betterment and protection of our country. I suppose his failure was in assuming that you understood right from wrong...."

"Excuse me?" complained Sherri.

"Well," replied Colonel Ron, "let me rephrase that. Your teacher obviously assumed you knew the difference between legal hacking and illegal hacking. I too would have assumed you knew the difference." Colonel Ron leaned back on his hands and said, "Sherri, please don't tell me you didn't know it was wrong to hack into a bank. I believe you knew it was wrong but did it anyway just to see if you could, like it was a challenge or something. Right?"

"A ... well ... I guess so. I mean, I did like the challenge. And it's not like I needed the money."

Adding my two cents, I said, "Any way you look at it, you were stealing something that did not belong to you."

"Listen to you, Miss I Stole A Gun," Sherri whined.

"Whoa now," warned the Colonel while sitting back up straight. "We don't need to go there. That was a long time ago, when Elizabeth was just a little girl. We're adults now, ladies, and we have to think like the moral, educated people we are. I hope when you leave here, neither of you will be doing things we know are wrong. Things that could jeopardize your freedom."

Sherri and I leaned forward to stare at one another. She smiled, and I smiled back.

Colonel Ron looked at me and said, "Okay, now it's your turn. What insight can you offer here?"

I thought for a few seconds. "I'm like Sherri. I miss a lot of things I have at home, some of my friends and all that, but nothing in Manhattan can compare to what I've learned here. I found my true identity. For the first time in my life, I can tell you things about my real parents, and I've been able to talk with my real grandmother. I've learned that the people who raised me were not as bad as I thought. They were just a couple of simple people trying to make a living by raising kids no one else wanted. I understand the issues that caused me to be angry for most of my life. And I understand more about those on the other side of those issues. Perhaps I'm becoming more emotionally intelligent."

"Bravo. Spoken like a true daughter of a psychiatrist. Dr. Green would be pleased." Bruno, standing below our feet, began growling, and then let out a series of deep barks. Bertha's bell began clattering, and the sound of hooves beating the ground disturbed the morning quiet. "What the hell?" Colonel mumbled quietly, as cow, calf, and horses scattered through the foggy field.

"What is it?" asked Sherri.

"Sshhhh," came from the Colonel as he placed his finger on his lips. Bruno did not advance, but continued a low grumbling growl. We all sat still, watching and listening, searching for whatever had startled the livestock. Suddenly, Colonel Ron tapped Sherri's arm, then mine, and then pointed toward movement midway in the field near the creek. I could barely make out two familiar caps floating just above the foggy mists. Colonel Ron spoke quietly, "Believe our boys are back to looking for treasure."

We all sat quietly for a while, watching Jimmy and William disappear out of the field and into the trees lining the creek. Colonel Ron seemed to be analyzing where he thought they might be heading. It was obvious they were going to go back up the hill. After a while, he said, "Let's go to the Inn."

On our walk back, I asked, "Thought Jimmy and William were in jail?"

"Loretta says they were only charged with public intoxication. Neither was driving or even in the car when the police arrived."

"Good point," commented Sherri.

"So," I continued, "aren't you gonna run them off?"

"No sense in it. They'll just come back. Unless they know something we don't know, they're no more likely to find treasure today than in the past."

Chapter 36

One thing is for sure: the grass never quit growing at Grayson Springs. Chores became such a routine for Sherri and me that we initiated the process without being told. Allowing the grass to grow too tall would only amount to extra work. Shortly after our barn conversation with Colonel Ron, I began my turn pushing the mower. He and Loretta had joined Sherri's efforts at removing honeysuckle vines that were strangling the azalea bushes along the back side of the patio. The shrubbery's red and pink blossoms complimented the nearby freshly-pruned flowerbeds. Just since our arrival at Grayson Springs, the area had become a bouquet of perennial colors. While working, I daydreamed about seeing Mary Elizabeth Pierce and her Lieutenant John Jordan Crittenden strolling along in some dreamy conversation. Stopping for a moment, I gazed out over the grounds and could somehow see the view as it would have been laid out in 1875— children playing along balconies of the massive 150-foot long, three-story hotel buildings. I could hear excited voices, young and old mingling with the wind, the clanging of horse and buggies, and the daily hustle and bustle of life at the glamorous Grayson Springs Resort.

An odd summer chill gave me goose bumps. As if drawn by some invisible force, I began cutting grass in the direction of the sulfur springs area. At the bottom of the same pathway that had sparked my interest soon after our arrival, I hesitated; pondering the nearly-ripened blackberries that speckled the entangled mess which had thus far kept me away. It appeared the briars only grew in about a ten-foot strip along the edge of the woods. Populated with underbrush and saplings, the woods at a distance looked clear enough for walking. From where I stood, nothing indicated rain. For a short piece, I could make out what I assumed to be the remains of a pathway winding uphill between the larger trees.

My great-great-grandmother, in her youth, had walked up that path with John Crittenden. Somewhere beyond those thorny briars, there had to be a sitting rock and the tree into which the young soldier had carved his and Mary Elizabeth Pierce's initials.

"Hey!" startled me. "What the hell are you doing?" Sherri asked. "And why are you even cutting grass here? I thought we were working near the entrance today."

I stood dumfounded, leaning against the idle mower. "I was thinking."

"About what?"

"How I need to go up that path."

"Girl, you are one strange mo-fo. You still think you're gonna find some kind of treasure up there?"

"Maybe."

"Well, good luck. My ass is not crawling in those weeds with a bunch of chiggers and blood-sucking ticks."

"It's just that something's been telling me to go up there ever since the day we arrived...."

"Is that right?" interrupted my thought.

Sherri and I turned in unison to find that Eli Clemons had joined us.

He asked, "So, what's up that path?"

Sherri answered, "If we knew that, we wouldn't be standing here wondering."

I asked, "Jesus, Eli, you always sneak up on people like that?"

"Didn't sneak up."

"Well, don't be."

"So," he asked, "you really think there's treasure up there?"

Sherri slightly shook her head. Like me, she figured it was best not to talk treasure with Eli Clemons. I answered him, "Who knows? Evidently Jimmy and William think so. We saw them heading up the hill about an hour ago."

"Is that a fact?" Eli grunted. "I thought Ben said they were in jail."

Sherri said, "Give me that thing," while reaching for the mower. "You two can stand around talking, but I'd like to be done."

As she stomped away, I couldn't tell if Sherri had been hinting for me to get rid of Eli or if she just wanted to give us time alone. Leaning toward the latter, I asked Eli, "So, what's been going on with you?"

"Not much. Spent the last week up in Shelby County, shoeing show horses."

"Show horses?"

"Saddlebreds. I hear you and Sherri snuck off the other night."

"Who told you that?"

"Ben."

"What else did he tell you?"

"What do you mean?"

"Did he tell you where we went?"

"Does he know?"

"Never mind. You know, Eli, this is my last week here."

"And you have to go back?"

"Yes, but maybe not for good."

"You ... you wanna come back to Grayson County?"

"I think so. I like it here. It feels like home.... Soooo?"

Eli's head tilted. "Soooo what?"

"So what do you think about me living down here, where I'm from?"

"I ... I think if you consider all things and that's what you want, then that's what you should do."

"What about us?"

"Us?"

"Never mind...."

"No. Don't 'never mind' me. What're you sayin'? What do you mean by *us*?"

"Eli, we've talked about this before. I've never had a boyfriend. I don't think I've ever even been friends with a boy who wasn't gay." I hesitated, waiting for his reaction. He stood silently, so I continued my rant. "For most of my life, I've avoided the idea of being with a man.

Now I find myself thinking about it. I'm not sure why. Not sure I want to. And I'm not sure I don't. But I suppose it probably is something I should try."

Eli suddenly seemed much taller than me. He stood staring down on my uncertainty. Unable to hold them back, my tears began to run. He reached and gently wiped my cheek. "You are one beautiful, sweet, confused girl. And I do believe there's a special person inside you just dyin' to get out. But let me ask you, do you really believe sex is something you just *try*? Shouldn't it be something that happens between two people in love, who are willing to make commitments? My father taught me not to play mommies and daddies with someone I'm not willing to be mommies and daddies with."

No guy I knew in New York thought or talked like Eli Clemons. His hesitations struck my curiosities, and I again wondered if he might be gay. "Are you telling me you've never been with a girl?"

"I ... didn't say that. There's already been someone special in my life." He seemed to be fighting tears. "Savanna was really sweet, like you."

Savanna. What a beautiful name. "Sooo, what happened?"

"She ... went away."

Without even thinking, I asked, "Where'd she go?"

Staring up into the sky, he said quietly, "I hope she's in Heaven."

My heart broke, and I felt stupid for having asked. "I'm sorry."

When I hung my head, Eli wrapped his arms around my shoulders, drawing me close. He whispered, "I hope you never hook up with someone just to see what it's like. You come back to Grayson County, we'll have time to get to know one another."

When he left me to my yard work, I watched Eli walk away, trying to imagine him as a knight in shining armor. I waited, expecting him to at least glance back, but he never did. At the Inn, he joined Colonel Ron, and the two of them walked toward the barn. As soon as they were out of sight, I ran to the back of the Inn. On the wall behind the spot where we stored the push mower, there were yard tools hanging on nails. I grabbed the hatchet and a pair of leather gloves, and then hurried back to the springs. While Sherri continued her mowing near the entrance, I went to my knees and began hacking at the bases of the blackberry briars. One by one, I cut, tugged, and pushed aside each woody stalk in a three-foot-wide swipe. Halfway through, I startled a long black snake that slithered off at an amazing speed. For a moment, I froze on hands and knees, scanning and wondering, *Are there others?* Confident of being alone, I continued. Eventually, I had created a tunnel wide enough and tall enough to crawl through the mess. Exhausted, I fell back on my elbows, admiring my work. Suddenly my butt was wet. Raindrops began hitting my head. "What the heck?" Though it hadn't rained for days, the ground seemed saturated. As I lay there on my back, it began to rain.

"What the hell are you doing?" startled me. It was Loretta. She stood at the other end of my efforts.

"Exploring," was all I could think to say.

She squatted to look through my passage. "Does the Colonel know about this?"

"No, and please," I pleaded, "don't tell him."

To my further surprise, Loretta began crawling. I remained on my elbows watching, admiring her audacity. Her flowing hair got caught in the bristles. Instead of turning back, she tugged herself free. In her struggle, a thorny branch swiped against her cheek and I saw a trickle of blood. The woman kept coming. I felt frozen, as if I were watching the approach of a wild animal. When she reached my feet, my petrification left her no choice but to crawl over me. And she did. I lay still as she emerged, straddling me on all fours. Her face came to within inches of mine. For a second, I swear I thought she was going to kiss me. When I held up the hatchet in my right hand, Loretta rolled over to my left side, then onto her stomach, propping up on her elbows, staring uphill. "So, you think it's up there somewhere?"

She knows what I'm up to. "Maybe."

"What the...?" She had become as wet as I had. Sun shine continued at the other end of the tunnel, yet she and I were being sprinkled with raindrops. "It's the curse," she mumbled.

"Whatever it is, it's wet."

Then, without looking at me she said, "I saw you talking to Eli. You think he's like Ben?"

"No."

"Me neither."

"Eli's not like any boy I've ever met."

"In case you haven't noticed, Eli's not a boy. He's a man."

"I've noticed."

"And?"

"I'd like to kiss him."

Turning to face me, she said, "No shit?"

"But I'd like to kiss you, too."

"Jesus." Loretta rose to her knees, and then stood. "Stand up," she said. I did, and the two of us remained silent for a moment, scanning the hill ahead. Large sandstone boulders spotted the slope.

I thought, *any one of them could be the one.*

Loretta said, "Regardless of what you think of Eli, I believe we should keep this treasure hunt from him."

"I agree."

"In that case, how about we get back before he and the Colonel come looking?"

Chapter 37

Standing on top of the railing on the balcony of our Manhattan apartment ... staring out across darkened treetops in Central Park ... warm breeze in my face ... muffled traffic below ... city lights sparkling in the distance.

"Here I come."

Spreading my wings ... soft liftoff ... floating ... flying ... new vision ... butterfly's view.

"I'm flying."

Behind me ... on the balcony ... Daddy ... Melanie holding her child...

"Daddy!"

"Brooke ... Elizabeth ... wake your ass up. What the hell's wrong with you?"

"What?"

"You're talking in your sleep. Crazy shit."

Just enough moonlight bled into the room for me to see Sherri standing over me with a pillow between us, as if planning to suffocate me. "What the... What's with the pillow?"

"It's my protection, weirdo, in case you woke up swinging again. What were you dreaming about?"

"Oh. I ... I think I was flying."

"Well, how about you land your ass so I can get some sleep."

A light knock on the door surprised us. Frozen in place, Sherri whispered, "Bet you woke up the Colonel."

"Yes?" I replied to the rap.

The door creaked opened and a soft image of Loretta slid in. She moved toward Sherri, whispering loudly, "What the hell are you doin'?"

"I'm about to suffocate this bitch if she continues talking in her sleep!"

Holding a finger to her lips, Loretta said, "Not so loud ... I heard her ... somethin' about her daddy."

"I knew she would wake somebody up."

"I was already up." Loretta sat on the edge of my bed. "I've been thinking about this treasure thing. Can you tell me exactly what it is you think you're gonna find on that hill?"

"What do you mean?"

"I know you think there's some sort of treasure up there, but how in the hell do you think you're gonna find it? What exactly are you looking for?"

"A rock."

"A rock?"

"And a tree with initials on it. Should be those of Elizabeth Pierce and John Crittenden."

Loretta frowned and asked, "And you know this because?"

"You're asking too many questions. Just trust me. Somewhere up on that hill, the young Lieutenant John Jordan Crittenden III carved his and Elizabeth's initials in a beech tree by a rock that looks like a bench. It's where they sat daily while talking."

Again, Loretta frowned and shook her head. "You two get dressed."

"Excuse me?" I whispered loudly.

"We're goin' up there."

"Why?" Sherri blurted.

"Something tells me there really is a treasure of some sort on that hill. Too damn many people been looking for too long. Eli said something to me about it earlier today. I played it off, knowing he was liable to repeat anything I might say to Ben. Those men are determined to find whatever is hidden up on that hill. Me, I'm just a little too stubborn to let them find if first. So, who's with me?"

Sherri whispered, "Have you been drinking?"

"Noooo."

"You're seriously going to walk around in those woods at night."

"Yeeessss. I thought you girls were into night adventures."

"And what about Colonel Ron?"

"Don't you worry none about the Colonel."

"How," Sherri asked, "do you plan on getting through those blackberry briars?"

"Elizabeth already took care of that."

A minute earlier I had been floating over Central Park in some crazy dream. If that wasn't crazy enough, now I had Loretta wanting to sneak off to treasure hunt in the middle of the night.

We slipped out the back door. Sherri mumble-bitched under her breath until we were well away from the Inn, and then she said, "Should we come across this so-called treasure, are we to divide it evenly?"

I joked, "Maybe we should divide it according to who winds up with the most chiggers."

"No shit. We'll all be itching for another week."

Loretta said, "You two quit worrying about chiggers. I didn't see anything looks like a chigger-weed on that whole hillside."

I had to laugh when Bruno nudged Sherri's butt and she jumped six inches off the ground.

"Damn dog! Get off my ass!"

"Not so loud," Loretta whispered.

The moon provided adequate light as we made our way across the lawn and into the sulfur springs area. In single file, we maneuvered the narrow paths until we reached the hill. At that point, trees blocked the moon, and darkness swallowed us. We were surrounded by a blend of loud, creaking noises created by tree frogs, katydids, crickets and God knows what else. Sherri stared into the darkness. "This shit's creepy."

Loretta made a ghostly, "Woooooh. You should know that some people claim to have seen a ghost in Colonel Ron's woods."

"Great," Sherri huffed. "And you avoided telling us this whyyyy?"

"By the way," I said, "you know it's going to rain on us."

"Rain?" questioned Sherri. "There are no clouds in the sky."

Loretta said, "She's talking about the curse of the woods. I've heard tell it always rains in a portion of these woods where we are going."

Sherri stopped walking and asked, "Is there anything else I should know? Like vampires or something?"

"Nope," Loretta replied. "At least, not that I know of."

Loretta had brought along an oil lamp. I held it steady on the ground while she struck a match and created light. She adjusted the lamp's stem until a bright halo illuminated the entrance to my tunnel through the briars. Lamp in hand, Loretta knelt and said, "I'll go first and then hold the light for you two."

Sherri squatted. "You did this?"

"Yes," I replied. "Yesterday, while you cut grass."

"Cool." She gathered her skirt and started crawling through. I followed closely. By the time I stood upright in the light, I had wet spots on my skirt. Sherri and Loretta already seemed spellbound by our surroundings. For a moment, we all three stood taking in the cursed woods. A mist had already begun. Drops fell from high branches, pecking the forest floor.

I whispered, "I've been here before."

"When?" Sherri asked.

"Not in this life, I assure you."

Loretta put her free arm around my shoulder. "When you were here, did you see the ghost?"

Before I could say 'no,' Sherri said, "I'm beginning to believe she *is* the ghost."

Creepy, long shadows expanded and contracted as Loretta rotated the lamp, searching for the path. Bruno trotted by, and I wondered if he used the tunnel or had his own way in. When he continued onward, I said, "Looks like he knows the way." We began trekking uphill, examining rocks and trees along the way. I asked, "Do either of you even know what a beech tree looks like?" Blank expressions answered my question.

When Sherri said, "This is impossible," something bolted in the woods uphill from us. Loretta raised the lamp as we all froze in our tracks.

"What is it?" I whispered.

"Not sure."

"Bet it's a bear," Sherri guessed.

Loretta acted unconcerned. "Not likely. I've never seen or heard of one around here."

Suddenly the woods echoed with the same blowing and snorting sounds I'd heard while riding in the woods with the Colonel. "It's a deer."

No sooner than we began walking again, from a distance, there came the most horrific sound I'd ever heard. It sounded like a woman being tortured in a horror film. Sherri grabbed onto Loretta. "Oh my god. What the hell was that?"

"Sounded like a wildcat."

"As in like a lion or something?"

"Jesus." Loretta pushed away from the wimp. "Haven't you ever seen a Kentucky Wildcat? It's the mascot for the University of Kentucky."

"Oh, I get it. But are they dangerous?"

"Never heard of one attacking a human."

Further uphill, Bruno began baying. "Now what?" I asked.

Loretta said, "He's tracking the deer. He'll be back in a bit."

Brush rattled close by, behind us. Barely audible pitter-patters tapped the wet ground. We all twisted quickly. I tried to mess with Sherri. "They're surrounding us."

"What?"

"The wildcats. They're going to eat us."

The sound continued as something meandered in the woods below us. Loretta held the light high. Sherri whined, "I can't believe I'm, like, hanging out in a rainy-assed, cursed woods in the middle of the night."

Loretta said, "Quit whining. You can head back anytime you want."

"Yeah right, and get eaten by a bunch of wildcats?"

"Honey, a wildcat wouldn't come near us. Whatever it is, it ain't gonna bother you."

Sherri asked, "Loretta, you do have a gun, don't you?"

"Yes."

Sherri seemed to be weighing out her options as the rustling sound moved closer. We stared into the shadows, hoping to catch sight of whatever it was. I turned quickly and caught a glimpse of something dark dashing behind a nearby rock. "It's over there."

"Where?" Loretta asked, rotating the lamp towards the direction I pointed.

A small black creature scampered from one shadow to another. Sherri squeezed my arm. "Is it a wildcat?"

"Too small."

The creature, black with a white stripe down its back, came out and started waddling right toward us. "It's a skunk!" shrieked Sherri, as she turned and blindly took off running.

Loretta tried to tell her, "Don't run in the dark, stupid," but it was too late. Sherri collided with something, shouted unrecognizable profanities, took off again, slipped, fell, and went silent. "Sherri?" Loretta whispered loudly.

With no answer, I said, "Shit!" The air had become filled with the most obnoxious odor I'd ever experienced. "Is that..."

"Yes, it is. Hope it didn't spray Sherri."

"Oh my god, it's nasty."

When we moved toward Sherri, the skunk scampered away. It was much larger than I would have expected. Larger than any house cat I'd ever seen. Sherri lay semiconscious, moaning slightly. It appeared she had struck her head on a rock. Blood trickled down the side of her face. Fortunately, she had not been hit directly by the skunk's spray. Loretta placed the lamp on a flat spot, and we helped Sherri up into a sitting position against the rock. Rain had begun to fall steadily. Sherri's clothes were wet, and she had lost one of her shoes.

While Loretta pulled back Sherri's hair in search of an injury, I used the end of my skirt to wiped away blood. "Doesn't look too bad."

Loretta said, "Just hope she doesn't have a concussion."

I said, "Wake up, dipshit. Talk to me."

Sherri's eyes opened slightly. "What's that smell?"

"Skunk."

"Is it gone?"

Loretta surveyed the area. "Yes, I believe so."

We helped Sherri up off the ground and onto the rock, which was suitable for sitting. She leaned back against a big tree trunk. "No concussion," I guessed aloud, since Sherri remembered the skunk.

While Loretta nursed Sherri, I observed the rock she sat on, the tree it leaned against. *No way?* I thought. And then I saw it. Faint markings in the bark of the tree. "Oh my god!"

"Ssshhh. Turn out the lamp," Loretta whispered. "Hurry!" I lowered the stem until the flame extinguished. "Stay low," she continued, while pointing out what appeared to be flashlights streaking to and fro below us, just outside the woods.

"What is it?" I whispered.

"Either someone's looking for us or they're looking for the treasure. If they're looking for us, they'll call our names. Otherwise, we remain still and quiet."

"Looks like they're coming through the tunnel."

Sherri tugged my skirt. "Only one person knew you were looking up this hill."

Eli. Is it him, or did he tell his brother?

We crouched in perfect silence, watching the two flashlights streak about. Loretta tapped Sherri and me and whispered. "We have to lie down as close to the ground as possible and hope they move on up the hill without seeing us."

"But it's wet," complained Sherri.

"Wet might be our best option."

We moved behind the rock and tree and got flat on our stomachs, settling in just as the two flashlights began up the pathway we'd traveled moments earlier. At that point, it seemed a blessing that Sherri had led us twenty yards or so off into the woods, away from the given path. Somewhere over the hill, Bruno's yelping continued.

It seemed like forever as the two intruders moved uphill, streaking their lights back and forth in search. One said, "Oooowee ... been a polecat in here." When they had reached our elevation on the hillside, he bent over and picked something up.

"My shoe," whispered Sherri.

The man's light flashed in our direction for a second and then back towards his partner. "Looky here."

"What is it?"

"A shoe."

"Is that right?"

"And it's still warm. Don't believe we're alone."

I recognized the voices. "It's them," I whispered, "Ben and that old man Simpson."

Ben joined Simpson, checked out the shoe, and said, "Guarantee that belongs to one of those two girls."

The old man started looking around. "You girlies come on out here. Ain't no sense in hidin'. Believe it's time we got acquainted."

Loretta reached under her jacket and withdrew a gun. She whispered, "Y'all stay put," and then began crawling uphill.

The old man shined his light toward her. "I heeaarrr you. Best come on out so we can talk. You know you can't be runnin' off in these here woods."

The mist turned into rain. I could barely make out Loretta's silhouette. She'd positioned herself behind a tree, and then shouted. "Bartholomew Simpson and Ben Clemons, you men are trespassing, and I sure don't care for the way you be talkin' about my guests. Best head on back down the hill right now."

Both flashlights went out. I heard whispering, and then, "Well, if it ain't that pretty little black police girl been sleepin' with Colonel Lee. What you doin' up in these woods, middle of the night?"

I figured Loretta's silence meant she was moving again. Seconds later, she spoke. "Better question is what are you two doing up here where you ain't supposed to be?"

"Hell, I just come to see you ... you and your big city girls."

"Ben Clemons, I know you're out there somewhere, sneaking around. Charlotte know what you're up to? What kind of man you've become?"

As she spoke, I heard a twig break close by. Ben had been slowly sneaking in our direction. It looked like he carried a long-gun of some sort. Feeling around, I found a rock the size of a baseball. Gripping it in my right hand, I waited. When Sherri looked my way, I put my finger to my lips and then pointed toward Ben. We both watched as he stepped past us in his hunt for Loretta. When she spoke again, she said, "You boys leave now, and we can talk this over tomorrow," Ben raised his gun in her direction. Sherri inhaled so loudly that he heard her.

Shit!

For a moment, Ben stared. I crouched behind the opposite side of the rock. Loretta spoke again. "Them boys told me how y'all beat on 'em the other night. Hope you understand what's gonna happen if you put your hands on my girls."

After Ben took a couple more steps, I'm sure he could see her crouched behind the wide tree. As he raised his gun again, I launched, screaming, striking him with a right hook, rock and all. Fire exploded from the end of his shotgun. I collapsed backwards to the ground as he staggered and went down. My left leg burned. To my surprise, Sherri attacked Ben while I struggled to rise. She kicked and screamed and pounded at him with her fists. Loretta's gun and someone else's filled the woods with percussion and flashes, over and over. Expecting another shot from Ben, I used a sapling to pull myself up. He was on his knees, resisting Sherri's thrashing. I somehow became upright just as he backhanded her, knocking her several feet. Limping forward, I reached him just in time. When he turned and picked up the gun, I kicked with my good leg. My foot caught him under the chin at the same time my shin struck the shotgun. Falling backwards, I saw the world in slow motion. Ben's gun tumbled in the air, following my fall. I reached out and caught it just as my ass struck the ground. When my elbows hit, the gun struck me in the face. Somehow, I held on to it, fumbled to turn it in my hands, pointed it in the air, and pulled the trigger. The blast lit the night. Recoil hit my shoulder like a punch, and

I felt my head collide with the ground. Debris rained from the trees above as I lay still. My weight seemed triple. I couldn't move. Gunfire ceased. Bruno's baying moved down the hill. Far off, I heard the Colonel's voice shouting ... Loretta shouting back. Sherri hovered over me, screaming, "Oh my god, he shot her! She's bleeding!"

.....Visibility had become almost zero. Through the dust cloud, painted horses carried painted men ... worriers, screaming and shouting. Some on foot, shooting, stabbing, chopping ... I emptied my revolver as did those around me. Ten feet away a savage used his knife to remove the scalp of one of my men who screamed to the end. My head throbbed. I prayed. I fought. I wished I were home in Kentucky. Back with.....

I began to see light and could feel the bumpy, wet ground under my back. Loretta's lamp burned brightly nearby, and Colonel Ron knelt over me. "Welcome back. You had us worried."

"My leg. My head."

"Your leg is gonna be okay. It's your head I'm worried about. Can you tell me your name?"

"John..."

"John? You really did take a fall."

"Ben ... Simpson, where are they?"

"They ran off. We'll deal with them later. Right now we need to decide if you need medical attention."

"Loretta and Sherri?"

"They're coming up the hill. They went to get first aid supplies. So, you do know *where* you are."

"Yes."

"Well, you just lie still."

"She awake?" Sherri hollered from a distance.

"Yes," replied the Colonel. "Can't keep a good man down."

His words brought me to tears. "I saw horses, and, and men killing men. They were ... Indians and soldiers and, I ... I think I was a man."

He grinned and said, "Just take it easy. You've been through a lot."

"Come here, Colonel." He lowered close to my face. "Man to man, I'm not a man, am I?"

He used his hand to brush the hair out of my bruised face. "You certainly are not. But you *are* one hell of a woman."

"How is she?" asked Loretta.

"She'll live, but she could have a slight concussion."

Ben's shotgun had grazed the skin on the outside of my left thigh. Colonel Ron said I got lucky. A few inches over and I could have lost my leg. Loretta applied alcohol to my wound, and it felt like she was setting me on fire. She then wrapped my leg while bombarding me with questions about my name, the day of the week, time of year, etc. Holding Sherri's hand, I was able to walk down the hill.

Bruno appeared to be keeping guard on the back porch as we sat in rockers discussing the night's events. It turns out, Loretta had hinted of searching for the treasure, so Colonel Ron wasn't completely caught off guard with our actions. I had my leg propped up in another chair. Ben's shotgun leaned against the porch post.

Loretta asked, "So, what do we do about Ben and Simpson?"

Sherri wasted no time giving her opinion. "It would be nice if we could, like, go find them and shoot them the way they did Elizabeth."

"Not that easy," replied Colonel Ron. "I'm sure Ben's gonna say it was self-defense and that his gun went off by accident when Elizabeth attacked him. I just can't believe he's gotten so caught up in this bullcrap. He's always been such a good fellow."

"Huh." I didn't quiet agree. "All I can say is those coins must be worth a fortune."

Loretta stood. "I'm goin' to bed. Elizabeth, you keep in mind that those coins are not worth getting killed or losing a leg."

Sherri rose, yawned, and agreed. "Come on, superhero. Let's go to bed."

"Superhero? Hell, the way I see it, you're my hero. You saved my life. You kept that asshole from shooting me."

"You're both my heroes," yawned Loretta. "Believe we all saved each other tonight. Now let's go to bed."

Colonel Ron leaned back in his chair. "You two go ahead. I wanna talk to Elizabeth for a bit. I'll help her up the stairs in a few."

After goodnights, Loretta and Sherri retired. Colonel Ron said, "I'll be right back." When he returned he had a half-pint bottle of bourbon. "This treasure thing is really starting to get on my nerves."

"Psychologists aren't supposed to have bad nerves. So, you plan on getting drunk?"

"No, ma'am. But I'm sure as hell gonna have me a drink. Believe I deserve one after this night." He broke the seal, twisted off the lid, and then sucked down a whole lot in one drink. He let out a long exhale and made an ugly face.

"That bad?"

"That good." He sat the bottle down on the porch between us, and then pulled my pack of cigarettes out of his shirt pocket.

"Where'd you get those?"

"Found 'em next to you on the ground. Figured they must have fallen out of your pocket. Didn't want 'em to get wet." Tapping one out, he asked, "You want one?"

"No thanks. You can keep them. After watching you struggle up the hill all out of breath, think I'll quit."

"Good decision." He lit one, leaned back in his chair, and said, "Beautiful night, ain't it?"

I reached down for the bottle, and before he could react, I took a large gulp. It burned like shit but I didn't want to let him know. When I sat the bottle down, he shook his head and asked, "That bad?"

I leaned back in my chair and said, "You're right about one thing."

"What's that?"

"It sure is a beautiful night." He did not reply. The night sounds seemed to increase in volume. After a long moment of silence, I said, "Thought you wanted to talk."

"I do if you do."

"Are there really wildcats in the woods around here?"

"Yes, ma'am." He reached for the bottle and took another drink. "Elizabeth, the hype around this treasure hunt bullshit has obviously escalated since your arrival. Now even Loretta's gotten caught up in it. I think maybe the best thing would be to find whatever it is people are after so all this chaos can stop. I don't want people digging up my property from now on. And I sure as hell don't want someone to get killed over it. At one time, I actually thought about faking a treasure find, just so people would stop looking."

"I have a better idea."

"Really?"

"Yeah. How about we just go get it and be done with it?"

"You say that as if you know where it is."

"I believe I do."

"On the hill?"

"Yes. I think we were right there tonight when Ben and the old man came along."

"Tell you what ... if you can reveal to me your source of information, I'll go with you in the morning, that is if you can walk that far, and together we'll either find it or figure out a scenario to fake a find. One way or the other, I want this treasure thing over with."

"I have in my possession a diary that belonged to my great-great-grandmother, Mary Elizabeth Pierce. She wrote it during the summer and fall of 1876. It mostly deals with her relationship with John Jordan Crittenden III."

"A diary. No shit."

"I'll show it to you later. Important thing is the diary pretty much authenticates your congressional document. Elizabeth Pierce wrote about how the young Lieutenant John Crittenden III, namesake of his grandfather, Senator Crittenden, had given her a box. She called it a fancy snuff box, with coins in it, to keep while he was away fighting Indians. Long story short, when Crittenden died at Little Big Horn, Mary Elizabeth Pierce hid the coins to keep her father from selling them. I believe she hid them at their sitting rock in the woods. For years, she visited that rock on the anniversary of his death, taking a bouquet of wildflowers to place there in his memory.

"And you think you found the rock tonight."

"Pretty sure. According to the diary, Crittenden had carved his and Elizabeth's initials into the beech tree that the rock leaned against. I don't know what a beech tree looks like, but I did see markings in the bark of the tree there tonight."

"Ain't but two decent size beech trees on that hill. Believe I know which one you're talkin' about." While smashing out his cigarette, he asked, "Why didn't you tell me about the diary before?"

"I ... I think I was afraid if you saw the diary, you would think I was lying about my dreams ... and my visions."

"I see.... So, did Mrs. White give you that diary?"

"No. She's never seen it. But she does remember the stories. I intend to show it to her when I return to Grayson Springs."

"Return?"

"Colonel, if I hadn't gotten into trouble, I would be going off to college in the fall. Most of my friends will be. But, but now I have a grandmother. She lives alone. It seems to me, I could live down here with her. If they don't let me make up my finals, I could get my GED and then go to college somewhere in this area."

"You really feel that way?"

"Yes."

"And your grandmother?"

"Believe she'll agree. We have a lot of catching up to do.... Colonel, I do hope you know how much I appreciate what you and Loretta have done for me, and Sherri, here at Grayson Springs."

"Thank you. Means a lot to hear you say that."

"I'd like to study psychology and sociology."

"Seriously?"

"Yes."

"Closest college is the community college in E-Town. It's a drivable distance. You could start there and then transfer to the University of Kentucky. Or you could just attend the university and live on campus until you're done."

"Believe I'd prefer the community college. I really need to spend time with my grandmother. If I go to Kentucky full time, she could pass before I'm done."

"Good point. Whatever you decide, I'll support you in any way I can."

"We really do need to find this treasure. I can use it to fund my education."

"I'd say Dr. Green has that taken care of already."

"Perhaps. If so, then we can use the treasure to fund your and Loretta's Grayson Springs project. Of course, I'll want to be a part of it."

Colonel Ron's eyes became glassy as he contemplated my words. He reached for the bottle, held it up, and said, "To the future."

He drank all but a swallow and then handed it to me. I repeated his words "To the future," and then finished it off.

"You tell anybody I let you drink whiskey, I'll deny it."

Feeling giddy, I asked, "Colonel, do you think I could be possessed?"

He chuckled and said, "What makes you think such a thing?"

"I do things I don't understand. I see things that make no sense, and ... and sometimes it feels like I have a man living inside of me."

"Is that all?"

"Asshole."

Colonel Ron helped me up the stairs. Good thing too since the whiskey had me buzzing. I had my arm over his shoulder and his around my waist. It felt good to be held. We entered the room quietly, not wanting to wake Sherri. I whispered, "I'm going to sleep in my clothes."

"Good," he answered as I fell back on the bed.

"By the way," he whispered, "you know what day tomorrow is?"

"It's Wednesday. Why?"

"It's June 25th. Anniversary of you-know-what."

"Little Big Horn?"

"Yep."

"You believe in omens?"

"Not sure, but it does seem an odd coincidence." He bent over and kissed me on the forehead. "If you were my daughter, I'd say it doesn't matter to me who or what you are inside, but on the outside, I see a precious, beautiful woman."

Bourbon talking? "Thank you."

"Goodnight, Elizabeth." On his way out, he closed the door.

Sherri whispered, "What the fuck was that?"

Chapter 38

Wednesday morning. Loretta's rooster interrupted my sleep. For thirty minutes, I remained in bed thinking about last night's events. My head hurt more from bruise and booze than my leg did from the gunshot. I didn't really want to get out of bed, but I did. As I removed my blood-stained skirt, Sherri rolled over, gawking. "Where you going?"

"Downstairs. I need coffee and any painkillers available."

"Your face looks like shit."

"Thanks."

"You should stay in bed. I'll get you something."

"Thanks again. And I really mean it, but I have to get up." I limped out of the room quickly as possible to avoid her request for further explanation. Mine and the Colonel's walk up the hill needed to be private. On my excruciating trip down the steep stairs, I met the promising aroma of Colonel Ron's strong coffee. He crouched, stoking the stove.

"Well, well. Look at you walking on that leg."

"It hurts."

"Too much to climb the hill?"

"It'll hurt regardless. If you're going, I'm going."

"Well, I'll be ready to go just as soon as I sit on that back porch and have my cup of coffee. You?"

"Please. Maybe two. You got anything for pain?"

He grinned and said, "Whiskey."

"Hell no. Believe that's half the problem."

"Excuse me?" questioned Loretta, as joined us. "What's your problem?" When I turned to look at her, she grimaced. "Ouch."

"I know. Sherri already told me I look like shit. Don't rub it in."

Colonel Ron began pouring. "Coffee, Loretta?"

"Yes, please."

We sat in rockers, savoring hot coffee and watching robins pull worms from the wild strawberry patch. A stubborn mist of fog lingered over the creek and around bases of sycamores. Back at the barn, that old rooster's crow became faint as he wound down the morning ritual. Loretta surprised me. "Wrong person hears you talking about drinking whiskey with the Colonel, we can kiss our project goodbye."

"What makes you so sure I did?"

"Smelled it on his breath and overheard you in the kitchen."

"My lips are sealed."

"Good."

"So you got close enough to smell his breath?"

Colonel Ron cleared his throat, and Loretta changed the subject. "He says you wanna study psychology and help us out here at Grayson Springs."

"That's right."

"Of course, you know you're apt to change your mind by the time you've finished your degree."

"Things always change ... ain't that right Colonel?"

"Things change."

"What about Eli?" Loretta continued.

"What about him?"

"You two gonna be a couple?"

"I like Eli, but I'm not sure I can trust him."

"Under the circumstances, I understand."

"So," I asked, "what's going to happen to Ben and that old man for what they did last night?"

"Trust me, I'll be filing charges before the day is over."

I stood to leave and said, "Colonel, you gonna take a gun with us up on the hill?"

"Does a bear shit in the woods?"

Colonel Ron had his gun holstered to his side and carried a spade. I struggled to carry myself. Fortunately, he knew exactly where the tree stood. Good thing, seeing as how the woods looked so different in daylight. He and I stood in the sprinkling rain, staring at the markings on the tree. They were faint, but without a doubt read JJC+MEP. Colonel Ron commented first. "Hell, I've stood here before trying to figure out who those initials belonged to."

"So, where do we dig?"

"Good question." Colonel Ron thrust his spade into the ground and hit rock. He scraped around for a bit and then admitted defeat. "Only way to dig here is with a pick ... or a stick of dynamite."

"It's been a hundred and thirty something years. Maybe the tree grew over the spot we're looking for."

"That's a possibility."

"So wouldn't we need a saw?"

He laughed and said, "You really wanna cut down this tree?"

"You really wanna find the treasure?"

"Honey, this tree *is* a treasure. I'd say it's at least three hundred years old. It was already pretty big in 1876. If she really did burry something here, we might destroy a few roots, but not the whole tree. You feel safe staying here while I go back down to get a pick and a pry-bar?"

After watching Colonel Ron disappear down the hillside, I sat on the rock, staring up the hill the way Mary Elizabeth Pierce must have with John. Relaxing against the big beech tree's trunk, I enjoyed the sounds of the woods—insects buzzing, songbirds whistling, crows cawing, light percussions caused by water drops from the leaves above. *Sapling branches rattled. I turned to see a young woman, dressed like me, walking up the hill. In her hands, she held a bouquet of wildflowers. Her face shined, and her red hair flowed in waves to her waist. As she drew nearer, her beauty took my breath. She had my eyes. Reaching the tree, she knelt down and placed the flowers at its base. Then she reached under the rock where it leaned against the tree as if looking for something. Rising, she stepped around and sat by my side. Facing uphill, she leaned back against the tree. We sat silently, listening to the sounds of the woods—insects buzzing, songbirds whistling, crows cawing, light percussions caused by water drops from the leaves above.* Sapling branches rattled. I turned to see Colonel Ron climbing the hill, carrying a pick in one hand and a pry-bar in the other. In my solitude, I heard the softly spoken words, *"Goodbye, John."*

Nearing, Colonel Ron spoke, "I see no one got you while I was gone." He looked winded. "Damn, I'm out of shape."

I turned and sat wordlessly.

"What's wrong?" he asked. I remained silent as he stepped in front of me. He put his hand under my chin, lifted my head, and asked, "You been crying?"

I tilted my head and gave him *the look.*

"What?" he asked. "What's goin' on?"

Again, I gave him the look.

"You're shittin' me. You ... had a vision?"

Wiping my face, I nodded, "Yes."

"And?"

"She came up that path the same way you just did, carrying flowers."

He stood staring at me like a detective waiting for a flinch. "You watched her?"

I nodded.

"So it's not a vision, dammit. You're saying you saw a ghost.... Did she speak to you?"

"I ... I think so. She said, 'Goodbye John.'"

Colonel Ron grinned. "She called you John?"

For a second, I saw Daddy's expression in the Colonel. That psychiatric look of disbelief. A look I'd seen from so many in the past, and I began to cry again.

"Elizabeth..."

"You don't believe me."

He sat beside me, right where Mary Elizabeth had moments earlier, and said, "Please, I'm trying to understand. You say she had flowers..."

"Yes. She put them on the ground by the tree." As I turned to look, so did Colonel Ron. There were no flowers. I turned back and continued to cry.

Colonel Ron shook his head and said, "Did she know why you were here? Did she mention the coins?"

"No."

"So what else did she say?"

"Nothing."

"What did she do?"

"She ... she stuck her hand under the rock ... down there, where it leans against the tree."

"Under the rock. No shit?"

"Look up there, Colonel." I pointed toward the ledge, some fifty feet above us. "In her diary, Elizabeth wrote about that ledge. John told her that this rock had broken off of it and rolled downhill until it lodged against this tree. He said Indians had used it to grind corn or acorns or something and that there was a hole drilled into it."

"Really." Colonel Ron stood and began moving around the rock, inspecting. "You see a hole? I don't. And it sure doesn't look like the rock has moved in years."

The tree actually had an indention where the rock leaned against it, as if it had grown around it. I went to the other side of the rock and dropped to my knees.

"Don't put your hand under there. It's a perfect spot for a copperhead."

"But that's where it's at. I know it is."

Colonel Ron went to his knees and looked. He took a twig and scrapped around under the rock. "No snakes."

I reached under and ran my hand over the rock's surface. It wasn't a deep hole as I expected, but it was there nonetheless. I felt the same sensation as when I had touched Mary Elizabeth's gravestone. "It's here. I know it is."

"Let me see." He too ran his hand along the rock's surface. "Not very deep." Something had drawn his interest. After clearing debris, he lay down on the wet ground to gain visual access.

"But in her diary, she said the hole went nearly through the rock."

With his pocket knife, he began scraping. "If she put it in here, she was smart enough to fill the hole with mud.... Shit's petrified!" He rose with a smile on his face, yet his hands were empty.

"What?" I asked.

"It does look like someone put something in that hole."

I went to my knees, ignoring the pain of my injury, and then rolled to my side. I could see the hole and Colonel Ron's scrapings.

He said, "I don't wanna tear up my knife gettin' it out. I'll need to go back and get a chisel."

I rose and said, "Not now."

"Why not?"

Chapter 39

Loretta rose from her chair. "Honey, I don't believe in ghosts!"

"I do," Sherri admitted.

Colonel Ron said, "I'm skeptical too, but it does appear someone put something in that rock."

"Visions. Ghosts." Loretta shook her head. "What next?"

I stood and vented. "Loretta, what do you want me to say? How can I explain things that I don't understand? You have to believe me when I say I had no way of knowing where that hole was in the rock. She showed me.... And, and what if I'm not the only one who's seen her?"

"Bullshit," snapped Loretta. "Now you're being silly."

"Am I? You guys both told me Ben's a nice guy. My grandmother says the old man Simpson wasn't always so mean. Something drives these people crazy about digging up that hill."

"And you think it's a ghost?"

"I don't know. But I will tell you this: she looked a lot like me. Same color hair. Same eyes. Same clothes. It was like looking in the mirror."

"I think you're delusional."

"Easy, Loretta," said Colonel Ron. "Remember what William Rice said on the hill. Said he'd seen her before, *on* the hill. And I recall Ben had much the same reaction."

"He said he thought we'd met before?"

Sherri chimed in. "Can't we ask them?"

On an ugly, cloudy Friday morning, our last scheduled day at Grayson Springs, a small, perplexed gathering met on the patio. There, on a picnic table, Sherri and I served coffee and homemade bread. Sheriff Godfrey, arriving late, parked his cruiser outside the entrance, and then walked his big fat ass back to the Inn. Even before he reached the crowd, Ben Clemons and Bartholomew Simpson were bombarding him with questions. I overheard the Sheriff say, "Guys, I'm as confused you are." Glancing my way, he added, "And trust me, we'd best get a damn good explanation."

Jimmy Jackson and William Rice stood talking with Eli Clemons and Father Ryan, obviously keeping distance between them and Ben, Simpson, and the Sheriff.

I asked Colonel Ron and Loretta if we could get started. For the first time since our arrival, Loretta wore her badge hanging around her neck and her gun openly on her side. To get everyone's attention, Colonel Ron rang the dinner bell several times. Like school children, the whole crowd shifted silently toward us. Rockers had been provided for my grandmother, for Charlotte Clemons—ready to pop any time— and for Sherman and Eloise Henry.

Loretta began. "Okay, everybody! First I wanna thank you all for coming out this morning. Some of you were reluctant, and I understand. We appreciate your presence nonetheless. Hopefully by the time we leave today, you'll be glad you came. That said, I'll turn this over to Colonel Ron."

"I think most of you are aware that today is the last day of our first session of the Grayson Springs Project. As you can see, our two guests, Sherri and Elizabeth, have really cleaned this place up..."

"Can you lend 'em our way for a while?" joked Eloise Henry.

"I hear you Ma'am," Colonel Ron replied, but unfortunately, they will be leaving us tomorrow."

Jimmy and William were looking at one another as if to say, *Who cares?*

Colonel Ron continued, "If you haven't already noticed, this isn't exactly the crowd you would expect for a going away celebration. However, as you will soon find out, we all seem to have something in common. Now, on that note I would like to turn this meeting over to one of Grayson County's own, Miss Mary Elizabeth White Green."

Heads were turning as I limped up, shook hands with the Colonel, and then faced my guests. Eli Clemons smiled, standing on one side of Charlotte, with Ben on the other. I glanced at my grandmother, the Henrys, and then the others one by one. "I too want to thank you all for coming. By now you all know that I was not born in New York. I was born over in the flats, at the Henrys' place. My mother was their foster child Cynthia. My father was Jamie White." Pointing at her, I said, "And that makes this lovely woman my grandmother, which brings me to the purpose of this gathering. All my life, I have been haunted by dreams and visions of things that made little or no sense. I've said and done things that left me and those around me wondering. This trip to Grayson County has not only revealed to me who I am, but it has also made some sense of the odd things I say and do." Glancing around the crowd, I said, "Each of you, in your own way, has helped me come to a better understanding of who and what I am." Father Ryan gave me a grin and a nod.

Everyone began whispering and glancing around. "Please," I continued, "as Colonel Ron stated, most of us have something in common. But before I explain, may I ask that each of you place your cell phones on this table? I cannot say what I must say if there is a chance it can be recorded." Colonel Ron and Loretta were first to comply.

"What kind of bullshit is this?" asked William.

"Trust me," Loretta replied, "you'll understand real soon, and you probably won't mind. Please humor us for a few minutes."

Grudgingly, everyone, including Sheriff Godfrey, placed their phones on the picnic table. "Thank you." I smiled and said, "Perhaps now you understand how Sherri and I felt six weeks ago when we had to give up our phones. So, back to what we all have in common. Ben, when I first came here, Colonel Ron and Loretta introduced you and Charlotte as two of the nicest people they know." Ben hung his head. I turned my attention to his old friend. "Mr. Simpson, my grandmother tells me in her younger days, you were one of the sweetest guys she knew.... Jimmy and William, though we've had our differences, I feel like you are both okay guys." Glancing around, I said, "What I'm trying to say is that the one thing we all have in common is the same thing that changed us ... possessed us, so to speak...."

Sheriff Godfrey asked, "What the hell are you talking about?"

"I'm talking about our desires to find something buried on Colonel Ron's property ... a treasure, sir ... a treasure that people around here have been talking about for over a hundred and thirty years. Please, we don't need to pretend anymore. We all know what I'm talking about. The reason I asked that you turn over your phones is simple. While I believe each of you will understand what I'm about to say, others may not. I don't want people to think I'm crazy, and I don't want them to think any of you are either...."

I took a deep breath. "Yesterday I saw someone in the woods ... a young woman dressed similar to me. She was beautiful, with milky white skin and long, wavy red hair. She carried a bouquet of wildflowers...."

Heads turned and faces lit up. Charlotte gave Ben a look. He said, "I told you."

"In 1876, a young soldier named John gave something of value to a 15-year-old girl who worked here at Grayson Springs. It was a fancy little snuff box. He asked her to hold it while he went off to fight Indians at Little Big Horn. He told her if he never returned, the box and its contents would be hers. Second Lieutenant John Jordan Crittenden III died at Custer's Last Stand. My understanding is that the box he gave to Mary Elizabeth Pierce contained coins, 1856 proofs of the flying eagle cent piece. The woman I met seemed to be showing me where the box is hidden...."

"Where is it?" Jimmy blurted.

"We'll get to that in a minute..."

"Why you?" asked Godfrey.

"This'll sound crazy, but I think I heard her call me John."

"She recognized your spirit," interrupted Father Ryan with a smile.

"Perhaps," I grinned back.

Sheriff Godfrey blurted, "You people sound crazy."

"I can understand you thinking that."

"You expect us to stand here and believe you saw some sort of a ghost...?"

"Pete, shut the hell up and let the girl talk," Bartholomew Simpson scolded the sheriff.

I knew then that old man Simpson had seen the ghost of Mary Elizabeth Pierce in the woods. I said, "The girl who hid the box back in 1876 was the grandmother of this woman, my grandmother, Mary Elizabeth White."

Sherman Henry spoke up. "And the little redhead showed you where it's at?"

Loretta seemed stunned at how many present already knew of the red-headed girl in the woods. I said, "Yes, I think so."

"You think?" asked Eli. "If you're so sure, why haven't you dug it up?"

"Good question," echoed Ben.

Father Ryan grinned and said, "Bet I know the answer."

"Eli, I touched the spot where it's hidden. A feeling came over me, just as it did the day I touched the grave of Mary Elizabeth Pierce. In my heart, I know it's there, the box given to my great-great-grandmother by John, which brings me to my proposal. Ben, yesterday Loretta filed charges against you and Mr. Simpson. You both could go to jail for harassing my grandmother and for what you did to William on the Grayson Springs Road the other night. And there's already been a complaint filed against you, Sheriff, for corruption in covering it all up. And shit, night before last, on the hill, you guys could have killed me and Sherri and Loretta.... And look at you, William ... even after getting beat up, you get out of jail, and the very next day, we see you and Jimmy marching your asses back up that hill. My point is ... I believe we are all good people here, possessed by our desires to find that damned treasure. I want to end the madness, and I want all those charges dropped so everyone here can be friends again."

Heads were turning, and chatter erupted.

"Please, let me finish. I have my great-great-grandmother's diary and a letter to her that was written in the fall of 1876. These documents prove that the coins, if they really are there, belonged to Mary

Elizabeth Pierce. Her heir would be my grandmother. She has agreed to allow me to use their value, whatever that might be, to return to Grayson County, to live with her, and to make sure Colonel Ron's dream for Grayson Springs can continue. I want other young people to be able to come here and learn, as Sherri and I have, that there is more to the world than cell phones and email and texting ... and while I am still working on the issue, I do now realize that cursing at one another reveals a lack of vocabulary and may be a sign of unhappiness, a sign that we need to hesitate in our rat race lives and look for the simple joys and moments in life that are hidden in the world around us."

Sherri said, "People, I admire Elizabeth for what she wants to do. I for one have no desire to live here. But believe me, I will never forget the things I have seen and done here. I feel like I have lived a part of history. I will always be able to close my eyes and see that meadow out beyond Colonel Ron's barn ... the morning fog and the sounds of the country."

As several present nodded their approvals of Sherri's comments, Ben spoke out, "You say you want the charges dropped. What is it you want in return?"

"Already told you. I want us all to be friends again. And I want all of you to accompany me while I remove the treasure that's been driving us crazy for so long. Sheriff, you and Father Ryan can witness. If that box is right there where she showed me, it'll be proof enough that there is and has been something unusual going on in what most of you call the cursed woods. In return, Grandmother has agreed that we will offer two percent shares of the eventual revenues raised from the find to Ben, Mr. Simpson, Jimmy, and William for keeping the dream alive. And I want to give another two percent to the Henrys in return for the love they expressed for my real mother." Looking their way, I added, "And if you two don't mind, I'll claim you as grandparents on my mother's side."

Eloise Henry's face wrinkled. She took her husband's hand and said, "You hear that? We got ourselves a granddaughter."

"So, how about it Father Ryan ... will you be happy if I give up ten percent to these fine people instead of the Church?"

"I believe *God* will be well pleased with your efforts and generosity."

"Good. And Father, if we do indeed find the coins, I would like your blessing in hopes that the soul of Mary Elizabeth Pierce can finally rest in peace."

He grinned. "Young lady, if you present what you describe, I'll gladly give my blessing."

Sheriff Godfrey asked, "How do we know this whole thing is legit. That it hasn't been staged?"

Colonel Ron said, "Believe me, Sheriff, if it's there, it's legit. The damn thing's buried inside a rock. We'll have to chisel it out."

An hour later, we gathered in the woods. Though a steady drizzle of rain had begun, Charlotte climbed that hill wearing a hooded jacket, cradled on both sides by Ben and Eli. She said she'd rather fight the rain than miss the excitement. Jimmy stood in front of the tree and said, "I'll be a son of a bitch. We seen them initials before, but never knowed whose they was."

On this trip, Colonel Ron brought a chisel and a hammer. All the men and Loretta took turns lying on the wet ground to inspect the shallow hole. Jimmy rose to his knees and said, "I'll believe it when I see it."

Ben said, "Colonel, you mind if Bart and I participate in the chisel work...?"

"Me and Jimmy too," requested William. "We spent a lotta time up here lookin'."

Before it was over, most of us took turns tapping the chisel with the hammer. When it was his turn, Mr. Simpson moaned and groaned as he rolled into place and began. After only a few whacks, he broke through. "Hot damn, believe I got it!"

"Can you see it?" I asked.

"No, ma'am. Can't get my head under here far enough." He came to his knees. "But by God it's there ... I can feel it. My hands are just too damn big to get in there and pull it out."

"Well, come on up here," ordered Colonel Ron. "Believe Elizabeth ought to do the honors anyway."

By then, the skies had darkened, the rain had increased, and the men had already wallowed the ground into a muddy mess. As I contemplated, thunder clapped and Loretta said, "Best hurry before this storm hits."

Sherri said, "Better you than me."

I lowered to all fours, stared at the small opening, and said, "Someone be ready to pull me out." Down on my belly I went. Slick as it was, I managed to squeeze under much farther than the men. "It's dark under here." I could hear the rain starting to pour and felt it beating on my legs. In order to see the hole, I had to roll over on my back. There it was inches from my face. "I do see it!" Rainwater from uphill began seeping in around the rock. The more I squirmed, the muddier I got. For my fingers to reach the hole, I had to pull my elbows up past tree roots. Suddenly, I felt trapped, seeing no way to get my elbows back down.

God, please don't let me be stuck here forever. Lightning struck, and seconds later thunder clapped.

"Best hurry!" encouraged Loretta. We're all getting soaked out here!"

I was stuck under a frigging rock, and they were worried about getting wet. I managed to get one finger on top, and one under the small box. "It's stuck!"

"Try to wiggle it," Eli encouraged.

"It's moving."

"Well, get it out," pleaded Sherri.

"Got it, but ... oh shit! I'm stuck!"

"Jesus!" Loretta complained.

Colonel Ron said, "Roll back over on your stomach so you can come out the way you went in."

Thunder continued to roar, and I could feel the steady stream of rainwater soaking into my clothing. Gripping the small leather box in one hand, I struggled to roll over, only to find my chin submerged. "It's filling up with water in here, and I can't move!"

Next thing I knew, hands were gripping my ankles. As they began pulling, I felt my skirt crawling up my sides. They quit. Ben joked, "Looks like a mud wrestler in bloomers."

Jimmy added, "Boy, wouldn't this make a good YouTube video."

"Best not be a camera out there!"

William said, "Believe that's the smallest butt I ever seen on a woman."

"I heard that!"

At that point, I even heard Father Ryan chuckle. Eli said, "Damn, don't think I've ever seen a woman in a more compromising situation."

"Elizabeth, honey," Loretta added, "I believe these men are in a position to negotiate another percent or two."

"Would you all shut up and get me the hell out of here?"

When they resumed tugging on my legs, I felt mud and my bloomers riding up my ass. Sherri said, "Good thing she's got small boobs."

By the time they dragged me out, I was a muddy mess. Leaning back against the rock, I held the miniature treasure chest in my hand while the pouring rain washed my face. It was exactly as described in Mary Elizabeth's writing—a small, leather, rectangular box. Everyone smothered in around me.

Charlotte squatted, offering her dress to wipe my face.

Sheriff Godfrey said, "You gonna open it or not?"

"I'm a little afraid to. It's so old ... might fall apart."

Colonel Ron said, "I wouldn't worry. Considerin' where it's been all these years, I'd say it's well preserved." Eli agreed.

It felt like opening a Christmas gift. All eyes were on the box as I released its two miniature, metal latches. Inside, the ivory porcelain snuffbox had been perfectly preserved. I can't imagine how hard it was to paint the scene of horsemen and hounds chasing the little red fox. Charlotte took a deep breath. "It's sooo beautiful."

Removing the snuffbox lid exposed five shiny coins. I took one out, inspected it, and held it up for all to see. On one side, the words 'UNITED STATES OF AMERICA' wrapped around the image of a flying eagle. At the bottom, the date read, '1856'. On the other side, it looked like a wreath of some sort around the words 'ONE CENT'. The woods came to life with hoots and hollers as everyone celebrated the find. More than a century and a half old, the coins looked brand new. Colonel Ron said, "Guys, I know we all want to look at them, but I believe we should keep them dry."

I placed the coin, the lid, and the snuffbox back into the leather case, and then held it up. "Here, Colonel ... you keep it safe."

After Eli helped me up, Father Ryan asked us all to hold hands in a circle. With the wind rocking trees and the rain coming down in sheets, he prayed. "Dear Lord, as it has been throughout history, you have an odd way of bringing closure to the lives of good people. By a strange set of circumstances, you have brought this unlikely group of people together to complete a task that began so many years ago. Today, it seems the spirit of Mary Elizabeth Pierce has led us to this place. She has finally delivered this, this treasure of sort to a young woman who intends to put its value to good use ... an honorable purpose that will help in the lives of many to come. May her intentions come to fruition. And now, hear us Lord as we pray that you allow the spirit of your servant, Mary Elizabeth Pierce, to enter into Heaven for eternal peace. Amen."

"Amen!" echoed about. Only those who were there could describe how the rain ceased, and the birds, insects, and even the squirrels chattered their approval. Everyone stood in silence, staring up. Sunshine beamed through clinging drops of rain, and the wood's canopy glistened like a giant crystal chandelier. Sherri whispered, "There really is a God."

Chapter 40

I stood at Casper's stall, whimpering as I rubbed the spot between her ears. A hand on my shoulder startled me. When I jumped, Sherri asked, "You okay?" I nodded. Then she asked, "Will you sit with me in the loft?" Her voice hinted that, like me, at least a part of her dreaded our departure.

For several minutes, we sat leaning shoulder to shoulder in the loft's opening, feet dangling, admiring the field, the fog, the birds, and Bertha's cowbell. Staring off into the woods, Sherri said, "When I get home, should I ask my father about his relationship with Loretta?"

At first I thought, *No.* But upon second consideration, I said, "I believe he'll want you to ... privately. You don't wanna hurt your mother. I'd say your father had to assume you would get to know Loretta. And, I'd bet he misses her and will cherish anything positive you might have to say."

Sherri put her arm around me and asked, "Why were you crying downstairs?"

"I'm not sure. Guess I'll miss Casper."

"And the hunk who gave her to you."

"Maybe."

"Maybe, my ass. Bet he'll miss you. You guys were good until all this treasure shit got in the way."

"You really think he was in on it?"

"No," she admitted, "but where the hell is he? Isn't he going to be here today to see you off?" I couldn't answer the question that I'd been trying to put out of my head. "You'll have your phone soon. Then you can call him." I cocked my head, looking at her. "Oh," she said, "he didn't give you a number?" She pulled me close and we rocked.

"I already said I'd be back, you know, to take care of my grandmother, but I wanna be around Eli too. He makes me feel ... different."

"You *wanna* be around him? God, you so belong here. You sound like a hick."

We retreated to our room in the Inn. There was nothing to pack. For six weeks we had longed for the return of our personal items, yet, as Sherri stripped off the 1800s, my heart feared the loss of what once seemed dreadful. The simple, backward culture of Grayson Springs seemed better suited for me than the hustle and bustle of Manhattan.

"Are they sagging?" she asked as she removed her homemade bra.

She flinched but did not resist when I reached out with both hands, brushing away her long, dark hair, exposing her, purposely letting my fingers drag across both nipples. "They're still beautiful, if that's what you are asking."

It surprised me when she spoke breathlessly. "Th ... thank you." She smiled, and then wiggled out of her bloomers as if I weren't even in the room.

"It no longer bothers you that I stare?"

"No. Don't think you're going to get turned on looking at all this hair?" Neither of us had shaved anything for six weeks.

"You don't know. I could be a freak."

"You *are* a freak. But remember, for Eli, not me." She stood there naked, as if waiting for my reaction.

I asked, "Are *you* okay?"

She tilted her head and said, "You know what, today is our last day, and since I know you desire Eli, there's something I want to give you." Before I could reply, she stepped up against me, wrapping her arms around my back. I couldn't speak. Her bare breasts were pushed against me. My arms went limp and I couldn't even hold her. She kissed me like Shauna does. I couldn't breathe. The bitch pulled away, glanced at the bulges poking through my blouse and said, "That's enough, girlfriend." Before I even understood, she turned her bare ass to me, began dressing, and said, "Now, when you come back, find Eli. Kiss him. If it does that to you, you're good." I stood in shock, ogling as she dressed, wanting to cry, wanting to clobber her. Fully clothed, she winked and, without a word, flounced out of the room.

With a deep breath, I dumped my clothes out onto the bed. Jeans, thong, bra, shoes, purse, phone, iPod, and my ball-cap, it was all there. I took off my blouse and bra, and then put on the Yankee's cap. I stared into the mirror while posing in several different positions. My nipples were hard. *Who am I? What am I? Why do I feel this way?*

A screeching drew me to the window. The red-tailed hawk perched fifty feet away in a white oak, surveying for a midday meal. Sun beaming through the window felt good on my bare skin. Suddenly, the hawk launched at the sound of horse hooves clip-clopping across creek rocks near the barn. It was Eli Clemons, high on his gelding. Approaching, he looked my way, stopped and gawked. I waved, and it was only after he shaded his eyes and tilted his head that I remembered my half-nakedness. *Too late now,* I thought.

I heard Eli's voice in the kitchen as I left the bedroom, carrying my bag. At the bottom of the stairs, I could see him through the kitchen door, leaning against the woodstove. He grinned as I entered the room. Sherri said, "What the hell?"

Loretta asked, "Why haven't you dressed?"

Turning to Colonel Ron, I said, "I did, but I couldn't wear the shirt."

Loretta smiled and said, "Told you that would happen."

"It still has blood on it."

"Turn it inside out," Sherri suggested.

"No, I want to wear these clothes home. My other clothes felt ... confining."

"Have you gained weight?" Loretta asked.

"Don't think so. But ... please, may I wear these?"

"Sure you can," replied the Colonel. "They're yours to keep. You too, Sherri."

Sherri said, "I'll keep mine, but I doubt I'll ever wear them again."

I asked, "How much time do we have?"

"We're out of here in forty-five minutes," Loretta replied, "Your plane departs at three o'clock."

I looked at Eli and asked, "Can we take a walk?" Even before he smiled, my tears were flowing.

"Sure. I'd love to."

As we left the kitchen, Sherri gave me another wink. When we stepped off the back porch, Colonel Ron barked, "You two behave...."

"Leave 'em alone," interrupted Loretta. I glanced back. "Forty-five minutes," she reiterated, "not a minute more!"

Before we reached the springs, Eli took me by the hand. "Where we going?"

"You'll see." I hurried him through the springs. Nearing the hill, he tugged me to a stop. "What's wrong?" I asked.

"Not sure," he answered as I squatted to crawl through the briar tunnel. He followed, and we found the woods different than before. Normally wet and dreary, everything appeared dry. Sunshine filtered through the forest canopy while a chorus of songbirds echoed loudly.

"My God," I said, "it sounds like a jungle." Wildflowers lined the pathway. Eli looked at me and shook his head. We ascended quickly. The ground, no longer mushy, invited us away from the path to the beech tree and the rock where I'd removed the treasure just hours earlier. Without speaking, I seated myself on the sandstone sitting rock.

Still standing, surveying the woods, Eli said, "Can't believe it's this dry already."

"I'd say the curse of the woods has been lifted. Sit with me, please." He joined me on the rock. I bumped him with my shoulder and said, "This is where they sat, Mary Elizabeth and John." Eli's attention seemed to be somewhere out in the woods. "Don't you have anything to say?"

He turned and asked, "You make a habit of standing naked in the window?"

"I was only half naked."

"And?"

"Don't ask me why," I snapped while rising from the rock. My tears were unstoppable. "Did I offend you?"

Glancing at my chest, he said, "Didn't get *that* good a look."

I began unbuttoning my blouse.

"What are you doing?"

Through tears I said, "Guess it's time you got a better look." I kept unbuttoning.

"But you're crying. Elizabeth, you don't have to..."

"I know that, Eli, dammit, but I trust you, and I wanna do this." I couldn't tell if he agreed or just gave in. He sat silently as I removed my blouse and then my homemade bra. "Bet these are the smallest boobs you ever saw."

"They're ... you're beautiful."

I stepped close and said, "Touch me." He put his arms around my waist, but turned his head and rested the side of his face against me. I pulled away and said, "What, you don't wanna touch 'em, or kiss 'em, or something? Isn't that what men do?"

He smiled and said, "Come here."

Loretta had already parked her cruiser at the gate. Instead of the old freight train, Sherri and I would return to Louisville in the back of a police car. Eli held my hand as we approached the Inn. Colonel Ron, Loretta, and Sherri sat in rockers as if they had nothing better to do. Colonel Ron tapped his watch and said, "You got five minutes."

I tried to avoid eye contact, but Sherri would not be denied. "Oh my god," she squealed. "Look at you."

The smile on my face would not go away. For the first time in my life I felt the love of a man. Was it real? Only time would tell.

Ten minutes later, Eli and I walked behind the others as we trekked to the front gate. By the time we got there, Colonel Ron had seated himself shotgun. Sherri sat in the back, already burying herself in electronics. Loretta took her driver's position as Eli leaned me against the back fender of the cruiser and kissed me. I felt hot all over again, as I had earlier in the woods. My legs became week, and had the cruiser not been there, I might have fallen. My head and mind were spinning.

It was like that warm and fuzzy spot right after one wakes up from a delicious dream ... that anxious moment before the details begin to fade. Instead of speaking, Eli kissed me again. This time I wrapped my arms around him and didn't want to let go. "We have a plane to catch," Loretta command.

Staring up through the back window, Sherri hollered, "Get a room already!"

Loretta put the car in gear and began tapping the gas, nudging forward. "You've got to go," Eli whispered.

I squeezed even harder and whispered back, "Do you really want me to come back?" He nodded yes. "But what if the judge doesn't let me? What if he puts me in jail?"

"Then I guess I'd have to wait until you get out, or come to New York and perform an old-fashioned jailbreak."

"You'd wait for me?"

"Elizabeth, remember when I told you sex is not something you do just to see what it is like?"

"Yesssss. You said it is something people do when they love one another and are willing to make commitments."

"Well there you have it."

"So this means you..."

"It means for the first time since Savanna went away, I feel totally alive."

Savanna, I thought, *what a beautiful name.*

I turned to get into the car. Eli stopped me and said, "You haven't told me how you feel."

I whispered into his ear, "Someday I'm gonna have you a baby girl, and we're gonna name her Savanna." Tears ran down Eli's cheeks as I kissed him quickly, climbed in and closed the door.

While we pulled away from Grayson Springs, I turned in the seat to watch Eli fade into the foliage. When I could no longer see his wave, I sat and fastened my seat belt. Sherri leaned over and whispered, "See what you've been missing."

I whispered back, "It was worth the wait." She took my hand in hers, and I knew I had a true friend.

Chapter 41

First morning home, I slept in until after 10:00. Daddy had already left for Saturday morning racquetball. With the baby napping, I found Melanie sitting on the balcony. For a while, I stood observing her through the sliding glass door. She drank coffee, but what moved me were the moments between sips, the way she stared out over Central Park. When I joined her with a cup of my own, she said, "I've never known you to drink coffee."

"I've gained an appreciation for it."

She grinned and patted the seat of the chair next to her.

I sat down, took a sip, and said, "In the past, when you came out here alone, I thought you were getting away from me." Instead of replying, Melanie stared ahead. Motherhood had been good to her. Sitting there with no makeup at all, she actually looked ... better ... tired, but somehow happier. She had a softer air about her. I asked, "Is this your chance to relax and enjoy the scenery?"

"If I said I never came out here to get away from you, I would be lying. But, for the most part, it *is* my way of relaxing."

"And I had to go away to figure that out."

Melanie set down her coffee and leaned back into her chair, staring off into the treetops. "Would it surprise you to know that I went through something similar with my mother?"

"Really?"

"During my high school years, we argued often ... a lot like you and me. Of course, I never struck her. Mother was adamant that all her children be home for dinner in the evenings. And to make it worse, she refused us the opportunity to watch TV during meals, said it was family time and the television would be a distraction, preventing proper conversation. I thought it was torture. Being the oldest, I rebelled. I remember complaining that we were a dysfunctional family and questioning why my parents couldn't be more like my friend's parents. When I left for Stanford, Mother and I were still on bad terms. After a while away, I began to suffer homesickness. Believe it or not, I missed our family meals ... the conversations. I came to realize we were the normal family and that my friend's families, though cool on the surface, were quite dysfunctional."

"Mom, we rarely eat meals as a family here. Does that mean we're dysfunctional?"

Melanie's face distorted, and she began to cry.

I said, "I'm sorry. Wasn't meaning to upset you."

Wiping her face, she said, "I know we're dysfunctional. That's not why I'm crying. You ... called me Mom. It's been years."

She was right. "Well, now you officially are a mother."

"Honey, I've been a mother since the day George introduced me to you. You were my baby girl. I held you every chance I got, which wasn't nearly enough, considering you didn't care to be held...."

I didn't want to be held?

"I took you shopping ... dressed you for school ... and look back at all the times I sat awake with you at night when you were ill or bothered by something."

"You wanted to hold me?"

"I can't believe you are asking that! And I can't believe you criticized your father for not holding you. Honey, you didn't want to be held. We both tried. Surly you remember."

Suddenly I did—there were times when one or the other tried to get me to sit close to watch TV, or when both wanted me to snuggle between them. Looking back, I should have felt safe, but did not. The closeness thing must have frightened me. "I ... I can't imagine how my rejection must have hurt you. I owe you and Daddy an apology for the way I have acted."

"It's ... okay...."

319

"No it's not. I said things about you. I thought you were cheating when you got pregnant. I couldn't imagine it being Daddy's."

"Technically it's not ... and I think you already figured that out."

"Yessss. I think I understand. I've seen the ads. Older men and their performance issues."

"No, honey. That's not it at all. It was more of a professional decision. When George and I got married, I had no intentions of having a baby. We had you. You were a precious little girl, so in need of love. You were mean at times, but George helped me understand. And I did fall in love with you ... still am. But at some point, you grew away from me, and you left a big hole in my heart. I wasn't done being a mommy. I needed more. When I told George I wanted a child, he said we could adopt. But I didn't want to do that again. I couldn't attach myself to another child, only to have it resist me later on, like you did. I needed a..."

"A child of your own. I took that sooo wrong."

"When George first said he couldn't be a father at his age, I thought he meant he was sterile. But then he showed me studies that document the high occurrence of schizophrenia and autism and even cancer among the offspring of elderly fathers. Honey, your father treats schizophrenia every day. He understands the pain and suffering involved for the patient and the parents of such individuals."

"I see, but technically Little George is not really his child. Will he be able to love him?"

"He loves *you* as much as any man loves a child. I know he will do the same by Little George."

I leaned back in my chair, feeling guilty for all I had put Melanie through. I had gotten so wrapped up in my own issues that I never stopped to think of things from her perspective. I closed my eyes, but the tears still escaped. She reached up, gently wiped my face, and whispered, "It's okay. Everything is going to be okay."

Without opening my eyes, I asked, "Will it be alright if I refer to Little George as my little brother?"

We held hands and cried together, ignoring the traffic sounds below, and seeing only the trees.

That evening, while Melanie breastfed Little George, I asked Daddy if he would join me for a walk in Central Park. He hesitated, but said, "Sure."

Moments later, as we waited to cross the street, he said, "Melanie told me you two have spoken. I know we need to, but I fear it will sound like a session."

The signal changed, and we began walking. "Then let's agree that it won't be. Colonel Ron and I spoke man-to-man. Can't we do the same?"

Stepping up on the curb, he stopped and said, "Kind of hoped for father-daughter, but I suppose man-to-man will suffice."

"Thank you."

As we walked, I described Grayson Springs, the animals, and how hard Sherri and I had worked on daily chores. He surprised me by revealing that he had visited Grayson Springs in the early 70s, before it began its deterioration. We sat on a bench, and I told him about sitting in the loft, admiring nature. At some point I gathered the nerve to say, "Daddy, I met someone in Kentucky."

He lowered his head and said, "That's not what I sent you down there for." When I refused to comment, he exhaled a deep breath and asked, "So, what's she like?"

I grinned and shook my head at his presumption. "Not a girl. Eli is a guy ... and, from your perspective, an unusually kind and respectful specimen of the male Homo sapiens."

Daddy grinned and said, "I sent you to Sacred Heart Academy, and you call your boyfriend a specimen."

Boy, did I deserve that.

Chapter 42

On Monday, July 11, I returned to New York Family Court. As in my last appearance, my parents sat behind me. Little George had been left with a nanny. It was nice to have Melanie in the room as an ally. Unlike my last trip, I felt comfortable making eye contact with her. More love, no hate. Two rows back sat Colonel Ron, Loretta, and, to my surprise and delight, Eli. He looked nice with no hat, his long brown hair hanging past his shoulders. The sight of him made me perspire. I smiled and then focused on Shauna, Jason and Darleen, who were all checking out Eli. Shauna turned and glared at me, and I could sense disapproval.

Instead of dressing up, as I had in the past, I wore my oldest pair of jeans and a white, short sleeved button-up blouse that, while plain, exaggerated my tan. My attorney had already expressed his disapproval.

"All rise!" demanded the sheriff's deputy. "This session of the New York Family Court is now in session. Presiding will be the Honorable Judge Bernard Stinson."

Like a recording, Judge Stinson entered the room, glanced around, and took his seat exactly as he had in each of my previous appearances. On this occasion, as he poured his glass of water, he seemed to be studying me. I heard doors open and looked back. Sherri Reid entered the courtroom, accompanied by a tall, dark, and handsome man. When he leaned his huge body over to kiss Loretta on the cheek, Sherri smiled at me. I gave her a thumbs-up.

An impatient Judge Stinson spoke. "If you people don't mind, I'd like to get started. Please have a seat." Sherri and her father sat behind

Colonel Ron and Loretta, and the judge began his litany. "Would the defendant please rise?" Mr. Sebastian and I stood, and I could see the judge checking out my attire. "Miss Green, let me start by reminding you and the court that you are now eighteen years of age. At your last appearance, there was an agreement that I, this court, would have the option of treating you as an adult when you returned from some sort of rehab innnnnn..." He paused, shuffling papers. "In Grayson Springs, Kentucky. Is that right?"

"Yes, Your Honor," replied Mr. Sebastian.

As the Judge hesitated, those from the prosecutor's office whispered to one another. The judge continued. "Mr. Sebastian, my decision today relies in part on my interpretation of the change or lack thereof in your client, Miss Green. Therefore, instead of hearing from you, I would like Miss Green to speak on her own behalf. You, Mr. Sebastian, may be seated."

Judge Stinson turned his attention to me. "I see, Miss Green, you have chosen to dress much less formally than in your previous visits. Should I assume this is some sort of a message for my court?"

Still standing, I said, "Permission to speak, Your Honor?"

He grinned and said, "Permission granted."

"Sir, in my previous appearances in this court I had been directed as to what I should wear and instructed on how to act and what to say or not say. This time, I have chosen to present myself simply as who I am. No fluff involved."

"And who exactly do you want this court to assume you to be?"

"May I speak freely?"

"Please do, with respect to the court I might add."

"Your Honor, since my last appearance here, I have had a unique opportunity to visit, or shall I say to walk in the shoes of my ancestors. In doing so, I have learned a lot about myself and about my roots. For the first time in my life, I know who I am, where I came from, and why."

"You found your roots in Kentucky?"

"Yes, sir. I was born near Grayson Springs and thus was given the opportunity to visit my past. At first I cursed the ground you and my father walk on for sending me back to where I was born. Even more so when I had to give up my cell phone, my jewelry, and my clothes, even my bra, in exchange for a wardrobe straight out of the 1800s."

"Is that right?" he asked, as if amused.

"Yes, sir."

He continued, "While I must say that your present attire does not offend me, I will have to question your suntan. Did you go to rehab, or to the beach?" Someone at the prosecutor's table laughed, and the judge gave them a threatening look.

"My tan, sir, is the result of daily outdoor labor."

"Young lady, I highly doubt you've done a hard day's labor in your entire life."

Colonel Ron stood, interrupting. "May I speak, Your Honor?"

Obviously offended, the judge asked, "And who, sir, might you be?"

"I am Colonel Ronald Lee, licensed psychologist and owner of Grayson Springs, the site of Miss Green's rehab."

"I read your report, Mr. Lee. You have something further to offer?"

"Your Honor, as part of her rehab, among other chores, Miss Green and one other young lady have continuously groomed more than an acre of grass with a push mower."

"A push mower?"

"Yes, sir. No gasoline engine involved. It's the old rotary blade version."

"So, you run a *green* facility?"

"Green in that we have no modern conveniences. No running water. No electricity."

"And you believe this environment to be an asset in the rehabilitation of your clients?"

"My preliminary estimate is yes. In eliminating the modern conveniences these young ladies are accustomed to, we get their attention much quicker. Thus, results are achieved earlier than in a more modern, technology-driven atmosphere."

"And the grass cutting is somehow therapeutic?"

"It gives them time to think and a taste of what it is like to suffer real labor. Trust me, Your Honor, grass cutting was only a portion of their workday. These ladies milked the cow, pasteurized milk, churned butter, cooked on a wood stove, and even caught and cleaned their own fish for supper. They rode horseback, fed chickens, gathered eggs, and..."

"I get the point, Mr. Lee.... You speak of a second young lady. Was she, like Ms. Green, a frequent flier of the court system?"

"No, Your Honor, I am not," blurted Sherri as she stood.

Frustrated, the judge said, "Is there some reason why people are blurting out in my courtroom today?"

"Sir, *you* spoke of *me* as if I were not present. So that you may avoid saying something you could regret, I felt I should introduce myself."

"And who are you to anticipate such recklessness on my part?"

"I am Sherri Reid of Los Angeles, California."

The judge stared for a moment, then said, "Is it my imagination or is Shayquan Reid of the Lakers sitting in my courtroom?"

Mr. Reid stood at 6'10" and said, "It's my pleasure, Your Honor."

"I'm the one honored," the judge replied. "Last time I saw you it was at the Gardens. Now, for the record, is this young lady your daughter?"

"Yes, Your Honor."

"Am I to understand that your daughter was also enrolled in this so-called Grayson Springs Project?"

"Yes, sir. And, if I may, please allow me to say that like Ms. Green, my daughter has come home a changed individual. I am astonished at the respect she has gained for me, my wife, and for herself. As her father, I must highly commend Colonel Lee's facility."

"Is that right? And are you and Colonel Lee former acquaintances?"

"No, sir. Though I have spoken to him on the phone, today is my first opportunity to meet him face-to-face."

"And how does a resident of California come to send his daughter to Kentucky?"

"Mr. Lee was recommended by a former classmate from the University of Georgia."

I sat hoping the judge would not ask who that classmate was. Instead, he said, "Georgia. I remember those days. Please be seated." Turning his attention back to me, he continued. "So, Miss Green, can you explain how visiting your so-called past is going to change your volatile behavior?"

I stood for a moment, staring at the table in front of me.

"Miss Green, I am waiting?"

It was a question I had not contemplated. I knew what I wanted to say, but was unsure how to say it. I looked back at Colonel Ron and Loretta. Both nodded. Turning back to the judge, I said, "Your Honor, for most of my life, I have lived in a stable environment. I have plenty of food, drink, and clothes. I have all the modern electronic technologies a person could want. Therefore, whenever I looked back on my early childhood, when I described it to therapist after therapist, the same conclusion developed. In my mind, I was convinced that I had been physically and mentally abused as a child, and to some extent, I'm sure I was. It's a wonder I'm not Sybil by now ... but I'm not. At first, I loathed the idea of returning to where I came from because I feared my past. But, Your Honor, the darnedest thing happened. In visiting my childhood ... in facing my demons, I realized that at least some of the memories of my childhood and the abuse I felt I'd been subjected to were possibly fabrications based on a child's perception of the truth. Some of what I considered abuse was exactly that, and while I am not making light of the acts, I will say that I have a better understanding of how it could happen."

"Excuse me!" snapped the judge. "Young lady, are you standing in my court making excuses for child abuse?"

"No sir, not at all. But what I have discovered is that those dirty, nasty boys, who put their hands on me when I was five-years-old, were that way before they came to my foster parents. Had they been good boys, they never would have been sent there in the first place. The Henrys opened up their backwoods home to a bunch of poor, homeless kids that no one else wanted. Obviously, the State decided that the

Henrys were not doing a proper job of it, and that is why they took the boys away from them, but that doesn't mean they were not trying. Your Honor, I have discovered that behaviors which may be considered odd or abusive to those of us living in Manhattan will not always be considered as such in a place like Grayson County, Kentucky ... a place where the culture is much different. For six weeks I got a taste of what it must have been like in the past. Hot, humid days and nights with no air conditioning. We used an outhouse and a swinging footbridge. And as the Colonel said, we pushed and pulled that old mower for several hours every day, and then did our other chores. I can't imagine how backwards things were for those who raised me. What they went through in *their* youths. Who knows what atrocities my real mother suffered, God rest her soul. She was deserted by her mother when she was but a child." My tears began to flow, but I couldn't stop. "I should probably be bitter towards my mother's mother for giving her away, but I'm not. Instead, I am curious as to the turmoil she must have been going through ... the pain she must have endured in those hills before and after she gave up her baby girl, my mother, who lived as a foster child in poverty for years and then died the night she gave birth to me.... Your Honor, I have experienced life-changing events in the last six weeks. My heart has been broken, but now it is healed. While I love Manhattan and will visit from time to time, I am a country girl, born and bred, and I have a desire to return to my roots. I beg this court's forgiveness for my disruptive past, and I beg for the opportunity to return to Kentucky to be with the grandmother I never knew I had. She is old now and lives alone. I am her only living relative. She needs me, and I need her. From her I can learn about the man who fathered me. He too died young in service to our country. Your Honor, I plan to receive my Master's in Psychology from the University of Kentucky. After that, I want to become a part of the Grayson Springs Project so that I might help others like me."

When I paused, Judge Stinson twirled his ink-pen between his fingers, and then asked, "You seriously want to work with girls who are plagued with issues similar or worse than yours?"

"Yes I do."

"You may continue."

"I ... I really don't know what more to say."

Here we go again, I thought as Judge Stinson began his standard stare into my eyes. This episode seemed to last forever, as if he were trying to read my mind. I refused to blink. Finally, he did.

"Be seated," he ordered before inviting the prosecution and Mr. Sebastian to approach the bench. I couldn't make out their mumblings. When they all returned to their seats, the judge continued. "Please rise again, Miss Green." I stood, trying to read his thoughts. "Miss Green. Six weeks ago I had visions of sentencing you to an adult facility. Your past behavior is unacceptable in the eyes of this court. However, that was then, and this is now. The change I see in your attitude is remarkable. Either you are a very good actress, or you have genuinely come to grips with reality. Today is the first time I have heard you speak on a level that corresponds with your intellect. Typically, I would sentence you to one year in an adult facility, with a suspended sentence and two years of probation. However, were I to do such, you would not be able to leave New York." After a glance to the back of the room, he said, "I may take heat from the press, but under the circumstances, I am releasing you, with no sentence and no probation, so that you may freely return to Kentucky. Every person deserves to know their past, their family's history. For you, that window may close at the passing of your grandmother. Do not make me regret this decision. If I hear of you causing trouble in Kentucky, I will personally come down there and use every ounce of my influence to have you put away. Do you understand what I am saying?"

"Yes, I do."

"Good. Go now and take care of your grandmother. Get your education. Do no wrong."

Outside the courtroom, small gatherings of defendants, lawyers, parents, and friends huddled in conferences awaiting their moments in court. It was my first opportunity to introduce Eli, now wearing his straw hat. Reaching for his hand, I said, "Eli Clemons, I'd like you to meet my father, Dr. George Green and my ... my mother, Melanie."

"Ma'am," Eli said, while tipping his hat and reaching for Melanie's hand. He then turned to Daddy. "It's good to meet you Sir."

They shook hands, and Daddy said, "Our daughter has spoken at length about you. We appreciate your support during her time away."

While Daddy used the conversation to analyze Eli's mind, Melanie seem to be analyzing the rest of him. She caught me watching, and we both smiled. Colonel Ron, Loretta, Sherri, and her father joined us. Loretta hugged me and said, "Everything seems to have worked out just the way we hoped."

Colonel Ron said, "Elizabeth, I got a call from my friend Walter about the coins. He says their uncirculated condition gives them a value of nearly twelve thousand apiece."

Sherri grinned. "You mean like, sixty thousand dollars for five pennies?"

"That's right," added Loretta. "And there's more."

Colonel Ron continued, "It seems the porcelain case the coins were in is rare also, and may be worth a lot. Walter's looking into it. He says if he can authenticate the maker, the case may be worth as much or more than the total value of the coins."

Eli winked at Sherri, adjusted his hat, and asked, "Did somebody say I was gonna get one of those two-percent shares?"

I said, "Ha, ha, ha," as everyone joked around, trying to lay claim to a share of Grandmother's money.

Daddy and Melanie stood silent, holding hands. Mr. and Mrs. Dr. George Green. *Not my real parents*, I use to say. Now they had a ... a look on their faces ... in their eyes. Like other parents at school functions. Happy. Not for themselves. Happy for me. As if my being happy made them happy. I stepped closer and said, "You guys still wanna hold me?" They did, and I think even Daddy cried. *They ... love me. They really do love me. They are my parents.*

As I wiped my eyes, my attention drifted down the hallway a short piece to the elevated voice of a girl, maybe younger than me, who stood ranting at what appeared to be her parents and an attorney. "You can all kiss my ass!" she blurted. "I don't need this! I don't need any of you!"

Halfway between the girl and me, Shauna stood throwing glances my way while ignoring Jason and Darleen's conversation. I excused myself and dragged Sherri over to meet them all. Jason and Darleen stopped their chat as I introduced Sherri. Shauna scanned her up and down and then stared at me. Tears ran down her cheeks.

"Stop that," I said. "You're gonna make *me* cry."

She wiped her face and said, "This could be the last time I ever see you."

"Don't be silly. I'll be coming back to visit, and all of you had best come see me. I think you'll like Kentucky. It's laid back."

"Trust me," Sherri commented, "it is nothing like New York. Other than chores, there's not a whole lot to do."

"I figured as much," Shauna sassed.

I said, "If you come down, I'll teach you how to ride."

"A horse?" Darlene asked.

"Of course."

"I'd like that," she replied.

"Me too," Jason added.

"And, Shauna, there's someone there I want you to meet...."

"A girl?"

"No. A priest."

Shauna looked befuddled at first, and then upset. "So, it was a priest who *converted* you. And now you think he will change me."

"No, silly. He didn't convert me. He helped me understand who I am. Why I think the way I do. Why I find women attractive. I don't believe Father Ryan would try to convert you. I think he knows better than that. But he does have an unusual theory as to why one might feel the way you do. He somehow makes better sense of it all." I hugged Shauna and whispered. "You've been my BFF for sooo long. I will always love you. But, you have to understand..." As I spoke, over Shauna's shoulder I noticed the ranting girl, some 15 feet away, watching. She tilted her head and then turned away. "Eli will make me complete. I deserve that. And I swear I hope someday you will meet someone who makes you feel the same."

Shauna separated from me and said, "I did. I met you."

As Sherri began motioning Eli to join us, I said, "Shauna, the complete thing has to go both ways, or it will never work. You can't tell me you didn't sense that in me all along."

My Amish knight in shining armor arrived, conveniently disturbing our conversation. While continuing my surveillance of the nearby gathering, I politely introduced Eli to my friends. He scanned all three and then directed his attention to Shauna, as if absorbing her. She apparently thought he wanted a handshake. When she reached, he took her hand gently and said, "Elizabeth speaks highly of you."

Shauna stood wordless, not daring to look into his eyes. That's her thing, you know. Anytime she expects someone is going to diss her, she refuses to look directly at them.

"I'm really glad I got to meet you ... all of you," continued Eli while glancing at Jason and Darleen, still holding Shauna's hand. Caught off guard, she looked up, their eyes met and neither spoke for an odd moment. I swear she blushed.

As Eli and Sherri continued chatting with Shauna, Jason, and Darleen, Miss Loudmouth stormed across the hallway and into the ladies room. I said, "Excuse me guys, I'll be right back."

Inside the lavatory, I found the distraught girl leaning against the washbasin, firing up a cigarette. She was bigger than me by a couple of inches in height and maybe 20 pounds. She delivered a glare that reeked of caution and distrust as I surveyed the room and then focused on her. She seemed a mix between white and something foreign. The hand she held the cigarette with had scabs across the knuckles. Blowing smoke my way, she asked, "What the fuck is your problem?"

"In the hallway ... I felt your pain."

"Yeah right. So you're some kind of fucking mind reader? Or do you just go around meddling in other people's business?"

"I was lost for years. Didn't really know who or even what I am...."

"Welcome to my world."

"I wanna help you."

"Fuck you."

"I ... I spent my whole life not trusting anyone. Thinking everyone was out to get me. I've hurt people with my words and my fists. Some deserved it, and as it turns out, some did not."

Instead of replying, the girl shrugged her shoulders and took another draw. When I reached for the cigarette, she hesitated, blew smoke in my face, and then handed it to me.

After a draw, I blew smoke back at her and said, "Recently, I met some people who are turning my life around."

"So you want me to kiss your ass, congratulate you, or what?"

Handing the cigarette back, I said, "I told you, I wanna help you, if I can. Trust me..."

"Fuck you again bitch. I don't trust you or nobody else. Every asshole I ever trusted was only interested in money or a piece of my ass, or both, and you ain't about to get either."

"I don't need your money, or you. When you were in the hallway, venting at those people, I saw *me* six weeks ago ... angry, scared, and about to go to jail, and I'm thinking, how did I get from where she is to where I am now? I've been in and out of this courthouse since I was eleven-years-old. Watching you made my stomach knot up again. And it makes me wonder just how many girls out there are going through the same stuff you and I are. Tell me you've never cried yourself to sleep ... or, or got stoned just to forget who you are. I never trusted a single man or boy because I thought all they wanted was to put their hands on me, or worse." As I spoke, the girl's eyes got glassy. "You don't have to say it, but I *am* willing to bet you're a whole lot like me ... we've both been there."

She took a draw, blew it away from me, and began wiping her face.

I said, "My parents sent me to a place far away from here. At first I hated them and the place they sent me. But, after a while I realized I was at least away from the people that were driving me crazy, and was actually around people I could trust. People who listened to what I had to say, and not just because they wanted my parent's money. They understood me and truly wanted to help. They made me work my ass off on some God forsaken, yet awesomely beautiful place in the hills of Kentucky. And you know what, the hard work was better than the bullshit I was going through here."

"So, you still hate the people here?"

"No, I've come to realize that the mother I despised really did love me, and wanted to help, but just didn't understand the crap that was going on inside of me. Now I know it was not her fault ... or mine. I just had to get away long enough to find out who I really am."

The girl offered her cigarette again, and asked, "So, who the fuck *are* you?"

As I took a draw, Loretta entered, badge flashing on her belt, waving her hand at the second hand smoke. "Are you kidding me? You just got out of trouble, and now you're smoking in a public building."

"It's my fucking cigarette," the girl spoke, as she turned to walk out.

I said, "Hey, you asked who I am. I *was* you. Now, I'm the happiest girl on earth." As she shoved open the exit door, I raised my voice. "I wanna help you!"

"You what?" asked Loretta.

"You heard me. And, if you and Colonel Ron are willing to help, I bet I can get her to quit using the f-word so much."

Half an hour later, Colonel Ron, Loretta, and Eli joined me in the courtroom one row behind the parents of Miss Connie Marie Johnson. We sat waiting for Judge Stinson to return. It was my first trip to court as an observer. The defendant sat silently, elbows on the table, face in her hands while her attorney conferenced at the prosecutor's table.

She didn't appear nearly as tuff as she had let on to be in the ladies-room, and yes, I could feel her pain, her anger, and her helplessness.

As the Court Clerk made his, "All rise," announcement, and Judge Stinson entered in his practiced fashion, Miss Johnson glanced back. I raised both hands, gesturing toward my friends. Her eyes closed, lips quivered, and she turned away.

Judge Stinson looked over his case papers, and then began scanning the room. When he spotted me, he grinned, and I knew that he knew I was serious.

39154619R00191

Made in the USA
Charleston, SC
25 February 2015